PRAISE FOR LISA GO

THE RED MAGICIAN

"Turns the hidden world of Eastern European Jews during the 1940s into a world of wonders, then transcends the Holocaust with a magical optimism."

—*The New York Times Book Review*

"[Goldstein] has given us the kind of magic and adventure that once upon a time made us look for secret panels in the walls of wardrobes, or brush our teeth with a book held in front of our eyes, because we couldn't bear to put it down."

—*The New Yorker*

THE DREAM YEARS

"A short book but an intense one. Like all Goldstein's work it's beautifully written and full of marvelous lingering imagery."

—Jo Walton, author of *Among Others* and *The Just City*

"This is an excellent little novel...Highly recommended."

—*Solar Bridge*

A MASK FOR THE GENERAL

"In transplanting the consciousness of the 1960s to the near-future, the author of *Dream Years* has created a brilliant parable of nonviolent revolution. Recommended."

—*Library Journal*

"Absorbing, quietly impressive, thoughtful work—welcome evidence of Goldstein's steady improvement as a clear-eyed fantasist of depth, range and charm."

—*Kirkus Reviews*

TOURISTS

"One of the great American novels of the 1980s."

—*Fantasy & Science Fiction*

"A charming tale of magic realism . . . A cool, quiet breeze in a realm too often filled with hot air."

—*San Francisco Chronicle*

Walking the Labyrinth

"This marvelous and (in the old sense of the word) fabulous book combines the best qualities of narrative, epistolary and personal journal novels. . . . *Walking the Labyrinth* is full of enchantments and illusions, wonders and delights, and the mysterious connections of a family. A highly satisfying read!"
—*Fantasy & Science Fiction*

"A modern morality play that says much about what it means to live, love and learn. Along the way, Goldstein confronts us with bold truths, as well as enchantment."
—*Locus*

Dark Cities Underground

"The novel moves rapidly, building momentum as each secret is revealed...the story's premise, and the questions that arise from it, should keep readers involved."
—*Publishers Weekly*

"Reveals and explores the connections among the worlds of Narnia and Never-Never Land, the Wind in the Willows and Wonderland, myth and legend.... This fine modern fantasy is also about archetypes, childhood, growing up, loyalty, immortality, death, and love."
—*Cynthia Ward*

The Alchemist's Door

"Meticulous research, pristine storytelling, and Goldstein's genuine affection for her characters make this historical fantasy a priority purchase for most libraries."
—*Library Journal*

"Aficionados of historical fantasy or simply of strong prose will love this fast-moving and entertaining novel."
—*SF Revu*

THE UNCERTAIN PLACES

"An exquisitely beautiful, eerily compelling modern fairy tale."
—*Library Journal*, starred review

"Goldstein's complex and ingenious plot transplants the forest realm of European folktale, where witches grant wishes with strings attached and you'd better be careful which frog you kiss, into the sun-drenched hills of Northern California in the 1970s—and beyond."
—Ursula K. Le Guin, author of *A Wizard of Earthsea* and *The Left Hand of Darkness*

"A gripping story that twists with compelling dream logic; Goldstein's fairy-tale family radiate believable unreality, and the faerie realm contained herein evinces the perfect mix of terror and attraction. Start reading this at your peril; once I did, I couldn't stop until I was done."
—Cory Doctorow, author of *Little Brother* and *Down and Out in the Magic Kingdom*

WEIGHING SHADOWS

Also by Lisa Goldstein:

Novels
The Red Magician
The Dream Years
A Mask for the General
Tourists
Strange Devices of the Sun and Moon
Summer King, Winter Fool
Walking the Labyrinth
Dark Cities Underground
The Alchemist's Door
Daughter of Exile (as Isabel Glass)
The Divided Crown (as Isabel Glass)
The Uncertain Places

Collections
Daily Voices
Travellers in Magic

WEIGHING SHADOWS

LISA GOLDSTEIN

Night Shade Books
New York

Night Shade books may be purchased in bulk at special discounts for sales promotion, corporate gifts, fund-raising, or educational purposes. Special editions can also be created to specifications. For details, contact the Special Sales Department, Night Shade Books, 307 West 36th Street, 11th Floor, New York, NY 10018 or info@ skyhorsepublishing.com.

Night Shade Books® is a registered trademark of Skyhorse Publishing, Inc. ®, a Delaware corporation.

Visit our website at www.nightshadebooks.com.

10 9 8 7 6 5 4 3 2 1

Goldstein, Lisa.
  Weighing shadows / Lisa Goldstein.
  pages; cm
  ISBN 978-1-59780-840-8 (pbk.: alk. paper)
  I. Title.
  PS3557.O397W45 2015
  813'.54—dc23

                              2015013599

Print ISBN: 978-1-59780-840-8

Cover illustration by Cortney Skinner
Cover design by Jason Snair

Printed in the United States of America

WEIGHING
SHADOWS

THE WOMAN WAS STALKING her again. She was keeping to the other side of the street and staying back a few paces, but Ann had no doubt about who it was. She had seen her a few days ago on her way to work, and a week before that, and now here she was again, almost not even bothering to hide her interest.

What did she want? Ann turned to look at her and the woman nodded. It was as though they were playing some kind of game, the rules of which were known to both of them. You know I'm watching you, she seemed to say, and I know you know, and you know I know you know . . .

We could stay here forever, Ann thought, trapped in infinite recursion. The woman was shorter than average, and because Ann was short herself she had wondered once or twice if the woman could be her biological mother, come to find out what had happened to the baby she had given up. And her hair was brown like Ann's, though Ann's was a few shades lighter, more reddish.

Ann turned away and continued on to Sam's Computer Solutions, and by the time the boss let her inside her stalker was nowhere to be seen. She went into the back room and dumped her coat and purse in her locker, then headed out to the office and started work.

She had gotten a reputation at the shop as a clever hacker, so the other two employees often saved their most difficult problems for her. It meant that she sometimes got to work on interesting things, but on the other hand it also meant that she failed more often than the other two, which gave Sam, the boss, more reason to pay attention to her. She disliked that, felt uncomfortable when people noticed her.

That dislike was probably why she had spotted the stalker so easily. She knew any number of ways of making herself inconspicuous, and it alarmed her that the woman was still interested in her. What could she possibly want? Some of Ann's excursions into the Internet hadn't been entirely innocent. Still, if the woman was her mother . . .

She fell into a well-worn reverie of reunion, an embarrassing fantasy in many ways but one she couldn't keep away from. It took her through the boring job she had started yesterday, retrieving data from a hard disk someone had wiped accidentally. A mix of off-the-shelf recovery utilities and her own custom code designed to predict missing sector data, based on file types and still extant CRC data, made it a pretty mundane task, but a distressingly common one. . . It was amazing how often people managed to screw up like that. PEBCAK, they called it at the shop: Problem Exists Between Chair and Keyboard.

It took her less than an hour to recover everything, and she sat for a moment after she had finished, summoning the energy for another job. "Ann!" Sam called from the front of the store. "Could you come here for a minute?"

She headed out to the front—and there, talking calmly to Sam, was her stalker.

"She asked for you by name," he said, and turned away to help another customer.

"Who are you?" Ann asked, shocked into rudeness.

"What?" the woman said.

"You heard me—I want to know who you are. You've been following me, haven't you? It's creepy, and it's probably illegal too. I could go to the police."

"No. No, you have the wrong idea. I want to interview you for a job."

"You—you what?"

Sam hurried over to them, probably drawn by the sound of Ann's raised voice. "Is there a problem here?" he asked.

"No," the stalker said. "Ann and I were just talking."

That's right, Sam said she knows my name, Ann thought. This is beyond creepy.

Up close Ann could see that the woman didn't look much like her at all. She had round cheeks and a snub nose, nothing like Ann's thinner face. Her hair was streaked with gray.

Sam headed back to his customer. The woman went on quickly, before Ann could say anything. "Look, I think we got off on the wrong foot here. I brought my computer to your store and you got rid of a virus for me. I like the way you solve problems, that's all. We might be able to use someone like you."

"So why were you following me? Do you do that to all your potential employees?"

Careful, she thought. She said she wants to offer you a job—don't alienate her.

"I'm sorry if I frightened you," the woman said. "We wanted to know more about you, that's all."

"Who's 'we'?"

"My company. Transformations Incorporated. We're—well, we're problem-solvers. Look, the easiest thing is to show you. Can you come to our campus, take a look around? When's your next day off?"

It sounded too good to be true, Ann thought. Things like this didn't happen to people like her. "I should tell you—I never went to college," she said, trying not to sound defensive. They'd find that out sooner or later; it was probably best to get it out of the way.

"That doesn't matter," the woman said. She seemed unsurprised, as if she'd known all along. And maybe she had; maybe they'd learned all kinds of things about her from following her around. "The important thing is how well you do on a series of tests we'll give you."

"I don't even know your name," Ann said.

"I'm sorry. I'm Emra Walker. I could shoot my data to your phone, if you like."

Ann nearly laughed. Did Ms. Walker really think she could afford a smart phone on the salary they paid her here? "My phone wouldn't take it. Don't you have a card or something?"

"No, sorry."

"Where's Transformations Incorporated, then?"

"I can pick you up and bring you there. When are you free?"

"Tomorrow's my day off—I guess we can go then."

Ms. Walker asked for her address and phone number, then made a show of programming them into her own phone. Ann had the idea that it was just a formality, that they already had all her information, including her work schedule. Why else had they made contact with her just before her day off?

ANN GOOGLED THE WOMAN that evening, as soon as she got back to her apartment. She found a website for Transformations Incorporated, written in language so vague that it seemed to be intentionally hiding something, filled with buzzwords like "proactive" and "forward-looking" and "forming new paradigms for time-honored modalities." She clicked on the "Contact" link but there was no street address, just some phone numbers and email addresses. Emra Walker herself she found listed under "Facilitators."

4

She surfed over to the Department of Motor Vehicles and snuck into its employee remote access interface, something she had figured out how to do a while ago. Once in the database, though, she couldn't find a driver's license for Emra Walker anywhere. Well, maybe she had moved here from another state. But when she hacked the Social Security administration she couldn't find a social security number either.

Walker rang her doorbell the next day. Ann felt her heart speed up as she opened the door and saw her standing there; some part of her, she realized, had not expected her to come.

They got into Walker's car, a late-model Toyota. Walker pressed a button and the engine caught, and Ann, who had never seen a car that started that way, had to keep herself from staring, from looking like some kind of technological ignoramus. It reminded her of ancient planes in World War I movies; she almost expected to see propellers whir into action.

Ann lived south of San Francisco, in a boring suburb on the peninsula. Walker turned onto the freeway and headed away from the city. They drove for several miles in silence, and then Walker took an off-ramp leading to an industrial neighborhood Ann had never visited before, filled with factories and warehouses. A few blocks later they turned in at a driveway leading to an empty lot. The lot was surrounded by a chain-link fence and concreted over; weeds were growing up through cracks in the pavement.

Walker slid a card into a machine by the driveway, and a gate in the fence opened. They drove a long way up a weed-filled road, then came to a large square building that looked like a warehouse. There was no sign in front to show what kind of business went on within it, or even that it was a business at all. Walker parked in a lot at the side and led Ann up the front steps.

Walker used her card again to open the door. It was very different inside, cool and quiet and softly lit, with white walls and pale wooden floors. A secretary at a front desk said something to them, too softly for Ann to hear. Ann looked at Walker, waiting for her to reply.

Walker didn't say anything, though. Now Ann saw that the secretary had a short wire leading from her ear, that she was probably on the phone, though Ann had never seen a telephone like that before. Where was the microphone, did she have it implanted somewhere?

The secretary murmured something and turned toward them, then buzzed them through a door behind her. "I'll give you a tour, then you'll have to get started on the tests," Walker said.

The tour was quick, fitful, as if Walker felt she didn't need to be polite once Ann had agreed to come along with her. She led Ann down a hallway lined with open doors, showing her classrooms, offices where people worked at computers, a laboratory filled with equipment she didn't recognize.

Ann stopped to look at a picture on the wall, a photograph of people running through a stone alleyway. A vast red fire, like a curtain, hung in the distance.

The people were wearing togas and sandals, she saw, and there were frescos on some of the walls around them. It looked like—she had read a historical novel about Pompeii once, and she had imagined it something like this. But a photograph? Well, you could do a lot with Photoshop these days.

Now she saw other photos, one of knights on horseback chasing a group of ragged-looking people without armor, another that looked like something she'd read once about Zimbabwe, men and women cementing bricks in an enormous circular tower. The photos looked surprisingly real; she could see the shadows of the ladders on the tower, and a dark stain of dirt, or maybe blood, on the flank of one of the horses. Someone had had a lot of time on their hands, she thought.

"Come along," Walker said. She sounded impatient.

Another door led into an open courtyard. For a moment, as she walked outside from the dimly lit corridors, the sun seared her vision, turning the green lawn black. Then her sight cleared and she saw fountains and trees, and groups of people sitting at tables or on the grass and eating and talking.

They headed across the courtyard and back inside, then down another hall to another classroom. This one was half filled with people, most of them, like Ann, in their early twenties. A laptop computer sat at each desk.

"This is where we'll be giving you your tests," Walker said.

She seemed to have assumed that Ann had already agreed to work for them. "Wait a minute," she said.

"Yes?" Another sound of impatience.

Ann had dozens of questions, and no idea which one to ask first. The tests could start at any minute, though; she had to hurry.

"It's just that I never heard of a company that gave classes before. I mean, I thought you were supposed to just go in and do your work."

"Ah. That's the difference between us and other corporations. We believe in skill-building, in staying on the cutting edge."

Could you fit any more clichés into that sentence? she thought. Still, she had to admit she liked the idea of being paid to study.

"Also, well, you never told me exactly what your company does," she said.

"That's proprietary information. We can't tell you that, not until we're sure we want to hire you."

For a brief moment Ann thought about backing out. She was already annoyed with the games the other woman played, with all the secrecy. Then she remembered something a teacher had once said. "It's like you want to fail sometimes, Ann. Like you're your own worst enemy."

The teacher had been wrong, though. The truth was that she didn't care whether she failed or not, that she didn't want to care. The worst thing was hope, was wanting something so badly that you'd be destroyed if you didn't get it. Because you didn't get most of the things that you wanted, so why go to all that effort?

But she wanted this job, she realized. Funny, since she didn't even know what it was. She went into the classroom and sat down at one of the desks.

The rest of the day passed in an anxious blur. A company employee appeared with stacks of forms for the candidates to fill out and sign, and then the computers booted up and a multiple choice test appeared on the screen. She skimmed easily through the first part, math and computer programming problems. The second part, history and foreign languages, was harder; she'd stopped paying attention in those classes a long time before she graduated high school. Still, she discovered that she'd read enough historical novels to answer a lot of the questions, and even the mysteries and science fiction she read were sometimes set in other times.

Then she was herded into another room, where a live interviewer posed a series of logic questions. Another room held another interviewer, this one asking about her personal life.

The logic questions were easy, the biographical information much harder. "Why didn't you go to college?" the interviewer asked, looking down at an open folder on his desk.

They had to know the answer to this. Probably it was in that folder he was staring at. "Well, my grades weren't good enough," she said.

"Yes, but why not? You're obviously intelligent."

She never talked about herself if she could help it, but sometimes, especially when she wanted to get someone on her side, she trotted out the story she called Pity the Poor Orphan Girl. She'd studied hard in grade school, she told the interviewer, but then, around the time she'd started high

8

school, she had been placed in a new foster home, one with seven children and one computer. "The teachers gave us homework you could only do on the computer, but the boys—there were five of them, and only two of us girls—they never let me use it, they stayed on for hours, watching porn and playing video games. I tried talking to the foster parents, but they weren't home very much."

"Why didn't you go to the library?"

Why didn't you? she thought. They all had advice for her, these people with their easy lives, they all knew what they would have done in her place. But would they really have taken the bus to the library, waited in line for their turn at the computer, and then managed to finish their homework in a half an hour, which was all the time the library allotted them? Wouldn't they have done exactly what she did, skipping classes and daydreaming through the ones she did go to?

She told him a little of this, trying not to sound as if she felt sorry for herself. And she didn't, not really. She'd managed on her own, she'd gotten free of that foster home, which had been far worse than she'd let the interviewer know. The parents were never around, leaving the kids to fend for themselves. The oldest boy had attacked her once, and thrown her to the floor of the room she'd shared with the other girl; she'd managed to stab him with a pen and he'd run away.

"How did you get hired at Computer Solutions?" the interviewer asked.

He would like this part, she thought; it showed initiative. "I worked at a fast-food place and saved up the money to buy my own computer, and then I got books from the library and taught myself how to program."

She was starting to get hungry; it had to be nearly noon. But when they finished the interviewer sent her on to another room, this one filled with only women. Another woman came through a door and told them all to strip and put on medical gowns for their physical.

She nearly backed out then, nearly turned around and just walked away. "This is the last thing on the schedule, and then you'll be free to go," the woman said.

Well, she'd come this far—she might as well get it over with. She took off her blouse and bra as quickly as she could, revealing the puckered scars on her torso for a few bare seconds, then shrugged into her gown. No one seemed to have noticed anything. Not that they would have mentioned it if they had: adults had mostly grown out of the cruelty of her high school gym classes, or at least they pretended that they had.

They lined up at a bathroom for a urine sample, and then a woman sitting at a table took her blood and temperature and peered into her mouth and ears. After that she was ushered into an examining room; it smelled astringent, like rubbing alcohol, with an undertone of an earlier woman's flowery perfume. A woman in a white coat came in, asked her to lie down on an examining table, and parted the front of her gown.

Ann held her breath and waited for the inevitable questions. Usually she said that she had fallen into barbed wire when she was a child. She had learned early on that if she told the truth, if she said she didn't know how or where she'd gotten the scars, the questioner would laugh or stare incredulously and then ask more questions she couldn't answer.

She'd tried to find out what had happened to her, but that information was gone, irretrievable. She'd gone through official channels and learned that her birth mother hadn't wanted to be contacted, then had tried unofficial channels, breaking into records for hospitals and foster homes. She'd already had the scars when she'd arrived at her first foster home; no one knew how she had gotten them. Someone somewhere along the way had given her the name Ann Decker; she didn't know why.

The doctor said nothing about the scars, though. She palpated her breast and stomach, then sat her back up and listened to her lungs through an icy-cold stethoscope. "Breathe," the doctor said. "No, deeper."

The doctor took away the stethoscope and fitted a blood pressure cuff around her arm. Her blood pressure must be through the roof, she thought. She breathed deeply, trying to calm herself.

"Okay," the doctor said. "We're done here."

"Now what?" Ann said.

"Now you find your contact person and go home," the doctor said. "We'll get in touch with you soon."

She'd expected something more ceremonial at the end, maybe even someone saying that she'd passed with flying colors and could start work tomorrow. Whoever these people were, they seemed terrible at social interactions. She left the examining room and found Emra Walker waiting for her in the room outside.

She tried pressing the other woman for information on the drive home, but Walker would only say that no one knew the results yet, that she would have to wait to be contacted. A week later she logged onto her computer and found email from Transformations Incorporated, with a heading that said "Congratulations." She made a fist and punched it, and shouted into the empty air.

07302014
108375

Strengths and Weaknesses of Cohort 15,
With Some Recommendations
Emra Walker

The 12 members of Cohort 15 were recruited in accordance with the guidelines set forth in Directive 24. All of them are outsiders in some way, with compelling reasons to leave their employment and/or domestic arrangements, making them eager to join our shell company, Transformations Incorporated. All are of superior intelligence, with either excellent grades or a good reason for poor performances in their places of education. All achieved high scores on our tests for creativity, problem solving, information retention, and flexible thinking . . .

There is one statistical anomaly regarding this group, however. Of these 12 members, a full 5 of them tried to break through the firewall on our computers while taking their tests, though none of them succeeded. These members are Francine Craig, Ann Decker, Maya Isaacs, Harry Leung, and Zachery Shaye. (See Table 3, attached, for the complete test scores of all 5. See also Table 4, attached, for a comparison with other cohorts, and note that previously only one or two members per cohort attempted this break-in during their testing period.)

Attempting to hack a computer is considered evidence of creativity and flexible thinking, and adds 5 points to the overall test score. I would like to go on record as disagreeing with this idea. To my mind breaking into a computer is a strong marker for antisocial behavior, and I would recommend that we stop rewarding these efforts. In fact, I would go further and subtract 5 points rather than add them.

Secondly, I would recommend that none of the members listed in Table 3 be sent together on any assignments, as their antisocial tendencies may combine and even intensify, causing unforeseen problems . . .

2

AFTER A WEEK AT Transformations Ann had learned very
little more about the company. She had to take two buses,
early in the morning, to the campus, where she spent a full
day studying everything from particle physics to ancient
history.

She discussed it, of course, with the other people in her
classes, but they had come to no firm conclusion. "Maybe it's
some kind of experiment," Franny said. She had long pale
crinkly hair and she laughed a lot; her mouth seemed wider
than most people's. She was another person with an easy life,
Ann had thought, and at first she was prepared to dislike her
because of it, but Franny seemed so friendly with everybody
that she couldn't keep it up.

They were eating lunch on the long green lawn, in the
shade of one of the trees. The lunches were available in the
cafeteria, and, Ann had been startled to learn, were free to
all the employees. She usually took as much advantage of
these meals as she could, and today she was eating a fish she
had never tried before, tilapia.

"What kind of experiment?" Ann asked. "What do they
want to prove?"

"I don't know. Maybe they want to see how long we go without asking any questions."

"Well, for God's sake don't ask any, then. I've never been paid to study before."

"Oh, the bill's going to come due sooner or later," a man named Jerry said. He was thin, intense, with long blond hair that flopped over his black-framed glasses. "It's all being funded by the CIA, or some secret organization we never heard of. They'll give us government jobs when we graduate."

"They're secretive, all right, but why does it have to be the CIA?" Ann asked. "Maybe it's something boring and obvious, like designing bombs."

"You're no fun," Franny said. "Anyway, I wouldn't do it. I'd never make bombs."

"You might have to. They made us sign those forms, remember? Did you read all of them?"

"Aliens," Zachery said suddenly, a man with a long thin face and a fuzzy beard. "Has to be. They're training us to colonize some distant planet."

Jerry turned to him. "You can't possibly believe—"

Zach laughed. Ann had already noticed that he didn't take very much seriously. "Well, Franny said she wanted something fun."

Franny ignored him. "And as long as we're asking questions, what's up with those mirrors they have in all the classrooms?" she said. "Do you think they're two-way mirrors?"

"Don't you mean one-way?" Ann said. "I mean, if you could see through it both ways it would just be a window, right?"

Franny laughed. "Yeah, I guess. But my question is, why would they bother looking at us through a mirror? They probably have cameras and microphones and whatnot."

"You think so? You really think they're watching us that closely?"

"Yeah, I do. At the interview they seemed to know things—well, they knew a lot about me."

"Yeah, I know what you mean," Ann said.

The others nodded. She waited, wondering if anyone would open up, confide their secrets, but no one said anything.

Chimes rang out over the lawn: lunch was over. As she cleaned up and headed to class with the others she felt a strange lightness building under her breastbone. It took her a while to figure out what it was, and then she realized: it was happiness.

"ALL RIGHT," PROFESSOR DAS said in their physics class that afternoon, with no preamble. "We're going to try an experiment."

He set a small wire cage on his desk. It looked like a hamster cage she'd seen in one of her high school classes, though there was no hamster inside it, or anything else. Instead it had a control panel on the side, with several buttons and a small LED display. Another table had been placed next to the desk, with a ragged baseball sitting on top.

"Now," he said. He looked out over the class. "You, Jerry. Come up here, please."

He took out another baseball, just as scruffy as the first one, and handed it to Jerry. "Write something on it, please," the professor said. "Anything you like."

Jerry thought a while, then scribbled something. He turned to go back to his seat.

"No, wait a moment," Das said. "I'll need you again." He looked at the ball, then showed it to the class. "He's written his name here—does everybody see it?"

The class nodded. Das put the ball in the cage and pressed some buttons. There was a high, nearly inaudible sound, a painful flash of light, and the ball vanished.

Everyone started talking at once, a murmur of soft voices. "So, what do you think happened to it?" Das asked, speaking over the various conversations.

"Well, it's a magic trick, isn't it?" Ann said. Even as she spoke, she felt amazed at herself. She had never volunteered first for anything in her life.

"A magic trick," Das said. "Anyone else? How would I have done the trick, anyone want to guess?"

"Mirrors," Franny said.

"Jerry?" Das said. "Do you see any mirrors here?"

He shook his head. He looked a little embarrassed up there, not sure what to do with himself.

"Could you go over to that ball there on the table?" Das said. "Okay, now pick it up. What does it say?"

"It—it says my name," Jerry said.

"Does it look like the ball I put in the cage?"

"Yeah. Yeah, exactly like it."

"Okay, so how did I do that? I mean, that ball was sitting there for a while, before I put the other one in the cage. Before Jerry wrote anything on his ball. Right? Did everyone see it?"

"Well, but it can't be the same ball," Zach said. "You and Jerry are working together—you told him what to say. He's your stooge."

Das laughed. "Stooge, is it? Jerry, did I tell you what to say?"

"No, sir."

"That's just what a stooge would say, though, isn't it?" Zach said.

"But if Jerry's right, if they are the same ball, how could that work?"

"Oh, no," Ann said. "No, no, no. I don't believe it."

"Yes?" Das said. "Ann?"

"No. It's impossible."

"What's impossible?"

"You sent the ball back in time."

Everyone started speaking at once.

"That's ridiculous—"

"Everyone knows you can't—"

"It's a magic trick, like she said—"

"Ann?" Das said. "Do you think I sent that ball back in time?"

"No," she said. Jerry had called Das "sir," she remembered. Was that what people did in college? "Sir," she added.

"Why not?"

"Well, because it's impossible. Things can't go back in time. Occam's Razor says . . ."

"Yes? What does Occam's Razor say?"

"It says not to multiply entities needlessly. That the simplest explanation is usually the truth. And the simplest explanation is, well, a magic trick. Sleight of hand."

"What would it take for you to believe that that ball went back in time?"

"I don't know. Well, if you sent *me* back. If I could experience it for myself."

"And we'll be doing that, eventually. But—"

"*What?*"

"We'll be sending you back in time. But there's a good many things you'll have to learn first, before we can do that."

Ann had barely heard him. "You'll be—you'll be sending us back in time?"

Das grinned. "That's right."

SHE SPENT THE EVENING in a daze, not even booting up her computer. This is either the biggest hoax ever, she thought, or they really do have a time machine.

But suppose it was true. Not that she believed it, but just suppose, just let Occam's Razor cut through all her disbelief. Where would she go? She couldn't think, could only imagine herself in one of those ridiculous costume dramas on late-night television, wearing a bodice and corset and curtsying to a king. She didn't know how to curtsy. No, the whole thing was insane. It had to be a joke, a test to see how much they would believe. But on the other hand . . .

The next day they were divided up into smaller groups in their history and language classes. Ann and Franny found themselves in one group, along with another employee named

Gregory Nichols. Gregory had been working at the company for a year, and he told them that he had already made several trips back in time—told them this with a straight face, yet another piece of evidence on the side of the company. Together they began to study ancient Crete, which Professor Strickland, their history teacher, called Kaphtor.

"You're going to learn to speak Kaphtoran in your language class," said Strickland. "It was spoken on Kaphtor for about a thousand years, from 2500 to 1500 BCE, and it—"

"Wait a minute," Franny said. "No one knows what they spoke there. It's what they call Linear A, isn't it? There are fragments of it, but it's never been translated."

"Well," said Strickland. "That's the advantage of having a time machine."

No one spoke for a long moment. "Why, though?" Ann asked finally. "Why are you doing all this?"

"I can only give you the outlines of our program," the professor said. "You'll learn more when you've been here longer. What happened is, well, things go very badly wrong in the future. The climate changes drastically, there are food shortages, and then a few countries get into a nuclear war over resources. There's starvation, plague, genocide, with huge numbers of people dying . . ."

"Wait a minute," Franny said again. "You're from the *future?*"

"That's right."

"But—but what are you doing here?"

"I'm getting to that. Our goal is, well, we're trying to make things right. We're going back and changing one or two things, performing some very small modifications, but the changes we make widen out, grow greater over time. And because of what we do, history is different, it turns out for the better."

"Why don't you just send people from your own time to change things?"

18

Strickland hesitated. "We—well, we're still struggling in our time," she said. "We don't have enough people to spare, for one thing. The most intelligent people we have are needed to do work there—we can't afford to lose them. So we came back here, to a time where we can take a few bright people from the population who won't be missed."

Thanks a lot, Ann thought. Though she had to admit that at least in her case it was probably true that no one would miss her. Even Sam hadn't seemed that sorry to see her go, when she'd given him her notice.

"What year do you come from?" she asked.

"I can't tell you that," Strickland said. "You can only know enough about the future as we think is safe."

"So is that what you want us to do? Go back in time and change things?"

"That's right. We'll ask you to make only small changes, though—move a vase from one room to another, or keep someone from getting to work on time. It isn't dangerous—you don't have to worry about that. Though of course you'll have to be careful."

Every day brought some new marvel. They watched holographic videos in their history class, videos that had been taken on Kaphtor by mobile cameras sent into the past. "The cameras look like flying insects—you'll probably see a few of them when you're there," Strickland explained. "Unfortunately we can't control them from the present—the best we can do is send them to a tace we're interested in and program them to come back. They home in on heat signatures, on groups of people. Then when they return we pull the data they've recorded. So our knowledge is a bit limited, but you'll know everything you'll need for a brief visit."

They took a drug that enhanced their ability to learn, and they were all speaking the Kaphtoran language after a month of study, though none of them was fluent. And they were introduced to another sort of language, one invented by the time travelers themselves, with words like "tace" for "time and place," and "thern" for "there and then." The language had extra tenses too, for events that had happened but had been erased, or events that existed but that the company planned to erase in the future.

The drug also made it easier to learn about the history of Kaphtor, and Ann grew fascinated by their customs, their society. Women wore long, frilled skirts, and blouses that opened in a V to their waist and left their breasts bare. The men were slender, athletic. They danced with bulls, they sailed to distant places, their art was renowned throughout the Mediterranean.

She worried about the open blouses, though it was not her breasts she feared exposing but her scars. She was working her way up to asking about them when Franny brought the subject up in their history class. Franny looked at Gregory as she spoke, as if daring him to laugh or make some lewd comment, but he seemed as serious as she was.

"We don't know what your cover story is yet," Professor Strickland said. "But one thing I do know is that you won't be from Kaphtor—you won't know enough to get away with that. Probably you'll be from Egypt, or Asia Minor. So no, you won't be wearing those blouses."

She returned to her lesson. "People out there don't know a lot about Kaphtor," she said, indicating the world beyond Transformations with a wave of her hand. "If they've heard of ancient Crete at all they think the inhabitants were called Minoans, because the man who discovered the ruins, Sir Arthur Evans, named them that, after King Minos. And they might have a vague memory of the myth of King Minos, who sent young people into the labyrinth to be killed by the Minotaur. In fact there was no King Minos—as I've said before, Kaphtor was a matriarchy, ruled by a queen. The word Minos was an honorific—there were men who were called 'the Minos,' which means Moon God.

"Even people who study Kaphtor don't know much about it. Some of that is because we're in the process of changing its history, because history itself is in flux. So if you read books in outside libraries you'll learn that civilization ended on Kaphtor because a volcano erupted on a nearby island, or because people revolted against the aristocracy in the palaces, or because the Achaeans, the ancient Greeks, invaded."

Ann felt a thrill at her words. She had always felt on the outside of things, looking in, had always wondered what it would be like to be part of an elite, someone in the know.

"The volcano isn't going to go off while we're on our assignment, is it?" Gregory asked.

Strickland laughed. "No, we wouldn't do that to you. The volcano erupted thirty years before your insertion. Some parts of Kaphtor still haven't been rebuilt, meaning it'll be easier to carry out your assignment."

"So what's our assignment?" Franny asked.

"We don't tell you that until you're in the field, actually," Strickland said. "The knowledge might change the way you act, make you self-conscious. Your Facilitator knows, and he or she will tell you what your specific tasks are."

"What about paradoxes?" Ann asked.

"What about them?" Strickland said.

"Well, when history changes, that means things change in the present, doesn't it? Can we change things so much that out parents don't meet, or our grandparents, and we end up not existing? And won't other people notice that things aren't the same? Or do we end up in a parallel world, where the present is different?"

"No, we'll still be in our world, this world. There wouldn't be much point in changing things if we weren't. As for things changing, and people noticing, well, as we told you, we only make very slight changes. There will be some small differences here, but no one outside Transformations will realize it. They'll think it's the way it's always been."

She smiled at them. "We'll feel it on the campus, though. You might have already felt a timeshift. The ground seems to move under you, like an earthquake."

They shook their heads. None of them had experienced a timeshift yet.

"If we changed something important, something that's in the history books and everyone knows about, the timequake would be huge," Professor Strickland went on. "If we went back in time and saved Lincoln, for example, or Kennedy—they'd feel it all through North America, maybe the world. That's why we only make small changes, and let the changes accumulate, add up. We don't want people becoming aware of what we're doing here."

Why not? Ann wondered. The company had already warned them not to share their knowledge with the world outside. Probably everyone would want to get their hands on a time machine if they knew about them; things would become chaotic pretty quickly

GREGORY HAD STARTED JOINING them at lunch, and they all pressed him for what he knew about the company and their travels in time. "Whern did they send you?" Franny asked.

"The Spanish Inquisition, the first time," Gregory said. He was as good-looking as a model, Ann thought, dark-haired but with startling blue eyes.

"Wow," Franny said. "That must have been scary."

"You know, it wasn't, not really. I was a priest from Rome, making sure that the other priests were following orders. People were afraid of me, not the other way around."

"Sounds like fun," Jerry said.

Gregory shook his head. "I didn't like it. Everyone was so terrified, all the time. They even smelled terrified—you could smell their sweat, and the mold in the prisons. I gotta tell you, I can't wait for Kaphtor. Sunlight and oceans. And I always liked the Greek gods and goddesses, Kore and Demeter . . ."

Ann would rather hear about Gregory's experiences, though; they'd talked enough about Kaphtor in class. So did Zach, it seemed, because he said, "So what did you do in Spain? Did you rescue someone, break them out of jail?"

"I had to cut through an axle on a cart, that's all. And before you ask me, no, I don't know why. Someone had to be stopped from getting somewhere, that's all I know."

"But Professor Strickland said—well, she said that we'll be debriefed when we get back," Ann said. "I mean, didn't they tell you anything?"

"I thought they would. But all they told me was that it worked out, whatever it was."

Ann sighed. If Gregory didn't know the answers to their questions, who would? "Why are they so secretive?" she asked.

"I wondered about that too," Franny said. "Do you think they're telling the truth, about being from the future?"

"What else could they be?" Gregory said.

"I don't know," Ann said. "One of those Internet hoaxes, maybe. You know—'We come from the future to save you.'"

"Why would they go to all this trouble—"

"Or a cult. Like when Strickland said they'll tell us more when we've been here longer. Like they're stringing us along, until suddenly we're all dressing the same and going door to door handing out pamphlets."

"Believe me, they're what they say they are. I really did go to Spain in the sixteenth century. And where else would they get all this technology?"

"I haven't seen any technology yet," Ann said.

"What—you want some guy in a blue box to land here in the courtyard?" Franny asked. "I don't think it's as easy as that."

"What about that drug they give us?" Jerry asked. "I had a look at it, in the lab. And, well, it isn't based on anything I know about. It has to have come from the future."

"Are you a chemist?" Franny asked.

"Something like that," Jerry said.

Franny frowned at the evasion, but Ann thought she could guess why he hadn't answered her. He had been manufacturing drugs, or something just as illegal. The people at Transformations weren't the only ones with secrets, she thought. Everyone here probably had a history they wanted to keep to themselves.

Ann had another question, but it wasn't one she wanted to share with the others. It had taken her a week after Professor Das's first time travel experiment to think of it, something that surprised her later, since the subject was usually at the forefront of her mind. Would it be possible to travel back to when she was born, see how she had gotten her scars? Could she finally get answers to the questions she had wondered about for so long? Who was her mother? Why had she given her up?

The conversation had moved on, and she tried to pay attention. "So where did they get the money for all this?" Jerry was asking, sweeping a hand at the complex in front of him. "The campus, and all the equipment—"

"Oh, man, you never read any science fiction, did you?" Zach asked. "They play the stock market, and bet on the races. It's easy if you know what's going to happen."

"I still think there's something strange here," Franny said. "Something stranger than just time travel, I mean."

"So what, you're going to back out?" Gregory said.

"Hell no," Franny said, smiling at him. "I can't wait to see Kaphtor."

A MONTH LATER PROFESSOR Strickland led her three students to a part of the complex they had never seen before, two floors up and through a long corridor. At the end of it they found a room filled with racks of clothing.

"Costumes!" Franny said.

"We don't want you to think of these as costumes," the professor said, though she was smiling as she said it. "They're your clothes, what you'll be wearing on your assignment. You're traders from Egypt, like I told you in class, but from Thebes, far to the south, beyond where anyone from Kaphtor has ever been. So you won't have to answer too many awkward questions." She smiled again. "And you can keep your names, your first names—no one will know what names from that place sound like."

She took a hanger down from one of the racks. It held a dress that looked surprisingly modern, a white linen shift with straps about an inch wide over the shoulders. She handed it to Ann and brought out another one, nearly identical, for Franny. "These were generally tighter, but we wanted you to have more freedom of movement," she said.

Gregory was given clothes from another rack, a pleated kilt and a nearly transparent shirt that tied at the neck, with wide pleated sleeves that fell in ordered waves to his elbows. Then they went over to a part of the room filled with rows and rows of shoes, and Strickland pointed to a rack of leather sandals. "Pick out a pair in your size, then try everything on, see if it fits," she said.

They each had a changing room, to Ann's relief. She pulled the dress over her head and slipped on the sandals, then looked up into the mirror.

The person who looked back at her seemed a stranger, a traveler from distant lands. A woman who sailed by the stars, with jasper in her hold, and carnelian, and rare perfume, coming back to Egypt with carved ivory and silver jewelry and beaten bronze. The gown left her shoulders bare, exposing one of her scars, but even that looked as if it belonged, evidence of her journeys.

And yet—wasn't she too pale? Wouldn't someone from Egypt be darker? Her initial delight began to fade.

She left the changing room diffidently. Franny and Gregory were coming out now, murmuring and feeling the fine linen of their clothing.

"Wow, look at Greg!" Franny whispered, nudging her. His kilt showed off the calves of his legs, which were roped with muscle.

It would never occur to Ann to express an interest in a man like Gregory, someone so far out of her reach he might as well be in another galaxy. Franny, though, she might be good-looking enough for him.

Now Ann remembered how much attention Franny had paid to Gregory at their lunches, how she had hung on his words as though he were the most fascinating person on earth. She felt a touch of sadness; she had enjoyed having Franny as a friend, and now Franny would probably start spending all of her time with him. It was a good thing she had not gotten close to Franny, or any of her fellow students.

"I look much too white for someone from Egypt," she said.

26

"Not at all," Strickland said, overhearing her. "Don't you remember? The ideal for women in Kaphtor is white, pale white, and the men are dark red. That's what we saw in the frescos, but of course the videos showed a different story— not everyone lives up to the ideal, in any timestream. Anyway, we want you to look enough like the people of Kaphtor to fit in, but different enough that you'll be taken for travelers. They'll think that you and Franny are perfect, beautiful. Gregory—" She studied him and then said, "We'll have to make you up a bit, give you some coloring."

Perfect, beautiful. No one had ever used those words about her before. They stayed with her, even after Professor Strickland told her that her hair was too thin and light, that they would need to give her a wig.

FRANNY ATE LUNCH WITH Greg the next day. Ann saw them walking to the cafeteria and laughing, but she was too excited to give it much thought. They were going to be briefed a final time that afternoon, and then leave the next day.

To Ann's surprise Emra Walker joined them at the briefing. She would be the Facilitator on this trip, she said, going with them to make sure everything went according to plan.

"We'll be meeting three other people from Transformations in Kaphtor, Preparers who left this morning and arrived thern a month before you do," she said. Ann blinked as the chronology twisted within her mind and then straightened out. "Their names are Meret Haas, Yaniel Elias, and Amabel Da Silva, and they've prepared the way for you. You haven't met them here on campus because we want the people on Kaphtor to think that they're strangers to us, and the best way to do that is for them to actually be strangers. Nevertheless, if you have any trouble and you can't find me, they'll be available to help."

She showed them holographic videos of the three earlier travelers, and Ann tried to memorize their features. Meret

Haas was a thin black woman with sharp cheekbones, a high arched nose, and long graying braids. Yaniel Elias had slightly lighter skin, black too perhaps, or Hispanic. He had shaved his head and, as if to make up for the lack of hair, had grown a huge mustache. Da Silva was white, a little plump, with dark hair piled on top of her head. All of them were older than Ann and her fellow students, in their thirties or forties.

Ann wondered briefly if Haas and Elias would stand out on Kaphtor. No, that was stupid, and probably racist besides—the company had to know what they were doing, know that it would be safe to send them into the past.

Walker went over the biographies the company had fabricated for Haas, Elias, and Da Silva, then said, "We'll be going to the palace in Knossos, and talking to a man called the Minos."

"And then what?" Ann asked.

"I can't tell you that," Walker said. "We want you to act naturally, with no preconceptions."

The next day Walker led them to the doctor's office, the same place where Ann had been examined. The same doctor was there, waiting for them. "Open your mouth," she said to Ann.

Ann complied, and the doctor swabbed the inside of her cheek. "What are you doing?" Ann asked, startled.

"We're changing your biome, your bacteria. Don't worry—it isn't dangerous. Your biome has to match the tace where you're going—otherwise you'll get sick, or they'll get sick."

After that they went up to the clothing storeroom and received their fitted clothing. A woman gave her and Franny necklaces made out of rows of beads, jasper, obsidian, garnet, lapis lazuli, and bracelets and earrings of copper and gold. Then a hairdresser placed a wig on her head, made of long braided black hair held back by an embroidered cloth band. A makeup artist circled her eyes with what she called kohl, though it was greenish instead of the black Ann had expected. Gregory got a wig of short black hair curled into rows, and then, poor man, he was taken into another room and covered with some kind of tanning cream that darkened his entire body.

Her heart was pounding hard as Walker led them into an elevator and up a few floors. They went into a room filled with semicircular rows of desks, where men and women sat and studied computer screens and LED readouts. A larger screen, this one blank, covered the front wall, and there were more people working on a platform below it. The leather bags they had packed several days ago were already there.

Walker ushered them up to the platform. "Don't move," she said.

Everyone but the four of them left the platform. Somewhere a voice started to count down. The room wavered, began to change. The air smelled of metal, and she heard a high ringing sound.

She fell down—on dirt, she saw. She was in a field, surrounded by trees. The sky overhead was startlingly bright, chrome bright; the leaves were neon green, the sun a white searchlight. She felt a brief, terrible nausea, which disappeared almost as soon as she noticed it.

"Shit," Walker said. "Oh, shit!"

ANN LOOKED AROUND. THE rest of them were getting up now, all except Gregory. The colors were fading back to normal, yellow, blue, green.

"What happened?" Franny asked.

Walker was bent over Gregory and pounding on his chest. "Shit, shit, shit!" she said.

"Is he—is he dead?" Ann asked.

Walker moved to give Gregory artificial respiration, then pressed rhythmically against his chest. "Get me my bag, someone. Hurry up!"

Ann was closest; she grabbed the bag and carried it over to Walker. "Take over here!" Walker said. Ann had never learned CPR, but she tried to copy Walker's movements as best she could.

Walker fumbled through the bag, coming finally on a plastic pouch. She took out a syringe, shoved Ann out of the way, and shot something into Gregory's heart.

Nothing happened. Walker pounded Gregory's chest again, breathed into his mouth, pumped his chest. Finally she sat back on her heels. "Yes, he's dead," she said.

"Oh my God," Franny said. Her voice was high and tight. "What happened? What went wrong?"

"Quiet," Walker said.

"You never said we could *die*—"

"Shut up, I said!"

Several people were coming toward them across the field. Even through her horror at Gregory's death, Ann felt a shiver at the realization that these were actual people from another time, another place. From Kaphtor.

Walker thrust the syringe back into her bag, then took out something else, too small for Ann to see. "What happened?" a woman asked. She glanced curiously at Walker's hand.

Walker dropped whatever she held into a small hole in the dirt, then covered the hole quickly. "We're traders, from Egypt," she said. "We were on our way to Knossos when our companion died."

The Kaphtorans put their fists to their forehead and murmured something, a prayer perhaps. "How did he die?" one of them asked.

"We—we don't know. He just didn't get up."

The group was looking at her with suspicion now. Did they think Walker had killed him?

"Well, you can't leave him here, unprotected and unreturned," the first woman said. "He has to go to the House of Return."

"The House of—"

The woman turned and said something to the group, too fast for Ann to follow. Another woman stooped to lift Gregory at his shoulders, and one of the men took his legs, and they set out along a dirt road.

It had happened so fast that the group was a good way ahead of them before they realized. "No," Walker said. She picked up her bag and ran after them. "No, wait—"

Ann and Franny hurried to catch up with her. "Why not let them take him?" Ann asked Walker in English.

"Why not?" Walker laughed harshly. "Because he has fake hair, and fillings in his teeth, and he's covered with tanning cream . . ."

She looked after the group, uncertain. More than anything that had happened so far, her expression terrified Ann, made her realize that they were on their own, and far from help. "We'll say that they can't interfere with his body," Walker said finally. "That our customs don't allow it."

Ann had already thought of that. She wondered why Walker was so slow, why she looked so worried. Was there more to this than a death, however terrible?

She followed Walker's gaze to the Kaphtorans. The women wore the clothes she had seen in her history class, the ruffled skirts and open blouses, their hair falling in long ringlets to their waist. But the videos had been unable to convey the extent of their confidence, the way they seemed to occupy the space they stood in, to move ahead like a ship under full sail.

The men looked as they had in the videos as well, wearing breechcloths in patterned fabrics, sandals, silver belts and armrings. The differences in color weren't as marked as in the frescos, but the men were darker than the women, as if the women were careful to spend more time in the shade.

The men and women both were small, none taller than about five and a half feet. So that was one of the reasons TI had recruited her, Ann thought, and Franny, and even

Walker—all of them were fairly short. She'd attributed her height to the bad food in the foster homes—who would have thought that it would turn out to be an asset?

The woman who had spoken to them first dropped back next to Walker. "My name is Itaja," she said. "What did you bring us to trade?"

"Our—our wares are in our bags," Walker said. Fortunately this was true; the company had selected objects for them that could have come from Egypt.

They followed Itaja through a land of rich red earth, checkerboarded with fields and orchards and vineyards. An aqueduct ran parallel to their path, raised up on high brick arches, and tall mountains marched with them on either side, far away in the distance.

They crossed a bridge over a small stream and came to the base of a low hill. The man and woman carrying Gregory looked barely winded, but they stopped and set him down, and two more people came forward and picked up the body. Walker was rummaging quickly through her bag; when she looked up the Kaphtorans were already climbing the hill and she hurried after them.

The path curved around the hill, and a tall mountain appeared in the distance. The Kaphtorans who were carrying the body nodded to it, and the others put their fists to their foreheads. It was a religious gesture, Ann knew; mountain peaks were sacred here. But unlike their gesture in response to Gregory's death it seemed more than just a ritual, not rote but heartfelt.

Near the top of the hill they came to a small stone hut, its walls painted with a fresco of a fleet of ships. "Stop here," Itaja said. "You'll have to wait for the guards."

A stack of wood was piled on the other side of the path, as tall as Ann. Was that a beacon, something they lit when enemies tried to enter the city? And what would they make of Walker, with her syringes and God knew what else?

But Walker had stopped and gone through her bag, Ann remembered. Had she been trying to hide everything that looked anachronistic? Did the bag have a false bottom?

A man and a woman came out of the hut and walked up to them, looking suspiciously at Gregory's body. "Why are you bringing the dead into Kaphtor?" the woman asked.

"He—our friend died suddenly, on our journey," Walker said. "We're traders, from Egypt."

"We're taking them to the House of Return," Itaja said.

"Good," the woman said to Itaja. She turned back to Walker. "Are you bringing any weapons into the city?"

"No."

"Could we see your bags, please?"

They dropped their bags on the ground and got them open. Ann watched the guards going through them, trying not to look at Walker. After a long moment the woman said, "You're free to go."

"Goddess show you your path," said the man.

Ann let out a breath, and they continued on. Finally another turn in the path showed them houses on the outskirts of a city, two and three story buildings of pale greens and blues and pinks, the colors of the candy hearts kids gave each other on Valentine's Day. Flowers twined up the walls or were painted on, surrounded by painted birds and bees and lizards, so lively they appeared almost real. The path broadened out, changed from dirt to smooth stone.

They saw people on the streets now too, all of them as self-assured as the men and women leading them, their heads high, their step firm. Some of the older men and women wore long robes tied with a sash instead of skirts or breechcloths. So Professor Strickland had been right—not everyone looked like the beautiful people on the frescos. She felt relieved to see it.

A few of them nodded to Itaja, and one or two stopped to talk. They spoke too fast to follow, but it was obvious that they were asking her about the body.

The houses grew higher and more complex, with rooms added on in every direction. If the city had suffered any destruction from the volcano they seemed to have rebuilt nearly all of it in the past thirty years. And it smelled surprisingly clean; no sewage, as she had expected, just a hint of jasmine and a hot, dry spice she didn't recognize.

Itaja put her fist to her forehead again, and Ann, following her gaze, saw a small painted shrine filled with fruit and flowers, shells and silver necklaces, at the base of one of the houses.

"This way," Itaja said finally, turning down a small street and into one of the buildings ahead of them. A fresco on the wall showed a line of tall women holding sheaves of wheat, stepping toward a queen or goddess on a throne.

The room inside was empty, lit by oil lamps made of stone. The two people carrying Gregory laid him carefully on the floor.

They could see little in the dim light. There was another shrine in the corner, with foot-high clay walls painted with a mural of a snake eating its own tail. Ann peered inside and was startled to see several snakes, moving as sinuously as flames. She could not hear anything from within the building, but she caught a brief odor of decay, overlaid with lavender and that dry spice again.

Finally a man and a woman came through a far door, murmuring to each other. Itaja went up to the woman and spoke to her, indicating the body. Suddenly Ann realized something. She had been about to talk to the man, figuring that he would be the one in charge. Their history classes had stressed that the Kaphtorans were matriarchal, but she saw now that she hadn't fully understood what that meant. Women hern were bosses, managers, artisans. Priestesses, queens. Her world turned upside down for a moment, swayed like when she had traveled through time, and then righted itself.

"Arudara here will help you with your friend," Itaja said. "Goddess show you your path." She and her group left.

Arudara called out. Several people came and picked up the body, then carried it further into the building. "Wait!" Walker called after them.

"What is it?" Arudara asked.

"Well, where are they taking him? When are we going see him again? We have—we have some customs, ways we have to arrange the body . . ."

"We can't embalm him, if that's what you mean. We don't have the materials."

That's right, she thinks we're from Egypt, Ann thought. "No—we don't do that either, where we're from," Walker said. "Just the opposite—we don't change the body at all, just wrap it and put it in the ground."

Arudara nodded. "And what token will you put in with him?"

"What—what do you mean?"

"To give the Bull. The Earth-Shaker."

No one said anything. They hadn't studied funeral customs in their history class—why should they, after all? No one had expected them to die during insertion.

"I'm sorry, I don't understand," Walker said finally.

"The Bull conducts his soul to the goddess," Arudara said. "Your friend has to have some gift, some token, to give him."

"What—what do you usually give?"

Arudara turned her head to look one way, then the other. It seemed to be a shrug. "A vase, some jewelry . . . Some object that meant something to him in life, that gave him *gove*."

She used a word that Professor Tran, their language teacher, hadn't been able to translate exactly. It meant "whole" or "entire"—"a whole loaf of bread"—but also something more, something the linguists at TI hadn't completely understood.

"All right." Walker looked through Gregory's bag and took out a carved ivory statue of a cat.

"Good," Arudara said. She smiled for the first time. "And he liked this cat? It was precious to him?"

"Yes," Walker said.

He had seen the cat exactly once, when he'd packed his bag. Ann realized that she hadn't given much thought to Gregory, that she'd been too fascinated with the newness and excitement of everything around her. She felt a wave of sadness, remembering how eager he had been to visit Kaphtor, how excited he'd been. Did he have a family, someone who would miss him in the twenty-first century?

She glanced at Franny, expecting to see her mourning as well. Instead the other woman looked furious, her expression hard.

Arudara was asking Walker about Gregory now, what he had been like, what he had done in life. "I didn't know him all that well," Walker said. "He was a trader, and—and he liked to travel."

"He was looking forward to visiting Kaphtor," Ann said. "He had heard a lot about it, and he was sure he'd like it."

"Ah," Arudara said. "Sad."

"When is the—" Ann began. She didn't know the word for funeral, she realized. Maybe there wasn't one. "When do you—"

"When will we take him to the Lands of the Dead, do you mean?" Arudara asked.

Ann nodded, then realized that the other woman didn't understand the gesture. "Yes," she said.

"The day after tomorrow," Arudara said briskly. She ushered them out into the street, and they found themselves alone for the first time since they had come to Kaphtor.

"All right," Franny said in English. She sounded mutinous. "You're going to answer my question now. Can time travel kill you?"

"No," Walker said. "Well, there was one person who died, in the early stages of the program. But it turned out that he had a heart condition."

"So what were all those physicals for? Shouldn't the company have found out if there was anything wrong with us? With Greg?"

"Sure. And we do, usually. But we can't find everything."

"You might have warned us," Franny said sarcastically. "You might have said, I don't know, 'We'll send you back in time, show you history, have you change things, and, oh, by the way, it might kill you.'"

"We did. In the release forms you signed, that day we gave you your tests."

"Do you really think we read those forms all the way through? There were pages and pages of them." She turned to Ann. "Did you read yours?"

Ann shook her head.

"Great, so you're covered," Franny said to Walker. "Good for you. Greg's still dead. And what about us? We still have to go back—are we going to die then?"

"You'll be perfectly fine," Walker said.

"Listen, if something happens to me"—Franny looked hard at Ann—"if I die, I want you to go to my husband and make sure he sues these bastards."

She had never mentioned a husband before. And if she was married, why had she flirted with Gregory?

This was obviously the wrong time to ask, though. "Sure," Ann said.

They looked around. It was growing dark; people were extinguishing their lamps and shutting their workshops. Some of them were in the street, heading home, but more, Ann knew, lived over their places of work. "We have to get to our lodgings," Walker said. "And I want some dinner—I'm starving."

Ann still had questions, what seemed like dozens of them. "What was that thing you buried, back when we first got here?"

Walker led them through the darkening streets, more confident now that she seemed to know where she was going. "It's a key. It'll take us back to your time, when we're ready to leave."

"Why is it all the way out there? Why don't we take it with us—wouldn't that be safer?"

Walker sighed. "I've never had a group that asked so many questions. It's 'all the way out there'"—Ann could hear the quotation marks in her voice—"because we always enter and leave a tace somewhere unpopulated, so no one sees us. And we don't carry it around with us because someone could search us and take it away."

"Well, but what if someone digs it up?"

"How could they possibly know about it? But don't worry—there are always backups."

"What did they mean by the Lands of the Dead?" Franny asked suddenly. "Where they're taking ... Gregory?" It seemed hard for her to say the name.

"Some cemetery, obviously," Walker said. "We'll ask about it later."

They came to a building painted with what looked like an orchard, the trees heavy with golden fruit, and they went inside.

They had reservations here, apparently, arranged by the three agents who had come before them. Ann was too tired, and too overwhelmed, to take much in. She ate dinner with Walker and Franny and then went to their room and fell asleep.

THE NEXT DAY THEY left the inn and followed Walker to the palace. The day had dawned hot, the sun already rising above the two and three story buildings. The roads led uphill and climbed back and forth, though Walker seemed to know where she was going. Sweat ran down Ann's scalp, beneath her elaborate wig.

She was thinking about the labyrinth in the famous myth, the one that hid the minotaur. It was supposed to be on Crete, but none of the insect cameras had seen it anywhere. She wondered if this spiderweb of streets could be it, if that was what visitors to Kaphtor remembered about the place.

She was about to say this when Walker spoke. "We're lucky that Gregory's—that what happened to Gregory was hern, in Kaphtor," she said in English. "Other taces have strict taboos about things like this—they would have thrown us out for bringing death into the city."

"Lucky, right," Franny said.

Walker said nothing, and they walked in silence for a while. Carts passed them, carrying grapes, olives, pottery,

and men and women on horses rode by, and even a chariot. The houses on either side were open, their wares stacked
in the doorways: patterned cloth, bronze figurines, double
axes. Craftspeople sat further inside, working at looms or
forges. On every street or so there was a restaurant or a tavern, where people sat outside around tables and talked and
drank—and there were other high, painted buildings that
gave no indication of what went on inside. Temples? Government bureaucracies?

People of every color walked by them in the streets, an
amazing diversity for a place still in the Bronze Age. Black
Africans, pale blond northerners, some Egyptians—how had
they all gotten here? The Kaphtoran navy had been destroyed
by the volcano, Strickland had said, but presumably some of
their trading vessels had been off sailing and had survived.

A man in a robe made of animal hide went by, his hair
twisted up into bull horns. A woman stood high on a scaffold-
ing, roughing out a mural on one of the buildings. Couples
passed them, arms twined around each other, first a man and
a woman, then two women, then two people in robes whose
sex she couldn't guess. Children ran and screamed and cartwheeled down the street, the girls as well as boys wearing
only loincloths. Some of them jumped on and off each other,
as if playing at bull-leaping.

The streets weren't crowded, though, not in the way modern cities were; there were only about 18,000 people in all of
Knossos. People walked, or sauntered, or idled at storefronts,
without any of the fretful hurry Ann was used to.

Finally they came to the palace. It was huge, so vast that
when she looked to the side she could not see where the outer
wall ended. And it was strangely mismatched, as if a giant
had piled stairwells atop terraces, balconies atop turrets.
Spaced irregularly on the roof were great bull horns, what
Arthur Evans had called horns of consecration. The stone
façade gleamed in the light like pearls.

Walker led them up a wide staircase, lined with frescos on both sides of acrobats leaping over bulls. A man stood at the top, in front of an open double door of bronze and silver.

"What's your business here?" he asked.

"We'd like to talk to the Minos," Walker said.

The man nodded and signaled to someone standing beyond him, further inside the palace. This second man took them through a long corridor that turned left and then left again, lit by stone lamps and lightwells. On the walls to either side stood a painted procession, men and women carrying tribute or trade goods. Hot sunlight fell on them as they walked past the lightwells, then dusty shadows, then sunlight again.

Their guide led them up another flight of stairs and through several more rooms and passageways. The rooms were lighter here, more open, and they saw painted banners, niches holding statues of women dressed in elaborate robes, a hallway with rows of double axes on wooden stands. Maybe this, and not the streets outside, was the labyrinth, Ann thought.

The guide stopped before an open door, said, "Throne Room," and bowed and left them. They passed through an antechamber and came to a room crowded with people, milling around or sitting on cushioned benches against the walls, so many that at first Ann could not see the Minos. Finally she spotted him, opposite the door they had come through, sitting on a chair made of the same luminous stone as the walls of the palace. A fresco of griffins and papyrus reeds spread out on the wall behind him, as if guarding him. There was a sunken floor in front of him, about a foot deep, and as Ann watched petitioners stepped down into it, put their fists to their foreheads, and began to speak.

The insect cameras had been programmed not to go into buildings—they were bigger than real insects, and someone was sure to notice them, maybe even capture one—so no one knew much about the inside of the palace. Still, the Minos was not very different from what Ann had expected. He was young and handsome and muscular, with long, thick, curly hair, and eyes as dark as pools of oil. He wore a robe made of some animal skin, bull hide probably, that left his arms bare, and he was heavy with jewelry: armrings, bracelets, signet rings, earrings. On his head was a crown of sharp bull horns that curved outward, facing his petitioners.

A woman stood next to him. She wore three long feathers in her hair, and she held a tall spear set against the floor. A drum sounded from somewhere whenever a petitioner finished talking, and the woman would indicate someone else with her spear, and then this new person would go down into the sunken floor and state their business.

As the crowds thinned out they were able to move close enough to hear the Minos talk with his subjects. A man wanted to donate a jar to an upcoming festival; a woman gave the Minos a carved gold ring as the fulfillment of some kind of promise, though Ann didn't completely understand what that promise was. He appeared bored by the whole thing—and it *was* tedious, she couldn't say that she blamed him. He smelled of a strong flowery perfume, of oil, of animal fur, of sweat.

After a while Ann noticed that the Minos seemed to be in charge only of small things, religious objects, the minutia of rituals. And why would it be different, after all, if this was a matriarchy? It was probably the queen who took care of the real business of the island. And according to Strickland a Minos was sacrificed every seven years—he would be a figurehead, nothing more.

"Wait," Ann whispered to Walker, urgently. "We're in the wrong place. He doesn't have any power here."

"Hush," Walker said.

"But we have to talk to someone else, a queen or somebody—"

"Shut up, I said!"

The spear-woman pointed in their direction. They stepped into the sunken floor and saluted the Minos, putting their fists to their foreheads. He reached for an alabaster cup, eggshell-thin, on a table next to him and took a sip. Then he nodded to them, his movements slow and heavy, and suddenly Ann realized that it wasn't boredom that she had seen on his face. He was drugged.

"Good morning, Your Grace," Walker said. "We come from a long way away, from Egypt, beyond the Great Green. We have heard wonderful things about your country, your artisans, and we would like to trade some of your goods for ours. We have—"

She bent down to look through her leather bag. The woman with the spear laughed, and Walker jerked her head up. "I—I hope I haven't given offense, Minos," she said. "Please believe me—that was certainly not my intention."

The Minos wasn't laughing. Alarm broke through his torpor, and he looked quickly at the spear-woman.

"You—you thought the Minos dealt with *trade?*" the woman said, her voice scornful.

"Forgive me," Walker said, still speaking to the Minos. "I didn't realize . . ."

"I don't know what it's like in Egypt"—the spear-woman's gaze swept over each of them in turn, until Ann was certain she had seen through all their disguises—"but on our island trade is very important indeed. Far too important to leave to the Minos here." Her voice grew low, amused, as if she was talking about a beloved pet.

"Then, well, could you please tell me who we should talk to?" Walker asked. "We're—we're staying at the Inn of the Pear Garden, if you could send someone—"

"I don't think so. If you know so little about Kaphtor that your first thought was to seek out the Minos, I don't see why we should bother with you at all. Your audience is over. You over there"—she pointed to another petitioner—"the Minos will hear you now."

The drum sounded, and they turned to go. Some of the people waiting for the Minos were talking in low voices, or smiling or laughing.

"Well, that was humiliating," Ann said in English, as they came out to the street. "And I told you, I said he wasn't—"

"Do you think I didn't know that?" Walker said. She had a way of looking down at people, over her snub nose, that made Ann feel small, ignorant. "It's part of the plan, our assignment hern."

Was that true? Ann had wondered about Walker's competence from the moment they'd arrived in Kaphtor. "Well, why didn't you tell us?"

"Because of your inexperience. This is your first assignment, after all. You wouldn't have reacted the way you did if you knew what was coming."

Ann knew herself to be an excellent liar; she was certain she could play any part Walker would give her. But of course Walker didn't know that—and it was never a good idea to boast about your skill at deception.

"So what happens now?" Ann asked.

"Now we go back to the inn, and wait for him to contact us. You did notice, I hope, that I managed to tell him where we're staying."

Suddenly Ann realized something. "So that's why he was drugged!" she said.

"Was he?" Franny asked. "Why?"

"The Minos is sacrificed every seven years, for the fertility of the crops. Remember when they told us that in history class? It must be getting close to his time."

"Very close," Walker said. "That's why he's going to come and talk to us."

They brought fruit and wine to their room at the inn and ate their lunch. When they finished Walker took out a small computer of a type Ann had never seen; it was rolled up like a scroll, and when Walker spread it out it hardened into a screen. There was a separate keyboard, made out of the same material.

"Is that—some kind of plastic?" she asked.

"I really don't know," Walker said.

Walker worked at her computer, but she and Franny had nothing to do but study the room they sat in, the benches along the walls, the rattan beds, the wooden chests inlaid with shells and ivory, the long windows just beneath the ceiling. "Can I see that computer?" Ann asked, when Walker paused to flex her fingers, but the other woman just shook her head.

The time passed slowly. Just as Ann was readying herself to ask if she could go outside and explore the city, the innkeeper knocked on their door. "Someone here to see you," she said.

She left, and a man came inside. At first Ann didn't recognize him; he had taken off his robe and crown and was wearing only a patterned breechcloth and a few armrings.

"Good afternoon, Your Grace," Walker said. "Won't you sit down, take some refreshment with us?"

His eyes were no longer as vague, or as dark. His gaze jumped from corner to corner of the room, as if he expected to see spies from the palace at any moment. He sat down on a bench, then stood, then sat back down again. The smell of his sweat, muted in the Throne Room, was very strong here.

Walker passed him a cup of wine. He murmured a few words over it and spilled some drops on the floor, then drank the rest of it down. She refilled it. "I—I have hopes you can help me," he said. "And in return I will make a trade agreement with your country—for very favorable terms, of course."

"I'll do what I can," Walker said.

"I—" He stopped, wiped sweat off his forehead with his arm, drank his wine. "There are factions at the palace, various groups, people at odds with one another. I don't have the power right now to—to deal with you as I'd like."

There's an understatement, Ann thought.

"You—you come from Egypt, from a land where men rule, is that true?" He looked at the group ranged around the room, seeming to notice only now that they were all women.

"That's right," Walker said.

"Ah. Good. I have friends at the palace who also believe in such things. And, well, what I need is, I need someone to disable the lookouts."

"The—the lookouts?"

"Yes, so that they don't raise the alarm." He held out his cup, and Walker filled it again. "Then my people, my allies, can come to my aid."

"How many lookouts are there?"

"Two. There's one post along the west road, and one to the north, with two people at each."

"And you want us to disable them? What do you mean by that?"

The Minos seemed uncomfortable with such a blunt question. "You understand. Overpower them somehow, or—"

The door opened and several people stepped inside, all of them wearing long feathers in their hair and armed with spears. The Minos threw down his wine cup and clambered up one of the benches, then tried to jump for the window beneath the ceiling.

One of them laughed. It was the spear-woman from the Throne Room, Ann realized. "You won't get out that way," she said.

The Minos turned and faced her, then climbed down from the bench. "You've been making trade deals on your own, have you?" the spear-woman said.

"No. No, I've been—been talking with these people, nothing more. I'm interested in Egypt, and they were kind enough to tell me—"

"Don't we give you everything you could want at the palace? Food, clothing, jewelry, women . . . If you wanted lessons about Egypt I'm sure we could have found you a teacher."

There was unmistakable cruelty in her voice. They both seemed to know what was really at stake here, and that it had nothing to do with Egypt or lessons. He gave her a look filled with hatred.

"And you." The spear-woman turned to Walker. "Do you think we didn't notice that you told the Minos where you were staying? We follow him everywhere, you know, and when he came here we knew it couldn't be anything innocent. What were you talking about?"

"It's as he says, my lady," Walker said. "We were telling him about Egypt."

"I wonder. You come to our city and the first thing that happens is that one of your party dies . . ." She laughed at Walker's look of surprise. "Oh, yes—did you think we didn't know? And now we find you talking to our Minos here." She thought a moment. "Take your bags and come with us."

"Come—where?"

"The queen will judge you."

Ann looked at the others, dismayed. Had Walker planned this as well? But Walker seemed frightened, uncertain.

The soldiers urged them toward the door, spears at the ready. "We'd better do what they say," Walker said in English.

"And then what?" Ann asked.

"And then—the queen will let us go, I'm sure, once she hears our side of the story."

Would she? Hadn't Walker just plotted treason with the Minos? And would the Minos be able to keep quiet about their conversation, or would he tell them everything as soon as he got back to his drugs?

She picked up her bag and then headed toward the door with the others, stepping over the puddle of wine from the Minos's spilled cup.

WALKER HURRIED TO CATCH up with the spear-woman. "Listen, our friend Gregory, the man who died," she said. "He'll be taken to the Lands of the Dead tomorrow."

"I'll send someone to escort you there," the other woman said.

She said nothing more as she led them through the twisting streets of the city. Finally she stopped at one of the houses and knocked on it with her spear. A woman came to the door, looking startled. No matter what era you live in, Ann thought, no one ever looks happy to see the police.

"Can you host these people while they're waiting for the queen's justice?" the woman asked, indicating Ann and Franny with her spear.

"Of course," the woman said. She opened the door wider, and the spear-woman motioned the two of them inside. "Goddess show you your path," she said.

The door closed behind them. "Wait," Ann said. "Aren't we going with—"

"Come," the woman said. "You must be hungry. I would be honored if you would take your dinner with me."

Honored? Weren't she and Franny supposed to be prisoners, criminals?

"Where is our friend going?" Ann asked.

"To another house," the woman said. "I don't have room for her here. Don't worry—she'll be shown the goddess's hospitality, just as you will be. Guests are sacred to us."

The ground floor of the house seemed to be a workshop, with a loom set up by a window and piles of cloth along the walls. The woman climbed the stairs and led them to a room with a table, with what looked like a half a dozen boys and girls crowded on benches around it.

"My name is Damate," she said. "These are my children."

"Can we eat now?" one of the girls asked. The table was set with empty plates, and Damate rummaged through some open shelves and added two more.

"Hush," Damate said. "Move over and let our guests sit down."

They found places along the bench. Damate went into another part of the room, opened a cupboard, brought out some food, and tested something sizzling over a brazier. The room began to smell deliciously of fish.

Damate took platters of food out to the table. She sat, lifted a cup of red wine, and spoke a long sonorous sentence over it. "Our Lady of the Sea, Our Lady of the Ear of Grain, accept this offering," she finished, and poured some drops of wine on the floor.

The children reached for the food. "Wait," she said, rapping one of them lightly on the hand with a spoon. "Our guests eat first—you know that."

Damate turned toward Ann and Franny, who helped themselves to fish and lentils and wine. The fish was seasoned with that sharp spice that Ann had smelled all over Knossos, a tang like newly cut wood warmed by the sun. Even the wine tasted spicy.

The children ate voraciously. When they were finally finished they sat back and started asking her and Franny questions. "Where are you from?" "Do you have any pets? I have a frog." "How many children do you have?" "Do you know any songs?"

There were only four of them, Ann saw—there had just seemed to be more. She looked at Damate helplessly, but the other woman made no move to stop them.

"We're from Egypt," Franny said. She turned to Damate. "Where's your husband?"

Ann frowned at her.

"I haven't found a husband yet," Damate said.

"Then how do you—"

Ann hurried to interrupt her. "Don't you have any—" She wanted to say "jails," but stopped when she realized she didn't know the Kaphtoran word for it. "—any places to put people waiting for the queen's justice?"

"Here," Damate said, clearly not understanding the question. "They stay with people until it's their time to see the queen."

"What if they're, well, what if they stole things? Or killed someone?"

"Those people are not the queen's concern. If someone steals something, she has to work to pay it back. As for a killing, that would depend. If it's an honorable killing there's no need for justice, of course. And if it isn't, well, the killer has to pay for that too. The queen is only brought into it if there is some question over the penalty."

Honorable killing? "But—aren't you worried about bringing us into your house?" Ann asked. "You don't even know what we've done."

"I can take care of my family," Damate said. She looked at the corner of the dining room, and Ann, following her gaze, saw a spear as tall as she was. "The queen wouldn't allow me to receive guests otherwise."

She had said it without boasting, but she did look as if she could defend herself. She was stocky and muscular, without the wasp waist of the women on the frescos, and her hair was piled up on her head instead of falling in ringlets. She wore a long robe of patterned cloth, tied with a sash at her waist.

Suddenly one of the children pointed to something above Ann's head. "Look," he said. "The little golden lady is here. She wants to tell you something."

Ann turned. At first she could see nothing there, and she thought, annoyed, that the boy was having a joke at her expense. Then a bee buzzed by her head, and she ducked away.

"Don't touch her!" Damate said. Then to her son, "What does she want?"

"She has a task for her, for the visitor." The bee flitted away, out an open window. "She goes," the boy said. He sounded sad. "She's gone."

All the children were staring at Ann now. Damate brought her fist to her forehead, and the rest of them did the same.

"It was just a bee," Ann said. She hated being singled out; it never meant anything good.

"You outlanders are very strange," Damate said. "Don't you recognize Our Lady of Honey, bringing you a message?"

"Well, but how do you know? When is it Our Lady, and when is it just a bee?"

"He tells us," Damate said, indicating the boy who had pointed to the bee. He hadn't been one of the children asking questions, Ann realized; he had kept to himself, quietly eating his food. Now she saw that he had a tattoo of a snake on one cheek, coiling up from his neck to next to his ear.

"He's very—" She used a word Ann didn't know. "He's dedicated to the goddess."

The boy looked up and mumbled something. "What?" Ann asked.

"She has a task for you," he said. He sounded matter-of-fact now, as if a visit from the goddess was an everyday occurrence. Maybe it was, for him.

"What kind of task?" she asked.

The boy looked to each of his shoulders, in the shrug she had seen before. "Good lady . . ." he began.

The others joined in; it was a prayer of some kind. "Good lady, garbed in green earth, we thank you for this favor, and for all your favors given. We live within your blessings."

The meal ended soon after. Damate took them into another room and showed them their beds, and then went downstairs. Ann had the idea that she usually slept in the room she had given them but that she had moved to her workshop to be close to the door, ready to come awake if they tried to escape.

Her legs shook as she got ready for bed. A part of her noticed it almost clinically, but another part still felt trembly, as if she had experienced something mysterious, numinous. It couldn't have been, though—she hadn't believed in a god, or a goddess either, for a very long time.

LIGHT COMING IN THROUGH the high windows woke her, and she stumbled into the bathroom. The Kaphtoran toilet had amazed her when she had first seen it at the inn: a wooden seat above two stones with a hole between them, leading down to sewers and out to sea. It could even be flushed, by moving a lever and allowing water to fall on the contents.

Damate was already up, opening cupboards and setting the table with plates and pitchers and a loaf of bread shaped like a coiled snake. The family and Ann and Franny ate breakfast together, and then Damate went downstairs to work.

The children headed downstairs as well, and Ann followed them. The workroom had a fresco along the wall, a line of women dressed in beautiful patterned cloth, and there was a small ivory statue of a goddess in one corner, with beads and silver charms in a bowl in front of it. Damate's bed stood in the center.

She had wondered how Damate supported herself and took care of the children without a husband, but she seemed to manage without any problems. A woman came to collect the boy who was dedicated to the goddess, perhaps to take him to the temple, and a girl and boy played with loom weights and some animals carved out of wood. Another girl scooped a frog out of a pitcher and watched it hop around the floor. They ignored Ann and Franny, who had not sung for them or given them interesting answers to their questions.

The girl with the frog had lighter skin than the other children, and Ann realized that they had had at least two different fathers, maybe more. What would that be like, to be able to choose your partners, to have children with whoever you wanted? To choose your husband—or not, if that was what suited you?

About an hour later a man knocked at the door. At first Ann thought he was the police, that the queen had sent for them at last, but he ignored her and Franny and rounded up the remaining children instead. Damate tried to explain where they were going, but Ann couldn't form a clear picture of it; it seemed to be a combination school, playground, and museum.

Transformations Incorporated had stressed over and over again that they weren't to offend the people in whatever era they found themselves, the ones the company called the time-bound. That was why Ann had scowled at Franny the night before, when the other woman had started with her personal questions; she didn't know how Damate would take being asked about not having a husband. Now, though, she was so puzzled by the arrangements here, and so tired of their forced idleness, that she was ready to ask her own questions. If Damate didn't want to answer she could always say so.

"Was that their father?" she asked.

"My brother," Damate said. She continued to work at the loom, not looking up, the shuttle moving in and out of the threads like a car darting through traffic.

"But what—why is he taking care of your children?"

"Well, he's my brother."

What on earth did that mean? She tried to feel her way toward an answer. "So . . . he's more important to you than a father of a child would be?"

"Of course. Your first family is always the most important."

"And if you had a husband . . ."

"A husband isn't blood. Not the way a brother is." She seemed to sense Ann's confusion; she stopped working and stared across the room, frowning. "Look," she said finally. "The woman makes the child, right?"

Ann said nothing. How much did these people know about biology? If they hadn't figured out the father's role in conception she certainly wasn't going to tell them, wasn't going to risk altering history that much.

"Well, of course the father does his part too," Damate said, to Ann's relief. "But the woman shapes the child within her, just as Potnia shapes the world. So the brothers and sisters shaped by your mother are the ones who give you *gove.*"

There was that word again, the one Arudara had used. Ann was beginning to get a better sense of it; it meant a feeling of harmony, of rightness.

Franny had come over sometime during this conversation. "Don't you want a husband, though? I mean, don't you get lonely?"

"Lonely? With all these children?"

"I mean lonely for adults. Adult conversation."

"Well, but I have my brother and the rest of my family, my sisters and my mother. And my friends, of course." She parked the shuttle in among the threads, seeming to settle in for a long discussion. "I did nearly take a man once though, my younger boy's father."

"What happened?"

Damate sat back against the wall, a distant look in her eyes. "Ah, he was a fine man, with beautiful eyes and a won-

54

derful smile. Not handsome the way the bull-leapers are handsome—more of a dreamer. A good love-maker, though."

Franny grinned, as if Damate had acknowledged she'd been right all along. She was a romantic, Franny, Ann thought. "What did he do?" Franny asked.

"Do? He's like his son, dedicated to the Goddess." Ann heard the capital letter as she pronounced the word.

"No, what I mean is—how did he earn his living? Support himself?"

"He doesn't. I just told you—he's dedicated to the Goddess. He lives at the palace, in Her temple."

"So you couldn't get married? Because they wouldn't let him out of the temple?"

"What does where he lives have to do with it? No, I didn't take him because—well, partly because he asked me, he didn't wait for me to ask him. I'm too traditional that way, I know that. All my friends say so, anyway. But also because the day he asked me was unpropitious—it was the day of Kore's death and descent to the Underworld."

"You didn't marry him because—because he asked you on the wrong *day*?"

"Not just the wrong day—the most dreadful day in the calendar. The longest night of the year, and what was worse, on this night the moon had gone to the Underworld too, and had not yet come back. We were at the temple, celebrating the mysteries, and, well, he couldn't wait to ask me. Perhaps if he'd left it for another day—ah, well. It's too late now."

Franny shook her head. "I don't get it. You loved him, right?"

A knock sounded at the door, and Damate opened it to a woman wearing three feathers in her hair and carrying a spear. The police, Ann thought. She had almost managed to forget them. Her heart jolted and then sped up painfully.

"I'm here to take your guests to the Lands of the Dead," the spear-woman said.

The words sounded as unpropitious as anything Damate's lover had said, but Ann had never felt as relieved in her life. She and Franny hurried to the door.

"I can only take one of you," the woman asked. "One must stay behind, as a pledge for the other's good behavior."

Ann didn't know what to hope for, to go with the woman or be left with Damate. Franny was closer to Greg and should see him buried, but on the other hand Ann was heartily tired of being cooped up indoors.

The woman pointed with her spear to Franny. "You, over there. You'll stay here."

"No!" Franny said. "No, I have to go. Greg and I, we were—we were dating." The woman's expression did not change, and Franny added, "We were in love."

The spear-woman looked one way and then the other, shrugging. "That's nothing to me," she said. "You." She pointed to Ann. "Come."

"No, she should go," Ann said, much to her own surprise. "I'll stay here."

"I'm not used to having my commands disobeyed," the spear-woman said. "Come along."

Ann looked at Franny and shrugged. "Thanks anyway," Franny said in English, and Ann followed the spear-woman out the door.

The cemetery was in the opposite direction from the palace, though as she followed the spear-woman through the streets she noticed that the houses here looked the same, the artists' wares spilling through the open door-ways. She saw another shrine by the side of the road, this one with a fire burning within it, and after that she spot-ted them all over, small ones tucked into corners, big ones almost the size of houses, standing in a plaza or where a group of roads met. They were all different, with differ-ent offerings: cloth, small double axes, goblets, necklaces. Were there many goddesses, or just one with many names?

That strange boy had called the one who had visited her Our Lady of Honey.

And now that she was looking for it she saw men and women with the same tattoo on their faces, a snake spiraling up from their necks to their cheeks. Other people were gazing at them with a combination of wonder and longing and fear, moving closer to them, even walking in circles around them. Were they hoping for a message from the goddess? But the men and women dedicated to her mostly ignored these people, and some of them were obviously crazy, muttering and gesturing to themselves.

Ahead of her the spear-woman turned onto another path, a winding road that led away from the city. The houses grew smaller and shabbier, and finally stopped altogether. "Here we are," the spear-woman said.

They had come to a flat rocky field. Two men were digging between stone walls about a room's width apart. Noises sounded behind them and she turned to see another spear-woman coming up the path, with Walker following her.

"Good to see you," Walker said in English, nodding. "How are you doing? Are they treating you all right?"

Ann blinked; Walker had never said anything remotely as pleasant to her before. "Better than I expected. What about you?"

"I'm fine. Where's Franny?"

"They kept her at the house, in case I tried to run away."

Walker looked at her significantly, but she said nothing more. They stood for a long while in silence, watching the men dig the grave. The heat beat down on them, and sweat poured down her sides and pooled between her breasts. For the first time she wished she could wear one of those light open blouses.

Walker looked around her. "When is it going to start?" she asked.

"No one can hurry the Goddess," the spear-woman guarding her said. It sounded like a proverb.

Finally they saw something riding up the path to the cemetery, a chariot drawn by horses. No, not horses—pulling the chariot were two animals with the bodies of horses and the faces of birds—and with open wings, though they weren't flying. Griffins, like the ones on the frescos.

Ann drew in a breath. Had they—gone extinct? But surely someone would have found fossils, bones . . . She looked at Walker, who was smiling.

"Where did they come from?" she whispered.

"We brought them hern. They're bioengineered."

"But then—why hasn't anyone found evidence of them?"

"We didn't bring very many. Just for the priestesses. We had to trade for certain . . . concessions."

Now she saw the priestess sitting in the chariot. She wore a robe made of animal hide; a pendant of a snake swallowing its tail hung at her breast. Her hair was down and her eyes were enormous, staring at something only she seemed to see. She looked otherworldly, numinous, as if she had just returned from the Lands of the Dead.

Then Ann realized that it was Arudara, the woman they had met at the House of Return. She wondered how many marvels her head could hold in one day.

A drum sounded, deep and complex. A horn blew. A waft of smoke drifted past her, a heavy smell. The priestess stood and began to speak.

"The year waxes, the year wanes. The snake grows thick and blind and seems to die. A man's life plays out like a thread and is cut.

"But spring returns, and the snake comes forth from her skin. The man finds rest in the arms of our Lady. Our Lady of the Evening Star, Our Lady of the Snake."

The odor of smoke grew stronger. It curled around her, disappeared, returned—like the year, the snake, the recurring rhythm of the drum.

Her thoughts blurred. She understood something important, fundamental, but when she tried to grasp it it vanished. Like smoke, like life . . .

The priestess rose into the air and hovered over the open grave. A snake was wrapped around her waist, and another coiled at her throat like a necklace. The gravediggers went to the chariot, brought out the body, and took it down into the hole.

Ann peered inside. The two men set the body on the dirt floor, folding it carefully so that its knees rested under its chin. Arudara dropped the statue of the cat inside the grave.

Ann looked up again. The priestess was holding her arms straight out to the side, like wings. Suddenly she screamed, a high fierce scream that went on and on, that echoed from every part of the cemetery. She was no longer a priestess, no longer Arudara; she had been taken by the living goddess, the ruler over life and death. Ann shivered.

Finally the scream stopped. "The sacrifice seems good, and is accepted," the priestess said. Her voice, her gestures, had changed completely, as though someone had slipped into her body as casually as pulling on a glove. "The man is at rest in the arms of our Lady. Our Lady of the Clod of Earth, Our Lady of the Worm. Now begins the time of growth, the time of the ear of grain."

The gravediggers were holding their fists to their foreheads, the same salute Ann had seen before. It seemed less a ritual this time, more an attempt to protect themselves from the radiance of the goddess.

The drum stopped. The men lowered their fists and bent to shovel earth into the grave. Ann looked up, and saw that Arudara had returned to her chariot. Or had she ever left it?

The smoke had mostly dissipated—and now that it was gone Ann understood that it had been some kind of drug. Well, of course, she thought, annoyed at herself for being so slow.

Walker headed toward the chariot. She'd been affected by the drug too, Ann saw; she seemed to be forcing herself through some medium thicker than air. Before she could reach Arudara, though, the priestess picked up the reins and rode away.

Walker turned to the gravediggers. "Do we—do we have to pay for the ceremony?" she asked.

The men continued to work, saying nothing. Finally they finished, and one of them spoke. "Pay? Pay to return a man to his Goddess? You people from Egypt have some peculiar customs."

"Come," Ann's guard said. "Time to go back."

They started down the hillside. The drug had not worn off completely, and everything seemed strange, heightened. She felt as if she understood the mysteries of life and death—no, more than that, as if life and death were the same thing, and it was only a foolish misunderstanding that had made her think they were different. When she followed the thought, though, when she tried to put it into words, the feeling grew confused, drifted away like smoke. But for a brief while, as they walked through the twisted streets of Knossos, it seemed as if death had no power to frighten her.

"She didn't really fly out of her chariot like that, did she?" Ann asked as they neared Damate's house.

"Fly?" Walker said. "I saw her turn into a—a lion, I think. Her face, anyway."

"It was a drug. They drugged us."

"I'd already guessed that, thank you."

Walker touched her hand. Ann looked down, saw that she was holding something small between her fingers. She opened her own hand to receive it.

"Don't look," Walker said. "We have our own drugs. Put it in your host's drink, and leave the house with Franny tonight, after everyone's gone to sleep."

"What is it?"

"It's a sleeping pill. Why? Did you think I wanted you to poison her?" She laughed harshly. "Meet me . . ." She looked around. "Over there, by that shrine."

"I thought we were going to wait for the queen," Ann said.

"I don't think the queen's on our side."

"What? Why not? Did the Minos say something?"

The two spear-women looked up at the word "Minos."

"Hush," Walker said. "I'll explain everything tonight."

They were coming up on Damate's house now. "Okay then," Ann said. "I'll see you."

"Goddess show you your path," her guard said, and knocked at the door with her spear.

FRANNY WAS SITTING IN the downstairs room, waiting for her eagerly. "How was it?" she asked.

"Pretty amazing," Ann said. She tried to tell her about the priestess, the drug, that final scream, but nothing she said managed to convey the wild strangeness of it, or that brief moment of understanding.

"I should have been there," Franny said when she'd finished. "I knew Greg better than any of you."

"You should have." She lowered her voice, though they were speaking in English. "Walker gave me a sleeping pill, for our host over there." She nodded at Damate, working at her loom. "We're supposed to escape tonight."

"A sleeping pill? Where'd she get it?"

"That bag of hers, probably. Do you think you'll be ready?"

"Definitely. Another day of this and I'll go crazy. But why doesn't she want us to wait, see what the queen says?"

"I don't know," Ann said. "She said she'll tell us tonight."

That evening she held the sleeping pill in her hand, and when they went to dinner she stayed close to Damate and sat next to her at the table. "Do you think your friend went on to the fields of the dead?" Damate asked her, after she had spoken her words and poured the wine to the floor.

What did she mean? "I don't know," Ann said. "Are there—does the goddess ever reject anyone?"

"Don't you know the tale of Kore?"

Kore was another name for Persephone, Ann knew. "She was kidnapped by Hades and taken to the underworld, wasn't she?"

"Kidnapped? You people have some strange ideas, truly. She was bitten by a snake and died, and became queen of the underworld."

"And so she ruled over those who had died," the boy with the tattoo said in a bright clear voice, "either sending them on to the green fields of the dead, or keeping them with her in the gloom a while, until she judged that they had the wisdom to go on."

Damate looked at him fondly. "I'm sure they don't want to hear that old story," she said.

"No, it sounds interesting," Ann said. If everyone was listening to the boy she could slip the pill into Damate's wine unnoticed.

"Go on, then," Damate said.

The boy nodded. "A long time ago the Lady Kore wandered away from the bull games and walked a while in the fields, gathering flowers," he said. He spoke very well, for someone so young. "But a snake came swiftly and secretly through the flowers and bit her on the ankle, and she descended to the Lands of the Dead."

Kore became Queen of the Underworld, said the boy, and took as her consort a bull that had been sacrificed in the games. Ann's hand was sweating now, and the sleeping pill inside it felt sticky; she hoped it still had some potency left. She leaned closer to Damate.

"But Kore's mother the Lady Demeter was worried about her daughter, and traveled the world looking for her," the boy said. "And while she searched she neglected the fruits and flowers, the living things of the fields, and they withered and died.

"Then Demeter learned of her daughter's fate. She descended to the Lands of the Dead, and she saw her daughter sitting on a throne and crowned with stars, and the bull sat next to her. And Demeter said, 'I have looked throughout the world for you, my daughter, and I have found you at last.'"

Damate was concentrating on her son, love and pride in her eyes. Ann's heart had begun to pound so loudly she could barely hear the boy's voice. She dropped the pill into the wine. Damate turned toward her and Ann met her gaze, forcing herself not to look down at the cup. Damate looked away, and when Ann glanced at the wine the pill had dissolved. Damate lifted the cup and sipped from it.

"But Kore said, 'If I go with you, who will judge the dead, and tell them when it is their time to go? And I have taken the bull as my consort, and cannot go back to your house.' Then Demeter saw how it was, that her daughter was a woman grown, and had taken a consort."

Damate drank more of the wine as the boy went on. "Demeter said, 'I will allow it, but for six months only. For six months you will dwell in the Lands of the Dead with your consort, and you will judge the dead, but for six months you will live with me in the world above, and all the living things of the world will grow and flourish.'"

The boy stopped; that was the end, apparently. "That was very good," Ann said, taking a long drink of her wine.

Damate took another sip as well. "Do you see now? The Goddess doesn't reject anyone, only decides when to send them on to the fields of the dead. Do you think your friend was ready?"

"I—I don't know."

"Well, he was young, you said, and his death was unexpected. It may take him a while to understand what has happened to him. He will stay with Kore a while, I think."

Ann nodded. "I guess so."

Damate yawned. "You've walked a long way today, but I'm the one who seems to be tired." She stood. "I'm going to sleep—I'll see you tomorrow."

6

SHE WAS IN A chariot pulled by griffins, flying over the streets of Knossos. The goddess came toward her in another chariot, this one drawn by an enormous bee. "Our Lady of Honey," she said, putting her fist to her forehead. "I thank you for this favor. Please, tell me what I must do for you, how I can fulfill your commands."

"The grain grows," the goddess said. "The grain is cut, and dies."

"What? I don't understand."

The goddess's voice blurred, grew indistinct. Suddenly she heard a loud clanking noise, and she looked down to see her chariot separating from the griffins that pulled it. "No," she said. "No, wait! Help me—"

She opened her eyes. The room lay in darkness, as black as the hole they had put Gregory in. Something clattered, and she realized the noise she had heard was Franny, trying to make her way through their room.

"Come on," Franny whispered. "It's time."

Ann had gone to bed fully dressed, with her bag next to her. She stood and picked it up, then moved carefully through the bedroom and downstairs to the front door.

She reached out for Franny, making sure she was still there, then felt along the wall of the workshop, trying to avoid Damate's bed at the center of the room. She had seen a torch by the door, which Damate had put out before going to bed, and when her fingers found the door she backed up, looking for it.

She felt the torch, reached for it—and it fell from the bracket and dropped to the floor. It was only wood, but the noise it made against the stone floor sounded loud in the quiet house. Damate stirred in her sleep, and an instant later one of the children cried out from their bedroom. She and Franny stood silent, waiting for Damate to wake up, to discover them unmoving by the door . . .

Nothing happened; the child must have gone back to sleep. Ann picked up the torch and they stepped outside, feeling the fresh air in their faces. She closed the door behind them.

"Do you know where we're going?" Franny asked.

"Yeah," Ann said. "Just let me get this torch lit first. There's a shrine around here . . . There it is."

They headed toward the fire they saw flickering in the distance. Somewhere far away a dog barked. A ridiculous number of stars shone overhead, more than she had ever thought were in the sky, and a great crescent moon sailed among them.

"After that, though," Franny said. "Because I want to see Greg."

"Greg?" Had Franny lost her mind, on top of everything else? "He's—"

"At the cemetery, I mean. I didn't get a chance to say goodbye."

"We can't go to the cemetery! Walker's waiting for us."

"So what? She didn't say what time she wanted us to be there, did she? Do you remember how to get to the cemetery?"

She did, but she didn't know if she should say so. Still, Franny deserved to see the grave—and this might be her last chance.

She lit the torch from the fire in the shrine and looked around. No one else seemed to be outside.

"All right—I think I can find it," Ann said. "But you have to be quick."

"Great," Franny said. "Thanks."

They walked for a while in silence. *Was* this Franny's last chance to say goodbye? Walker seemed to be saying that they had failed, that they would have to leave quickly, before the queen passed sentence on them. And what would happen once they got back to the company? How would that look, to have your first assignment recalled, to have that failure on your record? Well, she had always known it was too good to be true.

Something ran across the path in front of them. It was shaped differently than a dog or cat—a fox? For the first time Ann heard sounds in the night around them, rustling and chittering, loud in the silence. The Kaphtorans called Knossos a city, but it was really much smaller than that, groves and farms close around it.

Beside her Franny wiped her eyes, and Ann realized that she had been crying. You moron, she thought. She knew she had trouble guessing what other people were feeling, but any idiot could have figured out that Franny would be upset.

She should try to comfort her, but how? "I'm sorry about Gregory," she said finally.

"Thanks. You know, you're the first person to say anything."

"Well, nobody knew you were together. And Walker probably read your file, saw you were married."

"My file, right." Franny laughed bitterly.

"What do you mean?"

"What's in those files, do you think? If they can go back in time, how much do they know about us? How much privacy do we have?"

Ann thought of Franny as she was when she'd first met her, a woman who had laughed often and easily. She'd been another of those people who cruised through life, Ann had thought, with nothing to worry about, nothing to hide.

Now she saw how wrong she had been, that they had more in common than she'd thought. "Look," she said. "I— well, I grew up in foster homes. That's what they know about me. I think—I think they're looking for people who aren't connected to the present, our present. People who might be unhappy there, who would jump at the chance to leave."

She couldn't remember the last time she had volunteered anything about her life. Franny stayed silent, though, and Ann cursed herself for opening up, all for nothing.

"My husband used to hit me," Franny said finally. "He stopped, though. Well, he said he'll stop. He said that before, though." Her voice broke, though she was no longer crying.

"So I thought, well, if I got together with Greg, maybe I could leave him," she went on. "Maybe I could really do it this time. Okay, I knew it wasn't serious, that it probably wouldn't come to anything. It was fun to think about, though." She took a deep breath. "So, anyway. That's what they know about me. That I'd do anything to get away from my life. Anything they wanted."

Ann didn't know what to say. She wanted to ask why Franny had stayed with her husband, but she remembered all the stupid questions people had asked about her life, all the things they didn't know. She thought that Franny's story must be like that, something no outsider could understand.

"I'm sorry," she said finally.

"Yeah," Franny said. "Well. I'm sorry too. About you, I mean. The foster homes and stuff."

They had reached the cemetery. "Here we are," Ann said. "It—who's that?"

"What?"

"Over there. Someone—it looks like someone's digging up Gregory's grave."

They began to run. The person—a woman—looked up and saw them, but to Ann's surprise she stayed at the grave and continued digging. There was a light on the ground, a steady yellow like . . . a flashlight?

"Who are you?" Ann said when they had gotten close enough.

"Meret Haas," the woman said.

"From the company!" Ann said, feeling relieved. She had forgotten that Transformations had sent other agents to Knossos. "Can you help us? Did you hear what happened with the queen, and the Minos, and—"

"Wait a minute."

Meret picked up the flashlight and straightened, and Ann saw her clearly for the first time. Her wig had been knocked askew while she was digging, exposing short tight curls, black mixed with gray.

She had a strange expression, an amused half smile, as if she had just told Ann a joke and was waiting for her to laugh. Was she mocking them, did she feel somehow superior to them?

"Why are you digging up Greg's grave?" Franny asked.

"It's a long story. Have you ever wondered—well, what do you think about the company?"

"What do you mean?" Ann asked. "I think it's terrific. I mean, *time travel*."

Was it that terrific, though? Weren't they in a lot of trouble? What would the queen do if she caught them?

"But don't you wonder what they're doing?" Meret asked. "What their ultimate goals are?"

"They told us—they're trying to make things better."

"That doesn't explain what they're doing hern. Things seem pretty good in this tace, pretty stable."

"Not for the Minos."

"Not for the Minos, no. And all I know about your assignment is that you're supposed to contact him somehow. But why does the company want to come in on his side, someone so unhappy with the way things are? The only allies he could get would be from the mainland, Achaeans, warriors, people who worship Zeus, a thunder god. And Kaphtor's goddesses are peaceful, Potnia, Eileithyia, Kore . . . They haven't had a war in hundreds of years."

Professor Strickland had said the same thing. The Kaphtorans were safe behind miles of ocean; they had no walls around their palaces, no forts at any of the harbors. They had a strong fleet of ships, but their only security on the island was a few guardposts, the ones the Minos wanted them to disrupt.

"But we can't possibly know everything," Franny said. "I'm sure there are bigger issues here, more than they've told us."

"We can't know everything, you're right," Meret said. "But I've been with the company longer than you have, and I've seen some disturbing patterns. In nearly every case I know about the company's sided with warriors, with patriarchies, with hierarchical societies. Have you ever wondered why matriarchies have pretty much disappeared from the world? People say it's because they can't possibly work, but you know that isn't true—you've seen Kaphtor. A peaceful, prosperous, flourishing society that existed for thousands of years."

"Well, I'm sure they'll tell us everything when we get back."

"But that's strange, too, isn't it? That they don't even explain things until afterward?"

"Because we'd act differently if we knew," Ann said.

"Never mind that," Franny said. "You never answered my question. What the hell are you doing here?"

"I was wondering about Gregory's death. Why he died so suddenly. As if they wanted to get rid of him."

Franny looked stricken. "Why would they do that?"

"Because there are other people in the company, lots of us, who are starting to wonder about their policies. About the things they're changing, and why they're changing them."

"Was he—was Greg one of them?" Franny asked.

"I don't know. We don't know everyone who thinks this way. It makes it easier if we get caught—we can't give the others away."

"You make it sound like it's some big conspiracy," Ann said.

"It might be. To be honest, I don't know how many people there are."

"I don't get it," Ann said. "The company isn't this evil monolith. They're trying to save the world, to stop climate change and nuclear war."

"Look," Meret said. "Say you had a time machine. Say you started by helping people, preventing a war, like you said. And then, little by little, you saw ways you could help yourself, get some more power and resources for you and your friends. Wouldn't you do that if you could?"

"I don't know. I don't know who's in charge of all of this."

"Well, that's the thing. We don't know. They might be great humanitarians, it's true. But we've been watching them for a while, and we're starting to wonder."

"We can't stay here," Ann said, suddenly restless. "We have to find Professor Walker, and Franny still wants to say goodbye to Gregory." She drew Meret away from the grave, far enough so that Franny would have privacy.

"I hope—well, whatever you think, I hope you won't repeat this to Professor Walker," Meret said. "Or even tell her I was here."

"No, of course not," Ann said.

The words had come automatically, but to herself she thought that she would probably have to report this conversation to Walker. Meret seemed like a wingnut conspiracy theorist, but she might still be able to cause trouble for the company.

"Good. And remember what I told you." Meret smiled again, with that same look of amusement, almost complicity.

Franny turned away from the grave. "Okay?" Ann asked.

"Yeah."

They said goodbye to Meret. "Goddess show you your path," Meret said.

"Well, that was pretentious," Ann said to Franny as they left the cemetery. "Does she think she's one of the timebound or something?" She looked back to see Meret bent over the grave, returned to her digging. "So what do you think?"

"About what she said? It sounds crazy, doesn't it? There's this conspiracy, only she doesn't know who's in it, or how many people it has."

"Maybe it's just her."

Franny laughed. "Still, she's not the only one wondering about Greg's death," she said, looking thoughtful. "He seemed fine to me, completely healthy."

"But they wouldn't—they wouldn't kill him. Not like that. They'd court martial him, or put him in jail or something."

"Yeah. Yeah, I guess so."

"She told me not to tell Walker she was here, but I think I'm going to have to. If she hates the company so much she could do some real damage."

"It's weird that she trusted us so much, though. Why would she tell us all of that without making sure of us first?"

"Maybe it's some kind of test, to see if we'll report her to the company. And if it is, we'd sure as hell better say something to Walker."

There was a final reason Ann didn't believe Meret, but she said nothing to Franny about it, knowing that it wasn't logical. She had come to love the company, to feel a strong loyalty to it no matter what. How could she not, when it had rescued her from her boring wage-slave existence? And it had shown her marvels here in Knossos, with more marvels to come. She had all of time ahead of her.

They found Walker waiting impatiently at the shrine. "Where have you been?" she asked.

"We saw Meret," Ann said.

"What? Where?"

"At the cemetery." She told Walker about their visit to Gregory's grave, and Meret's questions about his death.

Walker drew in a breath. "So she's joined Core!" she said.

"What's Core?" Ann asked. "Is that the group she was talking about?"

"Lunatics is what they are. They believe in pretty much everything Meret told you, that the company leaders all have secret agendas, that they want to take over the world."

She seemed sincere, not at all like someone who had just set her a test. Ann continued to press her anyway. "So it's a real group? How many of them are there?"

"Oh, I don't know. No more than a dozen, no matter what she said. We try to find them and weed them out of the company, but they're clever, they keep slipping past us. And they recruit more people all the time."

"Do they do anything, though, or are they just talk? Could she—"

"Never mind about them," Walker said impatiently. "I have to tell you what we're doing next. Remember Yaniel Elias, the agent the company sent to Kaphtor in advance of us? He went to our inn, and the innkeeper told him we'd been arrested. So he asked around and got the names of people who act as jailers, and he found me at the house where I was staying. He told me a disturbing rumor—that the queen's displeased with some visitors from Egypt, so much so that she wants to, well, he thinks she wants to kill us."

"Kill us?" Franny said. "So what do we do?"

"Well, as I see it we have two choices. One is that we simply abort, go back to our own tace. But there's always some blame attached to agents who don't complete their assignment, even if what happened wasn't their fault."

"And the other choice?" Franny asked.

"We could stay hern, hide somewhere, and do what the Minos asked us to do. Drug the lookouts, so his allies can invade."

"Okay, then," Ann said. "I'm for staying hern."

"You misunderstood me," Walker said. "This isn't a democracy—I'm the Facilitator, I give the orders. I just wanted to explain my decision, so you won't have any questions." She looked meaningfully at Ann, making sure she understood. "And I say we stay hern, carry out our assignment. The company would expect it of us. And it looks bad if your first time out is a failure."

"So where are we going to hide?" Franny asked. "And how are we going to keep away from the queen's forces?"

"I don't think that'll be a problem. We'll just find some other inn, and we'll stay away from the palace."

"But we'll have to talk to the Minos again, won't we?" Ann asked. "Someone has to find out what his plans are, and tell him we'll do what he wants."

"That won't be a problem either," Walker said.

Really? she thought. She wondered how Walker was going to manage it.

"Looks like the sun's coming up," Walker said. "Let's go find a place to stay."

7

IT WAS DIFFICULT IN the dark to make out which of the buildings were inns and which were private houses or taverns or temples. They wandered around a while, Walker growing more and more impatient, until the sun rose fully and people started coming out onto the streets, and she was able to ask one of them for a recommendation. They found some new lodgings, went to their room, and fell asleep.

The sun was blazing through the high windows by the time Ann woke up. The others were still asleep and she stood quietly, trying not to disturb them. There was no partition in this room for a toilet, and when she went out into the corridor to look for one the innkeeper told her to use the hole in the field outside.

When she got back she noticed for the first time how shabby this inn was compared to their last one. The stone floor in their room had worn to dirt in some places and buckled unevenly in others, and their bedding was thin and tattered. The windows in the Inn of the Pear Garden had been covered by netting to keep the insects out, but in this place they were open to the air.

It was funny, she thought, what you ended up missing. She didn't care that she couldn't have a shower every day, that they had to go down to a creek to wash—or to a bath-house, though they hadn't had enough time to try one. But she craved coffee and chocolate, and several times a day she found herself reaching for her cellphone, to check the time or take a picture of something. On the other hand the air in Knossos, even when the days were muggy, even when she caught a whiff of offal in the streets, was astonishingly clear, untainted by chemicals; taking a breath was like drinking a glass of pure water.

The inn didn't serve breakfast, so after they had all gotten up they went outside and looked around. This neighborhood was not as good as the others they had seen, the houses lower and smaller, the people dressed in plainer clothing, without as many frills and colors. Even here, though, attempts had been made to brighten the houses, and many of the doors were painted in different colors: a pale sky blue, a dark pink like strawberries blurring into cream.

A few people gave them unfriendly stares, as if wonder-ing what they were doing there, or how much wealth they had on them, but most ignored them. Two women came down the street stumbling and laughing; prostitutes, Ann guessed, and drunk as well. Walker stopped them and asked about restaurants.

"Restaurants!" one of them said, laughing. She turned to her companion. "She wants to know about restaurants!"

"Well, where do you eat around here?" Walker said stolidly.

"At the palace, of course."

"The palace?" Walker asked. She regarded the woman with that imperious expression Ann had grown used to, clearly wondering if she was being made fun of.

"Sure. They give us grain every week, and wine, and whatever fruits are in season."

Ann remembered seeing pictures of the grain jars that had been found at the palace, a tall as a person. Historians hadn't been sure what their purpose was; one guess was that they had stored provisions in case of a siege. Now she realized that they had been used to give food and drink to the poor. Maybe, she thought, if the twenty-first century was as generous as the Bronze Age, they would have figured out what the jars were for.

The women tottered off, arms around each others' waists, leaning heavily against each other. They weren't prostitutes but lovers, Ann realized—historians weren't the only ones who saw what they expected to see. At least she had gotten the drunk part right.

"All right," Walker said in English, after the women had gone. "We have to see Yaniel anyway—he'll know where we can go eat."

"Why are we seeing him?" Franny asked.

"There you go asking questions again," Walker said. "You need to learn to trust me."

The more Ann saw of Walker's incompetence the less she felt like following her. But she said only, "Let's hope he can find us a better place to stay."

Walker said nothing, and they continued along the streets. Ann noticed that even here people had built shrines to the goddess, though they were much simpler and filled with smaller, less expensive things, shells and feathers and stones.

They came to a different neighborhood, a better one. A few moments later Walker knocked at a door, and Elias stepped out. "Emra, good to see you!" he said in English.

"Hello, Yaniel," Walker said. "Any idea where we can get some breakfast?"

"Of course." Elias led them down a few streets and into a building painted with swimming fish and squid and seaweed. An octopus flicked a tentacle over one of the windows.

They sat down and were given bread and lentils, and some beer that tasted like honey. "Glad to see you got away," Elias said.

"So are we, believe me," Walker said. "But we still need a place to stay, and we need your help with this assignment."

Elias frowned. "What kind of help?"

"We talked to the Minos and found out what he wants—we're supposed to disable the guards at the lookouts for him somehow. Unfortunately that's when we were arrested, while we were talking to him. So he doesn't know we've agreed to his plan, and we don't know any of the details, like when he wants us to put it into effect. But we can't contact him again—they know what we look like at the palace."

Elias continued to frown; Ann had the feeling that the company's assignments didn't usually go as wrong as this one. "Do you know where Meret went?" he asked. "She disappeared yesterday morning and hasn't come back."

"I have some news there as well," Walker said, and repeated what Ann had told her. She ended with, "We should go to the cemetery, see if she comes back."

"We can't spare anyone to wait for her," Elias said. "We'll put a camera there."

A camera? Right, one of those insect things. Ann hadn't realized they'd brought any with them, though.

"What'll you do if you find her?" she asked.

"We'll take her back with us to the company," Elias said. "They'll ask her questions, try to get more information about Core. And if we don't find her—well, if she doesn't join us at the pickup location she'll have to stay hern."

"People do that?" Ann asked. "Decide not to go back?" What would that be like, to live in Kaphtor? Her mind ran through a quick list of things she would have to give up: antibiotics, air conditioning, cars and planes and computers and books . . .

Still, there had been times when she had felt almost at home in this tace, more so than in the twenty-first century. A country where women ruled, where they chose their own lovers. Where the majority of people seemed happy and confident, and no one starved. Of course, as she'd said to Meret, there was the Minos; probably he wasn't very happy with the way things were arranged.

"It's happened once or twice," Walker said. "Not very often. Of course we know more or less whern they are, and we keep a close eye on that tace, just in case anything unusual happens."

"Can't the company—well, they know where she was, or they will know, when we tell them. Can't they send someone else back in time and find her at the cemetery?"

"If they'd done that, we'd have seen them already," Elias said. "They probably don't care, or they won't care, if she stays hern. They might have run all the calculations, realized that she can't possibly do any harm in such a distant tace."

"And extractions are expensive, if they're done without a key," Walker added.

"They could still pick her up, though, right?"

"I guess so, if they think it's important," Elias said.

Ann looked over at Franny, wondering what her reaction to all this would be; she had complained often enough that no one ever told them anything. She didn't seem to be paying much attention, though. "So Greg—" she said, slowly. "Greg wasn't killed?"

"Of course not," Walker said. "All this is someone's paranoid fantasy. I told you—his death was an accident. An unfortunate accident."

"Are you sure Meret didn't say anything more about Core?" Elias asked. "Didn't try to get you to join?"

Ann and Franny shook their heads.

"Did you tell her about our assignment hern? What the Minos wants us to do?"

"She knew about the Minos, that we're supposed to contact him," Ann said. "But she didn't know anything beyond that."

"All right, good," Elias said. "We need to think about how to get into the palace." He looked at Walker. "I can't go—your host has already seen me, and she might have given them a description. Probably not, but we can't take that chance. And of course we can't count on Meret. That just leaves Da Silva."

"Where is she?"

"At the inn. Still asleep, probably." He looked around the table. "And you three—you're going to have to keep off the streets, at least until our assignment. We'll see if you can get rooms where I'm staying."

"Look, none of this is my fault," Walker said. "Gregory died, and it all went downhill from there."

Sure it's your fault, Ann thought. You should have known the queen would take an interest in us after Gregory died, and been more careful. "How long are we going to have to stay there?" she asked.

"I don't know," Elias said.

They went back with Elias to his inn and rented a room. It was a lot like their room at the Inn of the Pear Garden, with benches, rattan beds, high windows, and stone floors. They all looked around them, realizing that this would be their home for a while.

Walker seemed to understand their boredom, though, and even sympathize with it, and she lent them her computer to play games on. Elias and Da Silva had gone to the cemetery and planted a camera, and in addition to playing games they were able to watch the feed from the camera on the computer. But whenever they checked they saw only the rocky plain of the cemetery, and within it the half-dug grave.

The computer would let them do only those two things, though; probably Walker had programmed it to block everything else. Ann waited until Walker wasn't watching and searched for other folders or drives, but it resisted everything she tried. It was too bad—she would have loved to program one of those cameras, watch it zoom across Knossos.

Elias brought them dinner and they went to bed soon afterward, still tired from their missed sleep the night before. It seemed to Ann she had just fallen asleep when she heard Walker's voice.

"There she is!" Walker said. "I knew she'd come back."

Ann opened her eyes and saw the glow of the computer across the room. She made her way over to it and peered sleepily at the screen, trying to focus. Meret was bent over the grave, shoveling dirt.

"Let's go," Walker said. She stood up; like the rest of them she had gone to sleep fully clothed.

Franny was up now, and coming over to the computer. There was something unsettling about spying on Meret like this, watching her while she worked, all unaware. It seemed a deep invasion of privacy, though Ann knew Meret had to be caught before she could do any more damage.

"Are we going to get Elias?" she asked.

"I suppose we should," Walker said.

They went to Elias's room and roused him and Da Silva. "We'll go," Elias said. "You should stay here—someone might see you."

"No one goes outside at night," Walker said. "We saw that yesterday, didn't we?"

Ann and Franny nodded. Still, Ann thought, Elias was right to be cautious. Was this another one of Walker's poor decisions? But she was feeling desperate to escape the closeness of their room.

"All right," Elias said. "But stay behind Da Silva and me."

They headed toward the cemetery. Elias and Da Silva were carrying lit torches, and Ann studied the other woman by their wavering light. She was plump, with a round face, dark hair, and kind-looking dark eyes. There were certain people, Ann knew, who fit some motherly archetype, and she had a tendency to look for comfort from them, sometimes with disastrous results. She would have to take care to put boundaries between her and the other woman.

Da Silva had also brought along something the size of an iPhone, and she glanced at it as they went, making sure that Meret was still at the graveside. Ann wondered how they powered the computers and cameras hern, but she knew if she asked they wouldn't answer her. It was yet another question to store away, to see if she could figure it out later.

Finally Elias raised his hand and went on ahead of them. "She's there," he said quietly as he came back.

"You two stay here," Da Silva whispered to Ann and Franny. Then Elias said, "Now."

Elias and Da Silva rushed forward. Ann followed them, and saw Meret running off in the opposite direction.

All of them hurried after her, going as fast as they dared, their torches flaring like flags. Meret's flashlight shone out ahead of them, its glare unnatural in the weaker light of the torches.

The road began to slope downward. Meret was still running quickly, as confident as if she knew the way. Ann found herself near the front, between Elias and Da Silva. Ahead of her Meret's light vanished behind trees or outcroppings of rock and then shone out again.

Then the flashlight disappeared for good, and they ran to where they had seen Meret last. The road forked into three smaller paths, each heading down the hill. Beyond that was darkness, too dark to see the way she had taken.

Elias cursed softly. He chose the largest path and hurried ahead with his torch. Da Silva stayed where she was. She shone her torch around her; the rough stone face of the hillside loomed up in the light. "She's gone, I guess," she said.

Something sounded from inside the hill. "What—" Da Silva said. She ran her hand over the wall.

The sound came again, stone falling on stone. Ann felt along the tall rocks next to her. The hillside ended abruptly, and air came from an opening within it.

"Here," she said, whispering. "There's an entrance over here."

"Stay there," Da Silva said—unnecessarily, since Ann had no intention of going inside without a light. Da Silva moved toward her and went through the entrance, and Ann and the others followed.

It led to a straight corridor within the hill. They walked along it as silently as they could, but still their footsteps seemed to echo all around them, a crowd marching in darkness.

The passageway ended suddenly. Two others led away from it, to the left and right. "It's the labyrinth," Ann whispered. Her voice echoed back to her, sounding full of portent.

"Yes," Da Silva said. She brought her torch close to the walls. They were nearly straight, an amazing feat of engineering. "There's a carving of a double ax on the left—look. Was that put there to show the way?"

No one said anything. "Let's go on a bit, see what we can find," she said. "Maybe Meret didn't go very far. Be as quiet as you can."

They turned left. It was chilly within the labyrinth, much colder than the night outside. At the next juncture Da Silva found another double ax to the right, then right, then left again, until Ann lost any sense of how many times they had turned, and where the entrance lay behind them. Her uneasiness grew.

They went right. A musty, animal smell wafted out toward them. Suddenly they heard an eerie sound echoing through the corridors, a deep groan, breaking occasionally into a high whine. It sounded mad, desperate, the cry of someone who had been imprisoned inside the labyrinth for centuries.

"What the hell is that?" Franny asked.

"I think—I think it's a bull," Da Silva said. "This must be where they keep them, until the games."

"So that's where the carvings lead," Franny said.

Ann looked at her in surprise. Franny hadn't said much since Gregory died, and when they'd met Meret she'd seemed to check out entirely. Maybe she'd finally accepted that Gregory's death was an accident, that they had to concentrate on their assignment. Ann hoped so, anyway.

"Well, she can't have gone down that way," Da Silva said. She sighed. "We should head back."

"I guess you're right—the company doesn't care about her," Ann said. "This would have been the perfect place for them to capture her, before she ran into the labyrinth."

They turned around and followed the carvings to the entrance. A short while later Elias returned, and they told him what they'd found.

"The labyrinth!" he said. "Man, I wish they'd let us do some research while we're hern."

"We're doing something much more important," Da Silva said. It sounded like an argument they'd had before.

"I didn't find her either, obviously," Elias said. "Let's get back—we can't do anything more tonight."

8

THE NEXT FEW DAYS were as dull as Ann had feared. She and Franny played hundreds of games on the computer, they checked the feed from the camera, they talked about movies they'd seen, or places they'd visited—but never anything important, nothing about Ann's foster homes or Franny's marriage. And they never saw anything more on the camera feed, just a rocky field and an empty hole.

Finally Da Silva and Elias came to visit them. "We made contact with the Minos this morning," Da Silva said. "We told him where we were staying and he came to see us, told us where the lookouts are and when we're supposed to take care of the guards. Here—" She took out a piece of papyrus with a crudely drawn map.

"Weren't the queen's spies following him?" Ann said.

"Of course they were. We snuck out the back door and took him to a tavern we knew, a place where we could sit in the back and not be disturbed."

Ann looked at Walker. This was how you did it, she wanted to say, how you kept the queen from following your every move. But she felt too hot, and too dispirited, for the argument that would certainly follow.

And of course Da Silva's instructions were much more important. The Minos wanted them to do their work during the bull games, when everyone but the guards would be at the palace. They would not overpower the guards, as the Minos had suggested, but use the drugs that Walker had brought with her. The five of them would split into two groups, one for each lookout; they would try to get to know the guards, drink with them, and then, when the bull games started, they would give them the drugged wine.

"Would drugging them really change things that much?" Ann asked. "I mean, the Minos told us he has allies, which I guess means foreigners, people off the island—but doesn't Kaphtor have a huge navy? How far would they get if they actually invaded?"

"We don't ask those questions until we get back," Walker said repressively.

Da Silva seemed to take pity on her, though. "Well, we do know that the navy was more or less destroyed thirty years ago, when the volcano on Thera erupted. They've started to rebuild, of course, but their whole infrastructure was wiped out, shipyards and lumber stores and so on, so it's going very slowly. That whole northern coastline suffered—even the chain of lookouts there are gone. So there's only this one slim tace to carry out our assignment and let the Achaeans in."

"Is that who's going to invade?" Ann asked.

Walker glared at Da Silva, but Da Silva laughed. "Well, who else could it be? Who else lives to the north, and is trying to expand their territory? Anyone could have guessed it."

"But why are we on the Achaeans' side in this?" Ann said. "How do we know their rule would be any better than the queen's?"

Franny caught the echo of Meret's earlier question and glanced at her quickly, a warning in her eyes. Ann ignored her.

"Those decisions aren't up to us," Walker said. "You know that."

"A lot of effort goes into these calculations," Da Silva said. "You can't imagine how complex they are. I've seen the computers on the fifth floor, the modeling they do for every situation, every possible outcome—and you will too, once the company decides it's time. All I know is that we can't possibly second-guess them—we don't know nearly enough. If they want us to help the Minos then we're helping the Minos."

"So when are the games?" Franny asked.

"Tomorrow."

"Tomorrow? Can we be ready by then?"

"Of course."

"What if the queen told the guards to look out for us?"

Da Silva shrugged. "We'll make you look different. I wouldn't worry about it, though. Even if they did have your description it wouldn't be terribly accurate—it's not like they have photographs. And the queen doesn't know what I look like, and probably not Yaniel either."

"And we can always stop them if our assignment goes wrong," Elias said.

"Stop them—how?" Franny asked.

"Stun guns."

Had Walker had stun guns all this time? Probably not, probably they were only issued to higher-level agents like Elias and Da Silva. And Walker would certainly have said something if she'd had one.

Elias was disappointed that he wouldn't get to see the bull games. "It's like going to Rome and not seeing the Colosseum," he said.

"Maybe you can watch it being built, your next assignment," Da Silva said, and Elias laughed.

THEY SPENT THE REST of the day disguising themselves. Da Silva took off Ann's wig and dyed her hair a pure black, and she added some padding under her robe. For Franny she had some reddish skin dye, making her look more like the men.

"They'll think you're both a bit ugly," she said. "Ann'll be too fat, and Franny too dark. But that's good—it'll keep them from looking at you too closely."

Da Silva gave Walker some padding as well, and a hood to cover her hair. Elias got a toupee, and Da Silva suggested that he shave his mustache. He grumbled, but he took her advice.

They woke early the next day and left the inn. They had come to Knossos from the south, in keeping with their story of having sailed from Egypt, but now they were leaving by the northern road. All of them looked carefully at the unfamiliar streets around them, seeming to realize that their time hern was coming to an end, that they would have this one last chance to try to remember everything.

They came to a fork and separated, Elias and Franny and Walker going to one lookout and Ann and Da Silva to the other. They would hear the roars from the crowd when the bull games started, Da Silva said.

All of Ann's boredom of the last few days had vanished. She was finally carrying out her assignment, doing what she had been sent hern to do. She would—well, if not save the world, at least help in some small way to fix things.

They came to the lookout. The hut was painted like the one she'd seen when she'd come to Knossos, with a mural of ships; probably they wanted to remind people of their great naval and trading fleets, even, or especially, after those fleets had been more or less destroyed by the volcano. And this place, like the earlier lookout, had a tall pile of wood across the roadway, a beacon.

The door was open; Da Silva knocked on the wall next to it. After a moment a woman and a man came outside.

"What do you want?" the woman asked.

"We don't require you to see us when you leave, if that's what you're thinking," the man said, and then laughed as if he'd said something funny.

"We're interested in your lookouts here," Da Silva said. "We'd like to do something similar where we come from. How do you know who to keep out and who to let in?"

"How do we know you're not spies, come to learn our secrets?" the woman countered.

Da Silva raised her hands. "You don't have to tell us anything if you don't want to. We're curious, that's all. And we have some wine, if you're interested." She bent and took out two pottery jars from a leather bag she'd brought with her.

The man laughed again. "Why not?" he asked. He looked at the woman, who made the shrugging gesture Ann had seen before.

They went inside. The hut seemed a cozy place, with benches against the walls and a table in the middle. The table held the remains of a meal, some chicken bones and crusts of bread. A cat lay curled up by a back door, studying the table lazily as if trying to work out the best way to get at the food. There was one window, looking out toward the road, and a stone shelf held an oil lamp and some pottery mugs.

The woman and man took down the mugs, set them on the table, and poured the wine. They sat at the table, and the woman spoke some words and let a few drops of wine fall to the floor.

"Where are you from?" the woman asked, taking a sip from her mug.

"Egypt," Da Silva said. "Beyond the Great Green."

"You don't look like folks from Egypt. We get a few of those from time to time, don't we?" She looked at the man.

"And they would have bowed to our cat," the man said. "All the Egyptians love our cat."

"We're from far to the south," Da Silva said. "I think we're the first people from our land ever to visit Kaphtor."

"Say something in Egyptian then," the woman said.

Da Silva was drinking from her wine glass; it was up to Ann to answer her. She opened her mouth, wondering what she would come up with.

"Here we are now, entertain us," she said in English, remembering the song she had listened to over and over again in high school.

The guards nodded, seeming satisfied. They were sharper than she had given them credit for, though. She and Da Silva would have to be careful.

"So," the woman said. "That's how we do it. We ask questions, and we see if everything matches up, if it makes sense."

"And if you're a foreigner we take your weapons," the man said.

"But anyone can buy weapons in Knossos," Ann said. "I saw dozens of shops selling axes."

The woman and man looked at each other, as if amazed that anyone could be so ignorant. "They'd never sell you one," the man said. "Only a woman may touch the double ax, and only a woman of Kaphtor."

"And the Minos," the woman said. She giggled, as if there was something inherently ridiculous about the Minos. "Karu here wanted to be a Minos once, didn't you?"

A distant cheer went up, somewhere beyond the walls of the hut. The bull games. Their mugs were empty, and Da Silva reached into her bag and took out another jar, then poured the woman and the man another round.

"Sure," Karu said, taking a sip of the wine. "All the sex and drugs and food and drink you could ever want. Anything you desire, you just have to say the word."

"Except freedom."

"Well, it seemed worth it at the time, when I was a boy. Fortunately she didn't choose me."

"Who didn't choose you?" Ann asked.

"The queen, who do you think? All the candidates line up, and the judges send home the ones who are too ugly or too old or too young, and then the queen chooses from whoever's left. She sleeps with him until she's tired of him, and after that he can have anyone he wants, if they're willing. And there's never any shortage of women wanting to sleep with the Minos."

"Your time would be nearly up now, if she'd chosen you."

He nodded. "'S why I'm glad she didn't. Seven years seems like a lifetime when you're young, but it comes soon enough."

Ann was starting to feel warm, though the stone hut had been cool when they'd first entered. Was it the wine? Had Da Silva made a mistake and drugged them instead? She glanced at the other woman and saw beads of sweat at her hairline, under her wig.

"How do you choose your Minos, in Egypt?" Karu asked.

"We don't have a queen where we're from," Ann said. "We have a—a king."

The language of Kaphtor didn't even have a word for king; she had to use the word for queen and make it masculine. It must have sounded funny, because the woman and man laughed loudly.

"A king!" Karu said, trying out the word. "Everyone knows men can't rule. They don't have the—the mind for it, the what-do-you-call-it? Focus, that's it. Give them a problem to solve and they're off hunting, or to the bull games. And it's the women who understand *gove*—how to bring a family into balance, or a country."

He was starting to slur his words now. But despite what he'd said Ann was beginning to lose her focus too, becoming unable to concentrate. "Why is it so hot in here?" she asked.

"Hot?" the woman said. "Are you hot, Karu?"

"No. Are you?"

"No, I'm not hot. Why do you think it's hot in here?"

"Because—look, you're both sweating," Ann said. "Of course it's hot."

"The beacon!" Da Silva said. She ran to the front door, but both the guards had gotten there before her.

Despite her confusion Ann understood what she meant immediately. She made a dash for the back, thinking, The back door, someone went out the back door and lit the beacon. The police are coming for us.

The door didn't budge. She hurried to the front. The woman swayed like a tree in the wind and fell to her knees.

"What—what have you done with us?" Karu asked. He took a step forward and stumbled, then righted himself.

Da Silva tried to get past him, but he was still strong enough to resist her. "We drugged you," she said. "Your friend fell asleep, and you will too."

He dropped back against the doorjamb, blocking the way out. His eyes closed.

"Help me get him away from here!" Da Silva said. They both pushed against him, but he seemed as immovable as a wall. Noises came from somewhere, the cheer of a crowd or the crackling of a bonfire. Finally, with a sound like a wall coming down, the guard fell to the ground outside the hut.

Ann and Da Silva hurried outside, then stopped. Several women and men stood before them on the path, all of them carrying spears and wearing three feathers in their hair. More were circling around the hut. They were surrounded.

THE GUARDS TOOK DA Silva's bag and tied their wrists together with rope, then marched them back to the city. At the fork they met Walker and Franny and Elias, also bound and closely guarded. The two groups shuffled together like a deck of cards.

"How on earth did they find us?" Walker asked in English. "How did they know?"

"Silence!" one of the guards said. "You've lost your right to speak, lost any rights you might have had."

"Where are we going?" Franny asked.

"Silence, I said. But you'll see soon enough."

They continued on into the city. The houses around them started to look familiar; they were headed toward the palace. They're taking us to the queen, Ann thought. And what we've done is treason. She saw a vivid picture then, her neck on a chopping block, the shadow of a double ax raised above her.

A loud shout came from somewhere ahead of them, and then a wild cheer that seemed to go on and on. They turned a corner and came to a gate, with rearing bulls atop the walls on either side. They had arrived at the palace, at the bull court.

The guards took them inside and pushed through the crowds of people at the back. They skirted another wall and came finally to a raised dais, with an embroidered canopy shielding it from the sun. Several women sat under the canopy, fanning themselves.

The guards forced them up a small staircase and onto the platform. "Here they are, Queen Ariadne," one of them said. All the guards put their fists to their forehead, saluting her.

A woman turned toward them. The queen, like Da Silva, seemed to embody an archetype, or several archetypes at once. She looked like a mother, though one who was not gentle but terrible, stern—yet at the same time she had the energy and grace of a young woman. And her eyes seemed different still, old and dark and filled with wisdom. She was white as milk, and as thin as any of the women on the frescos.

Someone shoved Ann into a chair near the queen and she landed heavily, unable to use her hands to brace herself. "Come and watch the games with me," Queen Ariadne said. Her voice was soft and pleasant. "And I'll consider what to do with you."

To Ann, already filled with terror, it sounded like a threat, as if the queen was about to throw them to the bulls. Walker must have thought the same thing, because she said, "Please, don't—"

"Hush," the queen said. "Watch."

Ann looked at the vast space in front of her. A bull came running into the arena. In front of it, almost unbelievably, stood a slight figure, and as the bull hurtled toward him he jumped, grasped the horns, somersaulted over, and landed on the bull's back. The crowd cheered and he turned to the queen, spread his arms, and grinned, accepting the people's love and excitement. Then he leapt off the bull and was caught on the shoulders of another acrobat.

The bull turned and lumbered off in another direction. A different acrobat, this one a woman, cartwheeled toward it until she stood in its path. She wore only a breechcloth, like the men, and she looked even smaller than the last dancer, a straight line against the solid mass of the bull. The bull saw her, charged—and she, too, jumped for the horns, somersaulted, came down on the bull's back, and dropped down onto another person's shoulders.

Ann had been holding her breath. She tried to applaud and was surprised to feel the bindings on her wrists holding her back. She had nearly forgotten them, forgotten the queen's threat poised above them like a sword.

Another woman stood facing the bull. It charged, she leapt—and missed catching one of the horns. She hung from the other horn for a moment, then dropped off and scurried across the court. The bull thundered after her. She reached a stone platform in the corner of the arena and climbed it quickly, then, as the bull came past her, dropped down on its back. She spread her arms, the way the others had done, but the cheers from the crowd were slight and scattered.

Go for that stone, if she throws you into the arena, Ann thought. Stay there, and maybe the bull will forget about you. But she knew she could never outrun the bull, and that it was tall enough to scrape her off the stone.

Her mouth was dry, and she tried to swallow. She wouldn't survive more than a few seconds against the bull. If the company wants to rescue us, now would be a good time, she thought, but she had the idea that the company had lost track of them.

The crowd gasped, and she realized something was happening on the court. A man lay on the ground, had somehow missed the bull's back when he'd somersaulted. The bull swung its massive head from side to side, then gored him through with its horns.

Ann looked away, and when she looked back a dancer was leading the bull toward a gate in the wall. When it had gone a woman climbed down from the queen's platform and walked slowly over to the man.

The crowd was silent. Two more women came out, one of them carrying a double ax, the other something that looked like a low table. The first woman lifted the man's head onto the table—a chopping block, Ann realized. The man was still alive.

She turned away again. There was a thud, and then the crowd cheered; a few of them were singing. She looked back for the smallest instant she could manage and saw the woman holding up the man's head.

Everyone was singing now. "What are they doing?" she asked. "Why on earth do they sound so happy?"

"Kore will feast him tonight," the queen said. "He was sacrificed in her name."

Incredibly, the games were continuing. The bull was led back out, and another woman faced it. Instead of a breechcloth she wore trousers made of bright colored patches, and she had a cap sewn with bells on her head.

The bull charged. She jumped, and like the earlier acrobat she missed one of the horns. She dangled from the other horn; the bull was close enough to the queen's platform that Ann could see her fear. But it was an exaggerated fear, a fear that made fun of itself, and the crowd was laughing.

The woman swung back and forth on the horn, her bells jingling. She looked puzzled now, as if trying to think of a way off. Then she grinned and twisted up and over, and suddenly she was sitting on the bull's head, her legs dangling over its eyes.

The bull roared and flung its head around in frustration. She scrambled up, slipped, recovered, slipped again, and dropped back down to the bull's horn. She swung back and forth between the horns, moving in a quick intricate pattern that Ann could barely follow. The bull roared again, and tossed its head, and she used the motion to somersault over the horns and land on its back. It trotted off and she sat down abruptly, then bounced along its back until she dropped to the ground.

The crowd cheered. The cheers went on for a long time, while the woman spread her arms and turned in a circle to take in the entire arena. The bull spotted her and charged, and she skipped away toward the gate in the wall.

Even after she was gone the cheering continued. Ann wondered at the Kaphtorans, who could go from contemplating the mysteries of the underworld to laughing at a comedian in a quick heartbeat. Were they children, unable to understand the concept of death? Or were they something else, something so sophisticated she would never figure them out?

The queen stood and spread her arms as if to embrace the crowd. As one, the people put their fists to their foreheads, saluting her. Then they stood and began to make their way down the stone steps.

"Get up," one of the guards said, prodding Da Silva with the blunt end of her spear.

The games were over. They wouldn't be sent into the arena after all. Ann's feeling of relief was so overwhelming that for a moment she couldn't move. Her legs seemed disconnected from her body, unfamiliar; she couldn't seem to remember how they worked.

"Take them to the River Room," Queen Ariadne said.

She left before they could ask what would happen to them next. The guards chivvied them up with the butts of the spears. Ann made an effort to stand. They were forced down the stairs, through an open door, and into the palace.

THEY WENT ON FOR a long way, through corridors and colonnades, past pillars and frescos and carvings. In one wing of the palace they saw a row of open doors and beyond them craftspeople at work, women and men spinning thread, beating metal, painting unfired pottery.

Finally they came to a wide staircase. They headed down and down, four or five floors, through a part of the palace that must have been carved into the hill. Then they were shown into a nearly empty room, with silk cushions scattered across the benches and over the floor. Frescos showed a flowing green river with fish and turtles, lilies and reeds.

The guards sliced through their bindings and left them. They heard the sound of a bar being dragged across the door and they ran to slam against it, but it held firm.

They dropped down to the cushions in the center of the room and started to take off their disguises: pulling out padding, taking off toupees, rearranging their clothing. "I want to know how they found us," Walker said. "No one knew where we'd be, except the Minos."

"Well, that's it then," Elias said. "He must have talked."

"Why would he do that?"

"He takes drugs, doesn't he? And he drinks a lot, too. He must have let something slip."

"You think so?" Da Silva asked. "This was his moment, his rebellion against the queen. Do you really think he'd jeopardize that, even drugged?"

"I don't think he's a very strong character, if that's what you mean."

"I'm with Amabel," Walker said. Amabel? Ann wondered. Right, Da Silva. "I don't think he would have said anything. So who did?" She looked at Ann and Franny. "Are you two sure you didn't say anything to Meret?"

Ann felt anger rise within her and take her over, so strongly that for a moment she couldn't speak. She'd told them about seeing Meret—she had squealed, as they said in the foster homes—and yet Walker still suspected her.

"Of course we're sure," Franny said. "And we couldn't have told her anything anyway—we didn't even know the Minos's plan when we met her. All we knew was that he wanted us to disable the lookouts, not when or how to do it."

"You could have seen her later, after we talked to the Minos again."

"When?" Ann asked scornfully. "We were cooped up in that room the whole time. Anyway, we wouldn't have mentioned seeing her if we were plotting in secret all this time."

"I'm sorry, but it's the only explanation. If the Minos didn't say anything—"

"Of *course* the Minos said something—" Franny said.

"Oh, who cares?" Ann said. "How are we going to get out of here, that's the important thing. You do realize that what we did was treason? That they're going to kill us? How many other agents were killed on their assignments?"

"I don't know if we *can* get out of here," Elias said. "You escaped from them once—they're going to watch us carefully from now on."

"And we don't have our bags, or we could have—" Walker said.

"God, that's right," Da Silva said, interrupting. "If they track us back to the inn they'll find our bags. The drugs and stun guns and computers—"

"Well, but everything is pretty well hidden," Elias said.

"But what if they find them?" Da Silva turned to Ann and Franny. "You know the company's policy on this, don't you?"

Ann remembered a lecture on it, but the other woman didn't wait for her answer. "Tell them nothing about anything," she said. "Not the drugs or the technology, not the company, not our meetings with the Minos and what we talked about."

"What if—what if they torture us?" Franny asked.

"Don't worry, they won't. This isn't the kind of culture that tortures."

Was that true? How could Da Silva know something like that? She didn't remember anything about torture in Strickland's lectures.

"Wait, what did you mean about the bags?" she asked. "What could you do if you had them?"

"Any number of things," Da Silva said. "Send a message to the company, use the drugs somehow—"

"You can—you can contact them? From here?"

"Well, of course. We can send them messages, if we need to be extracted without a key. We don't do it very often, and we can only send small bursts of text data—it uses a huge amount of energy. But this is an emergency."

Why didn't they mention that before? Why did the company have to be so secretive? Suddenly Ann couldn't bear to listen to them any longer; she felt trapped, suffocated. She stood and walked over to a partition and looked behind it. There was a toilet on the other side, and a large basin—it was the most luxurious prison she had ever heard of.

"Well, but they have to know where we are, don't they?" Franny said. "I mean, they'll come and get us sooner or later."

"I don't think—" Elias said slowly. He didn't want to tell them, Ann saw, and she felt ill with disappointment. "They know which inns we were staying at—that much was worked out ahead of time. But there's no way they'll guess that we're at the palace. I found you that first time because I knew that prisoners stayed in private houses—all I had to do was ask around and find the right one. But as far as I know, no one was ever jailed in the palace itself. They'll have no idea."

"Well, but they have all the time they need to work it out, right?" Ann asked. "They could figure it out in 2050 or something, and still come back for us."

"That's the problem," Elias said. "If they were going to extract us they would have done it already. They would have stopped us on the way to the lookouts, someplace where we were alone."

"So that's it. We're going to die here." No one said anything. "I wonder how long they'll go until they give up." She pulled her legs up and laid her head on her knees, feeling hopeless.

"They might send someone to look for us, I suppose," Elias said. He sounded dubious. "Time travel uses a tremendous amount of energy, though."

"So, what—they'd rather save a few bucks than rescue us?"

Elias looked at her with impatience, and she realized how stupid she'd been. It wasn't a question of money, she saw. The world the travelers came from had depleted most of their energy; they could not help but hate the way her tace had wasted all of its resources.

"They'll be doing everything they can," Da Silva said.

"But you don't think it'll be enough."

"There's no point in being pessimistic. We can't know what will happen."

A part of Ann wanted to believe her. She looked so much like a mother, the sort of kind, concerned parent who put you to bed when you were sick, and cheered when you got the lead in the school play, and commiserated when the boy you were interested in turned out not to be interested in you. But at the same time she knew that that wasn't true, that she had conjured up a mother out of a comforting smile and warm, compassionate eyes.

It was still afternoon, but she felt suddenly tired. She went to one of the benches and lay down, and in a short while she was asleep.

SHE WOKE TO A loud scraping noise, and then the door opened and what seemed like a crowd of people walked into the room. For a moment she could make no sense of any of it— the sounds, the people, even where she was. Then she realized that someone had drawn back the bar on the door, that they had visitors, and she got up quickly.

The queen stood in the center of the room. She wore a purple frilled skirt and a white open blouse, and her hair was twined with gold and beads and jewels. A circle of her women orbited around her, and surrounding them, like distant, outer planets, were servants with trays of food and guards holding spears.

"I thought we'd have breakfast together," Queen Ariadne said. If she noticed that they all looked slightly different, that they had removed their disguises, she gave no indication of it. "And I want to apologize for that trick I played on you yesterday, making you believe I'd send you into the bull games. I was angry with you, and it affected my judgment."

She motioned to the servants, and they set down plates of hot bread and dried fruit, and mugs filled with some kind of juice. She sat on one of the pillows, spread her frilled skirts around her legs, and gestured to the others to join her. The servants and guards moved back to the walls and waited.

"This was my daughter's room, when she was a child," she said, as Ann and the others gathered around her. "I want to show you the Goddess's hospitality, even though I don't truly understand what you hoped to accomplish here. We defeated your army, you know. The Achaeans had landed from the mainland, ready to invade the palace and take command while everyone was at the games. And what I want to know is why. Why would someone from Egypt send the Achaeans against us?"

No one said anything. The queen looked puzzled, as though one of her children had lied about something unimportant. Ann couldn't help feeling sorry for her: they had come into her country, taken advantage of her hospitality, plotted with her enemies, and she would never know the reason for it.

Ariadne took a sip of her drink. Ann brought her mug to her mouth. Her drink was dark red, like blood. She tasted it cautiously. Was it pomegranate? Would she be forced to stay here, like Persephone in the myth? She shuddered.

"We know much of it already, of course," Ariadne went on. "We know the Minos has been talking to the Achaeans, that he wants to rule here." She shook her head. "He's not a very strong person, you know—he didn't take much convincing to tell us everything. He would have made a terrible ruler. So help me understand, please. Why did you want to set him up here as queen?"

No one answered her. "He's a strange one," the queen said. "I've had two Minoses before him, and both of them lived their lives here without complaint. They know, when they begin their term, that they'll be sacrificed at the end of seven years, and they accept it. The fruits and flowers die each winter, and are reborn in spring. And the Minos is reborn too, though not in his own person. If he is not sacrificed to Our Lady of the Waning Moon at the proper time, what would happen to the fertility of the land? What would happen to us if the crops die within the earth?"

"Why do they have to die for that, though?" Ann asked. "Why is she so bloody, that waning moon lady?"

Elias and Da Silva and Walker all turned to stare at her, scowling in a clear warning not to talk. But she wasn't giving anything away, she just wanted to know.

The queen smiled. "As well ask why fire is hot, or why we take pleasure from eating and making love. People die, you know—you can't stop it. She is the mistress of birth and sex, but also of death." She paused. "Was that it? Do you think it's unfair that the Minos has to die?"

"No," Ann said. "I just wondered."

"Then what? Help me understand here. Was it money? A chance to trade with us, on better terms than I would have ever given you? Or did the Minos simply bribe you?"

Ann shook her head, wishing she hadn't said anything. The queen was still looking at her with that warm and understanding smile. She had thought Da Silva was motherly, but this woman seemed something beyond that, the pattern for all mothers everywhere. She remembered that Ariadne had said that this room was her daughter's, reminding them of a mother-daughter relationship from the very beginning. Be careful, she thought. She knows exactly what she's doing.

She drank the rest of her juice to avoid looking at her. None of the others touched anything; they thought it was poisoned, probably. She was willing to take that chance, though. One of the first rules of foster care was to eat while you can; you never knew when you might get another meal.

"Or did you truly think the Achaeans would make better rulers?" The queen looked at each of them in turn. "You're women here, most of you—you know how bad men are at making decisions, how they're ruled by their emotions. There's too much anger there, too much love of violence. I acted like a man when I got angry with you, and I'm sorry for it."

She finished her drink and stood up, and her women stood around her. "All right then. I'll be busy tomorrow, but some of these women will come and take a meal with you."

Ann had thought the women were ceremonial, ladies-in-waiting or something. Now she saw that they were part of a council, helping the queen make her decisions. They left the room, the queen first, and the bar slid into place behind them.

The servants had not taken the food, and the others seemed to realize that they wouldn't be poisoned while the queen still wanted information. "What are we going to do?" Franny asked, taking a slice of bread. "They'll keep asking us questions until we answer them. And after a while they'll stop being so polite."

"People die, you know—you can't stop it," the queen had said. And they knew more about death than Ann ever had, these people who had once seemed so untroubled and care-free. Was Ariadne saying that they wouldn't hesitate to kill if they needed to?

"What if we told them the truth?" she asked. "Would that really be so terrible?"

"Well, the problem with that is that they wouldn't believe you," Da Silva said. "I mean, think about it. What are you going to tell them? That you're from far in the future, come back to make things better . . ."

"I could tell them to look in our bags, at our technology. That would prove it."

"You'd change the past drastically if you do that," Elias said. "Imagine Kaphtor with an industrial revolution."

"They won't be able to figure out anything from our stuff. It's much too advanced."

"You can't know that."

"We can tell them we're gods," Franny said. "Show them the flashlights, the stun guns."

"They have their own gods," Da Silva said. "And we don't look anything like them."

No one said anything after that, each of them thinking their own thoughts, preparing themselves in their own way.

The time passed achingly slowly. There were no windows, no sight of the sun moving through the sky. Every so often someone would ask what time they thought it was, but no one ever answered, though once Walker snapped at the questioner and asked what difference it could possibly make.

Finally, around mid-afternoon, they heard the bar being lifted on the other side of the door. Franny grabbed Ann's hand. Ann didn't move away, though she couldn't remember the last time she had held onto someone for reassurance.

The door opened, and Meret came inside.

Everyone exclaimed at once. "Meret!" "What the hell—" "What are you doing here?"

"So you're working with the queen now?" Da Silva asked.

"I'm rescuing you, you idiots," Meret said. She was wearing a long Kaphtoran robe over her shift. "Get up, let's go."

They hurried outside, then rushed after her down the hallway.

"Just what are you doing?" Walker asked as they ran. "Whose side are you on?"

"Yours, right now," Meret said.

"Ann already told us you're part of Core. So why are you helping us?"

"Maybe I don't want to see you die here."

"How did you know where we were?" Ann asked.

"Stop asking questions—we have to hurry."

They ran through the maze of the palace, passing rooms and lightwells and staircases. They started through a long room lined with frescos of graceful dancing figures, and then Meret cursed and turned back. A ballroom?

Finally, after Ann was thoroughly lost, Meret stopped at a door and peered outside. "Come on," she said.

They went through and found themselves in the bull court. It was empty, but Ann remembered the crowds, the noise, and she felt anxious, as if the queen was about to enter and the games start up again at any moment.

"Hurry up!" Meret called to her.

They ran through the court and out onto the road. "All right," Ann said, slowing down. She was panting, unable to catch her breath. "How did you know where we were?"

"I made myself useful around the palace."

"So you *were* working for the queen!" Walker said. "Were you the one who told her we were at the lookouts?"

"Don't be stupid. If I was the one who betrayed you, why would I come and rescue you later? And keep running—we're not safe yet."

There was an answer to that question, Ann thought, but she was too exhausted to concentrate. They passed houses and taverns and shrines; then the path started heading down the hill, away from Knossos. "Where are you taking us?" she asked.

"To the key you buried, of course. You're going back."

"You aren't coming with us?"

"What do you think? They know I'm with Core—they'll question me every bit as hard as the queen would have questioned you."

"Oh, come on," Da Silva said. "You have a very strange idea of the company if you think that."

Meret said nothing. She ran out ahead of them and then jogged back. "There's someone coming, but she won't stop you. Stop running, pretend you have every right to be here."

They slowed to a walk. Ann took deep breaths, trying to calm the pounding of her heart. A shepherd passed them on the road, driving her sheep in front of her. "We could make you come back with us," Elias said.

Meret laughed. "Not really." She reached into her robe and drew out a small gun. "I took all your weapons."

The sight of the gun was enough to silence them. They continued down the hill, passing more people heading into the city. Finally they reached the small stream and the valley floor she remembered, and came in among the fields and vineyards.

"Where did you get the gun?" Da Silva asked. "Did you take our bags from the inn?"

"Yeah. I can use some of the things you brought with you."

"So you're really staying hern?"

"Of course. Where else would I go?"

"You could come home with us. We won't penalize you, I promise—we just want to know why you're doing this, what you hope to gain by it."

"I want to see the Kaphtorans survive for awhile longer, that's all. I'm sure the company will send in more agents in a generation or so, but I'm going to see that they're safe for now."

"Of course we will—we get what we want eventually. But it'll be harder the next time—the Kaphtorans will have had time to build up their navy again, and strengthen the lookouts along the coast. And who knows what else you've done hern, blundering around like this? You've interfered with years of careful calculations, snarled up the timelines. For all we know you've made things worse."

"I doubt that."

"I could show you what you did, on the computers."

"I told you, I'm not going back."

The trees ahead were starting to look familiar, and a short while later Ann saw the place they had landed. It was an olive grove, she realized, noticing for the first time the twisted brown trunks, the dusty green leaves. She'd been too anxious to look at it closely, the first time she'd been here.

"Where did you bury the key?" Meret asked.

Walker made her way through the trees. "Here," she said.

She stooped and dug up a round piece of metal about an inch across. It looked a little like a gyroscope, Ann thought—there were oddly-shaped pieces cut out of the outer layer, revealing another layer with more holes beneath it, and yet another layer underneath that.

"Okay, good," Meret said. "All of you, go stand over there with her."

Walker manipulated the key, twisting it like a Rubik's cube. "Hurry up," Meret said, waving the gun at them.

It was at that moment, as she went to join Walker, that Ann understood Meret's riddle. "You betrayed us because you were trying to keep the Kaphtorans safe, like you said," she said. "And then you rescued us because you didn't want to see us die."

"But how could I have possibly known that you'd be at the lookouts?" Meret asked. She was smiling again, almost laughing, as if Ann had told her a good joke. "You know none of you told me that."

The air wavered around her. Everything began to blur together, the brown of the trees, the green of the leaves. The sun skipped in the sky like a stone over water.

Meret's voice came from far away. "Don't worry—you'll figure it out," she said. Or did she? A dreadful ringing sounded in Ann's ears, drowning out everything else. Her stomach clenched and she nearly vomited.

Then lights blazed out in front of her, so bright she felt as if she was being stabbed to the brain. She fell down onto a flat surface, the platform that had launched them back in time. Somewhere there were people applauding, whistling, someone calling "Welcome back!" in English.

The nausea was gone, and she looked around. The launch room seemed exactly as they'd left it, as though no time at all had passed. She pressed her hands to the platform and stood up. How long had it been since she had felt anything truly smooth, anything not handmade?

A man walked up to them, smiling broadly, holding out his hand. He was pale, very pale; she wasn't used to men who weren't some shade of red or brown. "Good to see you," he said, shaking hands with Elias and then Da Silva. "But we didn't feel any timequakes here—what happened to your assignment? And where's Haas? And Gregory Nichols?"

"We couldn't do it," Elias said. "I'm sorry."

The man frowned, then smiled again. "Well, don't worry," he said. "Everything will turn out all right, I'm sure. Right now you're going to the infirmary, and then we'll start our debriefings. Anyone need medical attention? What about some food or drink before we start?"

"Water," Franny said.

Pomegranate juice, Ann wanted to say. "I'd like some water too," she said.

08092014
109575

Assignment 17 to Kaphtor, Supplement:
Some Notes about Core, Along with Recommendations
Emra Walker

In addition to the problems we encountered during our assignment (see "Assignment 17 to Kaphtor," attached, for my full report), there were several disturbing incidents that might shed some light on the problematic group known as Core. To begin with, Francine Craig and Ann Decker were supposed to meet me at a prearranged location after drugging their jailers, but I later learned that they did not do this. Instead, Decker brought Craig to the cemetery at Craig's request, to show her where Gregory Nichols was buried. While at the cemetery they met Meret Haas, who was in the process of digging up Nichols's grave.

Craig and Decker's account of what happened there made it clear that Haas had joined Core. Decker also mentioned that Haas had wanted to inspect Nichols's body because of her suspicions that the company had somehow killed him. When Decker asked her why the company would do such a thing, Haas admitted that Nichols might have been another member of Core. Craig and Decker denied that Haas had used the word "Core," though, or given any description of that group's workings.

We tried to bring Haas back with us, but, as I stated in my report, we were unsuccessful. It is possible that she was not working alone, that she had help from other members of Core. Certainly her actions seemed too coordinated to be the work of one person.

My recommendations are as follows:
First, we must review all of Haas's previous assignments for possible sabotage. (See Table 13, attached, for a list of those assignments.)

Second, if we discover previous evidence of sabotage, we may have to send more agents to the past to erase these efforts.

Third, we must continue to monitor this tace, to see if Haas manages to effect any important changes thern.

Fourth, we need to review the files of all of the agents who took part in Assignment 17. Craig and Decker's exposure to Haas is troubling, especially in connection with the indications of antisocial behavior I saw earlier. (See the report, "Strengths and Weaknesses of Cohort 14, Along with Some Recommendations," attached.)

Decker is scheduled to go on Assignment 21, to Alexandria. (See Table 14, attached, for a full list of agents on that assignment.) As you can see, Haas was sent on another assignment thern earlier, and will be in Alexandria at the same time. My fifth recommendation would be to give Decker an additional assignment, that of getting close to Haas and finding out more about her plans, and those of Core.

ANN AND THE OTHERS were checked out by medical personnel, pronounced healthy, and given separate living quarters within the company. They stayed there for several days, recuperating and being taken to various rooms for interviews.

Ann told her own story three times, to three different people. Each of them stopped her when she came to her meeting with Meret at the cemetery, and each asked her the same questions. What did Meret tell you about Core? Did she invite you to join?

She had trouble breathing; the air seemed filthy after the clean skies of Kaphtor. And she slept badly, and her dreams were filled with snakes and drums and axes, each shape shifting into another like the waxing and waning moon.

Finally one morning she was shown into a fourth room, where to her surprise she saw Da Silva waiting for her. Da Silva went to sit in a fat upholstered chair, and indicated to Ann to take the chair opposite.

"Well," Da Silva said. "You're probably exhausted by all those questions."

"I guess," Ann said.

"I know I am. I hate it, but it has to be done. The company has to know everything that happens, on every assignment.

And especially this one, because, well, because we failed."
She scrunched up her face in mock distress, and Ann smiled.

"Does that mean they won't send us on any more assignments?" she asked.

"Not at all. None of the things that went wrong were your fault, not by any stretch of the imagination. The first problem was Gregory's death, and things just got worse from there."

Ann hadn't told the interviewers one of the things that bothered her, which was that Walker had been so incompetent. From the very beginning, when she was thrown by Itaja's statement that they had to bury Gregory, to when the queen's police had followed the Minos to their inn, Walker seemed at the center of a lot of the things that had gone wrong.

Should she say something now? But they probably didn't like people complaining about their superiors—and she wanted to stay with the company for as long as she could.

They talked a little about the assignment, Ann repeating the things she had said to the others. But she found herself opening up, going into more detail about some of the things that had happened. Da Silva looked at her sympathetically, nodding and smiling as Ann talked.

"What did you think about the things Meret told you?" Da Silva asked.

"We thought she was some kind of whack-job, to be honest. Franny and me. We didn't really know what to make of her. When Walker said that there really was some kind of shadowy organization—well, I have to say I was surprised."

"And Meret didn't mention Core?"

"No, nothing. Like I said, I'd never heard of Core by the time I talked to Walker."

She'd been asked this question so many times that her mind began to wander. Why did they call it Core? What was it supposed to be the core of, anyway? Core, corps, Kore . . . Of course Kore was pronounced with two syllables—Kor-eh— but still . . .

Meret *had* mentioned Kore, hadn't she? "Kaphtor's goddesses are peaceful, Potnia, Eileithyia, Kore, all of them." What if it was some kind of a password, what if Meret had been trying to see if she or Franny belonged to Core as well, if they were allies?

And hadn't Gregory brought up Kore too? "I always liked the Greek gods and goddesses, Kore and Demeter . . ." he'd said once during lunch. She remembered that because at the time she hadn't heard of Kore, and she'd wondered if it was a god or goddess, and how Gregory had heard of him or her.

So did that mean . . . No. No, it couldn't be. Her mind hurried from one idea to the next. Gregory was a member of Core. Gregory had died while traveling through time. Meret thought the company might have killed him.

"Ann?" Da Silva asked. "You look like you've remembered something."

She forced herself to pay attention. "No. No, sorry. Just thinking about Meret, and if she said anything else. But I'm pretty sure I told you everything."

She couldn't stop herself from following the thought to its conclusion, though she tried to listen to Da Silva at the same time. What if Meret was right, what if the company had somehow arranged Gregory's death? Did that mean she was right about everything? Was the company lying to them, did they have some agenda that only benefited an elite few? All she knew about the company was what they had told her, after all. Maybe there had never been any climate change or nuclear war, maybe they had lied about that too.

No, it was ridiculous. Secret conspiracies, evil overlords, death sentences . . .

"Can I ask you something?" she said.

"Of course," Da Silva said.

"Why was the company on the side of the Achaeans? I mean, the people in Kaphtor had pretty good lives—they hadn't been at war for hundreds of years, and no one ever starved, and their art was as good as anything I've ever seen. Why did the company support the invasion?"

"Weren't you debriefed on this?"

"Yeah, but I still don't get it. It seems like we need more of the Kaphtoran way of thinking, not less. Like the Achaeans were a step backward."

"Well, the Achaeans were the forerunners of the ancient Greeks. And the Greeks gave us so much, philosophy and art and drama and mathematics . . ."

Ann nodded. That was what the first interviewer had told her too. But it seemed a shame—no, a tragedy—that the Kaphtorans had disappeared from the world. She thought of their easy grace, their strength, the way everyone had seemed to fit in, to belong. She wondered how they took care of their orphans.

"Anyway, we can't know exactly why the company does certain things," Da Silva said. She looked tired, as tired as Ann felt. And she seemed to have had difficulty returning hern as well; the skin on her arms was red with some sort of inflammation. "It's the result of hours of computer modeling—I don't know if they understand it themselves, up on the fifth floor."

Maybe they should, Ann thought. Maybe they should have to visit the worlds they were condemning to extinction.

She wanted to tell Da Silva her conclusions about Meret and the password, wanted the other woman to admire her intelligence. But Da Silva belonged to the company, after all, and the company might have sent Gregory to his death.

ANN RAN INTO FRANNY the next day, on her way to the cafeteria. "Listen," she said, when they had gotten their food and were sitting out on the lawn. "I figured something out, or I think I did. Remember when we saw Meret that first time, and she said something about Kore? About the goddesses in Kaphtor being peaceful, like Potnia and Kore?"

"Sort of," Franny said. Her voice sounded scratchy and she cleared her throat, as if trying to get the twenty-first century out of her lungs. "Wow, this pizza is good. I can't believe how much I missed tomatoes."

"So I was wondering, well, what if it was some kind of password? Kore, I mean. Like Core."

"Sorry. If what was a password?"

"The word Kore. If Meret used it to tell us that she was in Core, and to ask if we were too."

"That's a pretty big stretch, isn't it?"

"Okay, but look. Gregory said something about Kore once, at one of our lunches. So what if he was in Core too?"

"You're starting to sound like her. Like Meret."

"Well, suppose Meret was right? Suppose the company did kill him?"

Franny shook her head. She had gotten her broad smile back; she seemed to have put Gregory's death behind her somehow. Was that how she was able to live with her husband, by ignoring anything painful or upsetting?

"I don't want to talk about Greg anymore. Anyway it was an accident, everyone said so."

"Yeah, but they wouldn't tell us if it wasn't, right? They wouldn't say, Hey, we killed Gregory, and we can do the same to you, anytime we want?"

"Why would they want to kill us?"

"I don't know. If we joined Core, maybe."

"Look—the company was the best thing that ever happened to me. And you said the same thing, that you were unhappy, that you'd jumped at the chance to leave your old life. They aren't killers—I mean, the idea's ridiculous."

"Okay. Okay, I guess it is stupid. Don't tell anyone what I said, all right?"

"Sure," Franny said.

"So what about your husband? Are you going back to him?"

"Yeah. We've been talking on the phone, and it sounds like he really missed me." She laughed, then cleared her throat again. "Da Silva and I worked out a cover story, something to tell him while I'm recuperating. If only he knew!"

She had hoped that Franny would be her ally, that she could share her suspicions with the other woman. But it looked as though she had no allies, that she would be alone with her questions.

AFTER THE DEBRIEFING THE company gave them all a week's vacation. Ann spent the time reading and listening to music and playing computer games. She thought a lot about Kaphtor and the people she had met there; once, when she went out to get groceries, she saw a U-shaped antenna on the roof of a building and her first excited thought was, Horns of Consecration!

She thought about emailing Franny and getting together over the vacation, but she didn't want to get in the middle of a reunion between Franny and her husband. And she thought a lot about TI as well. Were they satisfied with what she had told them, or had Da Silva guessed that she had held some things back?

She realized for the first time that Meret, too, must be from the future, like Walker and Elias and Da Silva. Perhaps she knew things Ann didn't know, terrible things about the company, perhaps that was why she had joined Core. Why hadn't she thought to ask her?

When she got back on campus she learned that she and Zachery had been assigned to Professor Strickland's classroom. "We're sending you to Alexandria," Strickland said to them. "It's a sort of tricky assignment, because we're going to ask you to do two things. There's your regular assignment, of course, but we also want you to meet up with Meret—"

"Meret?" Ann said. "But she's in Kaphtor!"

"Well, yes," Strickland said. "But before that she was on assignment in Alexandria. We're going to send you to meet her thern. We want you to get close to her, talk to her, find out what she knows about Core. But remember, she won't have met you by this time—she won't know who you are."

For a moment Ann couldn't grasp this idea, couldn't make it lie flat in her mind. Then, when she understood it, it seemed to open doors within her, expand her ideas of what was possible. No one was ever gone, ever truly dead—everyone could be found somewhere along the timelines. She wondered if Franny had realized this, if she had ever thought about going back and seeing Gregory. And how many others wanted just one last moment with their husbands, wives, lovers, children . . .

"You, Ann, you're going to want to talk about your time together, in the cemetery and when she rescued you," Strickland was saying. "You'll have to be very careful not to do it, to say absolutely nothing about her future. The fifth floor's worked out the permutations of what she did in Kaphtor, and it looks like she didn't harm our overall strategy. But if she knows what will happen she could change her actions, do some real damage."

"What's Core?" Zach asked.

Strickland explained, repeating more or less what Walker said in Kaphtor. "Do you understand what I'm saying?" she asked Ann. "About approaching Meret?"

"Sure," Ann said.

"And do you think you can do it? We're asking you, in essence, to become a double agent, to pretend that you want to join Core."

Ann nodded. She *did* want to learn more about Core; the assignment wouldn't be terribly difficult.

"Okay, good. I don't like dealing with time etiquette—my subject is history, after all. And your Facilitators will tell you more about this, explain what you'll need to do."

"Who are our Facilitators?" Ann asked, hoping they wouldn't be saddled with Walker again.

"Don't worry—you've met them before. Yaniel Elias and Amabel Da Silva."

That was nearly as bad. She remembered how she had wanted to tell Da Silva everything, all her thoughts about the company and Core and Gregory's death. She would almost rather have had Walker; at least then she wouldn't have to watch everything she said.

"All right, then," Strickland said. "Alexandria. What do you know about it?"

"Well, they had a library," Zach said.

"A library, right," Strickland said. "The biggest library in the world, with something like six hundred thousand scrolls. More than a hundred plays by Sophocles, more than seventy by Aeschylus, if you can imagine it. All of them lost in a fire in 391 CE—only seven plays by Sophocles, and seven by Aeschylus, have come down to us."

"And we're going there to—prevent the fire?" Ann asked.

"We can't do that, unfortunately. The change would be so great it would cause a huge timeshift, a timequake people would feel around the world. No, you're going to do what we always do, which is to change something small, something subtle."

"And you can't tell us what that is," Ann said.

Strickland smiled. "Don't worry—your Facilitators will tell you, when it's time." She turned to her computer and displayed a map against the wall. "Alexandria is in Egypt, here, on the Mediterranean. It was founded, as you probably guessed, by Alexander the Great, and even in the fourth century, which is when you'll be there, the culture was mostly Greek. But by then it had been conquered by the Romans, and then Emperor Constantine moved the capital from Rome to Constantinople and converted to Christianity. So there's an amazing diversity of people there—Greeks, Romans, Christians, the native Egyptians, who are mostly pagans, and a large community of Jews—and people speak a lot of different languages, Greek, Latin, Egyptian, Hebrew. You'll be learning the Greek they used at the time, the language most of the people in power understood."

"The fourth century," Zach said. "So we'll be there when the library was destroyed?"

Strickland smiled again. "Yes, you will. But we're getting ahead of ourselves—let's go over the history first."

She turned off the lights, and they watched holographic videos taken over fifteen hundred years ago. The videos moved along the outside of the library, showing covered walkways, gardens with statues and fountains and shaded benches, scholars deep in conversation, clerks bustling back and forth with buckets stuffed with scrolls. Two statues stood in niches at the door of the library, a man with the head of a bird and a woman holding a staff—the Egyptian gods Thoth and Seshat, Strickland said.

"The destruction of the library is another one of those taces where the historians in your era don't really know what happened," she said when the video ended. "We know from the cameras we've sent that it burned down in 391, but all they know is that it disappeared sometime over the centuries. So one history, written back in Roman times, says that Julius Caesar burned all the books by accident, when he helped Cleopatra with her war against her brother, Ptolemy XIII. The problem with that is that other people still talk about the library after 48 BCE, which is when that war happened. And there were other wars, other taces it was supposed to be destroyed. One history says the Muslims burned the books when they conquered the city in 641. That was Christian propaganda, though—the Muslims had the greatest libraries in the world during that time and would have been more likely to have saved the books, if they still existed. So with all this uncertainty, we have room to make some adjustments in the timeline."

On weekends Ann surfed the web, looking for more information. She had the idea that upper management at TI would disapprove, that she wasn't supposed to stray from their curriculum, but she had disliked being on the side of the Achaeans and she wanted to be prepared for whatever might happen this time.

One of her links brought her to the biography of a woman named Hypatia. Hypatia had lived in Alexandria in the time they were going to visit, and had taught mathematics, philosophy, and astronomy. "In 415," said the website, "she was accused of witchcraft and killed by a mob."

The bare sentence hit Ann almost like a blow. She had been identifying with Hypatia, she realized, another intelligent woman working in a difficult time. Were they going back to rescue her? No, she would die twenty-four years after the destruction of the library, far too late for them. But at least they might get to meet her.

The next day in class she asked if Strickland had any videos of Hypatia. Strickland frowned for a brief moment, so quickly that Ann was not completely sure she had seen it. "You've been doing research, then," she said.

"Yeah," Ann said.

"Well, we would have gotten to her eventually. And as it happens we do have a video."

She called it up on the computer. They saw a group of people talking, gesturing, laughing, mostly men but some women, with a woman at the center. The websites had all agreed that Hypatia had been astonishingly beautiful, but no one would have ever said that about this woman: she was plump, shorter than anyone else in the crowd, her nose squashed in the middle, her eyebrows too heavy. She wore what Ann knew was called a tribon, a rough woolen cloak usually worn by the poor; some philosophers dressed in them too, to show their lack of interest in material things. Her unruly black hair had sprung free of most of the ribbons she had tied it with, and as they watched another ribbon came loose and fell to the ground.

Her face showed a fascination with the debate, a vitality that few of the others had. Her eyebrows arched high on her forehead at something someone had said and then stayed there for the rest of the conversation, making her look perpetually amazed.

When the video ended Strickland summarized the woman's life for Zach and then said to Ann, "You admire her, don't you?"

Ann nodded.

"Well, it happens. We all have our favorites, people whose lives we wish had turned out differently. It's hard, because you can't tell them anything they don't already know, including—especially—how they die. You can't help them in any way, no matter how much you want to."

Ann nodded again, surprised. Strickland had never volunteered anything so personal during class. She wondered which historical figure the professor had wanted to save.

A few days later Strickland gave them their cover stories. "This time you're going to be from Crete," she said, smiling at Ann. "We thought we might as well use your experience from your last trip. Of course in this era Crete has been conquered by the Greeks and then the Romans, so it's pretty different from what you remember. But the climate's still the same, and so is most of the food. And the best thing is you probably won't meet anyone who comes from there—it's a backwater now, far away from the centers of power. You're going to be scholars who are visiting the library to study. That'll give you a reason to be there, but it won't matter so much if you're not that sophisticated, if you don't know a lot about the customs of that tace."

Zach hadn't been sent on assignment yet, and when Strickland brought them to the fitting room he looked at the rows and racks of costumes in astonishment. The professor gave Ann a tunic and then what looked like a long blue shirt, so long, in fact, that when she held it up to her neck it dragged along the floor. "The tunic goes on underneath," Strickland said. "And the extra fabric of the chiton is bundled up over the belt."

Zach got a tunic, a shorter chiton, and a belt. "Shouldn't I be wearing a toga?" he asked. "Alexandria was part of the Roman Empire, you said."

"You'd get more attention than you want, in a toga," Strickland said. "Only Roman citizens wore them."

They picked out leather sandals and then went to their changing rooms. It took Ann a while to arrange her clothes the way Strickland had shown her, but finally, when everything was more or less in place, she looked up into the mirror. There was an embroidered band along the neckline and hem of the chiton, a beautiful pattern in red and gold.

She grinned at her reflection. A scholar from Crete, she thought.

Zach spent their free time asking her questions about her trip to Kaphtor. She told him about Gregory's death, the Minos and the queen, the bull games, their capture and rescue. She tamped down her cynicism, keeping to herself all the questions Meret had raised. Zach deserved to see things for himself, to make up his own mind. And she was still unsure what she believed; she found herself moving from one position to the other within the space of a minute, swinging like a broken needle on a dial from one end to the other.

AND THEN IT WAS time. They got their cheek swabs, and went to the fitting room and put on their clothing. A hairdresser arranged Ann's hair so that it curled above her forehead and fell straight in back. Another woman hung her with more jewelry than she had ever seen in her life, so much that she felt like a Christmas tree draped with ornaments: a gold necklace with garnets, matching gold earrings, some rings, and a snake bracelet that wound halfway up her arm.

She and Zach and Da Silva and Elias assembled in the launch room, received their bags, stood on the platform, heard the countdown. Colors blurred and then sharpened, and she felt a hard wrench in her stomach that made her double over and almost vomit.

The feeling passed, and she straightened up and looked around her. The others were getting up too, and her first reaction was an intense relief that everyone had come through safely.

They had landed, once again, in place without streets or people. Hard sand stretched all around them, with a few buildings and palm trees in the middle distance.

Elias dug a shallow hole in the ground and buried the key. "This way," he said.

He set off across the sand and they followed. It should have been hot, as hot as Kaphtor, but Alexandria stood between the Mediterranean and Lake Mareotis, and the breezes that blew between the two of them kept it cool.

Their walking brought them to a temple of white marble with statues standing on either side of the door, an older goddess and a younger one holding sheaves of wheat in their hands. Demeter and Kore, Ann thought. No, they'd call them Ceres and Proserpina hern, the Roman names for them. It lifted her spirits to see them in this new tace, like running into friends in a strange city.

Past the temple was a huge oval structure that she recognized as the hippodrome, and beyond that a city wall and the Canopian Gate. Two guards stood on either side of the gate.

"Open your bags, please," one of them said. "Did you bring any books?"

They confiscated books from travelers and then copied them, she knew, and returned the copies instead of the originals. Because of that the agents had not packed any books, not wanting to draw attention to them.

The guards looked inside their bags and motioned them through. A street stretched out before them, straight and smooth as a table, lined with columns made of red granite. They passed churches and temples, gardens and obelisks and statues, everything a strange combination of the light classicism of Greece and the ponderous weight of Egypt, so that they saw temples with painted columns in front and carvings of Osiris and Isis on the massive red-brick walls. Other streets crossed theirs at right angles, and she thought that no matter how much she had loved Knossos she was glad to have come to a tace you could map out on a grid. All of it spread out, open, displayed before them like goods for sale.

People passed them too, Roman soldiers on horses and camels, monks in black robes, citizens walking or carried on sedan-chairs, wearing cloaks and chitons and togas. Fortune-tellers sat next to cages filled with birds, offering to cut the birds open and read the entrails. Philosophers stood on the corners, calling out their wares like fruit-sellers: "You there—do you know what the perfect number is?" "What's the size of the world—have any idea?"

Zach was looking around him, trying not to stare, not to be too obvious. "I know," Ann said in English. "Isn't it great?"

A man in front of them stopped abruptly and bowed solemnly to a cat on a doorstep. Zach nodded, seeming too amazed to say anything.

The company liked to get their agents to a tace in late afternoon, giving them time to look around, eat a meal, and have a good night's sleep before they started on their assignment. They stopped at a restaurant and Ann had a surprisingly good dinner of fish and beer, with figs and melons and raisins on the side.

Elias led them to their inn. Ann was certain she wouldn't be able to sleep that night, but when she woke up it was morning, the sun shining through their window.

"All right," Da Silva said at breakfast. They were back at the same restaurant, eating rolls stuffed with fruit and drinking more beer. She was speaking English, though there was no one around to overhear them. "We're going to give you your assignments. Very simple this time. All you have to do is move some oil lamps in the library from one place to another. We're going to head over there today, show you where the lamps are and where we want them, and then we'll go back tomorrow, early in the morning. The disturbances will start tomorrow and spread to the library about an hour later, so we'll want to be well away by then."

"What disturbances?" Zach asked.

"I was getting to that. The Christian patriarch here, Theophilus, is taking over all the pagan temples, turning them into churches. Tomorrow he's closing the Serapeum, the most important temple in Alexandria, and a group of pagans has vowed to keep it open. They're going to barricade themselves inside it and fight the patriarch's forces. And then the fighting spreads to the library, and the patriarch's mob burns it down."

"The library's destroyed tomorrow?" Ann asked. "Isn't that cutting it a little close?"

"We try to spend as little time in a tace as possible, to minimize errors. You had more time in Crete because we didn't know how long it would take to gain the Minos's confidence. This tace, as I said, they've given you an easier assignment."

"When am I going to talk to Meret?" Ann asked.

"I don't know. I don't know if there'll be time. We'll have to play everything by ear."

They went out into the streets again. Alexandria was tiny, Ann remembered, only about two miles from east to west and one mile north to south, though it was one of the most important cities in the world.

They turned at the intersection of two main streets, marked by high red columns at the corners, then Elias took them through an outdoor market. She looked for evidence that something was about to happen, for displays of tension or temper, but everyone seemed to be going about their business. People all around them were stopping at booths and chatting to the proprietors, buying olives, lapis lazuli, cinnamon, ivory statues and golden charms in the shapes of gods and goddesses. And of course books—one section of the market was devoted entirely to venders selling scrolls.

How would she know what a normal day in the city looked like, though? Those people over there, whispering to each other, were they pagans discussing their tactics for tomorrow? Would that monk in the black robe take part in the fighting?

They came out on the other side of the market, into a garden the size of a city block. A group of people walked past them along the flowerbeds, talking loudly.

There was something eerily familiar about the scene, like the worst case of déjà vu she had ever had. The people were all leaning in toward the center, listening intently. Then the crowd parted briefly, and she saw a small woman with raised eyebrows.

Hypatia, Ann thought. Not only that, but this was the exact moment she had seen on the video in class. A ribbon came loose from Hypatia's hair, and as she watched it fell to the ground, forgotten.

She looked around for the camera, found it as it buzzed past them, the camera's wings glassy in the sunlight. If she watched the video again would she see herself on it this time?

Another woman stood at the outskirts of the group. Ann didn't remember her from the video; the camera hadn't photographed that part of the crowd. A black woman, with long black braids mixed with gray . . .

"Meret!" she said without thinking.

The woman turned toward her. "I'm sorry," she said in Greek. "Do I know you?"

God, that was stupid, Ann thought. Da Silva and Elias were both staring at her, looking shocked and angry. "I—I saw a video of you back at Transformations," Ann said to Meret in English. "They told us to find you if we had any problems."

Meret frowned. "They never said anything to me about being a Preparer," she said. She caught sight of Elias and grinned. "Yaniel! I didn't know you'd be here."

"No, this assignment was planned after you left," Elias said. "Good to see you."

"You too," Meret said. "Hey, what happened to your mustache?"

Elias scowled. "I had to shave it off. It hasn't grown back yet."

Meret looked around for Hypatia and her followers, but they had already gone past the obelisk at the center of the garden. "Well, I have my own assignment hern. Where are you staying?"

Elias told her, and she hurried away.

"What were you thinking?" Da Silva asked Ann after Meret had gone. "Didn't they tell you that she's never seen you before? That you have to be careful, very careful? The last thing you want is for her to become suspicious."

It was hard hearing Da Silva criticize her, worse than if it had been anyone else. "I'm sorry," she said. "It won't happen again."

"All right," Da Silva said, sounding mollified. "You recovered well, at least."

They headed across the garden toward a cluster of buildings. Excitement began to fill her, a different and more intense excitement than what she'd felt at the palace in Knossos. Here was an entire city that understood the importance of books, of knowledge and ideas and philosophy. And she would see it soon, the largest and greatest library in the world.

They came to the porch and walked between the two statues, Thoth and Seshat. "God of wisdom, and of writing," Elias murmured, indicating Thoth. "Goddess of time and measurement"—and now Ann saw that what she had thought was Seshat's staff was some kind of recording instrument, marked with a series of notches. It was topped with a star enclosed in a sort of upside-down bowl, or a crescent moon facing downwards.

The bronze doors stood open. A guard asked them for their proof of membership, and Elias showed him the papers the company had forged. Then Elias led them through an antechamber and into an open courtyard surrounded by columned passageways. They headed down one passage, past people talking, arguing, hurrying from one place to another with buckets of scrolls. Some of the people were head-down in their scrolls, and Ann and the others had to dodge out of their way as they approached.

Doors opened off the colonnade. She glanced through one and then stopped, her breath caught in wonder. The room was enormous. Tall marble columns held up a frieze along the walls, with bookcases in the niches between them. A statue of Minerva stood at the front, the drapes of her clothes swirling as though she had just arrived and planted her spear against the pedestal. Two rows of desks ran down the room, with people sitting at them and reading quietly. Marble of every color paved the floor, shining out where the sun hit it from the high windows and open door: blood red, sea green, fiery yellow-orange.

She took a step inside. The place smelled sour, organic, probably because of all the papyrus scrolls crowded together;

it reminded her of a health-food store. She looked up and saw another story above the frieze, with more niches, more bookcases, another statue. And this was just one section of the library, with more rooms elsewhere.

"Ann!" Elias called. "Come on."

She hurried after them. They passed a large amphitheater, probably an empty classroom, and then a smaller classroom, with young men and a few women sitting on the stone steps and taking notes. Boys and girls sat in the next room, ranging from about five to ten years old, and at the head of the class, pointing to some Roman numbers written on papyrus, was Hypatia, with Meret standing next to her.

Was Meret supposed to be there? What if she refused to follow orders again, what if she was teaching them calculus or Arabic numbers, things that hadn't even been invented yet?

"Is that what she's here to do?" Ann whispered to Elias, not wanting Meret to look up and see them. "Teach the kids?"

Elias peered into the classroom. "I don't know," he said. "We'd better let her get on with it, whatever it is."

The line of columns ended and they walked through another garden, this one with a reflecting pool at the center. Then they came to another colonnade, and another row of doors.

Elias consulted a piece of papyrus and went into one of the rooms. This room was small, about a third the size of the first one, but it was arranged along the same plan, with bookshelves and columns and another statue at the front. He pointed to an oil lamp on one of the tables and said, "That lamp there—that has to go on this table here, closer to the bookshelves. Like I said, we'll do that early in the morning, when the place is nearly empty. We want as few people seeing us as possible."

He studied them a moment. "Let's say—Ann, you're in charge of this one. Now come on and we'll find the rest of them."

He looked at the papyrus and headed down the passage-way, and they followed. Ann thought of Meret again, wondering what it would be like to work with Hypatia. She felt a dull prick of jealousy at the idea of the two of them becoming friends, especially when her own assignment was so boring in comparison.

And then, perhaps because she was remembering Meret from the graveyard in Knossos, she had a terrible thought. She saw the lamps knocked over, the flames leaping eagerly for the papyrus scrolls. "Why are we doing this?" she asked. "Are we trying to make sure the library gets burned down, or burn down more of it?"

Two clerks hurried by, arguing about where to shelve some scrolls. "Hush," Elias said, though she had been speaking English. "The librarians get very nervous when people talk about fire. Understandably so."

"But why do we want to move those lamps?"

"You know we can't tell you that," Elias said. "And to be honest, I couldn't tell you even if I wanted to—they don't explain things to the Facilitators anymore."

"Really? Why?"

"I don't know. It started when we got back from Crete."

"So they thought the problem was that Meret knew we were supporting the Minos? That if she didn't know she would have completed her assignment?"

"Maybe. I don't know."

But doesn't that mean they have something to hide? she thought. That if they told us the results of our actions we wouldn't do them? She said nothing, though. Clearly Elias and Da Silva didn't want to hear her speculations about the company.

They headed toward other parts of the library. Twice Elias went into rooms and pointed out oil lamps to Zach and Da Silva. Finally he found a lamp for himself, in a part of the library that seemed to be devoted to mending scrolls, and they headed back to the entrance.

The library was starting to close by then; people in Alexandria only worked from morning to early afternoon. It seemed like a good idea to Ann, and she wondered what Sam at the computer shop would have said if she'd told him she wanted to work Alexandrian hours.

"We have the rest of the day off, like the Alexandrians," Elias said as they went back through the first courtyard. "Unfortunately we'll have to spend it indoors—the cameras didn't pick up any fighting today, but they might have missed something."

Ann had had her fill of waiting at inns. "What about Meret? When am I supposed to talk to her?"

Elias thought a moment. "I suppose you can go look for her now. But be careful, and come back as soon as you can."

12

THEY HAD REACHED THE antechamber by then. Ann turned
and hurried back to the colonnade. Past the large room filled
with books, past the lecture room, running now toward the
classroom where she had seen Meret and Hypatia. She went
inside—

It was empty, the teachers and students gone. She
stopped abruptly and then ran through the door on the other
side and looked up and down the corridor. Empty, like the
classroom.

A girl of about ten came toward her. "Do you know where
the teachers are?" Ann asked. "Hypatia and—and the other
woman?" Agents usually kept their names for their assignments but not always; Meret might have changed hers.

"Teacher Meret," the girl said. "Of course—she's in the
Great Room."

"Which one is that? The room near the entrance?"

"I'll show you."

The girl was tall for her age, and more self-assured than
most ten-year-olds Ann had seen. She was slender, her legs
as about as thin as Ann's arms, and her nose and ears were
slightly too big, as though she still needed to grow into them;

she looked a bit like a gentle, friendly giraffe. She had long copper hair, an unusual color for her tace.

They headed back to the high marble room. Hypatia and Meret sat at one of the tables, rolling up their scrolls, but otherwise the room was empty. The girl ran inside, hair flying, sandals clicking against the marble.

"Teacher Hypatia," she said. "This woman wants to talk to you."

Hypatia looked at Ann. "No, not you," Ann said, flustered at coming close to someone she admired. Great—now the woman would think she was horribly rude. "I'm sorry—I mean, I'm delighted to meet you, but I have to talk to Meret."

Meret turned toward her. "All right," she said.

"Not here," Ann said.

Meret nodded and followed her out the door. Two men hurried down the passageway, nearly colliding with them. "Why don't we go to one of the gardens?" Meret said in Greek.

"I want to stay indoors," Ann said, answering her in English.

"Why? Is something wrong?"

"Not really. I just want to get away from the cameras."

Meret looked at her shrewdly but said nothing.

They went into one of the empty classrooms, and Ann studied the other woman. She seemed younger and more relaxed in this tace, the lines on her face not as deep. Her hair had grown out, and had been twined into dozens of braids. No, of course she hadn't grown it out—she'd cut it sometime between now and her assignment in Kaphtor.

She studied Ann with a focused, attentive expression, as though she expected to learn something interesting. She looked, in fact, a bit like Hypatia herself, as if she had picked up some of the other woman's attitudes while studying with her.

Ann had given some thought to her assignment, about how to start. She drew a deep breath. "My last assignment was in Knossos, in the Bronze Age."

"Oh, man, I'd love to go thern. I put in a request for it, but no one's said anything yet."

"I liked it a lot. I liked the way the women were in charge, and all the goddesses, Kore, Potnia—"

Meret stopped and stared at her. "Are you—" she whispered.

"In Core?" Ann said. She felt exultant. She had guessed right, it *was* a password. "No, but I think I want to be."

"Why? What happened?"

Ann took another breath. "They gave us our assignments hern," she said. "We have to go to the library, move some lamps from one place to another. I think they want to make sure the place goes up in flames. And I can't do that, I can't help burn it down. I'd never forgive myself."

Meret sighed. "That's not something I'd know, unfortunately. I don't even know a lot about my own assignment."

"What did they tell you?"

"Just that I'm supposed to keep an eye on a certain book, make sure it doesn't disappear. Some weird retelling of Genesis."

"Genesis? Why on earth?"

"I have no idea. Anyway, I already put a tracer on it, so I can follow it wherever it goes. Which means I can spend the rest of my time here doing stuff the company probably wouldn't approve of, like teaching Hypatia's students."

Ann grinned. She was liking this version of Meret more than the last one; teaching children seemed a better use of her time than digging up dead people. "What if they see you in the cameras?"

"I've been pretty careful. The only close call was when you yelled out my name. I looked at you just as that camera came by."

"God, I'm sorry! I was just so startled to see you. But don't worry—I actually watched that video before I left, and you weren't in it."

"Really? That's a relief."

A man put his head into the classroom. "What in Isis's name are you still doing here?" he asked. "The library is closed. Outside, both of you."

Ann waited until the man left and said quickly, "I wanted to ask—how do I join Core?"

"We don't really have membership, or regular meetings," Meret said. "We have to be very careful, because the company can send cameras to any location and find out what we're up to. I only know a few members, and they only know a few, and so on."

"And there's the password too."

"It's more than a password, really. We've been working on—well, on a kind of underground, something to help the time-bound resist what the company is doing to them. We start with their religion, their worship of Kore or whatever goddess they believe in—as far as we can tell the company nearly always backs gods or a god, taces with men in charge. Then we add other teachings, esoteric knowledge about the company and how to deal with them . . . So even if the cameras notice us, if they see us going into a temple or something, the company has no idea what's going on—they think it's just another local religion."

She mentioned a few names, the members of Kore she knew, but Ann had never heard of any of them.

The footsteps came back down the colonnade, and they stood quickly and left the room, passing the librarian on their way out. "Do you want to meet Hypatia?" Meret asked.

"I'd love to," Ann said, surprising herself with her enthusiasm. "Who was that kid with the red hair?"

Meret laughed. "She's amazing, isn't she? That was Olympia. I can't believe she isn't in any of the history books—she's as smart as Hypatia, or smarter. But of course the library burns down, so history doesn't find out a lot of things."

It had been easy getting into the library, but the guard wanted to search them thoroughly when they left, to make sure they weren't smuggling books. To her relief, he called for a woman to pat them down. "I never heard that Hypatia taught kids," Ann said, as they headed back across the garden.

"No. That's another thing the histories don't mention. But she thinks it's more important to teach children than adults—after all, they're the ones who are going to create the future."

They came out to the street, and Meret turned right. They walked in silence for a while, Ann glancing around her at the crowds. Everyone seemed to be speaking a different language, though the only ones she recognized were Greek and Latin.

"They all look so calm," she said, choosing her words carefully in case the cameras heard them. "Considering what'll happen tomorrow."

"That's how it goes, in a lot of taces," Meret said. "People want to believe that everything's fine, that things will go on the way they've been."

"I wish we could do something for Hypatia, though. That we could save her somehow. It was horrible, the way she died."

Meret looked at her for a long moment but said nothing. Was she silent because of the cameras, or because what Ann was saying was so impractical, a novice's wild idea?

They stopped at a house and Meret knocked on the door. A servant took them inside and led them to a room with a few reclining couches. There was a mosaic on the floor, pictures of birds surrounded by a frame of geometrical shapes, but otherwise the room seemed bare, austere, suitable for a philosopher. Though, Ann thought, she still had servants, or at least one. A door opposite them opened out into a courtyard, and when she looked through it she saw a bronze armillary sphere, showing the circles of the heavens.

Hypatia came into the room and went toward them. "This is my friend Ann, the woman I met in the library," Meret said.

Hypatia smiled and held out her hands. "They say that two things that are equal to a third thing are equal to each other," she said. "If Ann is your friend, and you're mine, then I'm sure Ann and I will become great friends."

Ann took her hands. Hypatia led them to the couches and called for her servant to bring them some food.

For the rest of her life, she knew, she would remember the conversation that afternoon. They talked about philosophy, and somehow Hypatia managed to make it seem interesting, even essential. But they discussed other subjects as well, politics, religion, all the things that people had warned her never to bring up in conversation.

"What religion do you believe in?" Hypatia asked her.

She remembered the foster parents that had taken her to church every Sunday, and said a blessing before every meal. But they hadn't seemed to live their life according to the Bible, the book they claimed was so important; instead they spent a lot of their time warning the kids about the dangers of homosexuality and abortion.

"None of them, really," she said.

"None?" Hypatia laughed. "But someone has to have created all this, don't you think? The world, and the animals, and the people?"

She had a sudden urge to tell Hypatia about the Big Bang Theory, about evolution. "Well, then, what do you believe in?" she asked.

"In number. Mathematics leads to understanding, and on to higher wisdom. It's in mathematics that you discover the perfection of creation."

Ann nodded. It was an attractive theory, one she thought she could believe in too. But then she remembered the goddess in Kaphtor, and how she had been drawn to her as well. So what *was* her religion then?

"I have to keep these ideas secret, though," Hypatia went on. "Most people wouldn't understand, and some Christians would call me a heretic—especially now, with the city so uncertain. So I tell everyone that my subject is mathematics, and I teach my students to say the same thing."

"What are you going to do when Theophilus closes the Serapeum?" Ann asked.

"Try to stay out of it. I don't bother with buildings, places built out of brick and marble. As long as they leave my mind alone I'm fine." She frowned. "My father wants to fight, though. He's one of the old pagans, he believes in giving the gods their due. I have to say I'm worried about him."

Theon, Hypatia's father, had died—would die—defending the Serapeum. And all of that would happen tomorrow. Ann looked away, feeling a sudden sadness for Hypatia, and a vague guilt for knowing what would happen. Would Hypatia be able to keep her philosopher's objectivity when she heard the news?

The courtyard had begun to fill with shadows, and she remembered, startled, that she had get back to the inn. "I have to go," she said. "The others are expecting me."

"I'll come with you," Meret said. She turned to Hypatia. "Goodbye—I'll see you tomorrow."

They headed toward the door. There was a silence behind them, and Ann had a horrible feeling she had forgotten something, something to do with those foster parents who had taken her to church.

Manners, that was it. That foster mother had tried to teach her politeness, accompanying her lessons with slaps and punishments. She still didn't completely understand manners, but she turned back and said, "Thank you for a wonderful afternoon."

"You're welcome," Hypatia said. "I hope we'll see each other again."

Ann and Meret began to walk. "That was incredible," Ann said.

"You don't get to meet famous people very often," Meret said. "I thought I would, when I started, but there are more ordinary people than famous ones, after all. Though they aren't so ordinary once you get to know them."

Meret stopped at a corner. "I'm going this way," she said. "Where are you headed?"

This was probably the last time Ann would see her—and all at once she made her decision. It wasn't anything the other woman had said; it was more the way she had acted, the compassion she had felt for the timebound. And the contrast between her and Walker, and even Da Silva, her behavior compared to the callous disregard of rest of the company.

She put her hand out to Meret's arm to hold her back. She looked around for a camera, but didn't see one. "Listen," she said. "I'm not supposed to say anything about this, but I think I have to. I met you before. In Knossos."

"You met—oh. You mean I'm going thern after all?"

Ann nodded. She told Meret everything that had happened, starting with Gregory's death. As she spoke she suddenly understood Meret's expression at the graveyard and afterward, her half smile, as if she and Ann were sharing a joke. Meret had been told everything she was about to do, she knew exactly what was going to happen, and on some level she expected Ann to know it too.

And now it was Ann's turn to feel as if she was acting, performing a role in a play that was familiar to both of them. It seemed impossible that Meret didn't know any of this; after all, they had experienced it together.

"And then you rescued us, at the palace," Ann said. "And—oh my God—that's how you knew where we were, because I told you, I'm telling you now. And how you knew what our assignment was, that we were supposed to drug those guards, and so you were able to go to the queen and tell her where we'd be, and she could arrest us. And I guess I was supposed to tell you all of this, because if I hadn't we'd never have been rescued, we'd still be thern today."

She spoke the last sentence in the time traveler's argot, using the tense for events that should have happened but had been erased. "Oh God, you're going to have to remember all of this, and say it all just the way it happened," she said. "I think I can recite it, maybe not word for word—"

Meret held up her hand. "It's okay, you don't have to. Things have a way of working out the way they've already happened—it's one of the weird rules of time travel. We call it the Law of Conservation of History. I'll just start talking when I see you, and probably I'll end up saying everything I'm supposed to say."

There was one more piece of information Ann had to give her, but she didn't know how to say it. Best just to get it over with, she thought.

"And then, well, you stayed in Kaphtor. In Crete. You said you didn't want to go back if the company knew you were in Core."

"I stay . . ." Ann had expected Meret to look apprehensive, but she had a dreamy, pleased expression on her face. "I've been thinking about that, actually, about hiding in the timelines, on this assignment or another one . . . And Kaphtor would be perfect, because whatever I started thern would be very early, would only get stronger as time went on."

Ann nodded. She liked the thought of an idea catching hold, becoming weightier and more momentous over the centuries, until finally, unstoppable, it appeared in some far distant time . . . "It's like you have your own time machine," she said, "only it takes a long time to work, and it only goes one way."

Meret laughed. "Exactly! Anyway, if you're ever in trouble and there's a temple to a goddess, whatever her name is, go there and see if they can help you. We've only influenced a handful of taces so far so it's a very long shot, but you might as well try it." She hesitated. "When are you leaving Alexandria?" she asked.

"Tomorrow afternoon."

"I might have something for you. I'll come find you at your inn."

"My assignment's in the morning."

"Well, I'll look for you in the afternoon, see if you're still around."

They said goodbye and Ann went on to her inn. The sun had not set yet; she still had time to make something up about Meret. She sat on the lip of a fountain; a cooling spray of water brushed over her like a consoling hand.

ELIAS AND DA SILVA started asking questions as soon as she got back to the inn. She gave them the story she had come up with, that she and Meret had discussed the impending riots and then gone to visit Hypatia. "Wait," Elias said. "You—you met Hypatia?"

"Yeah," Ann said.

"Well, I have to say I envy you. You didn't tell her what happens to her father tomorrow, did you?"

"No, of course not."

The questions continued over dinner at the restaurant and after they got back to the inn, until Elias and Da Silva seemed satisfied that Meret hadn't mentioned Core. They went to bed early, to be rested for the day ahead.

They woke in the dark the next morning and headed out. Da Silva and Elias were talking quietly, but Ann said nothing as they walked through the streets. Should she complete her mission? Why did they have to move the lamps? What would Hypatia do?

A man called out something in the distance. Another man shouted back, and a horse neighed. This was it, she thought. It was starting. Was Theon already at the Serapeum, building barricades with his friends?

Only librarians and clerks and guards had come to the library that day, as if the patrons had known something was up and had kept away. Elias led them into the courtyard.

"We have an hour before the riot spreads to this part of the city," he said. "So get away as quickly as you can, just do your assignment and go. We'll meet back at the inn."

They separated, each of them going to their assigned spot. Ann went into her room, picked up the lamp, and moved it to the table Elias had shown her. Then she sat down at a table in the far corner and waited.

She heard more shouts from outside, then the sound of horns blowing. A troop of horses galloped past, and someone screamed.

Her heart had started to pound like the beat of the hooves. What was she doing here? It was getting more dangerous by the minute, and Elias or Da Silva might come looking for her . . . She fidgeted, desperate to stand up, to hurry away, but she forced herself to stay.

It seemed as though an hour had passed, longer, when a man rushed into the room and looked around. He grabbed the lamp she had moved and ran over to the nearest bookshelf, then played the light over the scrolls, studying the tags on the end with the titles. He took two of the scrolls and turned to go, stopped, seized two more, and stuffed all four of them into his toga.

He stopped again when he saw her. "What are you doing here?" he said. "They're heading for the library—come on, we have to go."

She said nothing. He mistook her silence for disapproval. "I'm saving them," he said defiantly. "The patriarch's told them to burn the library, but people can't live without these books."

She saw now that he was younger than she had thought, eighteen or twenty, someone for whom books were still a matter of life or death. "Good for you," she said.

They hurried out of the room together. The library seemed empty, all the clerks and librarians gone. Suddenly a group of men burst out from the garden and clattered along the marble colonnade. Some of them were waving drawn swords, and a few of them carried torches. A man rushed into one of the rooms and out again, shouting gleefully.

"There's some more books no one will ever read!" he said. Threads of smoke twined out the open door.

"Praise God!" another man shouted.

Ann ran in the opposite direction. A high marble wall stood in the distance, enclosing all the buildings and gardens. She turned back and ducked quickly into an empty room.

"Hey, I just saw one of them!" someone shouted.

"Where?"

"That room, over there."

Ann hurried out the other side. There was a hallway there, lined with closed doors, the light fading as she headed away from the room.

Finally she stood in complete darkness. The sounds of the men were growing louder. She put her hand out and felt a door, pushed on it. It didn't open.

She went as quickly as she could down the hallway, running her hand along the wall, trying each door as she came to it. To her relief one of them opened, and she hurried through.

She was in another room lined with books. Fire bloomed like an exotic flower from one of the bookcases, and as she watched another case went up with a strong "Woomf!"

She rushed for the opposite door. The air seemed thinner, scorched, and she held her breath against the smoke. She ran through the door and back into the corridor. The men were past her now, she saw, their backs to her.

She jumped off the marble passageway, trying to make as little noise as possible, and headed for the garden with the reflecting pool. Suddenly a voice called out, "There he is!"

145

She looked back. The mob had turned and was running after her. "Look—it's a woman!" someone called out.

"Praise God!" another man said.

She reached the garden and ran past the pool. She forced herself not to turn around, but she could hear them coming closer, shouting, laughing.

"What does a good-looking woman like you want with books?" one of them called out.

"Come here—we'll show you what a woman's good for."

"We'll show you what those scrolls are good for."

"God, she's a fast one, isn't she?"

"I hope so!" someone said, and they all laughed.

Their voices sounded louder. She looked back quickly and saw that they were nearly upon her. There was a colonnade in front of her, fire flying out from a few doors, and after that the antechamber and the entrance. Her breath came fast and harsh in her throat, and she knew she would never make it.

"I'm going to kill that whore," one of the men said, panting. "After all the trouble she's put us through."

"Let me have her first, though."

Something hit her head, a thrown rock. Her vision starred, and she stumbled. She forced herself to stand upright, to keep going. The passageway ahead of her was blurred now. She stumbled again.

The passageway skittered, bounced, branched off into half a dozen paths. The light grew sharper, like a bank of strong bulbs, and then painfully bright. She felt a hideous pain in her stomach and doubled over.

She straightened as quickly as she could and looked around her. They men were gone. She was standing amid ruins, a fallen column at her feet. The men were gone, but so was everyone else. She was alone, with no idea of where or when she was.

SHE CHOSE A DIRECTION and began to walk, staring around
her in disbelief and horror. Shattered pieces of marble lay
on the ground, weeds growing up around them. She passed
a painted marble arm, then saw the rest of the statue lying
a few feet away.

Had she been knocked unconscious, awakening after the
mob had done its work? But the place felt different somehow,
as though she had been moved through space, or through
time.

How could that have happened, though? She hadn't been
anywhere near the key Elias had buried. Da Silva had said
that the fifth floor could insert and extract people, so perhaps
they had rescued her from the mob. But whern was she, and
why hadn't the company brought her back to her own tace?

She continued on, coming to a field choked by shrubs and
briars, and she picked her way through it carefully. After
that came a line of fallen columns next to a marble passageway, weeds pushing their way up through the cracks.
It looked familiar, and she realized it had been one of the
colonnades in the library. She was still at the library, then,
but sometime after the destruction.

Her head throbbed, and when she reached back to touch it she felt a lump the size of her thumb. That's right—she'd been hit with a rock, just before ending up here. And now that she'd noticed it it seemed worse, as insistent as a drum pounding in her ear.

Another statue lay on its back ahead of her, smashed into a dozen pieces. Its head remained whole, though, and she recognized it as Minerva, the statue from the Great Room. Her broken staff lay on the ground next to her.

The entrance had to be around here then, somewhere ahead. She went forward as quickly as she could and came to the door of the antechamber. The roof had fallen in in places, and the room was choked with wood and marble and water-logged papyrus.

She backed out and tried to walk around it, but the space between this building and the next was littered with wreckage, blocking it in all directions. Huge shaggy trees had grown up on the pathways. She worked her way forward and back, trying to break through the rubble, her frustration growing.

The sun was directly overhead by the time she made it outside. The garden in front of the library was still there, she saw, and so were the statues of Seshat and Thoth in their niches, chipped and faded but still whole. It was strange to see them like that, in the midst of all the destruction, looking like the survivors of an apocalypse.

People were walking through the garden, or sitting and eating and talking. She hurried forward, brushing off dust and leaves and cobwebs, hoping the places where she'd torn her clothes weren't too visible. "Excuse me," she said to a man walking toward her on the path.

"Can I help you?" the man said.

Too late, she realized she had no idea of what she was going to say. She thought quickly. "Do you know—do you know who's the patriarch now?"

The man looked at her strangely but said, "Patriarch Cyril."

"For how long?"

The man thought. "Three years. That's right, it was just around the time I had that rotten tooth, and there was fighting in the streets and I couldn't get out to have it pulled. They were fighting for Timothy, but if you ask me Cyril's done a wonderful job. It's about time we showed those pagans what the true religion is. Theophilus was a good man, God rest him, but he'd been too easy on them."

She'd been afraid of that. Hypatia had been killed in the third year of Cyril's tenure. Was that why she'd been brought here, did someone want her to save Hypatia? But who? The company wouldn't have sent her here without thorough training, she knew that much.

She left the man and continued on to the outdoor market. That at least had stayed the same, crowded and smelling of a dozen spices. People were studying her strangely, though, and looking down she saw that her chiton was still smudged with dirt and soot.

She had no money with her—the Facilitators were in charge of that in the taces they visited—but she was wearing necklaces and bracelets she could sell. She glanced around for a booth selling jewelry.

Now she saw that she'd been wrong before; the market *had* changed, though in subtle ways. A group of men in black robes stood at the edge, watching the crowd from beneath their hoods: Nitrian monks, called from their desert monastery to help Cyril in his campaign against the Jews and pagans. Soldiers rode past on horses and camels. The scroll merchants were gone, and so were the people who sold charms and statues of gods and goddesses, replaced by men selling crosses. Most of the people here were men, in fact; there were few women on the streets. Maybe that was why everyone staring at her, maybe it had nothing to do with her clothes.

What had that man said, that Theophilus had been too easy on the pagans? Theophilus had been the one to close down the Serapeum, and to order the library destroyed. It was hard to imagine what more he could have done to satisfy the Christians.

She went up to a booth selling jewelry and bargained with the stall-holder for one of her rings, then took the money he gave her to another booth displaying clothes. She changed behind the booth, leaving her old chiton where it dropped.

Now what? She should go back to the inn, see if the others had been transported here as well—that is, if the inn still existed twenty-four years later. And she hadn't eaten since breakfast, and her hunger along with the pain in her head was making her feel sick to her stomach.

She stopped at a restaurant and ordered roast goose. She hadn't asked that fanatic in the marketplace what month it was—he would have really thought her crazy if she'd done that, might have even reported her to the authorities—but it had been chilly outside, almost wintry. Hypatia had died in March.

Maybe it was December, maybe she was too late. But she felt strangely certain that Hypatia was alive.

She finished the goose and went back into the streets. The city had changed here as well, she saw: some of the columns had fallen and not been replaced, and every block held a derelict building or two, burned out by fire or broken into. A soldier wearing armor made of bronze plates studied her from a camel, and she felt suddenly conspicuous, though she didn't think she had violated any laws.

What had the others thought when she hadn't returned? Had the company started looking for her? Maybe she could find a camera, wave at it, scream, jump up and down. But there probably weren't any cameras hern; the company only sent them to the taces they called hinges, times and places that existed at some branching of history, where they could mold events into the shapes they wanted.

It didn't seem likely that they'd find her, out of all of history. She would have to stay hern. And do what? Unlike most of the people in the city she could read and write, but the Christians seemed to disapprove of women who worked. And she would not marry any of these men, not for anything.

No, she had to have come hern for a reason. Maybe once she saved Hypatia she would be rescued, picked up by whoever had sent her. She had to think so, anyway; unlike Meret, she didn't think she could bear to live outside of her own era.

The inn was still there. She went inside with relief and found the innkeeper, a middle-aged man with a fringe of hair around his head. "I'm supposed to meet my friends here," she said. "Three people from Crete, like me. Their names are Yaniel and Amabel and Zach."

He scowled. "Outlandish names you have. No, there's no one like that here."

"Are you sure? Zach is young, my age, and—"

"Believe me, I'd remember."

Maybe they'd used different names. But that was wishful thinking, she knew; there was no reason they should have. They would have wanted her to find them.

She hadn't realized how much she'd been hoping to meet them here. But she had to push aside her despair; she had work to do.

"I've been traveling," she said. "I wonder—could you tell me what day it is?"

He looked at her disdainfully, though whether it was because she had lost track of time or because she was a woman on her own she couldn't tell. "The twenty-fourth of March," he said.

She was right, then. Hypatia had died—would die—tomorrow, on the twenty-fifth. She remembered it because, ironically, it was the date they celebrated the vernal equinox in Hypatia's era. "I'd like a room for a night," she said.

He took her money—nearly the last of it, she shouldn't have splurged on that goose—and assigned her a room.

As she turned away she realized suddenly that this was the innkeeper's son, the young man who had talked and joked with them twenty-four years ago. The eyes still looked the same, and some of the lines of the face, but sometime over the years he had turned sour, like others she had seen in the city.

Well, it was a good thing he hadn't remembered their names from their previous visit. It would have been hard to explain why she hadn't aged in nearly a quarter of a century.

She found the room, went inside, and tugged the latch into place. A scratched and wavy mirror lay next to a washbasin, and she looked into it. No wonder people had stared, she thought. Dirt streaked her face, and a great cobweb draped the top of her head like a hairnet, leaves and rocks caught in it like jewels. She brought the mirror closer to study her pupils, worried about concussion, but it was too distorted for her to see them clearly.

It was still afternoon, but she felt as if she had been awake for the full twenty-four years. And she still had to find Hypatia, and warn her if she could. She washed herself with water from the basin and headed outside.

As she walked through the streets she remembered something Meret had told her: "If you're ever in trouble and there's a temple to a goddess, whatever her name is, go there and see if they can help you." But though she looked for them she didn't see temples to any goddess, Kore or Demeter or Isis; they had all been burned or converted to churches.

She found Hypatia's street easily, and the house she had visited with Meret. Just yesterday, according to her internal clock—and it had been only this morning when Theophilus's men had burned the library.

She knocked at the door, and a woman she didn't recognize came to answer it. "Does Hypatia still live here?" she asked.

The woman drew back as though Ann had thrown hot water on her. "There's no one by that name in this house," she said. She started to close the door.

"Do you know where she went?"

The woman studied her through a crack in the door. "I didn't even know she'd lived here. It's that witch you mean, isn't it? The astrologer?"

"Witch?"

"That's what Patriarch Cyril said she is. He preached a sermon against her just last Sunday, two days ago. If you do know her I'd suggest you don't spread it around."

"She isn't a witch."

"Oh, and you know theology better than our patriarch, I suppose. Well, I have things to do. Don't come back here, or I'll call the Parabolans." The Parabolans had started as a group of young men who did charity, Ann knew, but Cyril now used them as an army, to enforce his edicts.

The woman slammed the door. Now what? She could look for Hypatia, though she had no idea where to find her. Or she could go to the Church of St. Michael, where Hypatia would be killed tomorrow.

Her head was throbbing, and she wanted nothing more than to go to sleep—though she knew that if she did have a concussion it could be the worst thing for her. Still, she found herself heading back to the inn. Her thoughts were fraying, becoming confused, and she began to worry that Walker would be waiting for her, and that she had to come up with some story about where she'd been.

But when she got back to the inn she saw with relief that Walker wasn't there. She went to her room and fell asleep.

SHE WOKE TO LOUD chanting from the street. She stood, disoriented, and went outside. The sun was rising, its bright light lancing down the wide boulevards.

The chanting grew stronger; it sounded as if the mob had taken Hypatia already, or were just about to. She cursed herself for oversleeping, for missing what might be her only chance.

She could hear what the people were shouting now, along with the sound of their feet marching in step: "Witch! Witch! Witch!" The words echoed through the streets, making it impossible to tell where they were coming from.

She hurried to the Church of St. Michael. Her head pounded as she ran; it felt as if someone were trying to drill through it. Halfway to the church she was stopped by the crowd, black-robed Nitrian monks and ordinary men and women from the city, fathers carrying their children on their shoulders, all of them shouting, their faces twisted with hatred.

Men on horses rode among them, wearing the black dress of the priests. She looked around for Cyril and saw a bearded man in a chariot wearing a black robe and hood, shouting something to someone further up. Massy golden jewelry glinted on his chest in the sunlight.

She joined the crowd and eeled her way to the front. Finally she saw a group of young men a few feet ahead of her, the Parabolans. She thought that they had to be holding Hypatia, but they moved in such tight formation that she couldn't see her. Next to them marched a skinny man in a dirty chiton, his long hair and beard matted. Peter the Reader, the history books said his name was, a minor clergyman.

She struggled to reach the Parabolans, but the crowd pressed in on her, holding her back. Someone shoved an elbow into her stomach, and she nearly vomited.

When she straightened she saw that she had ended up next to Peter. "Witch! Witch! Witch!" he cried, his face distorted. Strings of saliva ran between lips.

Finally the crowd came to two great obelisks. They were the only things that remained from the Caesarium, a temple built by Cleopatra to honor Julius Caesar; the rest had been torn down to build the church. St. Michael, like nearly every church in this tace, was a simple rectangle faced with limestone.

The Parabolans went inside. The rest of the mob followed, crowding in at the entrance and pushing their way through. She was thrown against Peter, briefly smelling his foul unwashed clothes, then squeezed past him.

Four rows of columns headed toward the front of the church. The Parabolans marched down the aisles and flung Hypatia down on the mosaic floor before the altar. Her clothes were torn, her breasts exposed, and she was bleeding in half a dozen places.

Ann watched in horror, a cold current running through her. She had read about this, of course, but reading it was very different from seeing it enacted in front of you. You didn't hear the voices of hundreds of people, all of them crying out for blood. You didn't smell their sweat, their clothes, the wine they had drunk and the food they had eaten. You didn't see the satisfaction on their faces as they stared at Hypatia, helpless at last.

No, not helpless. She regarded her captors with composure, almost smiling, as though she were standing in front of her students and about to begin a lecture on mathematics. "What do you have to say for yourself, witch?" Cyril asked.

"Nothing—I have nothing to say," she said. "You all know my philosophy, know that I have no argument with Christianity. And if you don't understand that, then nothing I say now will make any difference."

Cyril turned to the crowd. "You all heard her—she has no defense for her actions." He looked back at her. "Will you at least confess your wickedness, and die with a clear conscience?"

"I've done nothing wrong."

"Nothing! You've worked your black arts in this city, luring your followers to you by witchcraft. Do you call that nothing?"

"My students follow me of their own free will."

"Nonsense. No decent person could possibly believe your filthy heresies."

"Hundreds of them do, though. You've seen them."

Ann slipped back into the crowd. Some historians had claimed that Cyril's attack on Hypatia had been motivated by jealousy, by the fact that she had more followers than he did, was more beloved by the citizens of Alexandria. Now she was alluding to those followers, and from the little Ann had seen of Cyril she knew he would not stand for it.

"They follow you because of witchcraft!" he shouted, his voice shrill. "How many times do I have to explain that to you? You're a woman, you can't understand theology, so the only reason—the *only* reason—you have any students at all is because you've bewitched them."

A man next to Ann found a pottery jug, communion wine probably, and lifted it to his lips. Someone bumped into him and the jug fell to the floor and shattered.

Ann turned and struggled toward the entrance. She knew what was going to happen now, had read about it in any number of history books, and she knew she could not bear to watch it.

Hypatia said something, but Cyril cut her off. "I'm not going to waste my time arguing with you. And cover yourself at least, witch. Or are you lost to all modesty?"

"Your thugs were the ones who tore my clothes. Let them see what they've done."

Ann had moved far enough away that she could no longer see the two of them. Cyril must have made some gesture, though, because the men around her picked up the broken shards of pottery and surged forward. Ann pushed against them but she was carried along by the sheer tide, back toward the altar.

Someone screamed. The men with shards had reached Hypatia, were scraping her skin from her body. Another jug of wine smashed. The screams rose, grew louder. Ann closed her eyes.

"Too much for you, girlie?" someone asked her. "Why don't you want to see it? You a witch too?"

She opened her eyes quickly and saw a man leering down at her. She stamped down hard on his instep and hurried away.

He cried out in pain. "Hey, come back, girlie!" another man shouted after her. "You need to see this, see what happens to witches!"

She pushed and jabbed her way through the mob, desperate to get out. Two or three of the others were hurrying as well, unable to bear the screams.

The crowd grew sparser as she reached the back of the church. Finally she saw the door ahead of her, the sunlight beyond it. She ran outside and vomited on the ground.

SHE SAT AGAINST THE wall of the church, her legs drawn up
and her head on her knees. Tears ran down her face. Why
had she thought she could save Hypatia, could overcome all
the forces of history that had brought them to this point? She
was an idiot even to have come to see her execution.

She had to stand up, get going. And do what? There was
nothing she wanted from this place, nothing at all.

Those men might come out at any minute, though. She
thought of their shards of pottery, their hands red and slip-
pery with blood. She shuddered and forced herself to her feet.

She wandered through the city, the afternoon a blur. She
passed a canal somewhere, and a harbor, where lines of men
were hauling cargo from one of the ships to a warehouse. She
found herself at the market again and she turned back reso-
lutely, having no desire to see the ruins of the library again.

I am Seshat, she thought once, goddess of time and measurement. I know the lengths of people's lives, the times of
their deaths. And I can't do anything about it.

She went out into the streets again the next day, and the
day after that. She searched for cameras, for temples to the
goddess. But she could find no cameras in the streets, and all

the temples and synagogues seemed to have been converted into churches, the gold and silver and ivory stripped from their walls.

A few times she had the feeling that something else should have happened to her, that she was living in a time-line that did not exist. In her timeline, the *real* timeline, she hadn't escaped from the rock-throwers at the library; something else had happened to her, something she couldn't remember. Had she blocked it out because it was so terrible?

It was only on her third day that she remembered the key Elias had buried outside the city. She went through the Canopian Gate and came to a spot that looked familiar, but when she dug there she found only sand.

Well, of course, she thought, feeling stupid once again. Walker had taken the key with her when they'd left Kaphtor, and Elias had probably done the same thing here.

But she'd been moved ahead in time without a key. Did that mean she could return on her own somehow?

On the way back to the city she passed the temple to Ceres and Proserpina. She'd forgotten all about it, and now she hurried toward it, feeling excited. But it too had been plundered, and the statues smashed.

She sold more jewelry, and spent the money she got on food and lodging. She thought about Da Silva and Elias, wondering what they were doing, if they were searching for her. Elias would visit the famous lighthouse if he were here, and the tomb of Alexander. It wasn't a bad idea, and every morning when she set out she resolved to go to the lighthouse at least, but every night when she returned to the inn she realized she had spent yet another day wandering mindlessly through the streets.

A few days later she passed a word scribbled on a wall: "Kore." It was a sign, she thought, a message from Core. She looked around for a temple or some place where people might gather, but she saw only burned-out buildings, their rooms open to the streets. Goddess show me my path, she thought, her mind filled with confusion.

There were people staring back at her, monks in black and men and women wearing crosses at their breasts. It was dangerous even to be here, standing next to such an incendiary word. She hurried back to the inn.

The next day she realized that she had been in the city for a week, and that she had only one ring left to sell. Fear shot like lightning through the fog around her, and she tried to concentrate, to come up with a plan. It didn't seem to matter, though. She would stay here for the rest of her life, and Hypatia was dead.

She started off through the city, choosing a direction at random. "You're here!" a woman behind her said. "Finally!"

Ann turned quickly. Was it Da Silva? Meret? But saw only a slender woman wearing a tribon, no one she knew. "What? Who are you?"

"She told me to keep looking for you," the woman went on. "But she didn't say it would take over twenty years to find you, and that you'd still look the same."

"What on earth are you talking about? Who said what?"

"Teacher Meret."

"Meret? Wait a minute. Do you know Meret? Is she here?"

"She left a long time ago. But she told me I might see you again, and she gave me something to give you."

Of course—Meret was in Crete. Ann looked closer at the woman. She was in her mid-thirties, her nose and ears slightly too big for her face, and she had red hair, a strange color for this tace.

Red hair. Wait. Ann tried to get her sluggish brain to work. Twenty years ago. "You're—you were Hypatia's student. Olympia."

"That's right. But why are you the same age as when I saw you last? Are you—are you a god?"

Ann tried to laugh. "No, of course not. I just look young, that's all."

Olympia looked unconvinced.

"You said you have something for me?" Ann went on. "Something from Meret?"

"I do. It's at my house, though. Can you come with me?"

Meret *had* wanted to give her something, Ann remembered. Probably she had gone to the inn on that horrible day, but Ann hadn't been there. Or maybe Meret had gotten caught up in the chaos in the city, had been unable to reach her. Whatever it was, she'd handed it over to Olympia for safekeeping.

Olympia headed through the streets, and Ann followed. "You—do you know what happened to Hypatia?" Ann asked.

Olympia nodded. "She knew it was going to happen, knew that Cyril hated her. She said she was ready to die, that she would meet her death philosophically."

Ann remembered the screams, the sharp pieces of pottery. No one could think about philosophy under those circumstances. She couldn't say that to Olympia, though.

"She was a wonderful woman," she said instead.

"She was. Teacher Meret said—Teacher Meret seemed to know all manner of things, like an oracle. She said that Teacher Hypatia would be remembered for generations."

"I'm sure she was right."

They reached a street crowded with wooden three and four story buildings. Olympia turned in at one of the doors and they came to a small courtyard littered with food and broken pottery. A dry fountain stood in the center, and rickety stairs climbed up to the landings. Young men stood out on one of the landings, talking and drinking and laughing loudly.

They went up a set of stairs and Olympia opened a door at the top. The room inside was small, with only a bed, a chair, and a wooden chest the size of a picnic basket. Ann remembered Hypatia's house, the mosaic, the couches, the courtyard with the armillary sphere. It had been simple enough, but worlds brighter and more comfortable than this.

"Are you—are you all right?" she asked.

"I'm fine," Olympia said. Her tribon had moth-holes, Ann saw, and was frayed at the hem. "A philosopher doesn't need much, just a place to work."

"Are you a teacher now?"

"The only people who study philosophy these days are Christians, to be honest. And they don't want to read Pythagoras or Euclid, just their own philosophers. My father says he can't support me any longer, and that if I don't find work soon I'll have to get married. But someone somewhere must need a mathematician or an engineer."

She didn't say that very few people these days would hire a woman, though Ann knew they both were thinking it. Could she help Olympia somehow? How, when she couldn't even help herself?

Olympia went to the chest and opened it. "Anyway, here it is. A necklace, I think."

Olympia took out something wrapped in cloth and gave it to her. She unwrapped it and saw a tarnished silver chain, with a matte-black thumb drive hanging from it like a charm.

"A strange-looking ornament," Olympia said. "I don't know where she got it."

Ann nodded, trying to keep her amazement from showing. It had come through a quarter of a century in good condition, she saw, free of dust, though whether it would still work was anyone's guess.

"Thank you," she said.

"Thank Teacher Meret," Olympia said. "I was just her messenger."

They said goodbye and Ann went back down the stairs, fastening the chain around her neck and tucking the drive beneath her chiton and tunic as she went. What on earth had

Meret been thinking? There were no computers hern, no way to access whatever she had put on the drive.

But Meret, of course, had been sure she'd return to the twenty-first century. And she had to think that way as well, had to somehow break out of the hopelessness that had clung to her like a dark cloud.

She went out into the street. Perhaps, she thought, she had been sent here to get the thumb drive, and she would be returned to her own tace at any moment. But nothing happened, and she headed back to the inn.

She lost track of days, of time itself. Her only reminder that time was passing was when her hunger forced her to eat. But she had to ration her food now; she had sold her last piece of jewelry.

She was walking aimlessly in the street when she started to feel ill. Her headache, which had never left her, was growing worse, and she felt so dizzy she had to stop and grip one of the pillars to keep from falling.

The nausea intensified. The road in front of her doubled, became two, four, eight. "What is the perfect number?" someone asked, and then a high ringing noise drowned out every other sound. Her stomach wrung like a dishcloth, the cramps so bad she thought she might die, and she let go of the pillar and dropped to the ground.

The ringing stopped. She took a deep breath, got to her knees and then her feet and looked around.

The buildings were subtly different; they seemed newer, cleaner. Had she traveled again? Was she back where she had started, in 391? But how had she gotten hern?

She hurried to the inn, looking around her, hardly daring to hope. Other things had changed as well, she saw. The columns that had fallen to the street in 415, cracked and broken, were still standing hern, and buildings that had been churches had turned into temples again. She went around a corner and there, to her vast relief, were Da Silva and Elias and Zach, waiting for her at the front of the inn.

"Where have you been?" Elias asked. "We've been waiting here for hours."

Hours? But when she'd returned from Kaphtor no time at all had passed.

What time was it? What *day* was it? She had to come up with something quickly, had to invent the best lie of her life. "I got caught up in the riots," she said. "I was hit by a rock, here." She touched the lump on her head.

"What happened to your clothes?" Da Silva asked.

Of course, she wearing something different now, a yellow chiton instead of a blue one. "They got torn in the fighting," she said. "I couldn't go on the streets like that, so I sold some jewelry and bought a new chiton."

"Are you hurt? How do you feel?"

"I think I have a concussion. I've had a headache for—ever since that rock hit me."

Elias and Da Silva turned to each other, looking worried. "What is it?" Ann asked.

"It's dangerous to travel if you're concussed," Da Silva said. "Come on—let's get to our room and I'll examine you. We might have to stay hern for a few days."

They went inside. The innkeeper's son smiled at them, and for a brief moment, overlaid above his expression, Ann saw the scowling man he would become. They climbed the stairs to their room, and Elias shut the door.

"Sit on the bed, here," Da Silva said. "Have you had any hallucinations?"

Ann sat. It felt good to be taken care of, to put herself in someone else's hands. Somewhere a high thin alarm was sounding, telling her that she was treating Da Silva as a substitute mother again, but she was too tired to care.

"No," she said.

"Are you sure? They could be auditory hallucinations as well as visual ones."

"Oh. Well, I did hear someone ask me, 'What is the perfect number?'"

"When was this?"

"Just before I got here."

Da Silva took her face in her hands and looked closely into her eyes. "Yes, well," she said, sighing. "Your pupils are different sizes—it doesn't look good." She told Ann to bend her head, and then parted her hair and touched the spot the rock had hit her. "That's strange," she said.

"What?" Ann said, trying to rouse herself.

"It looks like it's mostly healed. When did you say you got this?"

"After I left the library. This mob came, and one of them threw a rock at me."

"Hmmm. You must have wandered around for a bit, lost some time. What do you think?"

You have no idea, Ann thought. She nodded. "Yeah, you might be right.

Da Silva still looked puzzled, but Ann didn't offer any more explanations. The first rule of lying well was to keep your lies simple.

"Well, the best thing for you would be to go to sleep," Da Silva said. "I'll come back every few hours and wake you, so you don't go into a coma. And the rest of us . . ."

"I'm going to visit the lighthouse," Elias said.

Ann nearly laughed, she had predicted him so exactly. She was too tired, though. She turned over and went to sleep. Sometime after they had gone she made a tremendous effort and stood up, found her bag, and hid the thumb drive deep within it.

ANN SLEPT THROUGH THE next few days. Da Silva woke her every few hours, studied her pupils, and asked her questions, though fortunately they weren't about Ann's time in Alexandria but designed to see if she was growing confused again. What is your name? Where are you? Who's the president in your tace?

Once Ann asked Da Silva what would happen if she traveled while she was concussed. "You've experienced time sickness, right?" Da Silva asked.

Ann nodded.

"Well, unfortunately it gets worse the more you travel. Finally it gets so bad that we can't send you out on any more assignments."

"What?" Zach asked. "What happens to us then?"

"Don't worry, you'll still be working for the company. You'll be teachers or computer modelers or recruiters, whatever fits the skills you have. That's why we keep hiring new people, why we need new blood. And why we need young people—it turns out they don't feel time sickness as badly."

"How many trips can we make?"

"It's different for everyone. The average is . . ." Da Silva turned to Elias. "What did that last study say?"

"Four to eight," Elias said.

"That's all?" Ann asked.

"Well, that's the average," Elias said. "This is my seventh trip, and I think I can do a few more before I have to stop."

"So if you're good at traveling they make you a Facilitator?" Zach asked.

"Well, there's more to it than that, but that's certainly part of it."

"Anyway, a concussion can make it worse," Da Silva said. "People have traveled with concussions, and sometimes they have to retire afterward."

Retire, Ann thought. It wasn't fair—she had only just started. And she wouldn't even be able to tell the company that she had traveled while she was concussed, and they would probably wonder why her time sickness was so bad.

Three days later Da Silva decided Ann was ready to travel, and they packed up and left the city. Elias dug up the key and they stood with him while he manipulated the circles back and forth. The sand and sky grew brighter, became a white that seared her eyes. A high keening sounded, and she had a terrible fear that the noises would become words, that she would hallucinate again.

Her legs buckled. She fell, hitting her knees against the platform. Men and women came forward to lift her up. "We felt the timequake," someone said. "How did it go?"

"A success, I'm happy to say," Elias said.

People cheered, called out "Congratulations!" Then someone led her to the infirmary, and she slept for a long time.

09152014
108825

Preliminary Assessment of Assignment 105,
With Some Recommendations
Emra Walker

. . . Ann Decker's disappearance of five hours, after the burning of the library, remains problematic. It is especially suspicious because this is not the first time she has done such a thing. As "Final Assessment of Assignment 87" states, Decker and Francine Craig disobeyed instructions and went to the cemetery to visit the grave of Gregory Nichols, another company employee, and in that time they met Meret Haas, a former employee now known to be a member of Core. (See "Final Assessment of Assignment 87," attached.)

One unauthorized absence, especially during a first mission, may be innocent, but two are almost certainly not. And there are several other grounds for suspicion—Decker claims that she cannot remember where she went during those five hours, she returned with nearly all her jewelry missing, and, of course, she met with Haas before she disappeared. According to the report "Goals and Aims of Assignment 105," attached, one of the reasons Decker was instructed to meet with Haas was to allow the company to spy on them, to see whether Decker had been convinced to join Core by the other woman. But most of the conversation between the two of them happened indoors, away from our cameras, and so we could not tell if any meetings with Core took place. It is of course quite possible that this avoidance of the cameras was deliberate.

I would therefore recommend that Decker be questioned closely, and watched carefully in future assignments, especially since this surveillance may lead us to other Core members. It is even possible that, despite her obvious intelligence and her ability to learn, she will have to leave the company . . .

15

"AND AFTER THE ROCK hit you—what did you do then?" Da Silva asked.

They were in one of the debriefing rooms, and Ann was recounting what had happened for the third time. She had managed to tell her story the same way to her first two interrogators, but Da Silva still seemed suspicious.

She had not been able to shake her fatigue, and she was starting to wonder why she couldn't just tell Da Silva the whole story. The company had not acted badly this time; it had saved several books from the fire, books that would otherwise have been lost forever. Sometimes it seemed that she stuck to her story out of nothing more than stubbornness.

But she still didn't know who was right about the company, Meret or Da Silva. And until she figured it out she would have to keep Meret's confidences to herself.

"I don't remember that part very well," Ann said. "I think I just wandered around the city. Then I realized that my clothes were torn, and I sold some jewelry and got some new clothes."

"You seem to have sold *all* your jewelry," Da Silva said. "You came back without any of it. Someone got a bargain, that's for sure."

"I guess. I think I gave all my money to a man selling clothes."

"And what did you do with your old clothes?"

"I changed behind the booth and left them there."

"And then what?"

"Then I tried to get back to the inn. I got lost a few times, though."

"Do you know how late you were?"

"They told me—they said you were waiting for about five hours."

"That's right. And you really can't remember what you were doing all that time?"

"I remember some things. I saw a harbor, I think, and some ships. Some churches and temples."

"And you're sure you're all right now? You haven't even asked me what our assignment was about, why we had to move those lamps."

"Well, it was pretty obvious, wasn't it? We wanted people to be able to find books quickly, and get them out of the library before it burned down. How did it work? Do you know?"

"It went well—the company's done the computer modeling, and it looks like people saved books in three out of the four rooms we went to. They're fairly happy with us this time. What did you and Meret talk about?"

Ann blinked at the sudden change of subject. She understood it, though; Da Silva was still trying to trip her up. "About Hypatia. What a terrific person she was."

"Did she talk about Core at all?"

"No, nothing."

Da Silva asked some more questions, easy ones finally, and then Ann was free to go. She went back to the room the company had given her and studied the thumb drive, as she had every day since she'd gotten back. She was eager to access the information on it but she couldn't use the computer the company had supplied; they might have equipped their computers with keystroke loggers and been able to read everything she wrote.

She was surfing the net when her phone rang. It was Da Silva, asking if she wanted to visit the fifth floor, the place where the computer modeling was done.

Of course she did. And did that mean that they trusted her, that she was ready to be shown more of the workings of the company? She logged off the computer and hurried down the corridor to the elevator.

Da Silva was waiting for her there. Zach and Franny showed up a few minutes later, and soon they were all talking eagerly about the taces they'd visited. Franny had watched Chartres Cathedral go up in France, and Zach told them about all the things he'd seen while Ann had been ill. Normally she would have felt annoyed with Zach for being so insensitive, but ever since the destruction of the library she'd wanted as little to do with Alexandria as possible. Anyway, it didn't matter that he'd visited the lighthouse and the palaces of the Ptolemys; she'd met Hypatia, who was worth all the Ptolemys together.

The elevator came and they got on. Da Silva took out a thumb drive and plugged it into a port near the elevator buttons. A panel slid open and Da Silva moved in front of it, blocking Ann's view. Ann had gotten a brief glimpse of the drive, though, and she thought it looked like the one Olympia had given her.

The elevator opened out into a huge windowless room, one that seemed to take up most of the building. People sat at individual workstations, and others congregated around large screens in the center of the room. It smelled of electricity, and her skin prickled.

"Here's where it all happens," Da Silva said. "There isn't much to see, really, but I wanted to show it to you because you might be working here some day. These are the holographic computers, where we test our models. You can look around if you want, but don't bother any of the team."

The large screens were transparent, like glass. Ann watched as a man ran his hand across one of them, moving an image from one side to the other. A woman spread her hands apart and the image grew larger.

Ann went closer. Her fingers itched to touch the screen, to move the images and equations, to manipulate data with her hands. Well, it might happen sooner rather than later, if Da Silva had been right about time sickness.

"Look at this, Tarquin," one of them said.

Tarquin? Their speech sounded strange, too fast, the vowels slightly different from the ones she was used to. And now that she was looking around she noticed other differences as well. Most of them were not black or white but somewhere in between, ranging from dark to light brown—more like Elias than any of the others she had already met. All of them looked a little sickly in the harsh light.

She had known that these people were from the future, but for the first time she understood it physically, as a real thing. What had these people seen, Da Silva and Elias and Meret and even Walker? Did they know what would happen to her, to Zach and Franny? Had they, like Seshat, measured her life and death?

One of the screens in the center darkened, then switched to a three-dimensional scene of a man walking along a trail in a forest. More men and women clustered around to watch. Someone called out, "Joe, over here."

A tall thin man came over, sat down at a keyboard, and entered some numbers, his fingers moving so quickly they seemed to blur. The image on the screen changed, became the same man walking up to a cabin.

"Better," the man named Tarquin said. "One more jump, I think."

Joe entered more numbers. The man on the screen knocked at the door to the cabin, and a woman opened it.

The programmers cheered, as if they had just accomplished something enormously difficult; it reminded Ann of old videos she had seen of the moon landings. She found herself smiling, caught up in the spirit of celebration, though she had no idea what had happened.

"Weighing shadows," someone said.

"You pups ever heard that expression?" Tarquin asked her.

She fought the urge to melt back into the crowd. She hated being noticed. "No," she said.

"It's what we do here. Judging one shade of difference against another. It's slow and painstaking work, but it gets us there in the end. Gets you there, I should say."

He said something to the others and she continued through the room, looking around her. Their clothes weren't too different from hers, but all their colors seemed to clash; she saw a dress of orange, salmon pink, and red, and a shirt made up of checks of lime green and turquoise.

The room was open, plainly laid out. She headed over to the computers ranged around the sides. "Here's where we figure probabilities," Da Silva said, coming up behind her. "Do you know anything about Markov chains?"

Ann shook her head. She walked past them, and to her relief Da Silva went to talk to someone else. Finally she came to a closed-off space at the end. What didn't the company want them to see?

She opened the door. Inside were a platform and a large screen facing a row of computers. Another launch room, probably, a smaller one.

A man bustled up behind her. "Sorry, that's off limits," he said.

She turned around. The man made shooing motions with his hands, indicating that she had to leave, and closed the door behind her.

By the time Da Silva rounded them up and led them to the elevator she was starting to think retirement might not be so bad after all.

Back at her room, though, she began to wonder. Would she still be with the company when she couldn't travel in time anymore? Or would they find out about her involvement with Meret, with Core?

But she wasn't really a member of Core; all she'd done was tell Meret a few things. And if she hadn't, Meret wouldn't have rescued them in Kaphtor, they might still be there, locked in the queen's palace. Or the queen might have killed them, or sent them into the bull games.

And was the company really all that terrible, after all? They had saved books; you would have to say that, this time anyway, they had chosen the right side, had been on the side of the angels.

But what did that say about Core? Did she even know enough to make a decision, to come down on Meret's side or the company's?

There were other questions too, things she still didn't understand. Did her thumb drive give her access to the fifth floor, the place where the computer modeling was done? But why would Meret have wanted her to go there?

She went to her door and glanced down the hallway. It was empty. She hurried back to the elevator, and when it came she plugged her drive into the port Da Silva had used.

The panel opened. Behind it was an alphanumeric pad, waiting for her to enter a password. She pressed the button for the fifth floor, but nothing happened.

THEY SENT HER HOME and gave her another week's vacation. As soon as she got to her apartment she plugged the thumb drive into her computer.

The data was password-protected, as she had expected. She typed in "Kore" and "Core" and "Hypatia" and "Meret," but none of them worked. She tried some tricks, everything she could think of, but none of them gave up the contents of the drive. It seemed to be using standard file and encryption systems—her own computer could see that there was data there; it just couldn't unlock it. At least, she thought, the drive wasn't using some far-future operating system that she would have to hack at the bit level. She sighed. There were plenty of tools that could do what she needed, but it would take time. She would have to set up a brute force hack, running the most likely combinations of binary data to unlock the encryption. She didn't like this type of solution—it was inelegant, and would take a long time—but it was the only option she had left.

She bought a textbook about probability and Markov chains, thinking that she could get a head start if the company ever put her to work on the fifth floor. To her surprise the subject fascinated her, and she spent hours working out the problems.

The next day Franny called her, asking if she wanted to get together for lunch. Zach would be coming too, she said.

She didn't like going out much, and meals, especially, were filled with social landmines, opportunities for people to discover what a misfit she was. But this was Franny and Zach, people she already knew, and who knew her. Anyway, they were misfits too.

She had to take three buses to Franny's house. It was one suburb over, a town she had never visited, with huge comfortable houses and carefully tended gardens. She headed up the front path and rang the doorbell.

Franny opened the door and led her into an entrance hall with a tiled floor. A room with a pure white carpet lay beyond it. "Could you take off your shoes?" Franny asked.

Take off her shoes? Who did that? Still, Ann did as she was asked. Her socks had holes in them, she saw.

They headed through the living room, the carpet whispering against her feet. They went past a dining room with an enormous table and a chandelier, and then into the kitchen. Zach was already there, sitting in a breakfast nook with a pizza box in front of him.

"Is your husband here?" Ann asked, joining him at the table and taking a slice of pizza.

"No, he's at work," Franny said. Before Ann could ask any more questions about him she said, "Zach and I were talking about our next assignment."

"You got your assignments already?" Ann asked.

"No—we're just trying to figure out what they might be. Zach wants to go to Rome."

"Rome?"

"Sure," Zach said. "What we saw was just a colony. I'd like to see the real thing, the emperors, the center of all that power."

"It's too crowded there," Ann said. "You remember what they told us—they like to go where there aren't a lot of people. Less of a chance to screw up that way."

"Yeah, but that's the challenge. Going to Rome and fooling all of them. Fitting in. I bet I could do it."

"Anyway, they never ask us for our input, just send us where they need us. You'll see—you'll probably end up at the Black Death."

"Well, there sure weren't a lot of people there."

"Fewer all the time," Ann said.

They laughed. She'd noticed this before, the gallows humor people sometimes displayed about the timebound. It was because they could do nothing to change their lives, she thought, they could only stand by and watch as the people they lived among were overrun by history. As they grew old and died, or were killed.

She didn't want to think about Hypatia now, though. She looked away from Zach, toward Franny. There was a large bruise, dark purple, on Franny's upper arm.

Their eyes met, and Franny looked away. That day's newspaper lay on the table, and Franny reached for it.

"You know that company Rengstorff Media?" she asked. Ann didn't, but she let the other woman continue. "When we left the CEO was Gayle Shapiro, wasn't it? But now the paper says that it's some guy instead, that he's been there for seven years."

"Do I look like someone who knows about CEOs?" she asked. "I don't even know what CEO stands for."

"I remembered Shapiro because this was the highest a woman had gotten on the Fortune 500," Franny said. "But now that memory's getting fainter, and I have this other memory instead. I think this was something we did—some history that we changed. And no one noticed anything, no one except us, because we were in the center of it. The people here remember that this guy was CEO for seven years—and he was, for them. That's what they lived through."

"Huh," Ann said. "But why would the company want to change the CEO of—what is it? A media company?"

"I don't know. Probably he makes a decision that turns out better for the world."

"Or for the company."

"You aren't still thinking about Core, are you? About that weird woman Meret?"

"No, not really." But she could not help remembering what Meret had told her, that the company nearly always sided with men.

She needed to change the subject; the last thing she wanted was Franny reporting her to the company. "Hey, you never said where you want to go."

"I don't care," Franny said. "It's always interesting, no matter where they send us. All I want is someplace not too hot."

They finished the pizza, and Franny walked them back to the entrance hall. As they stepped outside something whirred at the edge of Ann's vision, and she turned quickly to look at it. "Hey, a camera!" she said.

"Where?" Franny asked.

"Over there."

"I don't see anything. Anyway, why would they send a camera after us?"

Because the company was spying on them, obviously. Franny clearly didn't want to hear it, though. Even if she had seen the camera she would deny it, would convince herself it hadn't been there.

She wished she could talk to someone, discuss her doubts, get things straight in her mind. Was the company watching them? Why? Or was Franny right, had she imagined it?

Maybe it was a bee, she thought. Maybe Our Lady of Honey had sent her another message.

WHEN SHE RETURNED TO work she learned that they were going to study the thirteenth century this time. Franny was in her history class, she was pleased to see, and so was Jerry.

"Your next assignment is going to be here, Carcassonne, in the south of France," Professor Strickland said, indicating a PowerPoint map. "That's where a new religion started, the Cathars. A heretical religion, one that didn't believe in following the pope or any feudal lord. So in 1209 Pope Innocent III called for a crusade against them."

"A crusade?" Franny asked. "I thought the crusaders went to the Middle East."

"They did, usually. But the church was very intent on stamping out this heresy."

"Why?" Ann asked. "What did they do?"

"It wasn't what they did—it was what they believed. They thought there were two gods, an evil god that made this world, an imperfect world full of suffering, and a good, perfect god of love and peace. And since this world was flawed, they didn't see any reason to follow its god, or any of his authorities. So you can see why the church wanted to get rid of them."

"We're not going to be there during the crusade, are we?" Ann asked.

"No, don't worry. We'll get you out before then."

A week into the lessons Ann realized something: she didn't like this time period as much as the earlier ones they had studied. The Cathars wanted to have little to do with the material world, and some, who called themselves Perfecti, tried to keep themselves as pure as possible. They refrained from sex, they ate only fish and vegetables, they dressed without ornament and owned no property.

The word "cathar," in fact, meant "pure," Strickland said. They didn't call themselves that, though; their name for themselves was "Bonshommes," which meant "Good Men."

And that was the problem, Ann thought—there seemed no room for women in that tace. Women had been important in their last two assignments; the Kaphtorans had even worshipped them. Did patriarchal societies grow stronger as the centuries passed, as they tightened their grip on power? Or, as Meret had said, had the company nudged them in that direction?

She said nothing about these thoughts to Professor Strickland, of course. She didn't want the company to think she wasn't interested in her next assignment. And really, she didn't care whern they sent her—it was certain to be fascinating, no matter what tace it was.

In their language class Professor Tran taught them a dialect of French called Languedoc, which had been spoken in the south of France. Most of the troubadours had come from there, Tran said, singers who were attached to the court of some noble, and to help them get a feel for the language she played them videos of local performances.

The songs were about unrequited love, usually the love of the troubadour for a married woman. They felt plaintive, sorrowful, filled with yearning.

There was another reason Tran had played the troubadours' songs for them, one they learned in Professor Strickland's next class. "The crusaders are all men, and the people in Carcassonne have known each other all their lives," she said. "So the only way we can insert you into this tace is by making you troubadours. Fortunately there were women troubadours as well as men, so your appearance won't seem too odd to them."

"Troubadours?" Ann said, alarmed, and at the same time Jerry said, "But—"

Strickland held up her hand. "Yes, I know, none of you can sing. But your Facilitator this time is Tarquin Charles, and he can."

Ann remembered the man called Tarquin from the fifth floor. A computer modeler and a musician, she thought. Pretty talented.

"All you'll have to do is carry his instruments, and hand them to him when he needs them," the professor went on. "It shouldn't be too hard."

"Roadies," Jerry said. Ann laughed, but Strickland didn't seem to know the word.

"You're going to be from the Rhineland this time," the professor went on. "That'll explain your accent, and the fact that you won't know some of the customs. There were troubadours there too, called minnesingers, and they had the same kinds of songs, the same tradition of courtly love. But according to the background we'll give you you'll have traveled all over western Europe, from Germany to Spain—that way you'll have a diverse repertoire, you'll be able to come up with whatever your audience wants to hear. Well, Charles will, anyway."

A few days later they went to the costume room and tried on their clothes. Ann got a long yellow dress with a belt that rested low on her waist, a green kerchief for her head, and high uncomfortable boots. Jerry's clothes seemed more decorative, more splendid—a tight-fitting coat that reached to his thighs, hose for his legs, and boots that ended in a sharp point. He had told the class that he couldn't wear contact lenses but the company had given him some new kind of lens so that he didn't need to wear his glasses. His face looked naked, skinned.

She nearly tripped over the hem of her dress as she came out of the changing room. Good Goddess, how was she supposed to walk in this thing? A woman bustled over with a tape measure. "Some women did wear their dresses this long," Strickland said, "but since you're supposed to be traveling it wouldn't look very believable on you."

"Glad to hear it," Ann said.

The days passed quickly, and suddenly it was time to leave. They got their clothes from the costume room and put them on, and Ann noticed with relief that her dress had been shortened and the boots stretched out to fit her. Then they went to the briefing room, where they met someone Strickland introduced as Tarquin Charles.

He wasn't the man she had seen on the fifth floor after all. He was short, like the rest of the group, and nearly bald. He seemed filled with nervous energy, pacing across the briefing room as Strickland went over their final arrangements.

It was weird that he was called Tarquin, though. Probably the name was in vogue in whatever tace he came from, like all the inexplicable Brittanys and Britneys in her own time.

They went into the launch room and stood together on the platform. People handed up their bags and the musical instruments, and someone began to count down to zero.

THE SHARP PAINFUL LIGHTS diminished, and Ann stood up. She felt sick to her stomach; Da Silva had been right about time sickness getting worse with each insertion.

They had landed at the edge of a forest, a few yards from a dirt path. Charles was bent over next to her, burying the key.

"All right," he said, standing up and brushing the dirt from his hands. "Let's go."

Everyone was standing now. Ann felt relieved to see it; a part of her still expected to find one of them dead. Charles motioned them over to the path and they began to walk.

They had arrived in late May. The sun burned hotly, a brooch of heavy gold in the sky. A warm breeze eddied past, bringing smells of pine and wild strawberries and lavender, and beneath that a sharp barnyard odor of stale food and animal excrement.

As they walked they saw whole families, out working in small orchards and along rows of grape vines. "Wait a minute," Franny said. "It looks like they're picking fruit over there. But it's only May—nothing can possibly be ripe yet."

"They're worried about war, about a siege," Charles said. "They're taking everything they possibly can and storing it behind the walls. They don't want to leave anything for the army."

Now they were passing clusters of stone farmhouses standing back to back. The ground floors seemed to be used as stables or chicken coops, and stone stairs climbed the outside walls to the area where the family lived. Other, smaller buildings lay scattered in the yards, barns, henhouses, dovecotes. And at nearly every house men and women and children were hard at work, harnessing horses, taking down laundry, piling their belongings into carts.

The path joined up with an old Roman road, wider and paved in stone. The road wound back and forth up a hill, until finally they saw the walled city standing in the distance.

"All right," Jerry said, impressed.

More people crowded the street here, going up to the city. Ann and the others edged around a flock of sheep, dogs nipping at their heels, and then passed the shepherd and his family. A cart drawn by oxen rode past them, stacked high with beds and tables, pots and dishes. Where would they put them all? she wondered, but no doubt the city had made plans for a siege.

Now they could see turrets rising above the walls, capped like mushrooms. A few more turns brought them up to the walls themselves, a patchwork of red brick and large pale stones from the old Roman fortifications.

A line of people had formed in front of the gates. The four of them shuffled forward slowly, finally coming to the gates as the sun began to set.

Two guards stood there. "We're—" Charles began.

"Troubadours," one of the guards said, squinting out at them. "I can see that. It isn't a good time, to be honest."

"We know the pope's thinking about a crusade," Charles said. "We'd like to come in anyway."

"You won't have much luck here. I doubt the viscount feels like music."

"That's our business, though, isn't it?"

"All right." He squinted again. "Don't say I didn't warn you."

He stepped aside, and they headed into the city.

"Not much of a reception," Franny said in English.

"Quiet," Charles said. "We'll talk when we get to the inn."

Charles was right, Ann saw. There were too many people here for them to talk comfortably. They hurried to their inn and went up to their rooms.

Charles shut the door behind him and began to pace. Ann, Franny, and Jerry sat on the beds. "The crusade isn't for two months yet, right?" Jerry asked.

"Well, but they don't know that," Ann said. "For all they know the pope's army's coming straight here, instead of Béziers."

"So what do we do now?" Franny asked. "What's our assignment?"

"We have to get close to the viscount," Charles said. "His name is Raimond-Roger Trencavel, and his territories include Béziers and Carcassonne. Ideally, we want him to invite us to a meal, or somewhere else private."

"But—well, you heard that man," Ann said. "He probably won't be interested in music."

"We'll just have to be extra charming then, won't we?" Charles said.

It was growing dark outside; as usual the company had sent them in during the afternoon, to give them time to settle in. "We'll go out and find dinner, and see Trencavel tomorrow," Charles said.

17

THEY SET OUT FOR the castle the next morning. Although Ann had seen the videos she had retained a picture of Carcassonne as a typical medieval town, with winding streets, small one- and two-story houses, churches, and a market square. But at every turn she came upon something new, surprising: a fountain covered in bright geometric tiles; a garden almost hidden from the street; a stall with a roof of striped cloth, selling meat heavy with spices. And the people were varied as well; she saw a man wearing a turban, and then a group of people with dark skin and straight hair who looked as if they might have come from India. Carcassonne itself wasn't a harbor but there were many towns in Languedoc that were, welcoming ships filled with spices and African ivory, sending out strawberries and pears, Cordovan leather and Toledo blades. And the city was next door to Muslim Spain, with its mathematics and medicine, architecture and poetry, perhaps the most advanced culture in Europe.

She had read historical novels, of course, but little from before the Renaissance, and she had always pictured the Middle Ages and earlier as very boring: a dull procession of peasants and landowners, men and women who worked without ceasing, breaking their routine only to go to church. Instead she had seen Copts and Jews, goddess worshippers and mathematicians—and now she was about to meet heretics.

"Trencavel isn't a heretic himself, of course," Charles said, breaking into her thoughts. "But he believes in what you would call freedom of religion, the right of everyone to worship as they like. And it's almost certain that some members of his family are Cathars."

Why was he explaining all of this? They had studied it with Professor Strickland, learned it until they could give the lectures themselves. Ann would rather look around her, take in the feel of the tace, the people's attitudes and expressions, the way she had done in Knossos and Alexandria.

Charles continued to talk, though, and she tuned him out. Probably, she thought, he was one of those people who liked the sound of his own voice.

She soon became aware of one difference between this city and the others she had been to. Garbage flowed down the middle of the streets, channels carrying offal and human waste. It smelled and looked terrible, and the channels overflowed in places; she had to be careful where she put her feet. As she watched a pig waddled to the edge and nuzzled at something, and she had to look away.

It was strange, she thought, that a city that had existed twenty-five hundred years ago had been cleaner than this tace. Progress was not the straight line she had thought it was; all through history things were discovered and then lost again. Someone in Muslim Spain had invented the steam engine, Professor Strickland had said.

The viscount's castle looked like the outer wall, with the same mismatched stone and squat towers. A stone bridge built over arches led to the castle doors. A guard on the other side of the bridge asked them their business, and when Charles said they were troubadours he nodded and let them in.

"That was easy," Jerry said, laughing nervously.

"Hush," Charles said.

They went through a series of cramped dark rooms, cold and uncomfortable-looking, with uneven floors. The castle smelled of burning wood and cooked meat, though none of the rooms they saw had fireplaces. Two dogs ran past, frisked and tangled in a mock battle, and hurried out again.

There were few hallways; instead, one room led into the next, and every so often they found themselves interrupting women at their sewing or men reading aloud. "Do we know where we're going?" Ann asked. Her voice echoed off the stone walls.

Charles said nothing. They came to a closed door guarded by two men, who ushered them into another room. This one was larger than the others, with candles glittering along the walls, tapestries to keep out the cold, and, Ann was glad to see, a fire burning in a fireplace. There was even a carpet, in knotted squares of red and gold and green.

A large man sat in a carved wooden chair. He wore crimson silks and velvets, and he was clean-shaven, like most of the men of the south. Charles bowed and introduced himself.

"Very good," Trencavel said. He grinned. "We love music, don't we?" Several people in the shadows murmured agreement. He hummed for a while and then broke off. "Do you know 'All the Birds Are Leaving'?" he asked.

"Of course, my lord," Charles said.

"Wonderful! And your own tunes? Do you have something new for us?"

"We do. Many things." Charles opened one of the sacks they had brought, but the viscount raised his hand to stop him.

"Not now," he said. "You'll play for us at dinner."

"Yes, my lord," Charles said. "Thank you."

"My man here will take you somewhere you can practice," Trencavel said. "Dinner is in an hour."

An hour? It wasn't even noon; dinner must mean something else hern. Even Charles looked a little panicky, though his face slipped back into blandness a moment later.

A man came toward them out of the shadows. "This way," he said.

When they got to their room Charles took a tablet out of his leather bag, unrolled it, and scrolled through it quickly. "Ah, here it is, by Bernart de Ventadorn," he said.

He brought out the lute, tuned it, and began to play. "We don't have a lot of time here," he said. "You'll have to learn which instruments to give me, and when."

"Do you really have your own songs?" Ann asked. "Something new you can play?"

"Not mine, no. But I can play songs that haven't been composed yet, things I know he hasn't heard before. 'I Dare to Claim'—Peire Cardenal will write that a few years from now."

He started another song, but Ann barely heard it. She felt as if she had just discovered new, unknown rooms within her mind, as if it had stretched outward in order to encompass this new idea. "But—but if this Cardenal comes to hear it, and he starts singing it, and then—well, who really wrote it? No one did, right? Not you, and not him either—it just appeared."

"We don't have time for those kinds of questions. Franny, you'll give me the guitar here. Then when I come to the end of this part I'll need one of the drums, that one over there."

Ann could not get the idea out of her head, though, and she thought about it while Charles practiced the next song, missing her cues once or twice. If she used a proverb hern, "A stitch in time saves nine," maybe, and it survived until the twentieth century and first time she heard it—where did it come from? What if someone introduced Bach's cello suites, or Einstein's theory of relativity . . .

"Ann," Charles said sharply. "The lute, please."

All too soon the viscount's man came to get them, and they followed him through the castle. They came to a hall holding a long table, and the man led them up a staircase into a gallery. A wooden screen stood at the front of the gallery, carved into diamond lattices.

Another group of men was already there, watching them as they took their places. "Who do we have here?" one of them asked.

"We're troubadours," Charles said. "We're—"

"Of course you're troubadours," the man said. "So are we—we're all troubadours. I thought we were the only ones playing today, that's all."

"He wants to see who's better, I suppose," someone else said.

"Who are you people?" the first man asked.

"My name's Charles, and these are—"

"Charles? Never heard of you. Well, I don't see any challenges here."

"I wouldn't be so sure of that, sir," Charles said. "And you never gave us your name."

"Peire Raimon de Tolosa," the man said.

The name was familiar from their classes. Charles nodded, and Peire Raimon seemed gratified to be recognized.

People were coming into the banqueting room now, the women in long gowns and fur, the men in jackets and hose. Jewels sparked as they moved, making glittering constellations in the candlelight. They found their places and stood behind their chairs, talking quietly.

Trencavel entered, a woman on his arm. She looked, Ann thought, a little like a fish, with protruding eyes and lips that seemed to lie flat against her face. "That's his wife, the Viscountess Agnes," Charles said softly.

The couple sat together at the end of the table, and the others took their places. The talk grew louder, boisterous, and a smell rose into the gallery, of unwashed bodies and heavy perfume. Dogs ran into the room, barking, and dived under the table.

The viscount clapped his hands and the noise faded. "We have two men to sing for our pleasure today," he said. "Peire Raimon de Tolosa, who I'm sure you've heard of, and—" He looked up at the minstrel's gallery. "I never asked who you were, did I?"

"Charles, my lord."

The company laughed softly, at the contrast between the melodic sound of the first name and the lone syllable of the second. "Charles. Why don't you start?"

Charles nodded. He did not look nervous, but his hand trembled as he motioned for his lute. As he played, though, his fingers began to move through the chords with confidence, and his voice sang out strongly into the room below. He was playing "All the Birds Are Leaving," Ann realized, the song Trencavel had asked for earlier.

The people below applauded when he finished, and then it was Peire Raimon's turn. He raised his lute, bowed to the assembled company, and set his fingers to the strings.

He sang about his love for a lady, a woman of high birth married to a nobleman. As he came to the second stanza he lifted his head and looked straight through the lattice at Trencavel's wife Agnes.

They had discussed this in class with Professor Strickland. It was a convention of troubadour poetry to address the lord's wife, Strickland had said, a way of flattering both the lord and his lady. But Ann had read the poems and seen the naked desire in them, the sexual yearning, and now, watching as the drama played out in front of her, it seemed to her as if Peire Raimon was courting Agnes. No, more than that—as if he was making love to her, before her husband's eyes.

She glanced at Trencavel but he sat silent, his face impassive. How could he bear to listen to this, to hear his wife's beauties praised so intimately? Agnes seemed unmoved as well, but as Ann watched she shook her head so that her hair fell to the sides of her face, and she smiled directly at Peire Raimon. No one in the hall would have noticed it, but Ann saw her clearly, her face changing, transformed into something beautiful under his magic.

After Peire Raimon finished Charles started on his "new" song, "I Dare to Claim," by Cardenal. It had been—would be—composed after the crusade and the conquest by the north, and it sounded different from all the other songs they had practiced—weary, resigned, done with things of this world. He was free of chains now, the troubadour said, speaking of his lover's hold on him—yet speaking ironically, since he had fallen under the chains of the northerners.

It was a new style, more cynical and less joyful than the songs written before the conquest. Peire Raimon turned to Charles, surprised and impressed, and Ann felt strangely vindicated. One for our team, she thought.

When it was his turn Peire Raimon sang about a man who wished that his lord was far away, so far that he could lie in his lover's bed and not worry about her husband interrupting them. With each stanza he sent the lord further and further from his castle, until finally he banished him to Jerusalem, where, he said, the lord became religious and entered a monastery.

Everyone laughed and clapped. Trencavel laughed too, and raised his wine cup in a salute, and Peire Raimon bowed to him and Agnes.

Charles began a song she didn't recognize, one they hadn't practiced. It was another poem about a man's love for a high-born lady, the wife of a lord, and as he sang it he seemed to change, to become more alive, intense. He'd gotten caught up in the competition, she saw, determined to meet Peire Raimon's challenge.

Lady Agnes turned toward him, her eyes shining, her lips parted as if in a kiss. The rest of the company watched the two of them with their mouths open, shocked and gratified at the same time. It was like looking at a car accident, Ann thought, or a sport that could turn violent at any time.

Finally the dinner ended. The viscount and his wife stood and the others followed, their voices louder now.

The troubadours went down into the banqueting hall, mingling with the diners. Her questions were piling up, threatening to spill out into the crowd, but she knew Charles would want her to wait until they were behind closed doors. Someone nearby praised Peire Raimon, and someone else said Peire Raimon had better look out, this new man was the best he'd ever heard.

"Listen, man," a voice said.

They turned. It was Trencavel, cutting through the crowd to speak to Charles. "God gave you talent, that's certain enough," the viscount said. "I'd like to offer you my hospitality, here in the castle. If, that is, you don't have somewhere else to go."

"I'd be honored, sir," Charles said, bowing.

"Wonderful, wonderful. This way, my friend."

Trencavel led them through more rooms, each opening out of the next like a honeycomb. If Peire Raimon did make love to Viscountess Agnes, Ann thought, where on earth could they go in this castle to be alone?

They reached a hallway, only the second or third Ann had seen in the castle, and the viscount headed down it. "Maybe my cousin's right," he said. "Maybe the world is a vile place, already lost to the Evil One. But you can't think that way, can you? Not when there's meat and drink, and companionship, and beautiful women . . . And that music you played—how can that be evil? It gives you joy—it even made me think of God. Not very often, I have to admit." He grinned, then became serious. "You have to take what happiness you can, especially now. The crusaders are on their way, you know. Who knows where we'll be, this time next year?"

He wasn't expecting an answer, of course, but Ann could have given him one. Trencavel would go to the crusaders' camp, thinking that he could negotiate with them, and he would be held as a prisoner of war until he died there soon after. Or was killed—the history books were divided.

The hallway was cold, but Ann felt a chill that came from somewhere else, the winds sweeping through the years. Seshat, she thought.

A group of men went into one of the rooms, singing loudly: Peire Raimon and his troubadours. Peire Raimon turned to look at them, briefly, then looked again. "Good day, my lord!" he said.

"You've met Charles here," Trencavel said. "He'll be taking the rooms next to you."

Peire Raimon scowled at Charles. Well, great, Ann thought. We aren't even here for a day, and we've made an enemy already.

"You can get some dinner in the smaller banqueting hall," the viscount said to Charles. "I'll see you tomorrow." He turned to Peire Raimon and said, "Both of you."

Ann waited impatiently until Charles had closed the door behind them and then asked, "What on earth was that all about?"

"What?" Charles asked.

"Is Peire Raimon sleeping with Agnes? How could he say those things? And how could Trencavel just sit there and take it—why doesn't he have him thrown in the dungeon?"

"They don't have a dungeon."

"You know what I mean. And you—" She wanted to ask him why he had sung the songs he had, if he was courting the viscountess as well. But she had vowed to be more professional, to finish this assignment without getting into trouble.

"You should have gotten all this from Professor Strickland," he said. "It's a convention, nothing more. No, Peire

Raimon isn't sleeping with the lord's wife. And I won't be either, if that's what you were going to ask."

"It sure seemed like it," Franny said. Franny the romantic, Ann thought, pleased the other woman was taking her side. "I wasn't expecting anything nearly that steamy."

"I bet they *are* sleeping together," Ann said. "We don't have cameras inside the castle, right?"

Charles sighed. "If they were, Trencavel would have thrown him in the dungeon, like you said. Figuratively speaking, of course. He wouldn't let the man stay here and give him gifts, that's for sure."

"Maybe he doesn't know," Franny said.

"That's enough of that," Charles said. "We have to find dinner, and then get our things from the inn—Franny and Jerry, you'll go and do that. And I have to practice. You're right about one thing—I wasn't expecting so many of those songs either. We're going to have to step up our game." He took out his tablet and scrolled through it.

The troubadours did not perform at the smaller meal that evening, to Ann's relief. Charles, she knew, had hoped to be seated near the viscount, but they were placed far from the fire and light, nearly in darkness.

Afterward they went back to their rooms; she anticipated more practice but Charles shook his head.

"They go to bed early here," he said. "They're zany careful about wasting candles, and we should be too. And it's better if we keep to their schedule."

The viscount had given them two rooms; she and Franny took one, and Charles and Jerry the other. It was far too early to sleep, and she thought that they would stay up and talk about the day's events, but to her surprise the other woman was soon snoring gently. Maybe she was tired from her walk through the city; they had gotten lost more than once, she'd said.

That was fine, though—she had plenty to think about. "They're zany careful," Charles had said, and she had once heard Walker say something similar. Did "zany" mean "very" where they came from, in the future?

But the most important thing, of course, was that strange triangle, Trencavel, Peire Raimon, and Agnes. A rectangle now, with Charles. Maybe she could find out where the viscountess slept and wait outside her room, see where she went. Ann would bet anything she ended up next door, with Peire Raimon. She should have made that bet, with Charles . . .

She fell asleep, and woke the next morning to see cold golden light coming through the windows.

THEY PLAYED FOR THE viscount and his wife that day, and for the next few days. Ann watched the couple closely, but Trencavel seemed as jolly as ever, and pleased with Peire Raimon's music. Perhaps it was true that these songs were normal for this tace, Ann thought, but there must be plenty of troubadours who took advantage of that convention, who seduced high-born women with heady poetry.

The poems themselves spoke in highly exaggerated terms about love—the lover burned, he writhed in fever, he would die without his lady. She had been envious of the clothing Charles and Jerry got to wear, had thought their finery meant that they had higher status in this tace, but now she wondered if the men dressed that way to impress women, if it was really the women who held the power hern. If, in some strange way, this was another Knossos.

One day Trencavel stopped Charles on his way to the banqueting hall. They were too far ahead for Ann to hear what he said, but she saw the viscount take a ring off his finger and give it to Charles, and then say something that made Charles grin. "Of course, my lord," Charles was saying, when she caught up with him.

He slid the ring over his finger and moved to catch the light coming in through a window. It was a ruby, its sparks flashing like fire.

"Whoa," she said. She wondered if he got to keep it, but she remembered her vow not to ask too many questions. "What did he say to you?"

"Later. You're supposed to be my servant—I'm not going to tell you my business in front of everybody."

Peire Raimon noticed the ring as soon as Charles put his hands to his lute. He scowled again; it was becoming habitual with him. Ann had already figured out that the viscount was making him jealous on purpose, stirring up rivalry between the troubadours so that each of them would strive to outdo the other.

Still, it wasn't the viscount who was on the receiving end of Peire Raimon's hatred. Their room had been searched the day before, some of their things moved from their places, and Charles was certain that Peire Raimon had done it. Fortunately Charles's tablet had been hidden, in a secret pocket deep inside his bag.

And what had Trencavel said to Charles that had him looking so pleased? She waited impatiently for the dinner to end, for them to be allowed back to their rooms.

"We've been invited to an evening meal with the viscount," Charles said, when the door had been safely closed behind them.

"And that's good, right?" Ann said. "You said that's part of our assignment. So now what?"

"Now I write to the company and tell them we've gotten this far. And then we go take a walk, pick up a package."

"I thought communication with the company took a lot of energy."

"That's right."

"But—" She tried to work it out. "So this package—it's important, right? But why didn't the company send it along with us?"

Charles said nothing. He worked at his computer for a while, then, when he was finished, he collected a few things and wrapped them in a blanket. As they left their rooms the door next to theirs opened, and Peire Raimon and two of his men stepped outside.

"You know what I wonder?" Peire Raimon asked. His men stood in front of them, blocking the hallway. "I wonder why I never heard of you. Someone who plays that well, who writes poetry the way you do—you can't have come from nowhere."

"I'm from the Rhineland," Charles said.

"The Rhineland." Peire Raimon leaned against the wall. He was drunk, Ann realized. "Well, *someone* should know your name. I talked to some people, some friends of mine . . . You know what we think?"

He stopped; he seemed to have gotten lost. "No, what do you think?" Charles said, prompting him.

"We think you're a spy. A spy from the pope. You're writing to him, telling him all about the castle. The vulner— vulnerable places, where they can get in and kill us all. I'm going to tell Trencavel."

"You do that. He could use a good laugh."

"All right then." Charles moved toward the men, and they backed away.

As soon as they stepped outside the castle they felt the welcome heat of summer. The streets were nearly empty, even the merchants gone; they passed the storefronts for a barber, a carpenter, a money-lender, all of them shut and dark. The few people they saw hurried past as if a storm were about to break. Rumors Ann had overheard in the banquet hall had the pope's army heading for Carcassonne.

"Do you think he'll really talk to Trencavel?" Franny asked.

Charles laughed. "Peire Raimon? I wouldn't worry about him."

They came to the gate. Several guards stood there; Ann looked for the man they had met earlier but didn't see him. "We'll be back this evening," Charles told them.

The guards stared at him in amazement. "The army'll be here any day now," one of them said.

"We'll take our chances."

The farmhouses were all deserted, along with the orchards and vineyards. A hen squawked somewhere, and a bird flew overhead, a straight line against the blue sky. The silence seemed eerie, even sinister, and without talking about it they drew closer together.

Finally they reached the grove of trees where Charles had hidden the key. He dug for it, lifted it out, and manipulated a few of its wheels. "You might want to close your eyes," he said.

Ann ignored him. Something shimmered, and then a whorl of colors shot from the key, colors that seemed wrong somehow, that should never have been put together in that fashion. Things moved to form impossible geometries, with too many corners, or too few. Her eyes closed involuntarily, and when she opened them she saw . . . an angel.

She blinked. Someone stood there, someone who would have looked like a man if it were not for the wings rising from his back. He had long golden hair, amber eyes, and, she could not help noticing, no genitals at all. She had never seen anyone with an expression like the one he wore, a look of innocent joy at everything around him.

Charles shook out the blanket. A few things dropped out but he ignored them and threw the blanket over the man's shoulders. Then he picked up a pair of hose and tried to fit them on over his legs. "Here—help me with this, one of you," he said.

Jerry moved forward and they struggled together. The man made no effort to help them; he seemed not to know about hose, or blankets, or anything from the human world at all.

"Who—who is he?" Ann asked.

"Bioengineered," Charles said. They'd gotten the hose on somehow, and he bent and picked up a pair of shoes. "Haven't you seen our bioengineering before? You shouldn't be that surprised."

That's right—she remembered the griffins in Kaphtor. She had never seen anything so beautiful, though. Even wrapped up, his body hidden inside the blanket, the man looked like something from the childhood of the world, before everything had gotten so messed up. He gazed around him and smiled.

"Does he talk?" she asked.

"No. We haven't been able to bioengineer anything with consciousness, unfortunately. He's about as intelligent as a bird. Jerry, could you get the other shoe?"

"What are we going to do with him?"

"I'll tell you when it's time." Jerry shoved the shoe on somehow and Charles turned the man around, back toward the city. "All you need to know is that we can't let anyone see him, not until we're ready."

"How are we going to get him through the gate then?" Franny asked.

"It'll be all right if he's wrapped up," Charles said. He stepped back and studied him. The man began to wander off, and Charles grabbed his arm and pointed him in the right direction. "They'll probably think he's a hunchback. I hope so, anyway."

Charles re-buried the key and they headed toward the road, Charles's hand still on the man's arm. Something moved through the trees behind them, and Ann spun around. Branches shook, and leaves pattered to the ground. Then whatever it was scurried off into the distance.

"What was that?" Ann asked.

"Nothing. An animal."

Was it? It had sounded big, the size of a human. But there were boars in the forests here, and deer, animals large enough to cause the disturbance she had heard.

Still, she couldn't shake the idea that someone had been watching them. We can't let anyone see him, Charles had said. But what if someone had been standing among the trees? What if he or she had already seen him?

They began walking. She turned back several times before they got to the gate, but once again the streets were deserted.

The guards only glanced at them before passing them through. Finally they reached the castle and their rooms, and they sank down gratefully on the beds.

"He can't leave here until we're ready," Charles said. "One of you will have to stay with him at all times."

The man squatted suddenly. Charles cursed and ran for the chamber pot, then struggled to pull the man's hose down his legs. But even as the man urinated into the pot he looked vaguely delighted, as though this was the first time he had ever done such a thing. He must have a hole there somewhere, Ann thought. But she didn't want to think about his plumbing, wanted to concentrate instead on his extraordinary beauty.

She volunteered to guard him the next day. When the others had gone she studied him as he moved around the room, looking at things, touching them, trying to put them in his mouth. The feathers on his wings were the color of pearls, of sunlight breaking through the edge of a cloud.

She reached out and stroked one of them, and he turned and looked at her, seeming puzzled. "Can you fly?" she asked, moving the wing up and down to show him what she meant.

He flapped his wings slightly. "That's right," she said. She smiled to encourage him. "Flying. Can you do that?"

He raised his wings high into the air. They were so huge that he couldn't straighten them completely, and they bent against the ceiling. Then he lowered them; there was a whoosh like a sail coming around, and a blast of air blew past her. But he hadn't managed to get off the ground at all.

Probably he was too heavy, she thought. Maybe they couldn't give him lighter bones, or they didn't need him to fly. He flapped his wings again and again, each time harder, but nothing happened.

His puzzled expression returned. They'd given him bird DNA, she thought, and somewhere in his mind he expects to fly, he knows instinctively how it would feel. She felt a sudden frisson of sorrow, of desolation.

They were too high-handed, those people in the company. They meddled in people's lives, not just in the past but in their own present. They'd changed so many things they thought they were gods, that they could do whatever they liked. Whose human DNA had they used to create their angel? Had they even asked his permission beforehand?

She remembered Meret, that first time they had met, at the cemetery in Knossos. "Say you started by helping people, preventing a war," she had said. "And then, little by little, you saw ways you could help yourself, get some more power and resources for you and your friends."

Even she and Franny and Zach had laughed at the time-bound, had felt themselves superior to people mired in history. What must it be like for the company, for a group able to influence anything they wanted, anywhere in time?

Her thoughts brought her back to Core again. Was the company wrong to meddle in history like this? She wished she'd had more time with Meret, that she'd been able to learn more.

The man had stopped trying to fly. He'd found a package of food Charles had left, wrapped in cloth, and was trying to put the whole thing in his mouth.

"No, wait a minute," she said, taking the package away from him. She opened it and held out a piece of beef. He pecked at it quickly, like a bird, and when he finished he smiled at her, clearly asking for more.

CHARLES WAS IN A good mood when they came back from the banquet. "We're having supper with the viscount tonight," he said. He paced back and forth in the small room, while the others sat on the bed. "So here's what we'll do. We're going to create a sort of theater for him, one where each of you will play a part. I'll be outside the dining hall for most of it, setting the stage, so you'll have to engage him in conversation. Are you with me so far?"

What did he think? It wasn't like his instructions were hard to understand. Though she didn't know what she could say to a viscount; it was difficult enough just talking to ordinary people. Well, at least Franny would be there, and she seemed to have no trouble coming up with conversation. She nodded along with everyone else.

"All right, good," Charles said. "We'll do some role-playing first—I'll be Trencavel. Talk to me."

They played through various scenarios, each of them suggesting different topics of conversation, and then Charles said it was time to leave. He looked around for the winged man and found him sitting on the bed, gazing out at them placidly.

Charles threw the blanket over him and herded him toward the door. "Come along, all of you," he said.

"Wait," Ann said. "Why are we doing all of this? What's going to happen?"

"Don't worry about that. I want you to react naturally, just like the viscount."

"Well, but that man's supposed to be an angel, right? That's what you want Trencavel to think, anyway. So you want him to have some kind of religious experience, make him think he's seen a miracle."

"That's right. Now come on—we have to get there before he does." He picked up the sack holding his lute.

They left their rooms, the winged man shrouded—like a corpse, she couldn't help thinking. Why did it bother her so much, that they were about to deceive Trencavel this way? Was it that religion was such a personal thing, that she thought people should make up their own minds, not be tricked into some belief or other? What if the company had shown her an angel with no explanation—wouldn't she think she'd had a true religious experience?

Or was it something to do with her earlier thought, that the company was playing god to these unsuspecting people? That they'd grown so strong they were just using their power for power's sake?

"How did they create him?" she asked. "The angel?"

"How should I know?" Charles said. "I'm not a bioengineer."

They reached the smaller banquet hall and went inside. A door connected with another room, and Charles slipped through it, pulling the angel along with him. "Don't sit down until he comes," he called back to them.

"Well, I know that," Ann said quietly to Franny. They went to the chairs and stood behind them.

The viscount and his wife came in soon after. "Where's Charles?" he asked.

"He's getting some music ready," Franny said, giving him the answer they'd rehearsed. "He wants it to be a surprise."

"A surprise?" Trencavel said. He rubbed his hands together and grinned benignly at the people around him. "Good. I like surprises, don't I?"

He and Viscountess Agnes took their seats, and the rest of them followed. Then, unexpectedly, another woman came into the banquet hall and sat next to the viscount.

"This is my cousin, Maheut," he said.

Maheut was wearing a simple black gown, with a black kerchief over her hair. "She thinks she's perfect," Trencavel said, winking at her.

"Don't listen to him," Maheut said, smiling. "I'm a Bonhomme. Or I suppose you could say a Bonnefemme."

A Cathar, a heretic. The viscount must have a great deal of confidence in them, to trust them with such a dangerous family secret.

"One of the Perfecti, though," Trencavel said. "As I said, perfect. Though don't worry, cousin—I've instructed the kitchen to make food you can eat."

Trencavel clapped his hands and a serving girl came in, carrying a heavy platter. She had come through a different door than the one Charles was hiding behind, Ann noticed. Well, of course—Charles would have scouted everything out first, found the best place to conceal himself.

"Swans, to begin with," Trencavel said. The girl brought the platter around to him, and he speared one of the slices eagerly with his knife. Another girl appeared with a platter of fish, which she carried over to Maheut. They began to eat—all except Maheut, who paused to say a prayer over her food first.

There was silence for a while, and then Maheut looked across the table at Franny. "You look as if you have some questions," she said. "It's all right—I won't be offended by anything you say."

"Watch out—she wants to convert you," Trencavel said.

"We don't convert people," Maheut said. "We simply tell them what we believe, and let them decide for themselves."

"Well, all right," Franny said. "Isn't it hard to—well, to give everything up the way you have? Don't you want to eat meat sometimes, and drink wine, and get married?"

"Are you married?" Maheut asked her.

Franny looked startled. She was single according to her cover story; no husband would let his wife run free all over Europe. "No," she said.

Maheut shook her head. "I thought you were, for some reason. Still, you must know that a great many marriages are unhappy. Especially among noble-born men and women—their marriages are arranged by their fathers, to make alliances between families. That's why so many of them enjoy your songs, the ones about falling in love, and lying with anyone you desire."

She took a sip from the cup in front of her; unlike the others, who were drinking wine, she had been given only water. "I think that's the question you really want to ask, about lying with a man. And yes, I do miss it, very much sometimes. But I know that it was the false god of this world who invented all of that, to snare us, to make us desire carnality and forget about the soul."

Professor Strickland had discussed this, of course. And yet Ann, who had never had any religious inclinations before she had gone traveling in time, who felt reverence for no one except possibly an ancient forgotten goddess, was shocked to hear the god that most people worshipped described in such negative terms.

"But don't you think—"

Franny stopped. Music came from somewhere, not lutes or drums but sounds the viscount and his family had never heard in their lives. A rising and falling wail like a theremin, that spooky wind that blew through a thousand horror movies. The worst kind of cliché, Ann thought—though of course it would not be a cliché for the viscount, or any of the people in this tace.

"By our Lady!" Trencavel said. "What—what in heaven's name is that?"

The winged man came into the room, wearing only his hose. A light shone around him, making his fair hair glow like a halo. His amber eyes were shot with gold.

The viscountess uttered a small scream and put her hands to her mouth. The viscount scraped back his chair and started to stand, then sat back down. Even Maheut, who had seemed unflappable, looked startled.

The music changed, to a soft chorus of soprano voices. "There is a higher world than this one," another voice said. It was Charles speaking, of course; the angel could not talk. Still, everyone stared raptly at the winged man standing in front of them. "One not mired in falsehood, in material things. You must change your life. You must turn to the true god. The god who sits above this world, who—"

The serving girl came into the room, carrying a ceramic bowl of fruit. She gaped at the angel, her eyes wide, then dropped the bowl and fell to her knees. The bowl smashed against the stone floor. The angel froze, his eyes filled with terror, and then fled into the hallway.

CHARLES SWORE LOUDLY FROM the next room. The music stopped. Charles rushed through the banquet hall and outside, following the angel. "What was that, man?" the viscount asked.

"Come on—we have to find him," Charles called back.

They all hurried out into the hallway, then split up in different directions. Ann found herself sprinting through rooms and corridors, looking around frantically, her mind replaying the scene in the banquet hall. Had they failed their assignment? Clearly Charles had wanted Trencavel to become a Cathar (though why?), but would he believe he had been visited by an angel? Or would he realize that Charles had tricked him?

The banquet hall. She remembered the winged man eating from her hand, taking tiny bites like a bird. A servant was heading toward her; she stopped him and asked the way to the kitchen.

It turned out to be a long way from the smaller banquet hall, a long way from nearly everything. They'd built it at a distance to keep fires from spreading into the heart of the castle, she remembered that from her lessons. Finally she saw the small arched hallway the servant had described, and she ran down it, breathing hard, and turned into the final doorway.

The angel stood there, calmly pecking at a chicken set out on a table. All of the kitchen servants were on their knees, watching him, their eyes wide with wonder. The serving girl was among them—so that was how he had found the kitchen, Ann thought, by following her. Someone was muttering a prayer.

Ann went toward him and grasped him by the arm. "Come along," she said.

He continued to eat, ignoring her. She broke off a chicken wing and held it out to him, and he followed it uncomplaining, out of the kitchen and down the hallway.

There was no one nearby, but she could not imagine that they could make their way through the castle without drawing attention. She hurried into one of the rooms, still holding his arm, and grabbed a blanket and draped it over his wings.

He ignored this and continued to peck at the chicken. When he was finished he pulled away from her, back toward the kitchen. "This way," she said, forcing him forward, trying not to become angry at him. She held onto the pity she had felt, the anger at what had been done to him.

He stopped pulling and became docile again. Probably he couldn't keep anything in his mind for very long, she thought.

She got lost more than once on the way back, but she kept going without asking for directions, thinking that the fewer people who noticed them the better. Finally, after a long time of wandering through the castle, she found their rooms.

They were the first ones back. The angel dropped to one of the beds as soon as they were inside and fell asleep a moment later. She was tempted to lie down as well, but she had to keep an eye on him, at least until the others returned. As she watched he made an attempt to turn over, but he was stopped by the bulk of his wings and had to roll back on his stomach.

A moment later the door opened and Charles entered, carrying the sack with his lute. "Where did you find him?" he asked.

No "Well done," or "Good for you," she thought. Why was the company so stingy with its praise?

"In the kitchen."

"Ah. That makes sense. Well—thank you."

He seemed to begrudge her the words, as though he had a limited supply of gratitude and was afraid it would run out. Still, at least he had said it. "You're welcome," she said.

The angel tried to turn over again, then whimpered softly and fell back on his stomach. "Poor guy," she said.

Charles looked puzzled, no doubt wondering why it bothered her. "Well, we aren't finished here, I'm afraid. We have to get him back to the company right away, before someone spots him."

He glanced around the room without taking any of it in. "Where were the others, did you see them?"

She shook her head.

"We can't wait for them. I'll leave them a note—" He looked around again, then seemed to realize that they didn't have any pens or paper. "Well, it doesn't matter. Come on, let's go."

He woke up the angel and threw the blanket over his wings, then picked up his sack. The door opened and Franny and Jerry came in.

"Hey—where was he?" Franny said, seeing the winged man.

"Never mind that," Charles said. "We have to get to the key."

"What about the viscount?" Ann asked. "Shouldn't we get back to the banquet?"

"It's best to leave him alone for now, to think about what just happened."

They hurried out of the castle and down to the gates, then back along the Roman road. As they went Charles told the others how Ann had found the winged man.

Finally they reached the grove. Charles handed the angel over to Ann, then knelt in the dirt and began to dig. He found nothing in his first few handfuls, and he frowned and dug faster.

"Are you sure that's where you buried it?" Franny asked.

"Of course I'm sure," he said.

The rest of them went to dig alongside him, but none of them found the key. Charles sat back on his heels and looked around him, studying the trees and the road.

"We align the key with various landmarks," he said. "I used that branch there, and this stone . . . It should be right here."

"I thought I heard someone watching us that time, remember?" Ann said. "Maybe they took it after we left."

Charles said nothing. He returned to the hole he had made and dug a while longer. Now what? Were they trapped here? No, wait—he still had the computer as a backup. "You can send a message to the company, right?" she asked.

Charles stood up again and brushed his hands together. "That's right." He opened the sack and brought out his computer.

"I was wondering why you were still carrying your lute," Franny said, laughing.

He ignored her, unrolling the computer and placing the keyboard on the ground, then typing for several minutes. "You're going to have to stand back," he said finally. "You don't want to be caught up along with him."

Ann let go of the angel, and they all moved a few feet away. "Here we go," Charles said. "Close your eyes."

Once again Ann kept her eyes open, and once again she was swept by a feeling of wrongness, of strange colors and unnatural geometries. Something doesn't want people to travel in time, she thought. Then a vortex of color reached out for the angel, and he was gone.

"All right then," Charles said.

His voice seemed to come from a long way away. Ann was still staring at the void where the angel had been, and she forced herself to look away. Charles rolled up the computer and headed for the road.

"Wait a minute," Ann said, hurrying after him. "What about the key? We need to get it back, right?"

"Well, I'd like to find it," Charles said. "I have to take it inside the walls, for one thing—the crusaders will get here in about a week. But it doesn't matter all that much."

"Really? But what if—if some archaeologist digs it up years later, and wonders where it came from?"

"That happens less often than you might think. The Law of Conservation of History. And even if they do find it, they'll just assume that someone made a mistake, that it came from a higher stratum, a later one." He paused, then said, "Still, keep your ears open, and if you hear something let me know. People who find things like that tend to talk about them."

"Can they use it?" Franny asked. "Turn it on somehow?"

Charles laughed. "One of the timebound? Can you imagine Trencavel learning how to travel in time? No, it's safeguarded against them."

"Well, that's a relief."

"What's going to happen to the angel?" Ann asked.

"How should I know?" Charles said. "He'll be used on another assignment, maybe. Probably."

"Why didn't we go back with him? Is there more to our assignment?"

Charles looked up and down the road but it was deserted; nearly everyone had gone behind the walls of the city. "Yes, there's more," he said. "We have to make sure the viscount has a conversion experience, that he becomes a Cathar. And if we can't be certain of him we'll have to stay here until August, to see if—"

"Why?" Ann said.

"What?"

"Why do we want Trencavel to convert? What happens if he does?"

Charles stopped. "Don't you listen to anything we say?" he said. "We can't know that. We have to finish out our assignment with no knowledge of the consequences, otherwise it might influence our actions. They'll answer all your questions when you get back."

"Well, but they don't, not always," she said, remembering what Gregory had told them, that the company had never explained why he had cut that axle during the Spanish Inquisition.

"Of course they do. You know, no one else has ever asked me so many questions. This isn't a democracy."

Walker had said same thing, very nearly, including the dismissive mention of democracy. Maybe they lived under a different political system. Maybe, if all your resources were nearly gone, if you had to conserve everything, you had to have someone at the top to give orders, to decide how portion out the little that still remained. It sounded unpleasant, like a dictatorship. She would have liked to have asked them about it, but she knew they would never answer her.

THE BANQUETS WERE CANCELED, and all of Trencavel's energy went into preparing for war. Soldiers drilled in the courtyards, and blacksmiths worked in shifts hammering swords and daggers and axes, their fires smoking day and night.

The four of them barely saw the viscount, who had to dash from one emergency to another: storing the food for a siege, finding places for everyone who needed shelter, meeting with his knights and vassals. Still, rumors reached them that he had become a Cathar, that he had been shaken by the appearance of the angel. That he had become, not just a Cathar, but a Perfect like his cousin.

Charles wanted to stay a while longer, to make sure of Trencavel's conversion. Since they were no longer giving concerts he asked the viscount if his assistants could work in the kitchen, and Trencavel was pleased to have the extra help.

Charles wanted them to pick up gossip, to be in a position to listen to servants and nobles alike, but the work was hard and exhausting and they all hated it. Ann, who was the only one of them who had experience in food service, sometimes felt as if her life had cycled back in time, that no matter what she did to get out of poverty she would end up carrying platters of food and trying to smile at the people she served.

As she got used to the work, though, she began to like the anonymity it gave her. No one ever looked at her twice, not the lords and ladies or the servants in the kitchen. And she did overhear gossip, though not the sort Charles was looking for. Two people she had never heard of were courting, and another woman had gotten pregnant and wanted to terminate it. A Cathar holy man or woman would have helped her—they wanted to bring as few people as possible into this evil world—but the pregnant woman knew of no Cathars besides the viscount's cousin, and of course she couldn't approach someone so much higher in status.

A cleaning woman told the servants how she had surprised Peire Raimon and the viscountess in bed. Ann felt vindicated by the story and wanted to tell Charles, but she was so harried by work she forgot, and when she finally remembered it seemed unimportant compared to everything else.

Some of the lords and ladies did talk about how the viscount had changed, how he was eating very little and losing weight, how he had stopped joking with them and was spending more time by himself. It could have been evidence of a conversion, Charles said, but it could also just mean that Trencavel was taking his responsibilities more seriously.

They began to hear things about the outer world as well. Count Raimond VI of Toulouse, Trencavel's feudal lord, had gone penitent to the pope, received a scourging, and joined the crusade. He was trying to save his people, but he would also not mind if his vassal the viscount were to die in the war to come. The two of them had clashed several times over the years.

Then the pope's army attacked one of Trencavel's feudal holdings, Béziers, a town forty-five miles from Carcassonne. The soldiers' orders were to slaughter all the Cathars, to show no mercy. Someone asked the pope's legate, Arnaud Amaury, how they could tell the Cathars from the Christians, and he was supposed to have replied, "Kill them all, God will know his own." In the end every man, woman, and child in the town had died, over twenty thousand people.

It was a deliberate act of terror, and in the historical record it had prompted Viscount Trencavel to go to the crusaders' camp and try to negotiate. But in this timeline, when the crusaders reached Carcassonne on August first and ringed the city in a siege, he showed no inclination to compromise but continued to plan for war.

"Well, I think that's it," Charles said the next day. "He's decided to stay here and fight instead of surrendering. We've done what we were supposed to—it's time to go home."

Why didn't the company want Trencavel to surrender? Wouldn't the crusaders slaughter everyone here, the way they had at Béziers, if he stayed and fought? Or maybe the viscount would win the battle, would defeat the crusaders, and Languedoc would survive a while longer, independent of the north.

She said nothing, though. She would have to wait, ask her questions when she got back.

Charles opened his sack and looked for his computer. Then he hunted through it, then turned it over and dumped everything out on the floor. A lute fell with a muted clang, then a snarl of strings, wrapped around the ring the viscount had given him.

"I—" Charles said. He sounded panicked. "The computer's gone."

"Where was it?" Franny asked.

"Here, in this pocket. Someone's taken it."

"Who do you think—"

"Who else? Peire Raimon, of course. Let's go."

They followed him next door to Peire Raimon's room. He didn't bother knocking but threw the door open, so hard that it slammed against the wall.

Peire Raimon was sitting on a bed, playing his lute. "What—"

Charles went to him and lifted him up by his throat. "Where is it?"

Peire Raimon tried to speak. Charles loosened his grip slightly. "Where is what?" Peire Raimon said.

"You know what. What you stole from my room. A—a kind of cloth."

"Let me go. I didn't take anything."

"No? What would happen if we searched your room?"

"Go ahead—I don't have anything of yours."

"Where are your assistants?"

"Out."

"*Where?*"

"I don't know," Peire Raimon said quickly. "Drinking, I think."

"All right," Charles said to Ann and Franny and Jerry. "You heard him—he doesn't mind if we search his room. Let's go."

They spread out. Charles threw the bed over, then stripped off the blankets and shook them out. Ann opened a leather bag and dumped out the contents, stale and sour clothing that hadn't been washed in months.

Peire Raimon shouted something. Ann raised her head to see that Franny had found a small bag. Peire Raimon took a step toward her, and Charles knocked him to the ground. "Open it, Franny."

It didn't seem big enough to hold the computer. Franny pulled the drawstring open and lifted out a golden necklace strung with what looked like emeralds. "The lady gave me that," Peire Raimon said, sounding defiant.

"Good for you," Charles said. He headed into the next room, and a moment later they heard things crashing to the floor.

It didn't take long to search the two rooms. Charles came back after the three of them had finished and asked, "Did you find anything?"

They shook their heads. He turned to Peire Raimon. "Where did you put it?"

"I don't know what you're talking about," the other man said. He had gotten up from the floor; blood trickled from the side of his mouth. He summoned up courage from somewhere. "And if I did have something of yours I wouldn't hide it—I'd burn it. You're a devilish, unnatural—"

Charles took two strides toward him. He cringed back. "You—you burned it?" Charles said.

"N—no. No, I said I would have burned it. I wouldn't keep anything you've touched. There's something uncanny about you—everyone says so."

"If I find out you've destroyed something of mine I'll come back and kill you. Do you understand?"

Peire Raimon nodded, all his boldness gone. "All right," Charles said. He turned to the three of them. "Let's go."

They followed him out. What would happen if they didn't find the computer? Ann wondered. Would they have to stay here? She felt claustrophobia enfold her, a terror of being trapped in this tace forever. At least in Alexandria, her concussion had kept her from realizing the true horror of her situation—and in Knossos she had had other things to worry about.

"Walker said once—she said you have backups," she said. "If someone finds the key."

"The computer's the backup," Charles said, his words clipped with impatience. "No one's ever had both of them go missing before."

Walker had said "backups," plural. But then Ann had never known her to be precise with her language.

"What do we do now?" Franny asked.

"We look for the computer, of course," Charles said. "And the key. You keep your eyes and ears open, and I'll ask the viscount if I can search the castle."

DAYS PASSED, AND THEY heard nothing about the lost computer
or key. It was high summer, and the crusaders' army tightened their hold on the city; Carcassonne, a mountain fortress
with no convenient river nearby, was already perilously close
to running short of water. Sometimes Ann heard, or thought
she heard, the heavy thud of stones hitting the city walls.

Trencavel had agreed to let Charles look through the castle and had given him one of his guards to help, but none of
his searches turned up anything. For once Ann was glad of
the drudgery in the kitchen; it kept her from worrying about
her possible futures. And the others didn't seem to want to
think about it either; they discussed it only once, after a long
hard day in the kitchens. "Do you think Peire Raimon really
burned the computer, like he said?" Franny asked.

"Of course not," Charles said. "He said he would have
burned it, not that he did."

Ann didn't think that was proof of anything, but as long
as they were talking she had another question to ask him.
"We have no idea what's going to happen from this point on,
right? I mean, in the history books Trencavel goes to negotiate with the crusaders, and they spare the city, mostly."

"They killed the Cathars," Charles said. "And they drove everyone else out, without their clothes or possessions."

He'd missed the point completely. "Yeah, but they let them back in," she said impatiently. "What I mean is, in this timeline he doesn't negotiate with them, so anything could happen. They could kill us all, make an example of us the way they did in Béziers."

"Don't worry—we'll find the computer before then," Charles said.

"What about the company?" Franny asked. "Won't they realize something's wrong and start looking for us?"

Ann hadn't even thought of that. But the company could only find them using the cameras, and they could only view the cameras after they'd retrieved them from the past. And didn't she and the others need to be outside for the cameras to pick them up? She decided not to say anything, though; it was probably good for them to stay optimistic.

"Of course," Charles said. "That's a possibility too."

The next day Trencavel invited them to dinner. Charles was happy for the invitation; he would be able to make sure the viscount had become a Cathar. Ann didn't see what difference it would make, though. If he hadn't converted, there was probably nothing they could do about it now.

"We won't be having a grand meal, I'm afraid," the viscount said, when they'd seated themselves in the smaller banquet hall. His clothes were simpler than before, but still not the plain black that his cousin had worn. He'd been carrying a book when he came in, his finger stuck between the pages, and now it lay on the table next to him. "We have to save most of our food for the siege ahead."

"Of course, my lord," Charles said. "But—well, forgive me if my question is too bold, but I've heard another reason for your simpler feasts. There are rumors that you've become a Cathar."

"By heaven, I'm surprised you haven't become one yourself," Trencavel said. "Anyone would, after seeing that angel, hearing what he had to say." He pulled down his collar, and Ann saw that someone had embroidered a design in black thread there. Cathars had taken to wearing black near their skin, hiding their identity in case the crusaders invaded.

"That's one of the reasons I've invited you here, to get your opinion," Trencavel went on. "You saw it too, am I right? It was an angel, telling me to change my life."

"I'm certain it was, my lord."

"But then—why haven't you converted?"

"I will, after all this is over."

Trencavel looked satisfied. "Anyway, I want you to know that I'm not being stingy with my fare because I'm a Cathar now. People can eat whatever they like—I don't mind. No, the stinginess is because I have to prepare for war."

"I understand, my lord."

"It's strange, you know, this whole religious thing. People still expect me to guzzle like a pig, and rut like a stallion. They don't know how to treat me. Well, except for my cousin. She's delighted, as you can imagine."

A serving girl brought out a pitcher of water for the viscount, and another pitcher of wine for everyone else. Ann recognized the girl from the kitchen and smiled at her, and she nodded back.

"Except that she tells me that a Cathar cannot kill another soul," Trencavel said. Who? Ann thought. Right, he was still talking about his cousin. "She has no idea what it's like to rule here, even a few towns. I can't just sit back and let the crusaders overrun Carcassonne, especially after what they did to Béziers. I have to think about my people. If that makes me less than perfect, then so be it."

The kitchen girl poured his water. "And my wife," Trencavel went on. "She's still going off to Peire Raimon a couple of nights a week. And she thinks I disapprove, when truthfully I don't care at all. It gives her something to do, at least."

"You don't care?" Ann asked. "Really?"

He looked across the table at her. "That's right—I forgot," he said. "Outsiders don't understand how we do things here—they're always either confused or horrified. Our marriages are made for us by our parents, to join us to other powerful families. And we do our duty, we produce heirs and make sure that the line goes on. But if we weren't allowed to take our pleasure, to choose our own lovers, we'd turn mad, or violent." He paused, seeming to realize that what he'd said was at odds with his new beliefs. "Well, until we grow up, anyway. Until we realize that this world doesn't matter."

He seemed so open that Ann decided to risk another question. "So your wife really did give Peire Raimon that necklace."

"Oh, I'm sure she did. An extravagant present, but then she does seem to like him."

The viscount studied her gravely, giving her his whole attention. No one had ever looked at her like that, not even the professors at the company. Was it because women had status here, because their opinions mattered? Or did he treat every woman the same out of habit, flattering them automatically because he might want to bed them someday? Her face felt hot and she turned away, hoping he hadn't noticed.

"Well, maybe she'll convert too, sooner or later," Trencavel said. "Though she didn't see the angel, she can't really understand." He picked up the book near his plate. "My cousin gave me this—she thinks it might help."

The cover was just a thick leather binding, with no title or other information. The first page, though, had a long title in illustrated calligraphy, something to do with Genesis.

He turned the page and began to read, a long confusing passage about the creation of the world. At the beginning there was light, or maybe Light, and its emanation Wisdom, who was female, and then some more Lights, or maybe Aeons, and then finally Wisdom created an emanation without the support of the others, called Ialdabaoth. Ialdabaoth turned out to be the creator of this world, but because he was imperfect, without Wisdom, the world was also imperfect, lacking.

Ann lost the thread after that, and began to think about other things. Meret had tracked a version of Genesis in Alexandria, she remembered. The books saved from the library had been scattered throughout the world, to Byzantium, Baghdad, Spain. Had one of them made its way here, and caused a heresy to catch fire? But why would the company want to support the Cathars, to strengthen their beliefs?

AUGUST THE FIFTEENTH CAME, the day Trencavel had gone to the crusaders' camp. In this timeline, though, he stayed in the castle and continued to plan for war. Although they were heavily outnumbered by the crusaders, and everyone had heard about the atrocity at Béziers, he still seemed confident, rallying his soldiers, listening to their boasts and worries, making them laugh.

The cooks and kitchen boys and girls were more pessimistic, though, whispering about a new terror, a brilliant northern commander named Simon de Montfort. They barely talked to each other, speaking mostly to give orders, working with their heads down.

"We'll be safe here," Ann heard one young man tell another. "The angel will guard us, after all."

Angel? She put down the knife she was using to chop onions. "What are you talking about?" she asked.

"We have an angel's relic," he said, his face placid. "It'll keep us safe from the northerners."

"What kind of relic? Where?"

"My friend Guilhem has it. He saw an angel appear near the forest, and after it disappeared he found a—a thing it had left behind. A ball made of metal, with more balls inside it. A map of the heavens, with circles nested within circles, and the outermost the most perfect."

She was surprised at the man's eloquence, and wondered if he could be a Cathar. She would have never thought of the key as an image of the heavens.

"Where's Guilhem now?"

"I don't know. He lives on the street with the church of St. Michael, heading away from the market square. It's the shoemaker's shop—he's a cobbler. But he could be in the castle with everyone else."

She left the kitchen and ran down the corridor, then hurried through a series of public rooms. She'd found the key—they might still get away, leave this tace behind them forever. Where was Charles?

She found him in their rooms, practicing on his lute. She was panting from her run and had to stop a moment, take several deep breaths, but finally she managed to tell him what the kitchen boy had said. "Go get the others," he said. "And then we'll find Guilhem."

Franny and Jerry were still in the kitchens, and she hurried back to them. Then another run through the castle, all three of them this time, and finally they were all together in their room, gathered around Charles.

"Ann and Franny, you go out into the city, try to find this man," Charles said. "Do you know where the market square is?" They both nodded. "And Jerry and I will look through the castle, see if he came here."

He gave them a handful of coins to bargain with. "Although," he said, "if Guilhem truly thinks the key was left by an angel, he might not want to give it up for any price."

None of the guards said anything as they walked out of the main door. Apparently people here were free to go if they wanted, though the expressions on the guards' faces said that they were crazy to leave the protection of the castle.

A loud crash sounded as they went down the road into the city. They both startled, and then Ann laughed. "It's just the catapults, throwing stones against the walls," she said.

"Just?" Franny said.

"I thought it was a bomb. That's one thing to be grateful for, anyway, that they don't have modern technology."

"They can do a lot of damage with what they have. You heard them in the kitchen—Simon de Montfort is here. Remember him?"

"Of course." Montfort had shown his abilities as a military tactician at the beginning of the crusade and had been promoted from the ranks. He would go on to win nearly all of the Languedoc for the northerners, and be given Trencavel's titles of Viscount of Béziers and Carcassonne.

"And it's nowhere near the time he dies," Franny said. Montfort had been—would be—killed nine years from now, when the defenders of Toulouse threw a catapult stone back at the crusaders' army. According to legend, it was the women and children on the walls who threw the stone.

"Well, we don't know when he dies in this timeline," Ann said. "He didn't have to invade Carcassonne in the history we know about—he could die in the fighting hern." She paused, thinking. "Doesn't it seem like the company is changing a lot more than they usually do, in this tace?"

Franny nodded. "I thought of that too. Anything can happen now—anyone can die, even people who survived in our timeline. Well, they must know what they're doing, up on the fifth floor."

They had come to a confusion of streets and pathways, what would look like a child's scribble on a map. Walls leaned outward, creating pools of shadows that kept out the heat from the sun.

"We should be paying more attention here," Franny said. "I think the market square is back that way."

They turned around and reached the empty market square. A few banners hung listlessly in the hot air, and Ann could smell cattle dung, but the market itself was deserted.

They reached the street the church was on, then turned right, away from the market. "What does a shoemaker's shop look like in this tace?" Franny asked.

"Oh, I don't know. Maybe it has a big old sign in the shape of a shoe. Like this sign here."

Franny looked up and saw the sign, then bumped her hip against Ann's, delighted. "Oh, thank God," she said.

They knocked on the door. "Who's there?" someone called out.

"Guilhem?" Ann asked. "We'd like to see the angel's relic."

Guilhem opened the door a crack, then swung it wider when he saw the two women. "Of course," he said. "Come in."

He led them through his front room, a cobbler's workshop. Wooden feet stuck up into the air, guides to shoe sizes; they looked like people buried head down, only their feet showing. They passed sheets of leather laid out on counters, and knives and needles and thick, heavy thread. The smell of leather saturated the air.

Guilhem reached under a counter and brought out the key. "Can I—can I hold it?" Ann asked.

"No," Guilhem said. He set it down on the counter. "It's a holy object—I don't want it to lose its virtue with too much handling."

"The Church of St. Michael sent us," Ann said, the idea coming to her at that moment. Franny, she was gratified to see, revealed only a small start of surprise, and then schooled her face to show nothing. "They want us to buy the relic from you, so all of Carcassonne can benefit from it."

"It's not for sale. I was the one the angel chose—he must have had a reason for it. I can't possibly give it to you, or anyone else."

"You have to," Franny said. "The city's under siege—you know that. All of us need the angel's help, his blessing, not just you. You have to share it with the rest of us."

"No, I don't." His face grew sly. "How do I know you're from the church, anyway? I've never seen you there. And why wouldn't the fathers come themselves, instead of sending two women—and two women I've never seen before, with outlandish accents?"

Ann felt a desperate impatience. The key was so close, almost within her grasp. "You're being selfish," she said. "What happens when the army invades? You'll get the luck of it, and everyone else will die, will be killed. You'll be condemned to hell for your greed."

"I want the fathers to tell me that, like I said. Anyway, the army won't invade. The relic will protect us, that and the strong walls."

At that moment, almost as if he had called them up, loud voices rose from further down the hillside. A trumpet sounded, and another answered. Someone screamed.

"They're here," Ann said.

21

THE COBBLER LOOKED AROUND, panicked. "No, they can't be. They can't. The angel—"

Ann caught Franny's gaze and grabbed the key, and the two of them ran for the street. The cobbler raced after them, shouting. Franny seized a hammer from the counter and threw it at him, and he groaned and fell to the floor.

They hurried outside. The shouts were louder here; it sounded as if the crusaders had reached the market square.

"Which way's the castle?" Ann asked.

"Over here."

They ran through the streets, away from the market. They got lost again almost immediately, finding themselves in a narrow road with three ways leading out. High rooftops blocked their view.

"Which one?" Ann said.

"God, I don't know. Here—this one goes uphill, at least."

They ran up the pathway and reached a dead end, hemmed in by the backs of several houses. They turned around, back to the narrow road and the three choices.

Ann took one of the two remaining roads at random. It let them out onto a larger street, one she had never seen before. Someone shouted, sounding very close, and someone else screamed.

They ducked into an alleyway and peered out. A horse and rider trotted past them, hooves striking loud against the cobblestones. A banner flew from the rider's lance, and he wore a red cross sewn to his tunic. Ten or twelve foot soldiers followed behind him.

As they watched, another group came around a corner. The horse neighed through its headguard, and the two companies clashed together.

The crusaders had more men, Ann saw, and they were better armed. And the soldiers of Languedoc didn't seem ready for battle, despite all of Trencavel's preparations. Like Ann they had probably expected the war to start only after the walls had been breached. But she hadn't heard the walls come down, and she wondered how the crusaders had gotten inside.

The man with the cross leaned down from his horse and swung a sword at his opponent. Ann looked away. She couldn't stop herself from hearing the sounds of battle, though: cries and groans and screams. One of the crusaders shouted triumphantly, "God wills it!"

Someone started singing. Others joined in, ragged at first and then louder. She looked back. Several men lay dead or dying, and more were hurrying away. The crusaders marched on down the street, still singing lustily. One or two kicked at the dead men as they passed.

Without talking about it she and Franny waited for a long time, until the crusaders had gone out of sight. Then they edged out into the larger street and looked around them.

They could see the castle now, and they headed toward it. Horses neighed from somewhere, and they heard hooves galloping over the cobblestones. Black smoke blossomed a few streets away.

Someone shouted behind them: "There's two of them, over there!"

They turned and saw another group of men coming around a corner. They began to run.

The men hurried after them. "Why are you running, ladies?" a voice called out. "Why aren't you safe inside the castle, with your menfolk?"

"Heretic women don't have menfolk," someone else said.

"We'll show them what they're missing, then!"

Ann looked around frantically. A row of houses, another church way down at the end of the street. Would it give them sanctuary? No, probably turn them over to the crusaders. Anyway, they couldn't possibly reach it in time.

Then she saw it, a word painted on one of the houses. No, it couldn't possibly say that. But as she got closer she saw that she'd been right: "Cor," it said. "Heart," in the dialect of Languedoc, but it could also mean . . .

"In here!" she said to Franny.

"What? Why?"

She was panting too hard to answer. Instead she grabbed her and thrust the door open.

"No, wait," Franny said. "Who lives here?"

She closed the door behind them and leaned against it, breathing heavily. "What is this place?" Franny asked.

"Shhh," Ann said. "I think it's—"

A section of the wall rotated around a central hinge. A woman came out from behind it. "Good day, my ladies," she said. "Would you take some refreshment, for your hearts' sake?"

"Refreshment!" Franny said. "There's an army—"

"Hush," Ann said. "Yes, we would love some refreshment. For our hearts' sake."

"We must hurry then," the woman said. They followed her into the next room, and the wall rotated back.

The woman wore a long white gown; it looked like Maheut's dress but opposite, like those photo negatives they used to have. Another woman, younger than the first, was cutting up some fruit and setting it on a plate.

The second woman held the plate out to Ann and Franny. Apples, sliced neatly through the middle. It looked like a ritual, or a sacrament. Was she supposed to say something, or do something? Would they throw the two of them out if she got this wrong?

A shout came from behind the wall. "Ann! Franny! Let me in!"

"Is that a friend of yours?" the first woman asked.

It was Jerry. How had he gotten here? Had he followed them?

"Yes," Ann said. "Could you help him please? Bring him inside?"

"We don't allow men into our gatherings," the first woman said.

"I saw you go in there!" Jerry called out. "You have to let me in—they're coming after me!" He pounded on the wall with his fists but it didn't move. "Please, they'll kill me!"

"Can't you—can't you make an exception?" Ann said. "You heard him—they'll kill him if he stays out there."

"I'm sorry, truly." The woman did look unhappy, even compassionate, as if she would have let him in if the rules hadn't made it impossible. "There are no exceptions. If one man finds out about us he'll tell others, and our safety would be gone."

"He won't tell anyone, I promise," Ann said.

"I know what you're up to," Jerry said, quieter now. "Charles told me to follow you, see where you go. You belong to Core, don't you? Look, I won't say anything to him, I swear. I'll tell him you went right to that shoemaker, that the company has nothing to worry about."

The woman had grown more and more alarmed during this speech. "How does he know about Cor?" she whispered.

"If you don't let me in I'll tell them everything," Jerry said. "Where you went, what you did. They'll round up everyone you met and—"

231

There was a terrible sound, a sort of squishy thud, and then Jerry screamed. Ann listened, horrified. Had someone run him through with a sword? Then another sound, a body falling to the ground.

"That's done for him," a voice said.

"He was talking to someone, though," another voice said. "Is there anyone else here?"

"No. Don't worry about him. He was crazy, terrified."

"All right."

They heard footsteps, and the door opening and closing. Then silence.

"You see?" the woman said. "He knew about Cor, he was threatening to tell others. We can never make exceptions, not even for friends. Now, let's eat."

How could she sound so unconcerned? Jerry was dead. Ann had worked with him, lived with him, gotten to know him—how could she eat anything now? It reminded her of Kaphtor, where life and death had lain so close together there was not even a breath to separate them.

She looked around her. Bright cushions lay scattered over the floor, covered with pictures of birds and fish and flowers. A third woman was sitting there, a very old woman with wrinkled face. Her mouth had collapsed inward; probably she had few teeth left. But her hair was still beautiful, long, the color of lustrous ivory.

Light came from oil lamps set in niches around the room. There was another niche at the front, larger than the others, with a statue of a woman. Mary, probably, she thought.

The two women sat, and she and Franny joined them. "My name is Azelaïs," the first woman said. "This is Hélis, and Giraude." She indicated the young woman, and the old one. "And since you don't seem to know the ceremony of the apples, I will perform it for you. But you must tell me how you knew the password, but not this ritual."

Azelaïs took the plate of apples from Hélis. Then she took out a knife from her belt and used it to cut lines between the five seeds of an apple, lines which, when she was finished, joined up in a pentagram. "Thus did Teacher Mara show us, in the long-ago time," she said. She scored the other apples on the plate, then held them out to Ann and Franny.

Ann had been glad of the ceremony; it gave her time to concentrate, to think about what she was going to say. In the end, though, the only answer she could come up with was the truth.

She took a deep breath. "We're from very far away, another country. We heard about Cor"—she tried to pronounce it the way Azelaïs had, with a nasal "r" at the end—"and we wanted to join, but we knew nothing else about it."

"Nothing? Not about Teacher Mara, and the prophecies?"

Mara? Did Azelaïs mean Mary? She glanced at the statue in the niche and noticed for the first time that the woman was black. There were supposed to be statues of Black Madonnas all over Europe, she knew, but Professor Strickland had not talked about them much in history class; they had nothing to do with the current assignment.

Azelaïs followed her gaze. "Yes, that's her," she said. "She gave us all our assignments in the long-ago time. And she spoke prophecies, told us about events that came to pass just as she said they would, down through the many years."

"Meret!" Franny whispered urgently, just as the same thought had occurred to Ann. Had Meret done what she said she would do, had she gathered a group of women around her in Kaphtor and taught them to resist the company? And could a group like that have survived for twenty-five hundred years?

"We heard something about Teacher Mara," Franny said cautiously. "How accurate her prophecies are."

"Very accurate," Hélis said. "More so than any soothsayer we have ever seen, or heard of."

Meret had to be Mara, then. Who else could have given such accurate predictions of the future? Meret had a computer with her, after all, which could have held all of human history. She thought of the scope of Meret's achievement and felt a thrill travel through her, starting at her heart and shivering outward.

"But we may have failed in our assignment," Azelaïs said.

"What do you mean?" Franny said.

"We were supposed to introduce the poetry of the Moors to the people here, in the south of France. Not us, of course, but our sisters in Cor a hundred years ago. And the people of that time took up the Moors' poetry eagerly, they composed songs that talked about their love for women, of their beauty. We had thought that this would remake the way men think of women, that they would remember her essential nobility before they raped a woman, or hit her, or killed her. And some men did change, some of the nobility, and among the troubadours. But for the most part they stayed the same, they continued to think of women as they always had."

Someone shouted in the street. Ann stirred uneasily. She had kept the key in her left hand, had held onto it through everything that had happened, and now she felt it digging into her palm. Shouldn't they be heading back?

But she wanted to talk to Azelaïs, to hear more about Core. And Charles could wait, she thought. He hadn't trusted them, had sent Jerry to follow them . . . Jerry. That's right, Jerry was dead, his body waiting for them just outside the doorway. How could she have forgotten?

She forced herself back to the conversation. "But you did change some things," she said. "Trencavel, he was always very polite to me, and I was only a servant, someone who worked in the kitchens."

"Have you noticed that they will call a woman beautiful, but they never say what she looks like?" Azelaïs said. "What color her hair is, or her eyes, or whether she is tall or short or fat or thin? Any of these women can be exchanged for any other."

Ann hadn't, but she realized it was true as soon as the other woman mentioned it. She nodded.

"They sing to a statue of a woman," Azelaïs said. "A woman they created."

Ann nodded again. She'd heard people talk about putting women on pedestals, but she'd never really understood it; no one before had ever singled her out, made her feel special. Now she got it, though. If you put a woman on a pedestal you didn't have to deal with her, her messy flesh and blood, who she really was. You could treat her as your own construct, a made-up woman, a receptacle for your fantasies.

"Still, it may not matter, about our assignment," Hélis said. "Things are changing yet again, in the way that Meret foresaw. The armies coming to attack us, to bring the end of the troubadours, and much else."

"Her book did not say that the attackers would be so brutal, though. So barbaric," Azelaïs said.

That's because they weren't, as far as Meret knew, Ann thought. We changed it. Wait a minute. Her book?

"She wrote things down for you, in a book?" she asked. "Can we see it?"

"No," Hélis said. "Only our sisters in Cor can be trusted with her book."

"Then why not make them our sisters?" Giraude said, speaking for the first time. "They knew the password. And we have already shared the ceremony of the apples."

Azelaïs looked at them. "Would you like that? To join our gathering? I should tell you first that there are great responsibilities here—it is not all secrets and apples."

"I'd love to," Ann said. "But unfortunately we have to leave soon, to go traveling with our master."

"They can still join," Giraude said. "At whatever new place they come to. And in the meantime we can show them Mara's book."

Did they really have that many sisters, all over the known world, that Giraude could be confident they could find a gathering wherever they went? "Very well," Azelaïs said.

She rose. For the first time the women's attention was on something beside Ann and Franny, and Ann fumbled for a pocket and tucked the key inside it. Azelaïs went over to the statue and touched a spot beneath it, and a panel rotated outward, like the door in the wall. Then she bent and took out a huge heavy book, about two inches thick.

It was old, Ann saw, but it did not go as far back as Kaphtoran times: it was written on parchment, not papyrus. They must have copied it again and again through the years, women bent over the pages, working by lamplight . . .

Azelaïs opened the leather cover to the front page. The title was in Kaphtoran, what the linguists had called Linear A; Ann had never thought to see that writing again. "The Book of Kore," it said, and underneath that the same thing in the dialect of Languedoc. It was decorated in bright colors with Cretan designs, fish and octopuses swimming through water, reeds growing at the edge.

"Look," Azelaïs said, whispering reverently.

She flipped through the pages, stopping at a drawing of a city. Enormous buildings loomed up in the background, a combination of the skyscrapers Ann was used to and the structures she had seen in Kaphtor, room piled on room, ziggurating into the air. They were painted in pastel colors, pink and turquoise and butter yellow.

Something stood in front of the buildings, a strange mix of chariot and automobile. "People will ride through vast cities in conveyances like this one, which moves by itself," Azelaïs said. "And it will be called after the Goddess, car. Like Kore."

Ann tried not to laugh. She didn't think that was where the word came from.

"You smile," Azelaïs said. "But all the world speaks the name of the Goddess. Here." She turned to another page, finding her way through the book easily. "Here is a list of the towns and cities named after her. Listen. 'Khartoum, Karnak, Carthage, Corinth . . .' And Carcassonne, of course. That is why we are here, in this city—we try to build our temples in these places. And that is where"—she looked up at both of them, her face grave—"this is where you will find our gatherings, when you are ready to become one of us."

Azelaïs showed them page after page. Drawings snaked around the words; some of them had the fluidity of Kaphtor, but there was also art from other times, Egyptian, Roman, Byzantine. She hurried through the book, not letting Ann read too much of it, but she caught phrases here and there: "He will be killed then, and it would be good to leave this place before the fighting begins . . ." "Despite being a woman, Queen Mary will cling to a life-denying version of her religion. The sisters in Kore must do these things to bring Elizabeth to the throne . . ." "The sisters in Kore must work to elect these candidates . . ."

The next page showed a snake with its tail in its mouth. Within its circle were a few lines in elaborate calligraphy. "The Goddess, by whatever name you call Her, works in harmony with the cycles of the world. She is Mistress of the birth and death and rebirth of seasons, of the waxing and waning moon. And the women and men that we fight see time as a straight line, always moving forward toward some bright future. In this way they seek to cut themselves off from half of the eternal mysteries, from earth and night and death."

Azelaïs looked at Ann and Franny and then closed the book. She had wanted them to read that, Ann realized. The other woman stood and returned the book to its place.

Ann stood as well. "Thanks for your hospitality, but we have to get back now," she said. "Our friends must be worried about us."

Horses clopped past them, out in the street. "It is unsafe for you to go outside, I think," Azelaïs said. "We will have to keep you here with us, until the fighting is over."

"No one rang the church bells today," Hélis said. "What time do you think it is?"

"Time for supper, of course," Azelaïs said, and the others laughed.

There were more cupboards ranged around the room, Ann saw now, with doors that opened normally. Azelaïs and Hélis stood and took out bread and cheese and dried beef and wine, and set them on platters on the floor. After they had eaten they got down straw pallets and some blankets, blew out the candles, and prepared to go to sleep.

"What about Charles?" Franny whispered to Ann, lying on the floor next to her. "Won't he wonder where we are?"

"The hell with him," Ann said. "He sent Jerry to spy on us, after all."

"Well, but he wanted to know if you were a member of Core. And you are, aren't you?"

Ann said nothing for a while. "I think I am, actually. Look what the company did here—they got the army to attack Carcassonne, to kill hundreds of people who didn't have to die. Thousands, maybe. And Core—the sisters of Kore—all they want is for women to be equal to men." She paused again. "You aren't going to tell Charles, are you?"

"No," Franny said.

Ann slept badly, waking several times during the night to hear shouts or screams or horses neighing. When she woke at dawn, though, everything was silent—an uneasy silence, the sound of a city battered into submission.

Soon the other women got up as well, and they had a breakfast of bread and oranges. Hélis ventured outside, coming back to tell them that the streets were empty. "Folks said the soldiers are all in the castle now," she said. "Keeping watch on their prisoners. And most of the people are hiding—they remember what happened in Béziers."

"Do they know how the army got into the city?" Azelaïs asked.

Hélis nodded. "They had friends inside, traitors who opened the gates for them. So they never needed to break down the walls."

"Well," Azelaïs said to Ann and Franny. "It might be safe for you to go back now. Could you help us with something first, though? We need to move your friend's body. Someone might stumble upon it otherwise, and want to know what goes on inside this house."

Jerry—she'd forgotten about him again, damn it. And they needed to move him for another reason; the company might find him with one of their cameras and wonder what he was doing there.

"Of course," she said.

Azelaïs opened the secret door and they went out into the next room. Jerry lay on his stomach; he'd been stabbed in the back, and his clothes were soaked a deep red with blood. He smelled terrible, and she realized with horror that he'd loosened his bowels as he died.

Hélis opened the front door carefully and peered into the street. "All right," she said, coming back to them.

Together the four of them lifted Jerry's body and took it outside. What is it about me, Ann wondered, that people keep dying on my assignments? Am I some kind of jinx, a Typhoid Mary of the timelines? Anachronistic Ann?

"Where were you headed?" Azelaïs asked. "It might be a good idea to leave him there."

"The market square," Franny said.

The square turned out to be only a few streets away; they'd gotten more confused than Ann had realized, the day before. They looked around for soldiers and then set Jerry down in the street.

"Goddess show you your path," Azelaïs said. "I hope you find your sisters in Kore, wherever it is you are going."

"Thank you."

"And keep yourselves safe," Hélis said. "This new commander, Simon de Montfort—who knows what he plans to do? He might kill everyone here, the way he did in Béziers."

"There's a prophecy about him, one Mara might not have written down," Ann said, thinking to encourage them. "It's said that he will die at the hands of women and children."

"No, I never heard that. Thank you."

Azelaïs moved to hug her. She had always hated being hugged, hated anyone breaking through her defenses, but she found to her surprise that she held onto the other woman for a long time. Another mother figure, she thought, but she couldn't summon up the sarcasm she would have liked.

Azelaïs hugged Franny and they said goodbye. Then she and Franny hurried through the deserted streets to the castle. They heard the sound of marching feet only once, and they hid in an empty house until the soldiers went past.

They said very little. Ann was thinking about the sisters of Kore, and she supposed Franny was as well. Apples, books, knives, statues . . . Suddenly she laughed.

"Quiet!" Franny said. "Do you want to get us killed? What's so funny, anyway?"

"That thing with the apple, that Meret taught them. It's about the core, the core of the apple. It's a pun, and it took twenty-five hundred years for someone to get it."

CHARLES WAS WAITING FOR them down the road from the castle. "Where were you?" he asked.

"Never mind that," Ann said. "We got the key."

She took it out of her pocket. Charles snatched it away from her. "Did you see Jerry?" he asked.

"He's dead. Crusaders killed him."

"Are you sure?"

"Of course I'm sure. We saw his body."

"Where?"

"Near the market square."

Charles nodded and began manipulating the circles of the key. Wasn't he worried that someone would see them disappear? But they were in danger of their lives now, and that had to outweigh any caution Charles might have.

Once again the colors around them blurred, her stomach clenched, bright lights stabbed her eyes . . . and then they were on the platform, the sound of applause ebbing and flowing around them like ocean waves.

"Congratulations!" someone said. "We felt a huge timequake here."

"We'll have to check the data, of course," another voice said, "but so far it seems zany successful. How do you feel?"

Charles started to say something, but Ann spoke over him. "Not so successful," she said. "Jerry died."

"Did he?" someone else said. She looked out at the technicians but everything still seemed fuzzy; she couldn't make out who was talking. Or was she crying?

"Don't worry—we'll look into it," a woman said.

Look into it? What the hell? Jerry would still be dead.

They were taken to the infirmary, poked and prodded and asked questions, given food and drink. Ann wanted to crawl into one of the beds and sleep for weeks, but men and women kept waking her up, shining lights into her eyes, insisting that she walk around a bit.

Even sleep didn't help, though. She had terrible dreams, nightmares in which they went out into the room where Jerry lay and found nothing, or saw Jerry struggling toward them, a sword in his back, his eyes beseeching. And when she woke she would have to take a moment to remember that he was dead, and she would feel a sorrow so powerful that it would seem like the first time.

Should she have disobeyed Azelaïs, brought him inside where he could be safe? But how? She would have had to overcome two women, both of them wearing knives . . .

"We're going to have to debrief you soon," someone was saying. She forced herself to wake up, to pay attention. "Do you think you'll feel ready tomorrow?"

She didn't, but she wanted to be out of the infirmary and back home, where it would be easier to concentrate. The program she had set up, to crack the password on the drive Meret had given her, had to have finished by now. Maybe she would find some information there, something that could help her.

And she needed help, she knew; she needed to decide what to do next. When she closed her eyes she saw the clash between the crusaders and Trencavel's army, saw the viscount's men fall, the fear and pain on their faces as they died. What kind of people would cause that to happen?

"All right," she said. "Yeah, I think so."

A woman came for her the next day. Someone had laid out the clothes she had worn before she left, cleaned and folded, and she put them on slowly, feeling like an invalid. Then the woman led her out of the infirmary and toward the elevator.

A man was coming toward them, down the corridor. Jerry! No, it couldn't be, Jerry was dead. But it *was* him, a thin man with white-blond hair . . . "Hello, Ann," he said.

Her vision closed down. Everything went very small, shot through with dark flashes. She struggled to stay conscious. Her minder hurried her away, around a corner and into an empty room.

"Sit down," she said. Ann sat, her mind a blank. "Put your head between your knees. There, good. Breathe."

Ann kept her head down until she felt stronger, then looked up at the other woman. "You weren't supposed to see that yet," the minder said. "We needed to prepare you first. I'll have to report someone for that, whoever the idiot was who let him wander around."

"How—" Ann said.

"How? Time travel, of course. We went back and took him home before he could be killed."

Her mind seemed to turn inside out, showing her the reverse of what she knew to be true. She saw—she *remembered*—two timelines, both of them equally valid. In one, Jerry stood outside the secret room and pleaded with her to let him inside. In the other he had been returned, and safe.

When did they take him? Was it before Jerry had followed her into the house or after? How much did Jerry, this Jerry, know about Core?

She couldn't ask the woman, of course, couldn't arouse her suspicions with questions like that. She would have to talk to Jerry later, try to sound him out.

"Are you ready to go on now?" her minder asked.

She was, but she wanted to deny her, deny the company. "No," she said. "I still feel weak. I think I'm sick."

The woman looked unhappy, and Ann felt a spiteful pleasure. "All right, then," the woman said. "We'll try again tomorrow."

WHEN SHE CAME INTO the room the next day she saw that Da Silva was waiting to debrief her. She felt happy to see her, and then a wariness, a reminder to be on her guard. Da Silva, she knew, was very good at coaxing out information.

"So what happened after we left?" Ann asked, before they could exchange pleasantries. "Did Simon de Montfort kill everyone again?"

"Not everyone, no," Da Silva said. "More than he killed in the previous history, though."

Ann thought of all the people she had met in Carcassonne—Maheut, the viscount's cousin, and the kitchen girl who had served them, and the cobbler, and even Peire Raimon and the other troubadours. And what about the sisters of Kore—had they remained safe in their hidden sanctuary? Who had survived, and who had been put to the sword?

"Why, though? Why did the company want all those people dead?"

"Well, the wars dragged on for forty years in the earlier history, and even after that the southerners kept rebelling. The Trencavel family even got Béziers and Carcassonne back for a while. And the Cathars were finally only wiped out a hundred and fifty years later. It turned out to be better to have a decisive win there, once and for all."

"But why?" She hadn't thought that much of the civilization of the south, but now that it was gone she remembered all the things she had liked about it—the mix of cultures, the beautiful songs, the fact that women could have a position of importance as a Perfect, or even as a troubadour. She even admired the strange way they dealt with their arranged marriages; at least no one seemed to get hurt, and they were able to enjoy themselves.

"I don't work on the fifth floor, so I don't know all the ins and outs of it," Da Silva said. "They're the ones who track all the repercussions down through the timelines, and they thought this was the best solution."

"It's just—these people don't seem like someone we'd want as allies. I mean, that puts us on the side of the guy who said, 'Kill them all—God will know his own.'"

"He didn't actually say that. The man who wrote the chronicle invented—"

"Well, so what? They still killed everyone."

Did the modelers ever feel guilty about what they did, all the deaths they caused? "What happened to Simon de Montfort in this timeline?" she asked.

Da Silva looked surprised. "I'm not sure," she said. Ann faced her, saying nothing. "Do you really want to know?"

Ann nodded. Da Silva went to a computer on a nearby desk and booted it up. "Well, he lived longer," she said, reading from the screen. "He wasn't killed in battle. He kept his titles, and put down more rebellions, and died of old age."

Maybe that had been the purpose of all their efforts then, to see to it that Montfort didn't die in battle. It seemed the worst kind of outcome to Ann: the commander alive and terrorizing the countryside, killing anyone who stood in his way. And it also meant that the prophecy she had given the sisters of Kore wasn't true after all. So much for encouraging them.

"Huh—look at that," Da Silva said. "There was still a revolt in Toulouse in 1218, same as in the earlier timeline. Looks like Montfort fought them and won. Apparently he didn't die there, the way he did in the earlier history."

Good for Toulouse, Ann thought. The more trouble the people of Languedoc could give him the better.

"What about Viscount Trencavel?" she asked.

"He died almost immediately, in the first wave of fighting."

"So he never tried to negotiate with the crusaders?"

Da Silva shook her head. "Look, we have to start the debriefing now—there's a number of things we have to get to before you can go home. The first thing is—well, you heard the technicians when you got back, there was a huge time-quake here. We changed a good deal, more than we usually do. So more things are going be different, and you'll probably notice some of them, before you start to get used to this reality. For one thing, there's a different president now. President John Henderson."

Ann blinked. "A different—you can do that?"

Da Silva smiled. "We did, apparently. They're very happy with all of you, up on the fifth floor."

Ann didn't smile back. She had never voted—she rarely paid attention to politics—but it still seemed wrong for these people to come here and change something so important.

Da Silva didn't seem to notice. "You should watch the news, get used to the changes. We don't want you making mistakes in your own tace."

She went over a few other differences, all of them minor, and then said, "So what happened during the time you were away from the castle? You went to get the key, and you stayed away for an entire day."

She wanted to trip Ann up with the change of subject, Ann knew. Still, she and Franny had discussed this on their way back, and she was ready with her story. "We were caught by the fighting, and we hid out in a deserted house. They'd left some food there, so we didn't starve. And we used their beds to sleep on."

"Where was the house?"

They hadn't thought about this part. "I don't really know. We got turned around a lot."

"All right. And then when you got back you told Charles you saw Jerry, and that he was dead. Where did you see his body?"

"Near the market square."

"And when? Before or after you hid out in the house?"

"After. When we were heading back."

"What did you think?"

"What did I *think*? Well, I thought it was terrible that he died. Why couldn't you have done that with Gregory? Bring him back like that?"

"Gregory? Right, I remember him. He died in Crete, didn't he?"

"Yeah. Why couldn't you just stop him before he left?"

"I don't know. If he died on the trip, my guess would be that he had some defect, maybe his heart, something they missed in his physical."

"So, what—he wasn't any use to the company so they didn't bother to bring him back?"

"I'm just guessing, like I said. I don't really know."

"Well, who does know? Wait, don't tell me. The fifth floor."

"That's right," Da Silva said.

THEY SENT HER HOME a few days later. She thought she'd answered Da Silva's questions fairly well, that they didn't suspect where she'd been in those missing twenty-four hours. They'd told her to be available for more debriefings, though, so she knew they weren't finished with her yet.

She went to her computer as soon as she got home. The program she had started was still running, and she saw to her annoyance that it hadn't unlocked the encryption yet.

She yanked the drive out of the port and threw it across the room. I'm sorry, Meret, she thought. If you wanted to tell me something you should have made it easier to get to.

Her refrigerator was empty, and she headed out to buy groceries. When she got to the supermarket she saw that several guards were standing by the doors, looking over the shoppers as they went inside. People seemed wary of them, almost frightened, and when she came closer she realized that they weren't guards at all but policemen. One of them said something into his phone as she passed.

She had forgotten Da Silva's suggestion to watch the news. What had happened at the market, that they had needed to call out the police?

She got a shopping cart and started down the aisles. There were great gaps in the shelves now, she saw, and one entire row had been taken out, leaving gouges in the lino-leum. Someone pushed in front of her to take the last box of the cereal she liked. What the hell? she thought. She got a different cereal and went to find milk.

The milk section looked as shabby as the rest of the mar-ket. Most of the cartons were past their sell-by date, and there was a sour, rancid smell coming from the refrigerator. It reminded her of the kitchen in Carcassonne, where the milk had been stored in a cool shadowed place but had still turned bad after three or four days.

She studied the dates on the milk cartons, looking for one that hadn't expired. She found one and took it—and a man standing next to her grabbed it out of her hand.

It felt like the last straw. "Hey, that's mine!" she said.

"Well, it's mine now," the man said, holding it out of her reach.

"You saw me take it."

"So?"

"So you know it's mine. Give it to me." She made a grab for it, and he moved it out of her way.

"Don't be ridiculous," he said. "I'm much stronger than you are."

He turned and put the milk in his cart. She felt her anger rise up inside her like a wave, until it seemed to take her over completely. She shoved her shopping cart at him, hit-ting him in the legs.

He whirled around and seized her by the arm. "You shouldn't have done that," he said. "Come along, girlie."

He pulled her down an aisle and then over to the produce section. A policeman stood there, looking out at the shoppers.

"This little thief tried to steal the milk out of my cart," the man said.

"No I didn't!" Ann said, more startled than offended. "He was the one—he took my milk, just grabbed it out of my hand."

"Did she, sir?" the policeman said, ignoring Ann. "Give her here—I'll take care of it."

"What!" Ann said.

The man shoved her over toward the policeman. She kicked out at his legs, but the policeman grasped her by the arm and tugged her away.

"You cut that out," he said, shaking her roughly. "You don't want me to add assault to your offenses."

"What offenses?" she asked. "I didn't do anything!"

Once again the policeman ignored her. "Do you want to press charges, sir?" he asked the man.

The man looked at the two of them, hesitating. Finally he shook his head. "It'll more trouble than it's worth," he said, sounding disgusted. "Just keep her away from me." He turned away, heading back toward the refrigerator.

"I hope someone stole your milk!" Ann shouted after him.

"You leave him alone, do you understand?" the policeman said. "He was kind enough to drop the charges—you don't want him changing his mind. Now let me see your ID."

My ID? she thought. She opened her mouth to ask why, then closed it again and took out her California Identification, what she had instead of a driver's license. It looked different somehow, but she wasn't sure how.

The policeman ran the ID over his phone, which sounded a quick tune when it had absorbed her information. Then he spoke a few words of explanation into the microphone. "All right," he said when he was done. "Let's go finish your shopping."

She headed back toward her cart. The policeman went with her, walking ostentatiously at her side. To her surprise she found that she was trembling, terrified that he might arrest her.

Why had she argued with that man? She was usually so good at keeping quiet, at never coming to the attention of anyone in authority. But how could it be right to steal like that? And why had the policeman been so ready to believe him over her?

The man had moved away from the milk, she was relieved to see. She picked up a carton that had expired and did the rest of her shopping as quickly as she could, the policeman staying with her as she headed through the aisles. It was only as she reached the checkout that he moved away from her, and even then he watched as she left the store.

She was still shaking while she waited for the bus, and as she got on. She fell into a seat and spread her bags out in front of her. "For God's sake, lady, put those away," a man said, walking past her. "You could break your neck."

She called Franny as soon as she got home and told her what had happened at the market. She had expected Franny to laugh at her fears, but instead the other woman said, "You know, now that you mention it I met some rude people too."

"People, or men?"

"You're right, it was mostly men. Though there was this one woman at the gym—"

Franny went to a gym? She was constantly being brought up against how different they were.

"Have you been watching the news?" Franny asked.

"Yeah, I was supposed to, but I never got around to it. I know we have a different president."

"It's not just that. There are food shortages all over the country, and gas shortages, and even martial law in some places. And they're talking about bringing martial law to California too, saying that people are rioting because of the shortages. You're lucky they didn't arrest you—they seem to be looking for excuses."

"Is this what the company wanted, do you think?"

"I don't know. And if it is, what can we do about it? Do you still want to—"

"Why don't we talk when I see you?" Ann said quickly. She wouldn't put it past the company to bug their phones.

"Sure. All right."

She hung up and went back to the computer to look at news sites. She saw very little about the shortages and martial law; instead the sites seemed to emphasize how stable the world had gotten, how few wars there were. Reading between the lines, though, she saw that there were more dictators as well, and more police states. The world seemed more peaceful, but also more oppressed, regimented, whole populations terrified into silence and obedience.

And yet—hadn't it always been like this? She rarely paid attention to the news, after all; maybe she had just never noticed how many totalitarian regimes there were. Or was she forgetting the world she had lived in, already taking this new reality as her own?

After a while she began to notice gaps in the net, like the empty spaces in the supermarket. Some of her favorite sites had disappeared, and others were missing links and posts she remembered from earlier visits. Finally she found an archive that hadn't been deleted, and she followed some hints in older posts to an underground site.

Here at last was a place where people exchanged ideas and information about the new government. But despite calls for rebellion, even revolution, there was no real opposition to President Henderson. The posters seemed to have been caught off guard by his swift proclamations of martial law, by the new laws giving him more power. Or maybe it was as she had thought so many times before, that most people in the United States had been lulled into sleep by reality shows and video games, that as long as they had a new gadget or television show to look forward to they would do nothing to disturb their easy lives.

That site led to others, and she ended up looking at a list of people who had disappeared into the prison system. It made her wonder if she had a record now, if that policeman had filed a report about her. She went on the city's police site, but it proved much harder to hack into than before. It took her several hours to break through the various firewalls, and then another hour to make sure her file was completely deleted.

While she was there she looked at some of the other arrest records. A great many people had been sent to jail for "disturbing the peace," which seemed to mean arguing with a policeman or someone else in authority. Franny had been right; she had been very lucky not to have been arrested.

THE NEXT DAY SHE got another email from the company, about another debriefing that morning. When she got to her assigned room she saw Franny arguing heatedly with Da Silva.

"That isn't what I'm talking about," Franny said. "You—you changed my country. You put someone else in as president. And martial law—"

"Look," Da Silva said. She nodded to Ann, indicating to her to take a seat. "As I told Ann here, I don't know all the ins and outs of this situation. But neither do you. There are things happening here that you can't understand, that you're seeing from only one perspective. Every tace has its own blind spots, believes in things that aren't necessarily true. Here in the United States you have a sort of fetish about democracy—"

"Fetish?" Franny said, appalled.

"Maybe fetish is the wrong word. But if you lived in my tace you'd see how much damage a democracy can do."

"Well, but we *don't* live in your tace."

Ann looked at Franny, trying to warn her off the subject. The other woman seemed to understand, and she shrugged at Da Silva as if she didn't want to argue further.

"Anyway," Da Silva said firmly. "That's not why I asked you here. I brought you in because it's time for you to see Jerry. Ann, I know you've already met him, and Franny, you've been told he isn't dead, but I still wanted to prepare you. You might feel dizzy, or see two realities superimposed, one where he died and one where he's still alive. Don't worry, though—you'll adapt pretty quickly to this new reality. And the other thing I want to warn you about is that you shouldn't make any reference to his death, or seeing his body. If you're confused by all of this, imagine how he feels."

She called out, and a woman led Jerry into the room. "Hi, guys," he said.

"Hi," Franny said, her voice barely audible.

She was struggling with the sight of him, Ann saw, trying to reconcile her memories. But the dizziness Ann had felt on seeing him earlier was gone; to her surprise Jerry's presence seemed natural, an established fact. It was true what Da Silva said, then—she had already accepted this reality.

"How are you feeling?" she asked him.

"Fine. Well, fine for someone who was dead for a while. Or so they tell me." He laughed awkwardly.

"Yeah," she said. "That must have been weird."

"You know, it isn't, not really. I don't remember dying, anyway. I was looking for that shop near the market, the shoemaker's, and then I was here, on the platform."

"So you were—you were following us?"

Da Silva frowned at her. Jerry ignored her, though. "Yeah," he said. "Charles told me to."

"But why?"

"Ann," Da Silva said. "It isn't good for him to talk about this."

"No, it's all right," Jerry said. "He said that you were part of some organization, but that's all I remember." He shook his head. "So are you? A member of whatever it was?"

"No, of course not."

"I didn't think so. I mean, how could you be? You didn't know anyone there, same as the rest of us."

Da Silva began to ask them questions, and before Ann knew it the interrogation had started again. They went over the same ground as before, her mind only half on her answers.

She remembered the flashes of feeling she'd gotten in Alexandria after her concussion, the sense that she didn't really belong there. Had the mob caught up with her in an alternate timeline, hurting her or—was it possible?—even killing her? And then had someone gone to the timeline before the mob had done its work and extracted her, sent her twenty-four years into the future? But who would do such a thing, and why?

They finished with Da Silva about an hour later. "Do you want a ride home?" Franny asked her.

"Sure," she said. Then, remembering all the rude people she had encountered the day before, she added, "Thanks."

They got in the car, and Ann directed Franny to her apartment. Franny began talking as soon as they got on the road, as if her frustrations ran off the same battery as the car. "Why do you think they wanted this—all of this—" She took her hands off the steering wheel and waved them at the passing streets, as if to indicate everything that had happened—Ann's policeman, martial law, the new president. "What do they get out of it?"

"Well, Strickland said they don't have a lot of resources up there, wherever it is they come from," Ann said. "This way they can take control of what there is a lot earlier, get a start on their problems before they become overwhelmed."

"I guess so. There do seem to be a lot more start-ups now, for solar power and wind power. More than I remember from before."

"Well, there you are."

"And there's more shortages too—gas and coal, food and water. They can't be transporting all of that to their own tace, can they? I mean, that would take a hell of a lot of energy, much more than they'd have."

Ann had never thought of that. "They wouldn't have to transport it, though. Just hide it somewhere and pick it up in the future."

"The food would go bad though. And how do you hide water?"

"I don't know. But coal—that wouldn't be too hard."

"So they could be stealing our coal, along with everything else. We don't even matter to them—they think they can do whatever they want to us."

"The real question is, what can we do about it?" Ann asked. "I want to join Core, but I don't even know who they are, or where."

Even as she said this, though, she remembered Azelaïs and her litany of names: Khartoum, Karnak, Carthage, Corinth . . .

"But Core can't really do anything, can they?" Franny said. "I mean, how do you fight against people who can change the past? The company'll just go back in time and stop them. Or kill them, like Greg."

"Well, look at what they did in Languedoc. They changed just one thing in the past, one battle, and we got this whole new reality. So maybe all we need to do is change something here, something small. Maybe Core knows what it is."

"That's another thing I wonder about. How did conquering Languedoc give us all of this?"

"Because, well, look," Ann said slowly, trying to put her ideas into words. "Everywhere we went, the same thing happened. The company supported a strong authority over a weaker one, a male-dominated world over one where women were more important. So the matriarchy in Kaphtor disappeared, and the troubadours in Languedoc, and in Alexandria . . . Well, I don't know what happened in Alexandria, but I think the books we rescued went on to help them somehow. And they didn't want to save Hypatia."

"Who's Hypatia?"

"Never mind. What I'm saying is, all of that added up to what we have now—a world filled with dictatorships, with authoritarian governments. With women being less and less important. That policeman yesterday—he didn't even pretend to listen to me, he was that sure that the man was right."

"You sound like a feminist."

"Well, of course I—" Ann stopped, surprised. "I *am* a feminist. Aren't you?"

"Well, I agree with some things. But who's to say women would do a better job than men at running things?"

"But—but you *saw* how women ran things. In Kaphtor." It was amazing that someone as intelligent as Franny hadn't realized that, Ann thought. But people were good at ignoring things that didn't match their beliefs. "They didn't have any wars, not for thousands of years. And they had enough food for everyone, and this amazing art and technology—"

"And they killed an innocent man, once every seven years."

"I'm not saying women should necessarily be in charge all the time. Just that they should be equal, should have equal chances."

They were coming up on her street; she didn't have nearly enough time to explain her point of view. She indicated her apartment building and Franny pulled over to the curb.

"Hey, why don't you just get a car?" Franny said. "You have to have enough money, with what they pay us."

Ann shrugged. She knew why, though. She needed to save as much as she could; she didn't know how much longer she would be with the company.

"I'll talk to you later," she said. "Think about what I said."

SHE SURFED THE NET after she got home, looking for other things that had changed in this world. By late afternoon her neck hurt, and she had the beginning of a headache. And she felt hungry; the meeting at the company had been at ten in the morning and she hadn't had breakfast or lunch. She leaned back in her chair and stretched.

There was something on the floor, near the wall. She got up and went to look at it. It was the thumb drive, lying where she had thrown it.

It looked different, though. It had opened up like a jackknife, revealing an LED display of a long string of numbers. A moment later the numbers changed, and then changed again.

She was an idiot. She didn't need a password, all she had to do was plug in the drive and enter the numbers it showed. Meret hadn't made it difficult for her. Just the opposite, in fact—she had made it as easy as possible.

She was eager to get started, but she forced herself to slow down and examine the drive. It was hinged, with the display hidden beneath an outer covering. She opened and closed it a few times, working carefully. You had to press a certain spot to open it; that had been the problem. Meret hadn't realized that she had never seen a drive like it before.

She went back to the computer and plugged it in, then entered the string of numbers it showed. Nothing happened. She bit back a scream of frustration and studied the drive again. Da Silva had plugged something like it into the elevator, to access the fifth floor. Could that be what the drive did, was it actually a key? Did Meret want her to visit the nerve center of the company?

Still, maybe it was just what it looked like, a flash drive. She worked at her computer some more, but she could discover nothing new. Finally she ate a sandwich, took some aspirin, and pulled her couch out into a bed.

Her mind raced in circles, though, refusing to let her sleep. What hadn't she tried? Did the drive have the answers to her questions, did it explain everything she wanted to know about the company? She felt an almost physical hunger for what might be on it. Information, tasty information.

No, it had to be a key to the elevator; she'd have to try it again, this time plugging in whatever numbers showed up on the drive. Had Da Silva said when they were going to summon her back to the company? She imagined plugging the drive into the elevator and riding up to the fifth floor, and then she fell asleep and dreamed about angels working at the company's terminals, and other angels flying overhead, carrying messages.

SHE HAD AN EMAIL waiting for her the next day, telling her to report for another debriefing. She felt a sudden excitement and sat down at the computer, staring at the message.

She should wait, should think about what it would mean to venture up to the fifth floor. She would have to pass herself off as a programmer from the future, would have to pretend to know how their computers worked, or find out in a hurry. It would be dangerous to go haring up there without a plan.

Still, how could she plan for something like this? She went through her sparse wardrobe, trying to find something with clashing colors. Finally she took out a purple skirt and pink blouse and tried them on together. Not as eye-straining as some of the outfits she had seen on the fifth floor, but it would have to do.

Her appointment was for ten in the morning again. She glanced at the computer's clock; it was just after six, plenty of time to get there by nine, when they opened. She worked at the computer for a while and ate some breakfast. Then she gathered together all the money she had in the apartment. It came to six hundred dollars, and she realized that she had been collecting it for some time, that for a while now she had thought this day would come. That she would have to run from the company, to hide somewhere the cameras couldn't find her.

She arrived at the company at nine. If she ran into problems, she thought, she could just say she'd gotten there early and skip the elevator until next time. But the receptionist, her first hurdle, just nodded at her and buzzed the door open.

She went down the hall to the elevator, walking as slowly as she could to avoid suspicion. Someone was coming toward her, a man who looked like Jerry. Damn—it was him.

"Hey, Ann," Jerry said. "I'm glad I caught you. I wanted to ask you a question."

She stopped. "Sure."

"I think I remembered something. After you left the shoemaker's you and Franny went somewhere else, didn't you? I was following you down a street, and I saw you point to something . . . Do you remember that?"

She shook her head. "A street? Where?"

"I don't know. It's been driving me crazy—I can almost bring it into focus, but not quite. You sure you don't remember?"

What if more of that trip came back to him? The street, and the word on the wall? What would happen if the company found the sisters of Kore?

"Yeah, I'm sure," Ann said.

"Well, think about it, okay? I'm pretty sure I saw it. What are you doing up so early?"

"What are you?"

"I'm going to talk to Charles. See if he knows anything."

"Okay. See you."

She hurried away from him, toward the elevator, and pressed the button to summon it. It came and she got on. She plugged in the drive, entered the string of numbers it showed her, and hit the button for five.

The elevator moved smoothly upward.

24

NO ONE PAID ANY attention to her when she stepped out onto the fifth floor. She hurried to the far end of the room and found a free computer and sat in front of it. Then she plugged in the drive and entered the numbers on the display.

A program seemed to detect the drive and automatically launch itself, then prompted her for a password. She tried all the ones she had used before: "Core," "Cor," and "Kore," then "Persephone," and finally "Hypatia." The screen cleared and changed to Meret's homepage.

She glanced down at the keyboard. It didn't seem very different from the ones she was used to, though there were a few keys she didn't recognize. She played around with them, figuring out what they did, and then called up the directory.

There were dozens of files, far too many to take in at once. At the head of the list was something called "Reminder." Every other file was in alphabetical order; did Meret want her to look at this one especially?

She opened it. It was short, just a few lines. "Reminder: Sending an employee only a few hours into the past or future requires a great deal of modeling; in fact, as the intervals in time get smaller and smaller the problems of insertion and extraction grow proportionally greater. It is far easier to move an employee decades or even centuries. If an employee is in danger and must be extracted at once it is better to send him some years into the future. After he has been inserted into a safe tace, you will have time to calculate when and where you can reinsert him.

"Remember also that this method does not involve a key but is instead done remotely, from the fifth floor. This means that you will have to work out both the traveler's beginning dates and his end dates from your station here. This is in contrast to travelers who use a key, whose time of extraction can be controlled from the past by that key and thus are open-ended. These two types of travel are called Closed and Open."

Ann understood Meret's meaning immediately, though the file was couched in such vague generalities she doubted if anyone in the company would get it. Meret was telling her that she had been the one to send Ann ahead in time, to 415, to get her out of danger while she calculated the safest way to return her to 391. Probably when Meret had gotten back from her assignment in Alexandria, before she had been sent to Kaphtor, she had looked through the archives and seen Ann on the camera feed, being attacked by the mob. And probably she had done exactly what Ann was doing, she had stolen moments on the computer, and had very little time in which to work. She had acted quickly, had sent Ann to 415 on the spur of the moment, maybe because they had discussed Hypatia's death.

And maybe she had wondered, just a little bit, if Ann could help Hypatia, could save her from the mob that wanted to kill her. But some historical events, the company had taught, could not be changed, no matter how many people they sent to solve the problem.

It was no wonder, Ann thought, that she felt so much out of place, as if she didn't belong in this timeline. She might have died, like Jerry, or survived and been left for dead, or been raped by the mob.

She shivered. This was the second time Meret had saved her life; it seemed she owed her for far more than just opening her eyes to the company's misdeeds.

She had discovered the answer to a smaller puzzle as well. She'd wondered how she'd been moved without a key, and why there had been a gap of five hours between the time she'd left Alexandria in 391 and when she'd been returned. Now she realized it was probably because Meret had been working in a hurry and hadn't had time to be precise. Meret's information also meant that she didn't need a key to travel now, a great relief, since she didn't have any idea where to find one. Though it also meant she would have to program her beginning and end dates beforehand.

But why hadn't the company found this evidence of Meret's meddling? They had been determined to discover where Ann had gone during the time she was away; she couldn't believe they hadn't checked the feed from the camera, the same feed Meret had used.

She looked through the directory and found a file called "Videos," clicked on it, and entered the time and place she was looking for. But although she found herself in Alexandria, along with film of Elias, Da Silva, and Zachery, there was nothing showing her and the mob at the library. Meret had somehow managed to erase it. She felt an extraordinary relief.

She studied the alphabetized list for other messages from Meret but found nothing. Perhaps they had been hidden to prevent the company from seeing them, but if so Meret had done too good a job of it; Ann couldn't find them either.

She did find a manual for the launch room, though, a tutorial for new employees. She opened it and paged through, fascinated by the technology.

She learned that the time machine had its own internal timeline, that voyages to the past took place in strict chronological order. So that, according to this timeframe, Gregory's assignment to the Spanish Inquisition had happened before his assignment to Kaphtor, even though, in the world's chronology, he had appeared in Spain in 1506 and in Kaphtor around 1,500 years before Christ. The company had found it necessary to impose this timeline in order to, as the manual said, "keep everything from happening all at once. If all our assignments occurred at the same time, we would never know which assignments caused which results, and everything would be in chaos."

She also discovered that the company could not travel into their own future, that they had no way of knowing how their manipulations had changed the world. Why, though, hadn't someone come back from the future to visit them? The company was divided on the answer. One faction thought that this silence meant that they had failed, that no one had survived much beyond 2327. Another group argued that the people of the future had kept away on purpose, that they knew that by simply being there they could change the timelines, could affect the company's project in negative ways. This claim had the virtue of optimism, of a belief that there would be a future, and that it was viable.

A loud commotion sounded at the door. "Ann Decker," someone called. "Is she here?"

She looked up quickly. No one pointed her out; none of these people knew her. But men were fanning out through the room, and although she was at the far end someone would eventually reach her station. She erased her tracks through the computer, logged off, and grabbed the thumb drive.

Now what? She couldn't head toward the door; one of the men would stop her, take away the drive. Arrest her for having it, probably. She was trapped.

No, there was one way out. She walked toward the room with the small launch pad, trying not to draw attention, to look as if she had important work to do. Once inside she closed the door and ran to the controls. The computer was already on, and set for 2327. She tapped the screen and hurried up onto the platform.

She felt the familiar time sickness, saw the piercing lights. She struggled to stay upright, to hold onto an awareness of her surroundings. When the nausea ended she saw that she was still in the launch room on the fifth floor, exactly where she had wanted to be. And the year was—she stepped off the platform and studied the computer—2327.

She opened the door and went outside. Once again no one paid any attention to her; everyone was focused on their own work. The computer workstations were where they had been in her own time, she saw. That made sense—people who traveled from one tace to another would want things to remain as familiar as possible. The machine she had used was occupied, though, and she went to a computer two stations down, far enough so that no one could peer over her shoulder.

She looked around her. The lights were more muted here, to save energy perhaps. Possibly in response to that the clothes were even brighter than in her tace, the colors more clashing. A lot of them were asymmetrical too, missing a sleeve or half a collar. Her own outfit, hastily put together, seemed even more out of place.

The keyboard looked more or less the same as the earlier one. She logged on, but she felt too worried about the men who had come looking for her to concentrate. When she hadn't shown up at the debriefing Jerry had no doubt told Da Silva that he had seen her heading toward the elevator. They couldn't know that she had the thumb drive, though, so they had almost certainly checked out the fifth floor just to be thorough. Maybe they'd thought she had snuck in with someone who had a key.

But it would probably never occur to them that she could use the time machine, and that she had gone into the future.

They had such low opinions of their employees in the past, after all. And even if they thought to examine the machine, there was already an explanation for why it was set for the year 2327: someone had used it before her.

Still, they could have ways of finding her that she had never thought of. She might not have much time. So now what? she thought. What should she do with the brief window she did have?

She knew the answer to that, though; it seemed she had always known it. She had to find a way to change history back to what it had been—and to do so in a way that the company couldn't change it back.

But she would have to go to a place where she already knew the language, and where her biome matched the existing bacteria. That meant she could only visit three time-frames, a pretty serious limitation. Or she could try some other tace, see how long she could survive there and how quickly she could learn the language.

Biomes, she thought, alarmed. She hadn't had a swab for the time she found herself in now—could she be missing some vital bacteria? She didn't feel ill, but there might be something here that would take a while to affect her. And all their teachers had said that the future was terribly polluted.

She should get to work, then. She searched the directory and found a tutorial for computer modeling.

It started off with Monte Carlo Markov chains, she saw, and she felt thankful that she had studied them earlier. But the tutorial grew more difficult to follow as she continued, and when she looked at her computer clock she saw that it had taken her twenty minutes to go through ten pages. And there were dozens of pages more, and those looked even harder.

She forced herself on, though, and twenty pages later she understood enough to think about modeling, about what events she could try to change. What if she went back, saw

Trencavel, and persuaded him not to believe anything the angel said? She entered the variables she needed, looked carefully through the code for errors, and clicked Execute.

The computer returned a probability of her desired outcome at 57%. Not great, she thought. Even worse, a list of possible negative events had appeared at the bottom of the page, and one of them was the somewhat unnerving prediction that she had a chance of seeing her earlier self. A jumble of equations followed, but all she could understand from them was that meeting yourself was strongly counter-indicated, that it could snarl the timelines like a ball of yarn.

She stretched and glanced at the clock, which said 13:23. It was afternoon, and she was starting to feel hungry. Did they have a cafeteria here? More importantly, what about bathrooms?

The man at the workstation two down from her caught her eye and said something. The words flowed into each other, gliding over her like a stream. Did they even speak English here, or something close to it? "What?" she said.

"I said, are you just back from the tributaries?"

She had been able to pick out individual words that time, fortunately. "Oh. Yeah."

"Good to be back at the headwaters, I bet."

"Yeah."

"What's your name?"

She thought quickly. "Tarquina," she said.

He laughed, though whether at the name or something else she didn't know. At least he seemed to accept it.

"What's yours?" she asked.

"Silas. Want to come for lunch?"

"Sure."

He rounded up a few other people and they left their workstations and crowded into the elevator. Two of them used wheelchairs, and she remembered once again that her professors had talked about the high levels of radiation and pollution in the future. Did they have a lot of birth defects hern?

The cafeteria was on the first floor, the same place it had been in the past. The familiarity relieved her, made her feel as if the future might not be too different after all.

She followed the others to the end of the line. Then she saw the men and women working behind the counters and she stopped, disbelieving. They all looked the same, tall and thin, almost exactly like the man she called Joe had seen on the fifth floor.

"Some of the mockmeat, Joe," Silas said, pointing to a tray of food she couldn't identify.

Were they all named Joe? They had probably been bio-engineered, cloned from a single original. Someone who was good at repetitive tasks, maybe. Someone named Joe?

Charles had said they couldn't give them consciousness, though. So the Joe on the fifth floor, the man who had worked so quickly at the computer—he was just a kind of machine. Weird.

A woman nudged her, and one of the Joes was looking at her quizzically. "Mockmeat, please," she said, and he ladled it onto a plate and handed it to her.

Another Joe, this one female, asked her what she wanted to drink. Or would she be a Josephine? Ann pointed to a drink on another tray and said, "That one, please."

"My, we are polite."

It was the woman next to her, one of the people in a wheelchair. For a moment Ann didn't understand what she meant. Then she realized that she had said "please" to the Joes, that probably no one used this sort of courtesy with them. "I'm just back from the tributaries," she said. "They're zany polite, where I was."

"Are you?" the woman said. "What was your go?"

What did that mean? She guessed that "go" referred to an assignment. "Kaphtor. Crete, about four thousand years ago."

"It sounds wonderful."

"It was. Sunlight and oceans, and the gods and goddesses, Kore and Demeter . . ."

They were the same words Gregory had used, a long time ago. Hundreds of years ago, now. But the other woman said nothing in response to her mention of Kore.

To her relief she found she didn't have to pay for her food; apparently the company still supplied free meals. She headed outside with the others, very conscious of the antique money in her purse.

There was something strange in the courtyard, something she couldn't identify, though it raised all the hairs on the back of her neck. Then she saw that a great part of the city had been covered over, that a barely visible dome stretched out far above them and a few miles on either side. It dimmed the light around them; even things several yards away were darker.

And there were no shadows here. Something deep within her had responded to that, something atavistic. She felt a strong sense of wrongness, as if an essential part of the world had gone missing.

The others were clustering around a picnic table that hadn't been there in her time. She hurried to join them. The woman she had talked to earlier rolled up next to her, at the end of the table.

"I'm Zarifa," the woman said. "What's your name?"

"Tarquina."

She took a bite of the mockmeat. It was heavily salted, though it seemed to have no flavor beneath that. "The food was prob better where you were, am I right?" Zarifa said.

She nodded, started to answer. Instead she began to cough, and went on for a long time before she was able to stop. She took a deep breath, then swallowed half her drink in one gulp. It was only water, slightly salty tasting like the food.

"Not used to the fine ambience at the headwaters?" Silas asked.

She tried to smile. "Not yet, no."

"It used to be even worse," Zarifa said. "Before the go to Languedoc. Were you here for that timequake?"

Ann shook her head. So she and the others had been responsible for a slight improvement in the future.

"You're so lucky," Zarifa said, her voice lower now, almost a whisper. "We all want to go out to the tributaries, get away from this awful place, even if it's just for an hour or two. It's wrong to admit it, but I know all of them feel the same way." She indicated the others at the table with her chin. "How did you manage to qualify?"

Ann shrugged. "I'm not all that sure, really."

"Don't be so modest," Zarifa said. "You must be some kind of brain."

She had sounded wistful. And probably she would qualify only for assignments to the twentieth century or later, where wheelchairs were more common.

Ann started to say something, then began to cough again. This time the fit went on for so long that Zarifa turned away and began to talk to the person on her other side.

Ann finished, then swallowed the rest of her water. Silas looked at her, a puzzled expression on his face. The people in this tace were used to the pollution, probably; they had to wonder why she was having so much trouble breathing.

"How did you know I was from the tributaries?" she said to Silas, to keep him from asking awkward questions.

"Are you kidding?" he said. "Who else would wear those clothes? Late twentieth century, am I right?"

Early twenty-first, she thought, but she nodded. She wanted him to know as little about her as possible.

Another cough began to tickle the back of her throat, and she stood. "I'm getting some more water," she said.

To her alarm, the others began to laugh. "Went native, then?" one of them asked.

She had no idea what he meant. She sat back down anyway, knowing only that she had blundered somehow.

"They didn't have rationing where you were, am I right?" someone else asked.

So that was it—they were only allowed one drink at lunch here. Still, she had to get inside, away from the bad air. "I'm going back to work," she said, standing up again.

Silas's puzzled expression had returned. She had made another misstep, but she couldn't stop to figure out what she'd done. She had to get into the building before she started coughing again.

To her relief she found a bathroom near the cafeteria. The plumbing inside was the most unfamiliar thing she had encountered so far, probably designed to recycle human waste. It took her a while to figure it out, but finally she finished and washed her hands. She was so thirsty she sipped the water that came out of the tap, but it was full of salt, undrinkable. Then she went back up to the fifth floor.

She continued working on her modeling, barely stopping to greet Silas and the others when they came back. The day wore on. A long time later she heard a group of people shout in triumph, and a few minutes after that another group entered the room and hurried over to them, setting up their own portable computers.

"Do you think you can finish modeling this today?" one of them said. "The second shift comes on in two hours."

"Sure," someone else said.

She glanced at her clock. 18:07. So they worked long hours here, until eight in the evening. It looked as if their minds as well as their bodies had been damaged by the pollution, that only a few people were intelligent enough to do the work the company needed. And these poor saps had to take on twice as much, to make up for everyone else. No wonder TI had recruited people from her own time period.

That lack of competent people would explain Walker as well. The company had had to lower their standards, to hire employees who weren't quite intelligent enough. And then, once Walker had joined the company, they would have found it impossible to dislodge her. In every tace Ann had seen the company had chosen hierarchies over democracies, had supported a strong person or group to rule over the great mass of people, from the Achaeans to Simon de Montfort. There was no reason to believe the company would not structure itself the same way—and Ann knew, from all her various jobs, that it was very easy to hide within this kind of organization, that responsibility could be spread around to different levels so that no one person ended up taking the blame. Walker's blunders would never have come to the notice of upper management.

What about the pills the company had given her and the others, to make them more intelligent, able to learn faster? But maybe they didn't work on the people in this tace, for one reason or another.

She shook her head. She should be working, not coming up with theories to explain the company.

What would happen when the second shift started? Someone would definitely notice if she stayed on; she would have to leave with everyone else. And what would she do then? Where could she go? She would have to get inside somewhere, or spend the night coughing her lungs out.

She turned back to the computer screen. She remembered her debriefing with Da Silva, and her speculation that the whole purpose of their assignment had been to make sure that Montfort survived. But what if Montfort had been killed at Carcassonne . . .

She typed in a few variables. 38%, the computer said. God, that was the worst yet. But in her timeline he hadn't died in Carcassonne but in Toulouse, nine years later. She set up the modeling parameters again and hit return.

272

84%. She was close now, the closest she had come so far. She worked on refining the parameters, getting a higher score each time.

When she stopped to look at the clock she saw that it was already 19:38. She worked as quickly as she could, keeping an ear out for the next shift. Finally the computer returned a score of 95%.

Yes! she thought. The manual had cautioned against using anything under 98%, but she didn't have time to refine her parameters further. And she was supposed to check her work with a holographic computer, one of the machines with visual modeling she had seen on her first visit, but she didn't have time for that either. Anyway, all the holographic computers were taken.

She went back to the directory, intending to erase everything she had done that day. Suddenly she stopped, her attention drawn to a file called Employees.

She hesitated, then tapped it. It opened onto an alphabetized list. She scrolled down and found her name.

The first thing in her file was a letter from someone she had never heard of. "I'm writing from Local Year 1989, where I was sent to look for recruitment possibilities, children with no families or other attachments. To this end I've stationed myself at a local hospital. Yesterday I saw an ambulance bring in a newborn with dreadful wounds to her torso. I overheard one of the medical technicians say that her mother had given her up, and so of course I immediately thought of her as a possible. I managed to get a look at the intake form and find her address, then programmed a camera to go there twenty-four hours earlier. The footage from that camera is attached."

Ann tapped the screen. Her hand was trembling. Here it was, the answer to the first question she had ever asked.

An empty garage appeared on the screen. The overhead door was open, the camera just outside it, looking in. A woman—no, a girl, around fourteen—ran through an adjoining door, screaming and crying. Her hair was tangled and matted with sweat, and she was naked from the waist down. She was carrying a baby, a newborn. She stopped and looked around frantically. The camera followed her as she went to a workbench at the side of the garage, with a set of tools hanging above it. She put the baby down on the bench and grabbed a pair of scissors, then cut her umbilical cord with shaking hands.

Then she looked down at the baby. Her expression had changed, become strange, remote. She raised her hand and stabbed the baby with the scissors. She stopped, looked at the wound she had made, and then brought the scissors down again and again. Five times, hitting each of the familiar places with terrible precision.

No. Ann closed her eyes. No, no, no—that couldn't have happened. She was watching something else, not her own birth.

"Stop it!" a voice said.

She opened her eyes and looked at the screen. A boy had come through the door. He grabbed the girl's wrist and wrestled with her a while, then finally snatched the scissors away from her.

He was still shouting, though—"Stop it! Stop it!" The girl screamed over him, "My life is ruined! It's ruined!"

Finally he seemed to realize that she had stopped, that he was holding the scissors. "Look," he said. He was trying to sound calm, but his voice still held a trace of hysteria. "We'll go inside, call an ambulance, get it to a hospital."

"No! No, we can't, they'll arrest me. Look, look what I did."

"But it's—she's bleeding. It's a girl, look. You can't just let her die."

"What if we . . ."

The girl's eyes fluttered closed and she began to fall. The boy was still holding the scissors, but he caught her with his other hand. He stood there for a long moment, in shock, Ann thought. Finally he laid the girl on the concrete floor, picked up the baby, put her down, and then went back into the house, still carrying the scissors.

The film picked up some moments later, with the arrival of two ambulances. Emergency crews ran into the garage and broke into two groups, one for the girl and the other for the baby. "Loss of blood . . ." someone around the girl murmured. "What the *fuck* . . ." someone else said.

Everyone was hurrying now, talking fast, doing things Ann couldn't follow. After a while she noticed that the boy was missing, that he had left before the ambulances had arrived.

The girl was loaded into an ambulance and driven away. The camera showed a cluster of paramedics around the baby, near the workbench. One of them—a woman—was holding her tightly and rocking her. A white bandage was wound around the baby's small torso.

"What name should I put on the form here?" someone asked.

"Shouldn't we wait, see what the mother says?"

"I don't think she wants anything to do with her."

"Well, Jane Doe, then."

"We should give her a real name—she'll have a hard enough time as it is," the woman holding the child said. "What about . . . Ann." She looked up at the tools on the workbench. "Ann . . . Decker."

Ann followed the woman's gaze. There was some kind of drill there, heavy and complicated. Black and Decker, it said on the handle.

The woman carried the baby into the remaining ambulance and they drove off, and the film ended.

Ann stared at the screen for a long time. After a while she noticed that Silas had turned to look at her, an alarmed expression on his face. She had been whispering under her breath, she realized: "No. No. No."

"What is it?" Silas asked.

"Nothing," she said.

She would go back, she thought. She would set the computer for 1989, walk into that garage, grab the scissors out of that woman's hand. Her mother. She was crying without making a sound now, thin tears running down her cheeks. She wiped them carefully, not wanting Silas to notice.

There had been adoptions that had not gone through because of her scars. She had overheard people talking about it, though no one had come right out and said anything to her. Prospective parents were horrified by them, or made queasy, even more so when no one could tell them who had attacked her, or why. The reason had been deliberately forgotten, Ann thought now, so that no one would ever have to tell her such a terrible story.

And after years of rejection she had become cynical, sure that no one would ever adopt her, and that had certainly not helped her chances. She had talked back to adults, made sarcastic comments far above her age level. She had set a fire in a foster parent's basement once, though that had been more in the nature of an experiment.

How much different would her life have been if she had never had the scars? She had been teased in every new school she went to, especially in gym class and other places where she had to change clothes. She had told some students that she had fallen into barbed wire as a child, and a group of girls—rich, popular, spoiled—had taken to calling her Barbie.

She could have been adopted, she thought. Could have had a family, gone to college, worked somewhere besides a crappy computer repair shop. She could have been named for something besides a tool company—and for a moment her hatred of the woman who had given her that name blazed so hotly she thought that Silas could probably feel it, two workstations down.

All her life she had disliked feeling sorry for herself, though, and this was no exception. She had learned to rely on herself, to make her own rules. She started to plan, to work out the steps she would need. Go to the launch room, set the computer . . .

The modelers around her were logging out of their computers and picking up their belongings, saying goodbye and moving toward the door. Silas was looking at her with that same puzzled expression, no doubt wondering why she hadn't shut down her own computer. There was no time to model probabilities; she would have to set the machine for 1989 and hope for the best.

But what about Core, and the reason Meret had sent her here? Should she fix her life, or fix the world?

The hell with the world, she thought. What had it ever done for her?

25

SHE SMILED AT SILAS—OR tried to smile, it probably looked like a rictus—and wiped everything she had done on the computer, then unplugged the drive. To her relief he picked up a canvas bag and headed out. She walked as casually as she could toward the launch room.

Once inside she locked the door and hurried over to the computer. Time to meet the monster who was her mother. The woman who had tried to kill her, who had blighted her life.

She remembered how drawn she had been to mother-figures, to Da Silva and Ariadne. She had even started to worship a mother goddess, though only in secret. But mothers weren't nurturing, or kind. They were killers, devourers.

Ariadne had even said so, or something like it. "She is the mistress of birth and sex, but also of death," the queen had said. "Our Lady of the Waning Moon."

They had known all about it, in Kaphtor. In so many ways they had been more sophisticated than the world in which she lived. Didn't she owe them something? Didn't she owe Meret, for all the sacrifices she had made?

Didn't she owe herself, though? No one had ever helped her, but now she had the opportunity to help herself.

Someone rattled the doorknob, then knocked loudly. "We get this room in five minutes," a man's voice said. "You need to clear out by then."

She had to decide. She couldn't decide; there were too many choices. The company had had no right to change her history. They should deal with their own problems, not foist them off on others. Just because they'd screwed things up in their own time didn't mean that she, that all the people of her time, had to live under martial law, with a policeman around every corner. She should use the thumb drive as Meret intended, to constrain the company's reckless meddling.

On the other hand, her last assignment had changed the world of 2327 for the better, Zarifa had said. Maybe she should just keep everything the way it was. Maybe changing things back would mean the failure of the company, even the end of human civilization. And if she didn't have to worry about that whole mess, about Core and the company, she would be free to travel to her own birth and confront her mother.

Variables cascaded through her mind. She thought of Da Silva again, of Meret. Of goddesses of death, and of life. Help me, Kore, she thought. What should I do?

But Kore had already told her. She had singled her out, had visited her in Kaphtor in the shape of a bee. The Goddess has a task for you, that strange boy had said.

Her end had been foretold in her beginning. The snake of the Kaphtorans, the snake of time, had eaten its own tail.

"Hey, open up!" the man's voice said. "It's our turn now—you can check the logs if you don't believe me."

She was out of time. She had come up with a way of erasing all her work on the time machine, of overwriting her destination after she had gone, and she programmed that in now. Then, almost without a conscious decision, she set the computer for Toulouse, 1218, with a return to her own time after ten days.

SHE LANDED IN A field. All around her were fallen trees, and old rotting stumps like decayed teeth. She could see no cities or towns, no farms, no roads.

Where was Toulouse? She had misprogrammed, had ended up somewhere unknown. And somewhen? What era was this?

Her nausea cleared. She slung her purse across her chest, then picked a direction and started to walk. Wherever she was, she had come to a land destroyed by war. There was only one reason to cut down trees like that: to destroy the crops before the enemy came.

The devastation stretched on into the distance. She had no way of estimating how far it went; she had never seen a landscape like this, without buildings or people.

It seemed to her that she walked on for hours. The sun moved through the sky, traveling so slowly she couldn't tell if it was rising or setting. Finally she realized that her shadow was growing longer; night was coming. She had forgotten to program in a time for her arrival, and the computer had given her the default, late afternoon.

What now? Would she have to sleep out here, in this exposed wasteland? And she was growing hungry; her last meal had been that tasteless lunch in the courtyard.

Something loomed up on the horizon. She hurried on, feeling relieved. A city wall, overlooked by towers. It looked enough like Carcassonne that she must have landed in the right timeframe, at least.

Then she saw the army camped outside. She cursed violently. The city was under siege, and she had no way of getting inside.

Why on earth had she thought she could do this correctly? People studied years to learn probability modeling, according to Da Silva. She would have to wait here for ten days, until she was returned home, and meanwhile nothing would have changed.

She couldn't spend that time out in the open, though. She had to find some new clothes, change out of her bizarre outfit, and then approach the crusaders' army, pretend to be a washerwoman or a cook. But what if they thought she was a prostitute? If they used her as a prostitute, no matter how strongly she denied it?

She would starve if she didn't join them, though, and she might as well go to them sooner rather than later. She walked around the army, staying a good distance away from it, looking for clothes. She was a good thief, she knew, had had to be of necessity. There had been times when she would have starved without her ability to steal food. And other times when she had had a different kind of hunger, had been famished for books, and she had stolen them from a bookstore, read them carefully, and then returned them.

Finally she saw a line of laundry spread out on the ground, drying in the sun. She headed toward it cautiously. The sun had nearly set, and at that moment several women left the camp to bring in the clothes before nightfall.

She dropped back quickly, but it was too late. One of the women saw her and started to scream. More women turned toward her, and then they were screaming too, drawing the attention of the soldiers nearby. Several men hurried toward her.

She ran. She was wearing flats, comfortable for her own tace but impossible for moving quickly. She tripped over a rock, stumbled to her feet, and hurried on.

The soldiers came closer. She could not hope to outrun them, she knew. She looked around frantically for somewhere to hide, but everything here was exposed, open, the land scraped bare.

One of them grabbed her arm. Another soldier said something in French, and a third answered him. She knew only the dialect of Languedoc, and she struggled to understand them. She thought one of them was telling the other to be careful, but it was hard to be sure.

The soldier who had hold of her said something she didn't understand. "Where are you taking me?" she asked.

He didn't answer. They dragged her toward a tent and threw her inside.

She struggled to sit up. Other men sat nearby on the tent floor, soldiers without the crusaders' cross sewn to their breasts. Prisoners from Toulouse, she thought, men who had taken part in sallies from the city and been captured, and were now waiting to be ransomed. Two crusaders stood by the front flaps of the tent, guarding them.

"Where are you from?" one of the prisoners asked her. He wore a padded jerkin, and an iron hat shaped like a bowl lay on the dirt beside him.

For a moment her mouth was too dry to speak. By the time she was ready to answer him, though, the conversation had moved on.

"She's from the east somewhere, I bet," someone said. "A long way away."

"They don't have those outlandish clothes in the east," another one said.

"How do you know, Gui?" Iron Hat asked. "When did you go traveling?"

"I've met men from the east," Gui said stubbornly. "And none of them wore those colors."

"Maybe only the nobility are allowed to wear them," Iron Hat said.

"Really?" the first man said. "And when did the nobility go skulking around a battlefield?"

"Maybe she's from Toulouse," Iron Hat said, lowering his voice. "Come to spy out the French weapons."

Despite her fear, Ann felt relieved to hear that she had arrived near Toulouse after all. "Are you?" Gui asked her. "From Toulouse?"

She had decided not to speak to anyone, not until someone in authority came to interview her. Anything she said in a careless moment to her fellow prisoners could be reported back to her captors.

"Come on, Gui," the first man said. "When did you ever see those clothes in Toulouse? Be consistent, in the Lady's name."

The Lady? Ann thought. Probably he meant Mary, though, and not Kore.

The men continued to argue lazily among themselves. One of the women she had seen earlier came in with a great cauldron of something hot and others poured it out into smaller bowls. "Broth again," the first man said.

A woman passed around the broth, leaving Ann for last. Finally she set down Ann's bowl and hurried for the entrance, crossing herself as she went.

The first man laughed raucously. "Never seen a woman from the east before?" he said, and the others laughed with him.

The woman turned back and let loose a series of harsh words in French, like a long string of firecrackers going off. Ann understood none of it until the end, when she heard the name "Simon de Montfort."

She'd come to the right time, then. Though she was not comforted by the thought; instead, remembering the stories she had heard about the man, she felt a cold terror uncoil within her. Montfort was the commander who had ordered the slaughter of the men and women of Béziers, who had thrown an old woman down a well and hurled rocks on top of her. Who had punished the defenders of the town of Bram by blinding the prisoners and cutting off their noses—all but one man, who had been left a single eye so that he could lead them into the next town as a warning.

What would Montfort do to her, and to these prisoners with her? In the history she had studied, he had died at Toulouse, and so had not had the chance to commit atrocities there. But that history had been changed, and Da Silva said he had survived.

Her hand was shaking as she raised the bowl to her mouth. The broth tasted mostly of water, mixed with a few gristly shreds of meat.

Eventually, several men came through the entrance. The man at the head was short and squat, with thick black hair and a black beard. His face was flat, his nose stubby, as if a giant thumb had pressed against it and squashed it inward.

He headed toward Ann. "So you're the woman they told me about," he said. He spoke good Languedoc, though with a strong accent. "With the outlandish clothes. Are you a witch?"

"No."

He scowled. "Do you know who I am? I'm Lord Simon de Montfort, Count of Toulouse, among other things. What's your name? Where are you from?"

She wanted to point out that he clearly wasn't the count of Toulouse, that he couldn't even get inside the city, but she knew better than to say it. "Ann, my lord. From the Rhineland."

"And what is an unaccompanied woman from the Rhineland doing near a dangerous battlefield?"

She had come up with an answer to this while she was waiting to be questioned. "I'm part of a group of *trobairitz*, my lord," she said, using the word for female troubadours. "We were separated in the war."

He scowled again. "I know what a troubadour does—he sings lewd songs to his lord's wife. Is that what the *trobairitz* do as well? Sing lustily to men not their husbands?"

"No, my lord. We—"

"And do they all dress as shamelessly as that? What do you call those clothes? Give me that sack you carry, let me see it."

She lifted her purse over her head reluctantly. Why hadn't she hidden it somewhere, before she came to the city? But she hadn't known she would be captured.

Montfort opened the flap and took out her wallet. He ran his fingers over the plastic surface, then lifted it to his nose and sniffed. He fumbled with the snap and took out all the money she had gathered before she left for work.

"What is this?" he asked.

"Nothing," she said. "Playthings."

"Look how carefully the scribes have worked here," Montfort said, showing the bills to the other soldiers. "The detail. 'Twenty dollars,'" he read, stumbling over the words. "Is that like *douleur*, pain? Is this some witch-work, to cause pain to your enemies?"

"No, my lord. Just a game, like I told you."

He handed the money to one of the soldiers and rooted through the purse again, this time coming up with her credit cards. "Look at this," he said, taking a card out of its plastic sleeve and bending it back and forth. It snapped suddenly, and he looked startled. "What material is this made of?"

"I don't know."

"Is this some Rhinish game as well?" Before she could answer he said, "Will your friends ransom you, do you think?"

It was an important question, she knew. If she couldn't be exchanged for money she was of no use to him; he could do whatever he wanted with her.

"Of course," she said, trying to sound certain.

"Where are they?"

"I—I'm not sure, right now. I could send off a few letters—"

"I'm sure you could."

He signaled to his men and they left. He was still holding her purse; it looked ludicrous in his huge rough hands.

"Ann, is it?" one of her fellow prisoners asked. "Is that your name?"

She nodded.

"And was he right? Is a woman troubadour as lusty as a man?"

"Shut up, Matfré," Iron Hat said, sounding tired. "We're not Frenchmen here. If you want to sleep with her why don't you just ask her."

"All right then," the first man said. "Will you sleep with me?"

She shook her head. All the men except Matfré laughed.

"It's late," Iron Hat said. "I'm going to sleep."

The men jostled for space on the floor and stretched out. Two guards carrying torches came in to relieve the men at the entrance. They set the torches in the ground and turned to look out at the crusaders' camp.

Flame and shadow washed over her. Noises sounded from outside: horses stamping, armor ringing out, men shouting and singing. The dirt floor felt uncomfortable, but she tried not to move around, to roll up against any of the men. So far they had not threatened her, but she knew that the French would not be nearly as courteous, that if a man wanted her he would take her, with no one to tell him no.

And she had wasted a day, one day out of the ten she had programmed for herself.

SHE WOKE TO HEAR noises at the entrance. Simon de Montfort and his men came inside and headed toward the prisoners. She sat up quickly.

"All right," Montfort said, lightly kicking the prisoner next to him. He looked fit and well rested, unlike Ann and the rest of the prisoners, and she realized that in this time-line he had not spent the last ten years fighting. "Get up— we're exchanging prisoners."

"What about me?" Ann asked.

"I'm sending you along with everyone else," Montfort said. "I still don't know if you're a witch or not, but that'll be someone else's problem."

"Can I—can I have my things back?"

This seemed to rouse him. "Back? Do you take me for an idiot? Who knows what those things are? I've burned them, burned them and then got a priest to speak holy words over them."

Luckily she didn't need a computer to get back this time. "Well, can I at least have some other clothes?"

"You want a good deal for a prisoner of war. Shall I fetch you some lark's tongues as well, my lady, and bouillabaisse in saffron? You'll be silent if you know what's good for you—I can still change my mind."

He led them outside and marched them through the camp, moving so quickly they had to struggle to keep up with him. The camp smelled of waste and spoiled food and unwashed men, with the rot of dead bodies underneath.

A group of men stood waiting for them in front of the walls. Montfort drew up to face them, and one of his soldiers read off the names of the prisoners.

"Ann of the Rhineland?" a man from Toulouse asked when they had finished. "Who's she, by the Lady?"

"I have no idea," Montfort said. "She showed up at our camp, just as you see her. Says she's a she-troubadour."

The man stared at her, and for a moment she feared they wouldn't take her with them. Then another man began to read the names of captured crusaders, and Montfort nodded, and the two groups exchanged places.

Cheers and exclamations went up from both groups. Ann and the others marched toward the wall, and a gate opened to receive them.

The men rushed into the city, still shouting. Someone started a song and the others took it up. Ann followed after them, at first tentatively and then, when no one made to stop her, running freely.

After a while she slowed and began to look around her. Houses stood deserted on either side, the doors smashed in or lying open to reveal the rooms beyond, their owners probably dead or gone to fight. Or maybe they were Cathars and had fled to the countryside; Montfort had burned heretics in all the towns he conquered.

She looked around her cautiously, then slipped into one of the houses. There was still furniture here, chairs and tables and rugs and cushions, all covered in drifts of dust. She moved on and came to the bedroom. A bed stood against the wall, with a small chest at the foot. The chest held a pair of neatly folded men's hose, a jerkin, and—she nearly shouted with relief—a woman's rough mud-colored gown.

She lifted it out, took off her skirt and blouse, and put it on. She would be able to blend in, finally; people would no longer stare at her, or cross themselves when they saw her.

She looked at her old clothes, lying on the floor where she had dropped them. They looked odd to her now, the colors like nothing else in this tace; she understood why people had called them outlandish. She would have called them outlandish herself.

She should burn them, she knew, in accordance with company protocol. But she was anxious to find people, and to join the defenders on the walls. And she was feeling hungry again; someone here would probably give her food in exchange for work.

She stuffed her clothes under the ones in the chest. Then she went through the house, looking for more things she could take with her. All the food had turned rotten, though, and whoever lived here had taken everything of value.

SHE MADE HER WAY to the city walls and began to walk alongside them. If the history books were right a group of women and children were defending the city by hurling boulders from a catapult.

Men and women hurried past her, carrying ropes and buckets and pieces of machinery. Someone called her over to some ladders against the wall, and someone else asked if she could help carry some heavy lumber, but each time she shook her head and told them she was wanted farther down.

Everyone moved purposefully, calmly, as if they had been practicing their defense of the city for years. Some of them were even singing, something she had read about but had never truly believed.

A little after noon she smelled some cooked meat, and glancing around she saw some women carrying food to a group of defenders. She went toward them, trying to look as though she had been on this part of the wall all morning.

The defenders climbed down the ladders and took their bowls from the women, then leaned against the wall or sat in its shadow to eat. A woman gave Ann a bowl and she drank it down greedily. It was more watery broth, nearly identical to the food in the crusaders' tent.

When they finished the defenders headed back up the ladders. "Come on," one of them said, looking back at her.

She glanced around her. Was this the group she'd been looking for? No—there seemed to be many more men than women here.

They were all staring at her now, though, and she had no choice but to follow them up the ladders. Defenders stood on temporary wooden battlements at the top, looking out through the crenellations in the wall. They reached into buckets placed at their feet and hurled rocks through the openings at the crusaders' camp.

A man handed her a bucket filled with rocks and pointed at the camp. "Over there," he said. "That big tent. That's the one to aim for."

He began to sing, and soon all the defenders had taken up the tune. It wasn't a song of war but of love, another troubadour's composition. "If I could find her all alone,/ While she is sleeping, or pretending to,/ I'd go to her, and steal the sweetest kiss,/ A kiss that makes my worthless life anew."

She picked up one of the rocks and threw it as hard as she could. It landed just short of the tent, and some of the defenders cheered. She took another rock, and then, after listening to the song for a while, joined in with the voices around her.

A line of archers formed up beneath the wall and drew their bowstrings. "Down, get down!" someone near her shouted. She ducked quickly.

A rain of arrows pattered through the openings in the wall. Some of them were tipped with flame, and fire burst out on the ground. Women hurried to pour out buckets filled with water, and when the all buckets were emptied they rushed off to fill them, going back and forth until the fire was out.

For a few hours after that her muscles would clench when she looked through the crenellations, and she would only relax when she saw that there were no archers below her. Then as the day wore on she felt less and less afraid, and finally the archers came to seem like a nuisance, of a piece with the hunger and dirt and bad food. The man next to her sent a bowman to his knees with a rock, and all the defenders stopped to cheer.

All afternoon she looked for a chance to slip away, but the defenders around her kept her busy. When she had thrown all her rocks someone brought her another bucket, and then another, and another. Finally she saw the sun going down past the crusaders' camp, and she realized she had lost another day.

It didn't matter, she thought; she still had time. She ate dinner with the defenders, then bedded down with them for the night.

She couldn't sleep, though. She had arrived safely, had reached her destination both in time and in space, and yet she felt as if she had forgotten something, had left something unfinished or unguarded. Could the company restore the data she had wiped from the computer she had worked on, or from the time machine? She didn't think so, but there was a lot she didn't know about their technology.

On the other hand, if they were going to come after her they would have probably done it already. Or would they? What if they waited until the very end, just before she killed Montfort and changed history? Or did the fact that they hadn't come mean that she hadn't managed to accomplish her goal?

She tossed and turned, her mind circling the same questions over and over. Finally she opened her eyes in near darkness and realized that she would not get to sleep again that night.

She stood and made her way along the wall, passing groups of men and women huddled together. Sometimes she saw lovers sleeping together, one curved against the other, and she felt a familiar loneliness. An army of lovers, she thought, then told herself firmly not to romanticize them.

A few lights glimmered on the walls, people keeping watch on the crusaders' camp. Then others began to stir, to stretch and yawn and climb up the ladders. She glanced quickly at the defenders as she passed, trying to look as if she had somewhere important to be.

A man rose and stood with his profile to her. Peire Raimon. No, it couldn't be. But she remembered now that he had given his name as Peire Raimon de Tolosa—of Toulouse.

He turned toward her. It *was* him, though a good deal older. Something sparked in his eyes, the beginning of recognition, maybe. She hurried on, and when she had put enough space between them she began to run.

She had been an idiot once again. She'd been worried about the company finding her and had ignored a far closer danger. Of course there were people in this tace who would remember her, and who would be startled, maybe horrified, to find her the same age as when she'd left, nine years ago.

And for it to be Peire Raimon, the man who had felt so much hatred for them, just made it that much worse. And this time the viscount wouldn't be around to protect her.

She turned a corner—and there, to her great relief, was the group she'd been looking for. Women and older children stood on the platforms, and younger children shouted and played beneath them, dancing around an ancient white-haired woman. At first Ann thought she was deformed somehow, her face sunk inward, and then she realized that the woman must have lost all her teeth.

Where was the catapult, though? Maybe they hadn't brought it yet, maybe it would turn up later.

She called up to one of the women on the platform. "Hey— do you need help?"

"Always!" the woman said, smiling down at her. "Come on up!"

She climbed to the wooden parapet. Her right arm felt sore from her work the day before, but the ache faded after she had thrown a few rocks.

A group of crusaders came close to the walls and she hurled a rock toward one of them. It knocked a knob off his shield, and the women cheered.

"Aim for their legs, if they're wearing armor," the woman next to her said. "They have great heavy plates on their chests, but only leggings below."

"Nothing there to protect, probably," another woman said, and the others snickered.

A crusader in mail brought his horse in close to the wall. "Like this," the first woman said, flinging a rock at him. It hit him in the thigh; Ann saw him clutch his leg and open his mouth in pain, though she could not hear him over the noise of the battlefield.

"One for Toulouse!" the woman called down to him in a taunting voice. "One for Richilde!"

"Who's Richilde?" Ann asked.

"My sister. She died in the siege of Carcassonne."

Wait a minute, Ann thought. Richilde—could she be the woman who would have killed Montfort? And was it because she had died in Carcassonne that Montfort had survived here, and had gone on to plunder and burn the southland, to kill its people?

"I'm sorry to hear that," Ann said. Sorry not least because Richilde hadn't survived to make history.

Richilde's sister seemed to have guessed how little Ann knew about defense, and she kept close to her all afternoon. "Duck to the side of the carnels, not below them," she said.

"Carnels?" Ann asked.

"These things," the woman said, pointing to one of the openings in the wall in front of them.

Oh, crenellation, Ann thought. She liked "carnel," though, another word possibly related to Kore.

She had picked up a rock and thrown it before she realized that the woman's use of the word might have been deliberate, that it could be a password. She struggled to come up with a reply, and finally said, "I hope they bring us a meal soon—it'll put heart into us."

The woman turned to her, puzzled. So much for that idea, Ann thought. Sometimes a word is just a word.

The day passed with much the same rhythm as the last one—throwing rocks, resting until someone brought more, pausing for food in the afternoon, in the evening. Archers loosing arrows, fires breaking out, being quenched. And the songs, sung out when the defenders slackened, or when the shadow of a passing cloud made them all pause.

Toward evening the crusaders wheeled a wooden tower close to the wall. "Shoot them, shoot them quickly," someone said urgently, and several women brought out bows, lit the arrows with fire, and took aim at the tower. Why? Ann wondered, but she said nothing; everyone else seemed to know what it was.

A few arrows thumped against the walls. Fires caught and ran along the wood for a moment, but the wind blew them out. Then men within the tower wrested off the wooden covering, revealing a catapult.

The arm of the catapult flung high into the air, and she ducked down below the wall. A great boulder crashed to the ground a few feet behind her.

Someone screamed. A woman cried out, a wail of grief. Ann looked back and saw a child pinned under the rock from the waist down. All the women nearby pushed against the rock to dislodge it, but with each thrust the child only screamed louder.

"Help!" one of the women shouted. "Someone help us!"

Ann climbed down the ladder. Defenders hurried over to them and clustered around the child. "Never mind that—you can't help him," one of them said. "Everyone with bows, get up the ladders—we have to stop them."

Ann had been looking at the boy as he said this. To the end of her life, she thought, she would remember his expression—somehow horrified and sad and resigned all at once. They really did have a different concept of death here, she thought. They knew that they could die at any moment, and they were ready for it, or as ready as they could be.

"It is you!" someone said behind her.

She turned. Peire Raimon stood there, among the people who had come over to help. She pushed through the crowd and ran.

"Stop her!" he called out. "Stop that woman!"

She sped quickly along the street by the wall. Evening had come; men and women crowded in front of her, climbing down the ladders, carrying food, stopping to eat. She dodged among them, looking for a place to hide. She heard feet behind her, more than one person.

"She's a spy," Peire Raimon said loudly. "The crusaders sent her."

Clever of him, she thought. He had no idea what she was, so he picked the worst crime he could think of, the one most likely to rouse everyone against her.

Why should they listen to him, though? She could make her own accusations, just as bad. Anyway, she was tired of running. She stopped and faced him.

"I'm not a spy," she said, as scornfully as she could manage. "He's the spy, and a thief as well. He stole something from us, when we were guests of the viscount of Trencavel."

The people chasing her had stopped. Several of them glanced from her to Peire Raimon and back again, looking confused.

"She's a spy, I tell you," he said. "Listen to her—does she sound like someone from around here?"

"I'm from the Rhineland."

"What are you doing here, then?"

"I'm a troubadour. I got separated—"

"Are you? Sing something for us."

Her voice was nowhere near good enough; they would know her for an imposter as soon as she opened her mouth.

"Why should I?" she said. "Why should anyone believe anything you have to say? You stole from us."

"Really? What was it I stole?"

That was clever as well; she certainly couldn't say "a computer." She was beginning to realize how badly she had underestimated him. "A necklace."

"And that's a lie," he said. "The viscountess gave me that necklace, as you well know."

He looked around him, his expression confident. A few people were nodding, probably more inclined to believe him than some foreigner. "I don't know any such thing," she said. "And you can't prove it."

"Of course I can. We'll ask Lady Agnes."

Agnes? She had thought Agnes was dead. "Is the viscountess—is she here?"

"She is indeed. Montfort spared her. How is it you don't know that?"

The crowd was muttering now. "If she's a spy . . ." someone said behind her. ". . . put her to death," someone else said.

"And where did you go when Carcassonne fell?" Peire Raimon went on. "No one saw you, or your friends—we thought you'd died. But here you are, healthy as a priest. Montfort must have rewarded you well for your work."

A man with a sword at his belt stepped forward and grabbed her by the arm. "All right, let's go," he said.

"What?" she said. "Where?"

"Where? Do you want holy ground, a priest to shrive you before you die? We don't have that luxury, I'm afraid." He glanced around him, looking for a good spot to lay her head. "Right here, I think."

She struggled to pull away but he held on tightly. "Wait," someone said behind her.

They turned. Then everyone was dropping to their knees, their heads bowed, as a man came up to them. His hair was dark gray, the color of ashes, and his face was deeply lined.

Ann bowed as well, though she had no idea who he was. "What's happening here?" he asked.

"Lord Raimond," the man with the sword said. "We captured a spy, my lord."

Raimond VI, the true count of Toulouse. No wonder he looked so tired, so careworn. "I'm not, my lord," Ann said. "I swear it."

"She's not from here, my lord," Peire Raimon said.

"What does that matter?" the count said. "Many people come here from somewhere else—that doesn't make them spies. Is she from the north?"

"No, my lord," Ann said. "From the Rhineland."

"Well, then," Raimond said. "Why do you say she's a spy?"

"She's—she hasn't aged," Peire Raimon said. "Not in ten years. No, nine—she was at the siege of Carcassonne. And she looked as young as that, twenty years old, and she hasn't changed a day."

She was twenty-five, but no doubt she seemed younger to these people, with their hard lives. The crowd was muttering again, looking to her and backing away. "I have a young face, my lord," she said. "That's not an offense, I hope."

"And why should that make her a spy?" Raimond said. He sounded exasperated.

"It makes her strange, uncanny," Peire Raimon said. "I saw her in Carcassonne nine years ago, among the viscount's court, and she looked exactly the same. How does she explain that? Ask her, my lord."

"She already explained it," the count said. "She has a young face."

"It's more than that. Find Lady Agnes and ask—"

"Move!" someone shouted from the walls. "Move away, my lord, please! The bowmen are lining up below us."

"All right," the count said. "Both of you are coming with me. We'll solve this mystery somewhere else."

With a few gestures the count ordered some of his men to take charge of Ann and Peire Raimon, and he led them into the city.

She looked around her as they went. She had expected Toulouse to look something like Carcassonne, but now she saw that the war had devastated it. They passed more empty houses, and men and women with missing arms or bandages tied around their eyes, and small children wandering aimlessly. Stones had been torn from the streets and buildings to be used as weapons. The siege had lasted nine months, and already the people looked hungry, and somehow lost.

The count's castle rose up in front of them. The men dragged them inside, and Raimond led them through a series of small dim rooms. Finally they came to a narrow corridor.

"In here, both of them," Raimond said, indicating one of the rooms. "And I want that bar kept across the door at all times, unless someone's in there with them."

The men pushed them inside. "And bring them some food," the count said.

He and his men left. The door closed, turning the room so dark Ann could not see the opposite wall. She heard a heavy bar slide across the door. "I hope you're happy," she said to Peire Raimon. "Your stupidity got us both arrested."

"You're the one who's arrested," Peire Raimon said, his voice coming out of the darkness. "He'll let me go, but you'll be here forever."

She felt her way to the wall and sat against it. A while later some of the count's servants came into the room, bringing candles and trays of food.

Peire Raimon was visible now, but what she saw made her wish for the darkness back. He was staring at her, taking in every detail of her face, clearly marveling at how little she had changed.

"Stop looking at me," she said.

Peire Raimon laughed. "I'll do as I please."

"I'll tell the count."

He laughed again. "And why should he care? A man's allowed to look at a woman."

Of course he was. All the veneer of chivalry had been stripped away, his true purpose laid bare. He could do whatever he liked to her.

"Are you immortal?" he asked her.

She bent her head to the food in front of her and said nothing. Perhaps if he thought she was immortal he would leave her alone.

"Don't think you're too good to talk to me," he said.

"Stop staring at me and I'll talk."

He laughed again and started to eat. The servants had brought them the ubiquitous broth, but this time it seemed mostly water, with only a faint ghostly taste of meat beneath that.

Now she could see a low cot on either side of the room. She finished the broth and went to one of them to lie down. Peire Raimon took the other one, then leaned over and blew out the candles.

She nearly protested, not wanting to be alone in the dark with him. Then she realized that he was trying to conserve the candles, and she said nothing.

The room continued to smell of whatever they had made the candles out of, mutton fat, she thought. And she could smell her gown too, the sweat of whoever had worn it last.

That soon faded, though, and she thought of Peire Raimon's taunt to her. "You'll be here forever," he had said. But she had to get to the walls, back to the defense of the city. What if he was right, what if they never let her go?

She had programmed the machine to bring her back in ten days. Seven days, now. She nearly laughed. Peire Raimon already thought she was uncanny—what would he do if she disappeared before his eyes?

But if she stayed here she would lose her only chance. Montfort would live, and her own time would be condemned to the timeline she had seen, to men with more power than anyone should be trusted with.

27

SHE WOKE WITH AN urgent need to use the chamber pot. She slipped out of her cot as quietly as she could, hoping that Peire Raimon was still asleep. He opened his eyes and watched her sleepily, then, realizing what she was doing, turned his head away to give her privacy.

Servants brought them breakfast soon after. She spent the rest of the day pacing back and forth in the room, measuring it with her footsteps. Ten paces one way, twelve the other. Peire Raimon asked her what she was doing but she felt too impatient to answer him, too anxious about what was happening out in the city without her.

The minutes crawled by. Then suddenly it was evening again, and the servants brought more food and light for their candles, and carried out the chamber pot. Another day lost, she thought as she dropped onto her cot.

The next day she found a twig in the corner of the room and used some mud to make a calendar on the wall. Four days gone, six to go.

"What are you counting?" Peire Raimon asked when he saw it. "And why four marks? You've only been here two days."

She said nothing.

The days continued to pass. She marked five days on the wall, then six, then seven. Every day she would ask the servants if she could talk to Raimond, and every day they told her that the count was busy with the war.

Finally, on the eighth day, she heard noise outside her room. Raimond came in, and with him Lady Agnes, the viscountess of Trencavel.

"My lord," Peire Raimon said, dropping to his knees. "My lady."

Were he and Agnes still lovers? Would they collude together, against her? She went to her knees, and by the time she rose Peire Raimon was already talking to the viscountess.

"Do you remember Ann, my lady?" he said. "She was a *trobairitz* with Charles, the man from the Rhineland, during the siege of Carcassonne. And she hasn't changed at all since then, not in nine years."

Lady Agnes studied her. Ann held her breath. "I can't remember," she said finally. "It was a hard time—I don't like to think about it. And of course my fool husband only made it worse, becoming a Cathar."

"Look at her," Peire Raimon said urgently. He mentioned the titles of the songs they had sung, then hummed "I Dare to Claim." "Don't you remember Charles? He tried to pay court to you."

"I—I think so. Maybe."

"There you go, my lord," Peire Raimon said to the count.

"My lord," Ann said. "I haven't done anything. It isn't a crime to have a young-looking face. And Lady Agnes isn't even sure if she remembers me."

Lord Raimond sighed. "I don't have time for this," he said. "I'll talk to Agnes later, see what she says."

"I've been a help to you on the walls," Ann said. "Let me go, and I'll fight for you again."

"And why is she here, fighting with us?" Peire Raimon said. "She isn't even from Toulouse."

"Why shouldn't I? I hate Montfort as much as anyone."

"Yes, why shouldn't she?" Lord Raimond said. "Doesn't all the world hate Montfort?"

Ann tried not to grin. She had won one round, at least.

But the count didn't return the next day, when the marks on the wall stood at nine. She resigned herself to the idea that he wouldn't make it back in time, that she would simply vanish from the room. It was too bad, she thought, that she wouldn't be able to see Peire Raimon's face when she disappeared.

The next day, though, one of the serving women stopped to talk to her. "Are you the woman they talk about?" she asked Ann, handing her her broth. "The one who doesn't age?"

Peire Raimon looked at the woman quickly. "No, of course not," Ann said. "It's this idiot here who thinks so."

"She doesn't," Peire Raimon said. "I remember her from nine years ago, in Carcassonne, and then—"

"Maybe you just have a terrible memory," Ann said.

She had grown very tired of Peire Raimon's company, these past seven days. He had stopped staring at her—chastened, perhaps, by the thought that she could truly be a witch—but he had only one topic of conversation, the fact that she hadn't grown older. At least, she thought, he hadn't attacked her. Maybe the songs he sang had made him slightly more courteous, as Azelaïs had said, or maybe he'd always respected women more than the other men in this tace.

"My religion speaks of a saint that never ages," the woman said.

What religion was that? Was the woman a Cathar? But Ann could not remember anyone like that among the Cathars. "What saint?" she asked.

"Her name is lost. She goes out among women and eases their hearts."

Cor, the woman had said, the Languedoc word for heart. Ann's own heart began to beat faster. "I know who you mean," she said. She lowered her voice. Peire Raimon had already stopped listening, though, apparently not interested in women's religion. "Is her name Mara? My heart is eased by her as well."

"A friend of Mara's. She met another one of Mara's friends in the long-ago time, and then met her again twenty-five years later, and she looked exactly the same."

Good lord—the woman was talking about her and Olympia, in Alexandria. She was a saint, a legend, her story miraculous enough to have survived for nearly a millennium. It was an extraordinary feeling; something she had done had mattered.

"I'll come back for you," the woman said, whispering. "Be ready."

"I need to leave today," Ann said in the same low voice. "I have to—to do something for Core."

"Today? It's best to take you out at night."

"Please. It's important."

"I'll try," the woman said. "I'm Hermesende, by the way."

She left. Ann heard the sound of the bar drawn across the doorway. Peire Raimon sat on his cot and slurped his broth, seeming unconcerned.

She had expected to spend the rest of the day nervously awaiting Hermesende's return, but instead she felt surprisingly calm, almost fatalistic. Whatever happened had already occurred, was already history to the people in her own tace. Hermesende would come or she wouldn't; Ann could do nothing about it either way.

Sometime later the door opened and Hermesende bustled inside. "Come along," she said to Ann. "The count wants to see you."

Peire Raimon looked up at that. "Ah, he's finally taking an interest. Is he going to burn her?"

303

"That's for him to say," Hermesende said. Her tone was so matter-of-fact that for a moment Ann thought she was truly about to be killed. Then she caught the woman's expression, saw her grin.

They left the room. There were no guards outside; everyone was probably needed on the wall. They raced through the castle, and then out into the city.

"I have to get to the walls," Ann said.

"All right," Hermesende said. "Should I leave you, then?"

Her voice sounded strange, different from anything Ann had ever heard. She seemed awed, wondering perhaps if Ann was the woman in the story, if she might be immortal. No one had ever addressed Ann in that tone, or anything remotely like it.

"Come along if you like," she said.

As they came closer she heard the boom of boulders hitting the walls, the skirl of trumpets, the sounds of shrieks and war cries. A company of men carrying knives and swords passed them, heading toward another part of the wall. One of them turned to stare at her as they went by.

"Look—it's her!" he shouted. "The woman the count arrested—the witch!"

He broke away from the others and hurried after her. She started to run, but when she turned to look she saw that he was closer now, gaining on her. He raised his sword, slashed out at her. The sword whistled as it cut the air.

She looked away, pushed herself to run faster. She heard him behind her, hurrying even closer, and then felt a line of pure pain down her upper arm. She cried aloud.

They were close to the company of women now. "Shoot him!" Hermesende shouted. "He's a spy—he's trying to kill us!"

One of the women on the battlements turned and pointed her bow at the man. The next moment Ann saw an arrow protruding from his chest, and he fell back against the wall.

"Lady!" Ann said, panting. "That was close. Thank you."

"My pleasure," Hermesende said.

The catapult she had read about had finally arrived, Ann saw, and had been set up next to the wall. As she watched the arm flung upward, and a boulder flew out over the crusaders' camp. "Nothing!" a woman on the wall shouted, and the woman operating the catapult swore.

The pain on her arm blazed up, and she forced herself to look at it. Bright red blood dripped from a long line scored in her flesh. She felt an instant of nausea and fought against it, forced herself to stay upright.

"I can put a bandage on that," a woman at the catapult said.

That was all she needed, a dirty bandage infecting the wound. "No, it's all right," she said. She blotted it with her gown. "Can I help with anything?"

"Of course," the woman said. "I need to take a break—I've been here all day. Do you think you can load the catapult?"

Ann nodded. She bent down for one of the boulders, hearing as she did so Sam's voice telling her how to pick up the computers. "Lift with your legs, not with your back," he'd said.

Even so, she couldn't seem to manage it. She had lost a lot of blood, and she was starting to feel dizzy again.

Hermesende took hold of the other side, and they lifted it together. Women began to sing, a bawdy song about the love of the two catapults for each other, their yearning for the others' touch.

"It's him!" someone called from the battlements. "The devil Montfort!"

The boulder slipped from her hands. Her vision turned gray, then black, not from the wound, she realized, but from time sickness. She was about to be recalled to her own tace.

"Up!" Hermesende called. "Put your heart into it!"

She made one final attempt to lift the boulder. "For Meret," Ann said. She could barely hear her own voice. "For Kore."

"What—what's happening to her?" someone asked.

Someone else said something, but the words pulsed in and out of her hearing. "Drop it!" Hermesende said, and she heard the boulder thump into the cradle.

"For—" someone said.

The word extended through time, became meaningless. She doubled over with nausea. A spear of light stabbed her eyes.

28

HER KNEES HIT A hard metal floor. She struggled to open her eyes and saw that she was on the small launch pad. She knew where she was, then, but when was she? She had programmed the computer to take her back to her own time, but she had had very little time in which to work. Had she returned to 2327, or, even worse, become lost in time somewhere?

She stood shakily and went over to the computer. 2014, it said. She'd done it.

She wanted to sit down, put her head in her hands, but she knew she had to keep going. She wiped the blood from her arm, then noticed a few drops on the floor and bent to wipe those too. The drops were small but dangerous; to the company, with their sophisticated devices, they would practically shout her DNA from the floor.

Her vision faded when she stood up. She reached out to hold onto something but there was nothing there and she fell again, this time with a hard thump. Great, she thought. If they hadn't known she was here they certainly knew it now.

She stood, wiped her wound again. Then she gathered her gown around her and stepped off the platform. No way to prepare for this, she thought, and went out into the larger room.

Only a few people turned from their workstations to look at her. "You've been in the wars," one of them said.

You have no idea, she thought. She nodded, not wanting him to hear her voice.

She was still worried about what tace she had come to. She could have messed up somehow, skipped a step or added one; the computer might have shown her the date she had programmed while taking her somewhere else. She studied the people in the room, but the clothing here told her nothing; the colors were still as bright and clashing as before. She hurried through the room, looking around quickly for Silas and Zarifa, or else Elias and Da Silva.

"I'd get to the infirmary before I went for debriefing," someone else said.

She nodded again. She stepped out of the room and headed to the elevator. It was only as she got there that she realized she didn't have the thumb drive that served as its key. She remembered putting it in her purse when she got to 1218, which meant that Simon de Montfort had it now. Had it then. She leaned against the wall, trying to clear her mind, trying to think.

Someone came up behind her. Ann turned, saw a man pressing the button for the elevator. "I lost my key on my go," she said.

The man frowned. "Did you report it?" he asked.

"I'm going to do that now." She hesitated. "Did you—did you feel a timequake here?"

He shook his head. The elevator came and they got on. He inserted his key and entered the code numbers, then pushed the button for the first floor. Then he turned back to the pad and pressed three as well.

"Go see the administrator," he said.

She was so tired; all she wanted to do was lie down somewhere. But when the elevator stopped at the third floor the man watched her closely until she got out. She headed slowly for the stairs.

What did it mean that they hadn't felt a timequake? Maybe they would only feel it at the place she left from, at the headwaters. Or maybe she hadn't changed anything, maybe everything was exactly as she left it.

She passed the room that supplied their costumes. Should she go inside, find something closer to her own tace? No, better to get out of here as quickly as possible, to take her chances with the gown.

She headed down the stairs and came out on the first floor. The receptionist frowned at her. "Where's your street clothes?" she asked.

"It's an emergency," Ann said.

To her relief the woman buzzed her out, and she headed for the front door. This was the important test, more so than the date on the computer, she thought. Was there a dome overhead, or would she see the clear sky, and shadows on the ground?

She glanced up and saw the sky—though it was not the blue she remembered from 1218 but overcast, filthy. Still, her relief returned, this time nearly overpowering her. She had come back to her own time, thank the Lady.

She had left her own tace on July 17, but had programmed the machine to return her to July 7, so the company would not be searching for her yet. It gave her some breathing space, but it also meant that she had to keep away from her own apartment, to take care that she didn't cross timelines with herself.

But had she written the code correctly? She needed a newspaper, a computer, something with a date.

She went through the parking lot and headed away from the factories and warehouses that surrounded the company. A while later she started passing more office buildings and street malls, and more people as well. Some of the people stared at her, clearly wondering what she was doing dressed in clothing from centuries ago.

She sat down on a low concrete wall and examined her wound. It had dried to almost the same color as the gown. Now what? she thought. Her mind was muddled; she could not seem to come up with a plan, could only manage one step at a time. Had the wound gotten infected after all?

All right, then. The first thing she had to do was go to a pharmacy.

She stood up. She had no money, which complicated things. No transactions with a friendly pharmacist—and no bus rides, no restaurants, no hotels.

Still, she'd rarely had much money; her situation wasn't all that different from other times in her life. She'd spotted a pharmacy in one of the malls and headed toward it. It wouldn't be the first time she'd had to steal something.

But it was the first time she'd tried to steal something while dressed in clothing from the middle ages. Everyone stared at her—the cashiers, the pharmacists, the customers browsing in the aisles. Someone headed in her direction, all set to ask if she needed help, and she hurried away.

She felt exhausted. She sat at a table outside a coffee shop, ready to jump back up if anyone complained. Her wound had opened up again, she saw. How much blood had she lost? How bad was her time sickness?

A woman sat down next to her, took out her phone, and scrolled through her emails. Her purse hung over the chair closest to Ann. A few years ago she wouldn't have felt bad about what she was about to do, but her recent paychecks had changed her, made her more sympathetic to people with money. Had made her softer.

Still watching the woman, she quickly unzipped the purse, dipped her hand inside, and took out the wallet. Then she stood and walked away.

A few blocks later she stopped and counted the money. A hundred dollars and change, better than she had expected. She had passed a secondhand clothing store a while back, and she went back to it and got a shirt and a pair of pants. There was enough left over for her to go to a pharmacy and get bandages and rubbing alcohol—a different pharmacy this time, so they wouldn't be suspicious. Then she sat on a bus bench and dressed her wound.

When she was done she went through the wallet again. It had several credit cards but she couldn't use them; the woman might have cancelled them already. And the company was probably tied into law enforcement here, and might look for stolen cards as a way to track her. Still, it was growing dark, and she felt sorely tempted to check into a motel, to sleep for several weeks. Instead she found a car that had been left unlocked and stretched out in the back seat.

She had expected to be up all night, listening for the car's owner to come back, wondering if her attempt to change history had succeeded. She'd forgotten to look at a newspaper, she realized, and she swore softly.

Had she made it to July 7? Was there another Ann here somewhere, asleep in her own bed? No, it was too early in the day for that—what would the other Ann be doing now? She tried to figure it out, but she fell asleep instead.

She woke to see the night around her growing lighter, cars and buildings separating themselves from the darkness. Dawn had come; she hopped out of the car and hurried away.

The next few days were more of the same. She stole money, food, more clothing. She couldn't steal a backpack without someone noticing, so she bought one and carried her things around in it. She remembered to look at the date on a newspaper finally, and counted back, and saw that she had managed to return on the day she wanted, July 7. She splurged on a motel for a night and washed herself thoroughly, watching the dirt of the thirteenth century sluice down the drain.

When she had taken care of the day-to-day stuff she went to a bank and opened a checking account. The only identification she had came from the wallets she had stolen, so she used the name she found in one of them. Then she went to the library and got on a computer.

For the next few days she tried to break into the computer networks of large, wealthy corporations. It took her longer than she had expected, but when she finally managed it she instructed the company to send a check to her account, and to continue to do this every two weeks.

She should have done this earlier, she thought, back when she'd been desperately poor. It had not been morality that had held her back but a fear of getting caught. She had grown more confident in her abilities since then, though. And now they had no way to locate her; she had no name, no job or money or apartment. If they found the account she created she could simply walk away; she'd proven she could take care of herself.

It was dangerous to use a real person's name, she knew, and she worked on tracking down someone who did fake licenses. Then she looked through the library's phone books for something innocuous, closing her eyes and pointing to names at random, and finally settled on the name Carla Bowen.

It was only later that she realized her new name had "car" in it, another Kore name. She decided to keep it anyway; maybe someone would think it was a password.

By then it was July 21. She had to leave, she knew; the company would be looking for her. They would be angry, too, furious that she had eluded them for so long.

She took down one of the library's atlases and studied it. It was astonishing, she thought, how many place names started with "Cor" or "Car." Had they all been named after

Kore, as Azelaïs had said? In addition to the ones Azelaïs had mentioned she found Corsica, Carmel, the Carpathian mountains, Cartagena . . . the list went on for several columns. And Chartres, which, when she looked it up in a reference book, turned out to have a labyrinth, and a black Madonna, and whose location had once, long ago, been sacred to the Mother Goddess.

When she got her fake license she looked on Craigslist and bought a secondhand car. It took her a while to get used to it; she had learned how to drive in some long-ago high school class, but she hadn't been behind a wheel since then. As she headed away she remembered Franny asking her why she didn't have a car, and her noncommittal answer. Should she try to get in touch with Franny? But the company would be watching both of them; no doubt they had a key-logger on Franny's computer, and one of their ubiquitous cameras parked outside her house.

Still, Franny deserved to know what was going on. And she was a friend, one of the few Ann had managed to make in her life. She decided to contact her when she got to wherever she was going, when she knew more.

She bought a book of maps of the United States, and set off.

She started in California, driving through Carmel and Carmel Valley, Carmichael near Sacramento, Corcoran to the south, Cartago to the east. As she passed through the small towns and villages, and listened to the radio, she saw that the country had returned more or less to what she remembered, the place it had been before the company had meddled in its history. There were no indications of martial law, or of a dictator poised to take over the government; the president was the same, and the vice president, and the people no more rude than they'd been before, or more dismissive of women.

At first she went through each town without a plan, not sure what she was looking for. She read the local newspapers, went through the classified ads, walked around the parks and restaurants and city halls.

As she continued, though, she began to get a feel for what she wanted. She studied graffiti, and looked at the books in the libraries, and talked to shopkeepers and waitresses and librarians.

She sat through a meeting of Wiccans in Carmel, listening as they planned a naked dance in the forest under a full moon. Their view of the goddess was far too simple, she thought; they seemed to regard her as an oversized mother, wiping away tears and handing out sweets. But she was also the crone, the goddess of death, the woman who killed the Minos once every seven years. Ann could have told them something about that.

She broadened her search to the rest of the country, to Carthage, Texas, and Carthage, Missouri; Corinth, Mississippi, and Corinth, New York. Then Carmel, New York, and a swing back to Carlisle, Pennsylvania.

In one small town in upstate New York she found a listing for a club called Daughters of Demeter, a group that, reading between the lines, sounded exactly like what she wanted. When she got there, though, no one seemed to know the password, or the ceremony of the apples. Even worse, they believed only in praying to the goddess; they had no book of prophecies, no knowledge of history, no plans to change the world.

She did find some similarities, though, after she had listened to them for a while. She thought that they might have split from the sisters of Kore a few hundred years ago. Schisms like that were bound to have happened at some time in history; the only surprise was that there weren't more of them.

They hadn't heard of other groups like them, groups that did more work out in the world. They seemed offended by the question, in fact, and a few of them lectured her on the importance of keeping pure in a polluted world, of not getting her hands dirty, of trusting to the Goddess to know what was best. She wondered if they were telling her the truth, if perhaps they were covering up the existence of a rival group, but she got nothing more from them and finally took her leave.

After weeks of not finding anything she thought about trying Europe or Africa, somewhere closer to where Meret had worked. When she stopped off in libraries she read about the island of Karpathos, close to Crete, and Corsica, and Carthage in Tunisia, Corinth in Greece, Carmel in Israel. And Chartres, of course.

There were an amazing number of black Madonnas in Europe, considering the whiteness of the population. No one seemed to know why they were there or what they represented; one unlikely theory postulated that the statues had simply grown dirtier over the years. They couldn't all be of Meret, she knew; there was something deeper here than she could understand, and she longed for a time machine to solve the mystery. But some of them had to be her.

She started collecting words that seemed in some way to do with Kore: charm, chariot, charter, carnal, court, courtesy. Karma, maybe. Carmine, cardiac, *corazón*.

The summer was extraordinarily hot, or extraordinarily cold, the start of global warming, some people said. She thought about the terrible pollution in 2327, all the problems their teachers had told them about. Things had improved for them after she and the others had changed history in Carcassonne, Zarifa had said, but then Ann had changed it back, had returned them to their contaminated environment. Had she even had the right to do that? But did the company have the right to make things worse for everyone else?

Even worse, what if the future wasn't able to solve its own problems without forcibly changing the past? What if what she had done meant the end of civilization, or at least the beginning of the end? Didn't she have some responsibility to help them?

She thought she did—which meant she would not only have to work against the company, she would also need to work at healing the planet, improving the environment for everyone, the present as well as the future. And here too the sisters of Core might be able to help her, she thought. They worshipped the goddesses of the earth, after all; to harm the earth was to harm their goddesses.

And sometimes, very seldom, she thought about her mother. She had hated the woman for a long time, before she had even known who she was and what she had done. Now she had an additional reason for her hostility: the knowledge that her mother had viewed her with horror, that she had wanted to kill her.

But, in fairness, the girl Ann had seen in the video had just gone through a painful childbirth, and was still in shock. And she was far too young for any of it, nearly half Ann's age. That didn't excuse what she had done, of course, but it did change the story, add a few variables. She understood now that her mother too was a part of the goddess, mother and crone, life and death in one person.

She had enough clues now to track her mother down. Maybe, she thought, after she had found what she was looking for, she could go searching for her, confront her, and then . . . And then what? No, it was better to let it all go, to leave things as they were.

After a month on the road she began to grow discouraged. How could a group like the sisters of Kore have survived for all those long years? The last she had heard of them had been in 1218. Even if they still existed, how could their message have remained intact throughout the centuries?

And what was she planning to do when she found them? How could she even think of working against the company, an organization with unimaginable technology, people who had *time machines*, for the Lady's sake? But if there was one thing she had learned from the company, it was that small gestures could change a world.

Then, in the middle of the country, in a town so small she had nearly driven past it, she saw the word "Kore" scrawled on the side of a boarded-up house. The library had no information on any group that studied or worshipped the goddess, and when she asked more questions the librarian told her proudly that they were all good God-fearing people here. And she could find nothing on the Internet about the town itself, something she had thought to be impossible in this day and age.

She got a motel room in a neighboring town and visited every day. She stopped asking questions and instead spent her time walking around the town itself, and when anyone questioned her she told them she liked the place and was thinking about settling down there. None of them looked as if they believed her—the town was dying, and most of the young people had fled—but they left her alone after that.

She went to a convenience store in the larger town and bought two disposable phones, one for her and one for Franny. She put one of the phones in a padded envelope and addressed it to Franny at the house next door to her; that way, she hoped, the company wouldn't see it and Franny's neighbor would bring it over sometime after the mail had been delivered.

Then, driving around one night after a long day of hiking past farms and pastures, she saw lights on in the abandoned house. She stopped the car and walked up to it. Her heart fluttered in her chest.

She knocked at the door and a woman opened it. "Hello," the woman said.

She was dressed all in white. Candles flickered behind her, and more women in white looked up from their places on the floor.

"Would you do us the courtesy of joining us?" the woman asked. "And would you eat an apple with us, for your heart's sake?"

About the Author

Lisa Goldstein has written fourteen novels and dozens of short stories. Her novel *The Uncertain Places* won the Mythopoeic Award in 2012. She has also won the American Book Award for Best Paperback for *The Red Magician*, and the Sidewise Award for her short story "Paradise Is a Walled Garden." Her stories have appeared in *Ms.*, *Asimov's Science Fiction*, *The Magazine of Fantasy and Science Fiction*, and *The Year's Best Fantasy*, among other places, and her novels and short stories have been finalists for the Hugo, Nebula, and World Fantasy awards. She lives with her husband and their irrepressible Labrador retriever, Bonnie, in Oakland, California.

Goldstein's web site is www.brazenhussies.net/goldstein.